SEE JANE RUN

"INTELLIGENT . . . EXTRAORDINARY . . .
A CHILLING STORY . . .
An entertaining page-turner"
Newport News Daily Press

"WONDERFUL . . . COMPELLING . . .
Creates a suspenseful situation
and mines it to its fullest"
Houston Home Journal

"THE STUFF OF NIGHTMARES . . .
Readers are frightened out of their wits"
San Diego Union

"A TALE FULL OF MYSTERIOUS,
PSYCHOLOGICAL TERROR"
Oklahoma City Oklahoman

"TAUT, SUSPENSEFUL—
yet eminently believable . . .
leads to a surprising and satisfying conclusion"
Library Journal

"DESIGNED TO KEEP THE READER
TEETERING ON EDGE"
Arkansas Democrat

"DIFFERENT AND UNEXPECTED . . .
You have to read
Joy Fielding's latest thriller"
Mobile Press Register

Other Avon Books by
Joy Fielding

TELL ME NO SECRETS

SEE JANE RUN

JOY FIELDING

AVON BOOKS NEW YORK

AVON BOOKS
A division of
The Hearst Corporation
1350 Avenue of the Americas
New York, New York 10019

Cover photograph by Richard Basch
Published by arrangement with the author
Library of Congress Catalog Card Number: 90-22603
ISBN: 0-380-71152-4

Published in hardcover by William Morrow and Company, Inc.; for information address Permissions Department, William Morrow and Company, Inc., 1350 Avenue of the Americas, New York, New York 10019.

First Avon Books Printing: September 1992
First Avon Books International Printing: March 1992

Printed in U.S.A.

RA 10 9 8

For Warren
and for Shannon and Annie

SEE JANE RUN

1

ONE AFTERNOON IN LATE SPRING, JANE WHITTAKER went to the store for some milk and some eggs and forgot who she was.

It came to her suddenly, without prior hint or warning, as she stood at the corner of Cambridge and Bowdoin in what she recognized immediately was downtown Boston, that while she knew exactly *where* she was, she had absolutely no idea *who* she was. She was on her way to the grocery store to buy some milk and some eggs, of that she was sure. She needed them for the chocolate cake she had been planning to bake, although *why* she had been planning to bake it and for *whom,* she couldn't say. She knew exactly how many ounces of instant chocolate pudding the recipe required, yet she couldn't recall her own name. Furthermore, she couldn't remember whether she was married or single, widowed or divorced, childless or the mother of twins. She didn't know her height, weight, or the color of her eyes. She knew neither her birthday nor her age. She could identify the colors of the leaves on the trees but couldn't remember whether she was a blonde or a brunet. She knew the general direction in which she was headed, but she had no notion of where she'd been. What in God's name was happening?

The traffic on Bowdoin slowed, then stopped, and she felt people being pulled from her sides, drawn as if by a magnet to the other side of the street. She alone stood rooted to the spot, unable to proceed, scarcely able to breathe. Cautiously, with deliberate slowness, her head lowered against the collar of her trench coat, she glanced furtively over each shoulder. Pedestrians breezed past her as if barely aware of her existence, men and women whose faces betrayed no outward signs of self-doubt, whose steps carried no noticeable hesitation. Only she stood absolutely still, unwilling—unable—to move. She was aware of sounds—motors humming, horns honking, people laughing, their shoes alternately shuffling or clicking past her, then halting abruptly as the traffic resumed.

A woman's angry whisper caught her attention—"the little slut," the woman hissed—and for an instant she thought the woman was speaking about her. But the woman was clearly in conversation with her companion, and neither seemed even vaguely aware that she was beside them. Was she invisible?

For one insane second, she thought she might be dead, like on one of those old *Twilight Zone* segments in which a woman stranded on a deserted road makes a frantic phone call to her parents, only to be told that their daughter has been killed in a car accident, and who is she anyway to be calling them at this hour of the night? But then the woman whose mouth had only seconds ago been twisted around the word "slut" acknowledged her presence with an almost beatific smile, then turned back to her confidante and moved on.

Clearly, she was not dead. Just as clearly, she was not invisible. And why could she remember something as idiotic as an old *Twilight Zone* episode and not her own name?

Several more bodies appeared beside her, tapping their toes and swiveling on their heels, impatiently waiting to cross. Whoever she was, she was unaccompanied. There was no one ready to take her arm, no one watching anxiously from the other side of the street wondering why she had fallen behind. She was all alone, and she didn't know who she was supposed to be.

"Stay calm," she whispered, searching for clues in the sound of her voice, but even it was unfamiliar to her. It said nothing of age or marital status, its accent nondescript and noteworthy only for its undertone of anxiety. She raised a hand to her lips and spoke inside it so as not to attract undue attention. "Don't panic. It'll all come clear in a few minutes." Was she normally in the habit of talking to herself? "First things first," she continued, then wondered what that meant. How could she put anything first when she didn't know what anything was? "No, that's not true," she corrected herself immediately. "You know things. You know lots of things. Take stock," she admonished herself more loudly, glancing around quickly to ascertain whether or not she had been overheard.

A group of perhaps ten people was moving toward her. They've come to take me back to wherever it is I escaped from, was her first and only thought. And then the leader of the group, a young woman of perhaps twenty-one, began speaking in the familiar broad Boston tones that her own voice strangely lacked, and she realized she was as inconsequential to these people as she had been to the two women she had overheard earlier. Was she of consequence to anyone?

"As you can see," the young woman was saying, "Beacon Hill is one of the areas that makes it easy for Bostonians to walk to work. Long regarded as Boston's premier neighborhood, Beacon Hill has steep cobblestone streets lined with private brick houses and small apartment buildings the construction of which began in the 1820s and continued through the latter part of the nineteenth century."

Everyone took due notice of the private brick houses and small apartment buildings as the young woman continued her well-rehearsed speech. "A number of the larger and more elegant homes have been turned into condominiums in recent years because of the housing shortage and Boston's soaring real estate prices. Beacon Hill used to be a Yankee stronghold, but while many of

Boston's old families still live here, people of all backgrounds are now welcome . . . as long as they can pay the mortgage or the rent.''

There was some benign twittering and much nodding of heads before the group prepared to move on. ''Excuse me, ma'am,'' the tour leader said, her eyes opening wide as her lips popped into an exaggerated smile, so that she resembled a happy-face button brought to life. ''I don't believe you're with this tour?'' The statement emerged as a question, the last few words curling upward along with the speaker's mouth. ''If you're interested in a walking tour of the city, you have to go to the tourist office in the Boston Common, and they'll sign you up for the next available tour. Ma'am?''

The happy-face button looked in distinct danger of losing its happy thoughts.

''The Common?'' she asked the young woman, whose easy use of the word *ma'am* suggested she must be at least thirty.

''Just keep heading south on Bowdoin until you hit Beacon. You'll pass the State House, the one with the gold dome? It's right there. You can't miss it.''

Don't be too sure, she thought, watching the tour group cross the road and disappear down the next street. If I can misplace myself, I can lose anything.

Inching one foot in front of the other as if she were stepping into unfamiliar and potentially treacherous waters, she moved along Bowdoin, paying little attention to the ninteenth-century architecture and concentrating on the road ahead. She crossed Derne, then Ashburton Place, without incident, although neither these streets nor the State House that suddenly loomed before her evoked any sense of who she might be. She turned the corner onto Beacon Street.

Just as the Happy Face had suggested, the Boston Common stretched before her. Ignoring the Granary Burying Ground, which she had no trouble recalling contained the tombs of such diverse notables as Paul Revere and Mother Goose, she hurried past the Visitors' Center toward the large Public Garden, knowing instinctively she had done this many times in the past. She was no stranger to the city of Boston, no matter how much of a stranger she might be to herself.

She felt her knees go weak and forced her legs toward a waiting bench, letting her body fold into it. "Don't panic," she repeated several times out loud, using the words like a mantra, knowing that no one was close enough to hear her. She immediately began a silent recitation of known—if largely unimportant—facts. It was Monday, June 18th, 1990. The temperature was an unseasonably cool sixty-eight degrees Fahrenheit. Thirty-two degrees Fahrenheit was the temperature at which water would freeze. One hundred degrees centigrade was hot enough to boil an egg. Two times two equaled four; four times four was sixteen; twelve times twelve was 144. The square of the hypoteneuse was equal to the sum of the square of the other two sides. $E = mc^2$. The square root of 365 was . . . she didn't know, but then something told her that was all right—she never had. "Don't panic," she heard herself say yet again as she began smoothing out the wrinkles of her tan coat, feeling slim thighs beneath her fingers. The fact that she was a veritable font of useless information was reassuring because how could a person retain such knowledge and not, at some point, remember her own name? She would remember. It was just a question of time.

A little girl came racing toward her across the wide expanse of park, arms extended, her portly black nanny running to catch up. She wondered for an instant whether this might be *her* little girl and instinctively reached her arms toward her, but the nanny quickly pulled the child out of reach, steering her toward a nearby set of swings, eyeing the bench suspiciously. Do I have children of my own? she mused, wondering how a mother could forget her child.

She glanced at her hands. At least a ring on her finger would tell her whether she was married. But her fingers were devoid of jewelry, although there was a thin line on the third finger of her left hand where a ring might once have been. She studied it closely, unable to say for sure, noticing that her muted coral nail polish was chipping, and the nails themselves were bitten to the quick. Her gaze dropped to her feet. She was wearing low-heeled, bone-colored patent-leather shoes, the right one of which pressed rather too tightly against her big toe. She pulled it off, recognizing the name Charles Jourdan printed across its instep, and noting she was a size nine, which meant that her height was probably at least five feet six inches. Even with her coat buttoned tightly around her, she knew from the way her hands grazed her sides that she was slim. What else had she been able to figure out? What else did she know about herself beyond the fact that she was white, female, and if the Happy Face and the backs of her own hands were any indication, well over twenty-one?

Two women walked by, their arms entwined, their large purses slapping at their sides. Her purse! she thought with great relief, feeling for a strap at her shoulder. Her purse would tell her everything—who she was, where she lived, what color lipstick she wore. Inside would be her wallet with her identification, her driver's license, her charge cards. She would once again know her name and address, the year of her birth, the kind of car she drove—if, in fact, she drove at all. Her purse contained all the mysteries of life. All she had to do was open it.

All she had to do was find it!

Stuffing her foot roughly back inside her shoe, she leaned against the dull-green slats of the park bench and acknowledged what she had known all along but had been too frightened to admit—that she *had* no purse. Whatever identification she might have been carrying when she began this strange odyssey, she wasn't in possession of it now. Just to make sure, to satisfy herself that she hadn't dropped her bag carelessly to the ground when she sat down, she took a concentrated look around, checking, then rechecking, the grass at her feet. She even circled the bench several times, once again catching the suspicious eye of the black nanny, who was pushing her young charge on the nearby swing. She smiled at the dark-skinned woman, then wondered what exactly she had to smile about, and turned away. When she looked back several seconds later, the nanny was hurriedly ushering the loudly protesting youngster out of the area. "There, now you've scared her," she said out loud, automatically feeling her face for any signs of disfigurement. There didn't seem to be any, so she allowed her fingers to continue their Braille-like reading of her features.

Her face was a narrow oval, her cheekbones high, perhaps a touch too prominent, and her eyebrows were full and untended. Her nose was small and her eyelashes were caked with mascara, although it seemed to have been applied unevenly and with a heavy hand. Perhaps she had been rubbing her eyes, she thought, causing the mascara to cling to certain lashes while abandoning others. Perhaps she had been crying.

She pushed back her shoulders, stood up, and abruptly marched out of the park, ignoring a stoplight and running against the traffic toward a bank at one corner of Beacon Street. She knocked loudly on the glass door, catching the attention of the manager, a prematurely bald young man whose head seemed several sizes too small for the rest of his body. She deduced he was the manager because he wore a suit and tie and was the only male in a room full of women. "I'm sorry," he told her gently, opening the door just wide enough for part of his large nose to protrude, "but it's after four o'clock. We close at three."

"Do you know who I am?" she asked desperately, surprised at the question she had not meant to ask.

The man's frown indicated that he interpreted her remark as a demand for special treatment. "I'm really sorry," he said, an unmistakable edge creeping into his voice. "I'm sure that if you come back tomorrow, we can take care of you." Then he smiled, a stubborn pursing of his lips that brooked no further discussion, and walked back to his desk.

She remained on the other side of the glass door, staring in at the tellers until they began whispering among themselves. Did they know who she was? If they did, they soon tired of her presence and, prompted by their manager, who was gesticulating wildly, returned their attention to their computers and balance sheets, ignoring her as if she no longer existed. Did she?

Taking a few deep breaths, she proceeded along Beacon to River Street, back toward the steep cobblestone streets lined with private brick houses and small apartment buildings from whence she had sprung fully grown and totally lost. Did she live in one of these nineteenth-century homes? Did she have enough money to cover the mortgage or the rent? Was she concerned at all about money? Was she a wealthy woman? Did she work for a living or did she hire others to work for her? Maybe instead of living in one of these fine old homes, she cleaned them.

No, she was too well dressed to be a cleaning lady, and her hands, while undeniably a mess, were too soft and uncallused for someone accustomed to physical labor. Perhaps instead of cleaning these houses, she *sold* them. Maybe that was what had brought her to this part of town. Maybe she had come to meet a client, to show off a recently renovated home and had . . . what? Been hit over the head with a falling brick? Despite herself, she quickly felt her head for bumps, finding none and ascertaining only that her hair had come loose of its tight clasp and was hanging in stray wisps at the base of her neck.

She turned right on Mt. Vernon, then left on Cedar Street, hoping that something would transmit the necessary signals to her brain. "Something please look familiar," she coaxed the tree-lined streets as she turned again at Revere, walking toward Embankment Road. The sun had disappeared behind a great gray cloud, and she felt cold, though the temperature remained steady. She recalled that the winter had been a relatively mild one and that the experts were predicting another hot summer. The Greenhouse Effect, they called it. Greenhouse. Greenpeace. Acid Rain. Save the Rain Forests. Save the Whales. Save Water—Shower with a Friend.

She felt suddenly overwhelmed with exhaustion. Her

feet were sore, the big toe on her right foot now completely numb. Her stomach was starting to rumble. How long had it been since she'd eaten? For that matter what sort of foods did she like? Did she know how to cook? Maybe she was on some sort of kooky diet that had affected her brain. Or maybe she was high on drugs. Or alcohol. Was she drunk? Had she ever been drunk? How would she know whether she was drunk or not?

She covered her eyes with her hands, wishing for the telltale pounding in her head that would signal an approaching hangover. Ray Milland's *Lost Weekend,* she thought, wondering how old she would have to be to remember Ray Milland. "Help me," she whispered into her closed palms. "Somebody, please, help me."

She checked her wrist for the time, an automatic reflex, and saw that it was almost five o'clock. She had been walking around for almost an hour and had seen nothing in that time to give her any clue as to who she might be. Nothing looked familiar. Nobody had recognized her.

She found herself on Charles Street, an easy and attractive mix of shops, from the local grocery mart to a variety of jewelry and antique stores, everything from hardware to fine art. Had she been heading here to buy her milk and eggs?

A man brushed past her and smiled, but it was the smile of one weary soul to another at the end of a trying day, and spoke nothing of acquaintance. Even still, she was tempted to seize this man by the shoulders, to plead with him for some indication that he knew who she was, if necessary to shake an identity from him. But she let the man pass unmolested and the moment was gone. Besides, she couldn't just accost total strangers on the street. They might call the police, have her locked away. Another crazy lady trying to find herself!

Was she crazy? Had she just escaped from an asylum? From jail? Was she on the run? She laughed at her own histrionics. If she hadn't been crazy before all this started, she certainly would be by the time it was over. Would it ever be over?

She pushed open the door of a small convenience store

and went inside. If she lived in this neighborhood, there was a good chance she frequented this little shop. At the very least, she hoped she had shopped here enough times to be familiar to the man behind the counter. Slowly, she made her way between the rows of canned goods toward him.

The proprietor, a ponytailed young man with uneven features and a straight line for a mouth, was busy with several customers who had converged on him simultaneously, each one claiming to be the first in line. She took her place behind them, hoping to catch the young man's eye, praying to hear a crisp, "Hello there, Ms. Smith. Be right with you." But all she heard was someone asking for a large pack of cigarettes, and all she saw was the proprietor's skinny back as he swiveled around to reach for it.

She glanced over her left shoulder to a row of impossibly beautiful young women, who stared back at her from the covers of several dozen magazines. Allowing her body to drift toward the magazine rack, she found her eyes riveted to the sultry face of one model in particular. CINDY CRAWFORD, the name beside the face proclaimed in bright pink letters, SUPERMODEL. No doubt who *she* was.

She lifted the magazine from its slot and studied the model's face: brown eyes, brown hair, a mole to the left of her slightly parted lips that distinguished her from the hundreds of other equally pretty faces that were everywhere. So beautiful, she thought. So young. So confident.

It occurred to her again that she had no idea what she looked like, no conception of how old she was. Her fingers gripped the sides of the magazine, bending its edges, curling them inward. "Hey, lady," a male voice called out, and she turned to see the proprietor waving an admonishing finger, "you don't handle the magazines unless you're gonna buy them."

Feeling as guilty as a child caught shoplifting a piece of candy, she nodded understanding of the rules, and clutched the magazine against her chest as if it were a lifeline. But she didn't move.

"Well, you gonna buy it or not?" the young man asked. The other customers had departed, leaving the two of them alone. Now was her best, perhaps her only, chance to confront him.

She threw herself toward the counter, watching him take a quick step back. "Do you know me?" she asked, straining to keep the panic out of her voice.

He stared at her without moving, his eyes narrowing in concentration. Then he tilted his head, his ponytail grazing his right shoulder, a smile creeping across the straight line of his mouth, twisting it into a flattened U. "You somebody famous?" he asked.

Was she? she wondered, but said nothing, waiting, holding her breath.

He mistook her silence for affirmation. "Well, I know there are a few movies shooting in the city right now," he said, taking several steps to his right so that he could study her profile, "but I don't go to a lot of movies, and I don't recognize you from anything I watch on TV. You on one of those soap operas? I know that them actresses are always coming to shopping malls and stuff like that. My sister made me take her once. She had to see Ashley Abbott from *The Young and the Restless*. 'The Young and the *Useless,*' I call it. You on that one?"

She shook her head. What was the point in continuing this charade? Clearly, he didn't know her any better than she did.

She watched his body tense, then stiffen. "Well, you gotta pay for the magazine, whoever you are. Celebrity or not, it's still two dollars and ninety-five cents."

"I . . . I forgot my purse," she whispered, starting to feel queasy.

Now the man looked angry. "What, you think that just because you're on some dumb TV show that you don't gotta carry money around like the rest of us? You think that because you're kinda pretty, I'm gonna make you a present of whatever you want?"

"No, of course not. . . ."

"Either you pay for the magazine or you get out of my store and stop wasting my time. I don't need people making fun of me."

"I wasn't trying to make fun of you. Honestly."

"Two dollars and ninety-five cents," he said again, extending his hand, palm up.

She knew she should simply hand over the magazine, but something would not allow her to give it up. CINDY CRAWFORD looked so lovely, so happy, so damned sure of herself. Was she hoping that such boundless self-assurance would rub off on her? She reached inside the pockets of her trench coat in hopes she might be carrying some loose change. Her hand moved rapidly from one pocket to the other, refusing to believe what it had found. When she finally brought her hand back out, she saw that it was filled with crisp, new hundred-dollar bills.

"Whoa," the man behind the counter whistled. "You rob a bank or something?" Then, "You just print these up, or what?"

She said nothing, staring with wonder at the money in her hand.

"Anyway, I got no use for hundred-dollar bills. I give you change of a hundred, I don't have any change left for anybody else. How many of those you got, anyway?"

She felt her breath pushing its way out of her chest in short, shallow bursts. What in God's name was she doing with two pocketfuls of hundred-dollar bills? Where had all this money come from?

"You all right, lady?" The man behind the counter looked anxiously toward the door. "You aren't going to be sick, are you?"

"Do you have a bathroom I can use?"

"It's not open to the public," he said stubbornly.

"Please!"

The desperation in her voice must have convinced him because he quickly raised an arm and pointed toward the storeroom to his right. "Look, I just washed up in there. Try not to be sick on my clean floor, okay?"

She quickly located the small bathroom just inside the storage area. It was a tiny, crowded closet of a room, containing an old toilet and a broken mirror above a stained sink. The walls were lined with boxes of supplies. A half-filled bucket of water, a mop balanced precariously at its side, rested by the door.

She dashed toward the sink and twisted open the cold water tap, burying her magazine underneath her arm, quickly catching the icy water in her hands and splashing it against her face until she felt as if she could straighten up without fainting. What was going on? If this was a nightmare—and this *was* a nightmare—surely it was time she woke up!

Slowly, she lifted her face toward the mirror, then had to clutch the sides of the sink for support. The woman who stared back at her was a complete stranger. There was nothing even remotely familiar about her face. She scrutinized the pale skin and dark-brown eyes, the small, faintly upturned nose and full mouth painted the same shade as her nails. Her brown hair was perhaps a shade lighter than her eyes and pulled back into a ponytail by a jeweled clasp that had come loose and was threatening to fall out. She pulled it free of her hair, shaking her head and watching her hair fall in soft layers to her shoulders.

It was an attractive face, she thought, objectifying it as if, like CINDY CRAWFORD, it was on the cover of a magazine. Kinda pretty, the young man had said. Maybe slightly better than that. Everything was in its proper place. There were no unsightly blemishes. Nothing was too big or too small. Nothing jarred. Everything was where it was supposed to be. She estimated her age as early to mid-thirties, then wondered if she looked older or younger than she really was. "This is so confusing," she whispered to her image, which seemed to be holding its breath. "Who *are* you?"

"You're nobody I know," her reflection answered, and both women dropped their heads to stare into the stained basin of the white enamel sink.

"Oh, God," she whispered, feeling a bubble of heat explode inside her. "Please don't faint," she cried. "Whoever you are, please don't faint."

But the wave of heat continued to wash across her body, sweeping past her legs and stomach into her arms and neck, getting caught in her throat. She felt as if she were melting from the inside out, as if, at any minute, she might burst into flames. She splashed more water on her face, but it did nothing to cool her off or calm her down. She began tearing at the buttons of her coat in an effort to free her body, give it more room to breathe. The magazine under her arm slipped to the floor, and she quickly bent down to scoop it up, pulling open her coat as she stood up.

She took a deep breath, then stopped dead.

Slowly, as if she were a marionette and some unknown force were manipulating her strings, she felt her head drop toward her chest in one seamless arc. What she saw—what she had seen when she was down on her knees retrieving the magazine but had managed to ignore—was a simple blue dress, the front completely covered in blood.

She gasped, the soft, frightened cry of a small animal caught in a trap. The sound quickly grew into a moan, then emerged as a scream. She heard footsteps, the sound of other voices, felt herself surrounded, overwhelmed.

"What's going on in here?" the proprietor started, then stopped, his words retreating into the open hole of his mouth.

"Oh, my God," a young boy groaned from somewhere at his side.

"Gross!" his companion exclaimed.

"What have you done?" the store owner demanded, his eyes searching the tiny cubicle, undoubtedly for signs of broken glass.

She said nothing, returning her gaze to the front of her bloodied dress.

"Look, lady," the man began again, shooing his two young customers away from the door, "I don't know what's going on here, and I don't want any part of it. Take your blood and your hundred-dollar bills and get out of my store before I call the police."

She didn't move.

"Did you hear what I said? I'm going to call the police if you don't get out of here right now."

She looked toward the frightened proprietor, who suddenly grabbed the mop from the bucket and brandished it at her as if he were a matador and she the bull. "Blood," she whispered, her disbelieving eyes drawn back to the front of her dress. The blood was reasonably fresh, still a little damp. Was the blood hers or someone else's? "Blood," she said again, as if the repetition of the word would pull everything into place.

"You got ten seconds, lady, then I'm calling the cops. Now, I don't want any trouble. I just want you out of my store."

Her eyes returned to his, her voice so soft she noticed that he had to bend forward in spite of himself to hear it. "I don't know where to go," she cried, and felt her body crumple, like a piece of paper in someone's clenched fist.

"Oh, no, you don't," the man said quickly, catching her before she could fall. "You're not fainting in my store."

"Please," she began, not sure if she was pleading for understanding or unconsciousness.

The young man, while not very tall or muscular, was surprisingly strong. He gripped her tightly around the waist and marshaled her quickly to the door. Then he suddenly stopped, looking uneasily around the store. "Is this one of them hidden video shows?" he asked warily, a hint of embarrassment creeping into his voice, as if he might have been had.

"You have to help me," she said.

"You have to get out of my store," he told her, regaining his composure and pushing her outside. She heard the door click shut behind her, saw him angrily shooing her away.

"Oh, God, what do I do now?" she asked the busy street. Again, the puppeteer took charge, buttoning her coat, tucking her magazine beneath her arm, directing her gaze toward the traffic. Seeing a taxi approach, the string pulling her right hand shot up, jerking her arm up and out. The taxi came to an immediate stop at the side of the road in front of her. Without further thought, she opened the cab's rear door and climbed inside.

2

SHE WASN'T SURE WHAT MADE HER CHOOSE THE LENnox Hotel. Maybe because it was one of downtown Boston's older hotels and therefore smaller and somehow more lifesize than its more modern counterparts, or maybe because fond memories of earlier visits still lingered in her subconscious, she didn't know. It was even possible that she was already registered here as a guest, she told herself hopefully as she approached the front desk, praying, as she had earlier in the convenience store, for a kind smile of recognition.

She had to wait in line behind a couple and their two young sons, towheaded little devils in matching sailor suits, each clinging to his share of their mother's ample hips and wailing their collective discomfort for all the lobby to hear.

"I'm hungry," the younger of the two, a boy of maybe four, complained, lifting up his mother's skirt and exposing her knee, as if contemplating taking a bite.

"I want to go to McDonald's," his brother, older by no more than a year, immediately elaborated.

"McDonald's! McDonald's!" became the rallying cry as they danced circles around the helpless adults who were their parents and who were doing their best to pretend that none of this was actually happening.

"Let Mommy and Daddy get us a room, then we'll find a nice restaurant, okay?" the young mother pleaded, fixing her husband with a stare that begged him to hurry things along before she started screaming.

"McDonald's! McDonald's!" came the expected and immediate response.

And then they were miraculously gone, guided inside a waiting elevator by a solicitous bellhop, and the lobby once again assumed the air of a refined, European-styled hotel. "Can I help you, ma'am? . . . ma'am?"

"I'm sorry," she said when she realized that the young man behind the reception desk was addressing her. Obviously she had better get used to being called *ma'am*. "I'd like a room."

His hands began tapping at the keys of his computer. "For how long?"

"I'm not sure." She cleared her throat, once, then again. "At least one night. Maybe two."

"A single room?" He looked past her to see if she was alone. Automatically, she did the same.

"Just me," she whispered, then louder, "Yes, a single room. Please." Mustn't forget my manners, she thought, and almost laughed.

"I have a room," the young man recited, reading from his computer screen, "at eighty-five dollars a night. It's on the eighth floor, no smoking, and it has a double bed."

"That's fine."

"And how will you be paying for that?"

"Cash."

"Cash?" For the first time, the young man's eyes shot directly to hers. She noted that he had the bluest eyes of anyone she'd ever seen. At least she *thought* he had the bluest eyes of anyone she'd ever seen. She couldn't be sure. God only knew the things she'd seen.

"Isn't cash all right? Don't you take cash?"

"Oh, yes, of course we take cash. It's just that we don't often see it. Most people prefer credit cards."

She nodded, saying nothing, thinking that she was undoubtedly one of those people in her other life, and wondering how anyone could be born with eyes so impossibly blue.

"Is something wrong?" the young man asked, the rest of his resolutely nondescript features arranging themselves into something of a question mark.

"I'm sorry," she stammered, "it's just your eyes. They're so blue!" She rolled her own eyes toward the ceiling. Whoever she was, she was an idiot! The boy would probably think she was trying to pick him up!

"Oh, they're not mine," he said, and returned to his computer screen.

"I beg your pardon?" The thought was beginning to form in her mind that she was a visitor from another planet.

"They're contacts," he explained cheerily. "Two nights you said?"

She was having great difficulty keeping up with the conversation. The familiar panic, which had temporarily subsided during the cab ride over from Beacon Hill, was returning. "Yes, no more than two nights." And then what? Where would she go after that if she still didn't know who she was? To the police? Why hadn't she gone there directly?

"I need you to fill this out." The young man slid a piece of paper across the counter in her direction. "Your name and address, etcetera," he said when he sensed her confusion. "Are you feeling all right?"

She took a deep breath. "I'm very tired. Is this necessary?" She pushed the piece of paper back across the reception desk, untouched.

It was his turn to look confused. "I'm afraid we *do* need a name and address."

Her eyes darted from the young man's face to the revolving front door, then finally settled on the magazine she still clutched fervently in her hands. "Cindy," she said a touch too loudly, then again more softly, more firmly in control, "Cindy."

"Cindy?"

She nodded, watching him reluctantly take up a pen and write the name on the information card.

"Is there a last name?"

Why was he doing this to her? Hadn't she told him she was tired? Didn't he understand she was paying cash? Why did he have to know things that were really none of his business? She thought of the young couple and their two little boys crying for McDonald's. No wonder the youngsters were whiny and impatient. Had he given them such a hard time as well?

"McDonald!" she heard a voice exclaim before realizing it was her own. "Cindy McDonald!" She took another deep breath before continuing. "One twenty-three Memory Lane . . . New York."

His fingers stalled on the word *Memory* and she had to bite her lip to contain her budding hysteria, but in another few seconds the form had been completed and it was all over but for her signature and the cash exchange. She watched her hand scribble her new identity across the bottom of the form and was pleasantly charmed by the strength and swirls of the letters she produced. Then she reached into her pockets and pulled out a couple of crisp, new hundred-dollar bills, trying to keep her face from registering amusement at the young man's growing discomfort.

"Any luggage?" The wariness of his tone indicated he already knew the answer, so when she shook her head, he merely shrugged and handed over the key to her room along with her change. "Enjoy your visit with us. If there's anything we can do to make your stay more comfortable, just holler."

She smiled. "You'll be the first to know."

As soon as she was inside her room, she hurled the magazine toward the double bed and tore off her coat, throwing it to the floor. The blood that covered the front of her dress hit her square in the eyes, like a ripe tomato hurled at her face. Forming a giant, angry fist, it reached into her throat and dragged forth a low, unwilling scream. "No, oh, no. Go away. Oh, please, go away."

She scratched at the front of her dress like a cat caught on a high perch. In the next instant, the dress was on the floor and she was searching her skin for signs of injury.

There were none.

"Oh, God, what does this mean? What does this mean?"

She spun around, as if the answer was located somewhere within these blue-and-white patterned walls. But the walls spoke only of floral prints and nothing of blood and injury. "Whose blood is this if it isn't mine?"

She ran to the armoire across from the bed and threw it open, catching sight of her frightened image in the mirror on the inside of the door. "Who are you, dammit? And whose blood are you covered with?"

The woman in the glass said nothing, mimicking her as she frantically searched her body for cuts or wounds. But although there were a few stray bruises on her arms, there was nothing to suggest serious injury.

She quickly reached behind her and undid the clasp of her flesh-toned lace brassiere, casting it aside, and staring at the small breasts that popped rather proudly into view. She wondered momentarily whether these breasts had ever fed a baby. They were nice enough breasts, she thought, in a conscious effort to calm herself down by concentrating on the everyday details of everyday existence. Would such concentration eventually lead her back to her own everyday existence?

It didn't. Her breasts told her nothing. Not whether they had ever nursed a child, not when they had first felt a man's caress, not even if they had ever been admired. She scoffed, feeling a laugh catch and die in her throat, thinking that she must be losing her mind. Here she was in a hotel room in the middle of Boston, a city she knew but didn't know what she was doing in, her pockets filled with money, her dress covered with blood, and she was standing in front of a mirror staring at her bare breasts and wondering whether they had ever been admired.

Well, why not? she thought, grabbing at the elastic of her panty hose and pulling them off along with her beige bikini panties, staring at her now naked body. What information was she hoping to glean from her exposed flesh?

Her body was a good one, she decided, studying herself from all angles. It was tight and muscular, almost boyish. Perhaps even athletic. Her calves were well developed, her legs strong and shapely, her stomach flat, her waist not particularly defined. More childlike than womanly, even at her age. It was a body that would definitely not make the cover of many magazines, she thought, glancing toward the discarded magazine on the bed. CINDY CRAWFORD stared back at her with a mixture of pity and indulgence. *Eat your heart out*, she seemed to be saying, and the woman in front of the mirror nodded defeat.

She grabbed at the crumpled blue dress at her feet, her hands careful to avoid the blood-covered bodice. Could her dress tell her anything? The label identified it as a size eight, pure cotton, Anne Klein. It had a round neck and large white buttons to the waist, a simple A-line skirt, and was probably as overpriced as it was understated. Whoever she was, she obviously had enough money to buy the best.

"The money!" She vaulted to where her coat lay discarded on the floor, pulling the cash from the coat's deep pockets, thinking only briefly of how ludicrous a sight she must appear. The stream of hundred-dollar bills seemed inexhaustible. How much money did she have? Where had it come from? "What am I doing with all this money?" she demanded, trying to arrange it neatly on the bed.

She was surprised to discover that most of the money was contained in thin, neat little stacks, as if straight from a bank. But why and how? Could it be possible that she was, in fact, a bank robber? That she had taken part in a robbery, pocketed the money, and then been splattered by somebody's blood when something went hopelessly awry? Could she possibly have shot someone?

She was seized with a terror so strong her whole body shook. *Because it felt possible*. The unwelcome thought that she might have been able to kill someone *felt pos-*

sible. "Oh, God, oh, God," she moaned, curling into a fetal position on the blue-carpeted floor. Had she shot some poor innocent in the course of an ill-executed robbery? And had she acted alone or with an accomplice? Was she some latter-day Bonnie, missing her Clyde?

She heard herself laughing and the laughter brought her back to a sitting position. While it seemed altogether possible that she might have killed someone, the notion that she could have taken part in a bank heist struck her as just plain silly. Unless, of course, she was desperate. But what would make a well-dressed woman in her early to mid-thirties desperate enough to kill?

Even without her memory, she knew the answer to that one. A *man* could make you that desperate. *What man*? she asked herself, no longer expecting any answers.

She ran a shaky hand through her hair, grown sticky with nervous perspiration. She hoisted her upper torso back over the bed, the tips of her breasts grazing the nine neat stacks of hundred-dollar bills that she had shaped into a doll-sized bedspread.

She grabbed at the first packet of bills, snapped off the paper clip that bound the bills together, and proceeded to count each one. After several false starts, she determined that there were ten hundred-dollar bills in each packet. Nine packets of ten hundred-dollar bills came to nine thousand dollars. That and the money she had already spent on the hotel and cab fare plus a few loose hundred-dollar bills and some change brought the total to just over nine thousand six hundred dollars. What had she been doing with almost ten thousand dollars stuffed inside the pockets of her coat?

She felt chilled and saw her arms were covered with fresh goose bumps. Forcing herself to her feet, she edged her naked body around the bed and retrieved her coat from the floor, noting the presence of dried blood on the inside lining as she wrapped it around her and stuffed her hands inside her pockets. She quickly pulled out some money she had missed and tossed the loose bills onto the bed beside the rest.

Something was clinging to one of the bills. It was a

scrap of paper, she realized, uncrumpling it and smoothing it out, grateful to discover that she didn't need glasses to read. She recognized the bold, sweeping strokes as coming from the same hand that had earlier signed the name *Cindy McDonald* to the hotel registration form, so she knew that she had written the series of seemingly inconsequential words she now read. But when? Scraps of paper had a way of lying dormant for weeks, even months, in forgotten coat pockets. There was no telling when she had written this. *Pat Rutherford, R.31, 12:30,* the note read, followed by *milk, eggs*. What did it mean?

Well, obviously that she had needed some milk and eggs—she was on her way to buy them when her memory failed, but how long ago had she left?—and that she must have had an appointment with someone named Pat Rutherford. Who the hell was Pat Rutherford?

She repeated the name several times with growing frustration. Was Pat Rutherford a man or a woman? Maybe *she* was Pat Rutherford. But why would she write her own name and room number on a piece of paper and put it in her pocket? Unless losing her memory was something she did on a regular basis, and experience had taught her to keep a record of who she was with her at all times. Sure, and make appointments when she wanted to see herself. Enough of this nonsense!

Had she kept her appointment? Had she gone to see Pat Rutherford at the agreed-upon time, collected just under ten thousand dollars, and then killed the unfortunate soul? Was it Pat Rutherford's blood that covered the front of her dress? Had she been blackmailing Pat Rutherford? Had Pat Rutherford been blackmailing her? Had she completely lost her marbles? Where were these ideas coming from?

"Pat Rutherford, who are you?"

She located a Boston phone book in a night table drawer, and fumbled for the R's: Raxlen, Rebick, Rossiter, Rule, Rumble, pages of Russells, Russo, Rutchinski, finally Rutherford, half a page of Rutherfords in the Boston area alone, forget about the suburbs. There was a Paul and two Peters but no Pats, although there were three unexplained P's. She debated telephoning each one, then immediately dismissed the idea. Just what would she say to Mr./Mrs./Miss/Ms. P. Rutherford? Hi, you probably don't know me, and God knows *I* don't know me, but did we have a meeting anytime lately in room thirty-one somewhere at twelve-thirty? And, by any chance, did I injure you severely?

So much for that idea.

She discarded the phone book, her eyes darting around the decidedly old-fashioned room, afraid to linger longer than a few seconds at any one place. "So, what am I supposed to do now?" she asked, staring up at the high ceilings, feeling exhausted and hungry. "Do I go to the police or do I try to figure this thing out for myself? Do I head straight for the nearest loony bin or to the nearest bathtub? Should I do anything now or wait till morning? What should I do?" She paused, absently fingering the large menu that room service provided. "When in doubt," she heard herself answer, "eat."

Just where this philosophy had originated she wasn't sure, but it seemed as good a solution as any, so she picked up the phone, dialed room service, and ordered a steak and a caesar salad. She needed only a moment's pause to answer medium rare, sour cream for her baked potato, and mineral water instead of red wine. She eliminated the possibility that she might be a vegetarian, and prayed that she had no weird food allergies. She was too hungry for any such unnecessary complications.

Twenty minutes, room service told her. Twenty minutes to get cleaned up before dinner. She made her way to the large white-tiled bathroom, discarding her coat on a high-backed wooden chair outside the bathroom door.

How nice it would be to simply disappear, she thought as the water from the shower streamed across her cheeks like tears. My mind is gone: take my body too. Whatever I've done, whoever I am, perhaps it's better that I don't know. Maybe I'm better off. Maybe whatever it is I'm running away from is worth *staying* away from.

Surely, she would be missed. Surely, someone somewhere was looking for her, not knowing where to look any more than she did. Her parents or her husband, if she had one; her boss or someone in her employ; her teacher or her students; her friends or her foes; maybe even the police! Surely, someone somewhere was looking for her! Why didn't she just turn herself over to the police and find out?

Because everything will have straightened itself out by morning, she told herself, emerging from the shower and hearing a knock at the door. She wrapped herself in a towel, then covered the towel with her coat and walked to the door. She knew who it was but asked anyway, her voice hoarse, barely audible.

"Room service," came the expected reply.

"Just a minute." The voice was firmer now, more in control.

Her eyes caught sight of the quilt of money lying at the foot of her bed just as her hand reached for the door. She froze. For an instant, her mind played with the idea of leaving everything just the way it was, allowing the unsuspecting waiter to come inside and deposit her dinner on the table across from her bed, to test his reaction to the sight of all that money spread so nonchalantly in front of him. Would he pretend that the money didn't exist, or that it was the most normal thing in the world to check into a hotel room and spread almost ten thousand dollars across the foot of one's bed? Didn't everyone?

There was a second knock. How long had she been standing here? She checked her wrist, recalling vaguely that she had taken off her watch along with her dress, remembering that the dress was still in a bloody heap on the floor. "Just a second," she called out, scooping up the dress and tossing it inside the armoire, snapping her watch back on her wrist as she pulled the towel out from underneath her coat and threw it across the neat stacks of hundred-dollar bills, at the last minute grabbing at one of the loose bills and squeezing it into her fist.

She reached the door visibly out of breath, as if she had just completed a marathon run. It required almost super-human effort to pull the door open, to back away, and let the elderly gentleman inside. Her eyes darted between the waiter and the bed, but if he noticed her nervousness or wondered at the fact that she was wearing her coat despite the fact that she was obviously dripping wet, he said nothing, his eyes directed resolutely at the cart he was pushing.

"Where would you like this?" he asked, his voice pleasantly nondescript.

"Here is fine." She indicated the desk by the window, amazed at how easily the words came.

He deposited the dinner tray on her desk, and she quickly thrust the crumpled hundred-dollar bill into his hand and told him to keep the change. He seemed to hesitate, then glanced with disapproval at the bed.

Her heart fell to her knees and she had to clutch the side of the desk to keep from falling forward. Had he noticed the money? Had it beckoned to him from beneath its damp confines like the telltale heart in the story by Edgar Allan Poe?

"I'll send someone to turn down the bed," he said.

Her own voice was sudden, shrill. "No!" she cried out, startling them both. She cleared her throat, heard herself laugh, mutter something about having work to do, not wanting to be disturbed. He nodded, pocketing the money in his hand, then made a hasty retreat.

She waited until she was sure he had gone before reopening the door and throwing the DO NOT DISTURB sign across its handle. Then she walked to the desk, removed the silver lid from her dinner, and sat down to eat. After only a few bites, however, she felt her earlier exhaustion return, and she stumbled toward the bed, drunk with fatigue. Not bothering to push the money aside or to remove her coat, she tugged at the bedspread and crawled underneath the heavy blue blanket. Her final thought before giving in to sleep was that when she awoke, everything would make sense again, everything would be all right.

But when she opened her eyes at six o'clock the next morning, nothing had changed. She still had no idea who she was.

3

THE FIRST HOUR WAS THE HARDEST. OPENING HER eyes to the knowledge that the supposedly restorative powers of sleep had done nothing to restore her memory sent her reeling into the bathroom to throw up whatever of last night's dinner she had managed to get down. When breakfast arrived—the fresh orange juice, croissants, and coffee she had ordered when her hunger returned—she noticed it came with a complimentary morning newspaper. Her eyes moved restlessly between the newspaper and the television set, afraid to land on either.

What was she afraid of? Did she seriously expect to find her photograph plastered across the front page? Did she think she might find herself the topic for the day on *Oprah Winfrey*?

She forced her fingers to the television dial and turned it on, half expecting to see herself staring back. But instead she saw some pretty blonde in her twenties delivering the news in a voice so cheery that it made her want to be sick all over again and heard not a word about a pretty brunet in her thirties who was missing, although a man in North Carolina reported seeing Elvis as he was emptying the trash.

Nor was there anything in the morning paper: no mention of an escaped prisoner in the vicinity, no word of a psychiatric patient having wandered off, no woman wanted for questioning in connection with any kind of mishap, no mention of anyone having staggered dazed from the scene of a serious accident. Nothing.

The thought occurred to her that if she were not a Boston native, if she came from some other part of the country, had merely ended up in Boston, then there would be no reason for her to make the local papers. And yet the blood covering her dress had still been damp when she discovered it, which would seem to suggest that whatever had happened, it had not happened too far away or too long ago.

She recalled the piece of paper she had found in her pocket—*Pat Rutherford*, R. 31, 12:30. Was there any mention in the paper of this Pat Rutherford? She reread the morning paper, finding nothing. If it was Pat Rutherford's blood covering her dress, Pat Rutherford had either made a quiet and unspectacular recovery or was still lying somewhere undiscovered.

Deciding she would learn nothing from the newspaper, she concentrated instead on the TV, switching channels continually, moving between *Good Morning America* and the *Today* show, between Phil and Oprah and Sally Jessy and Geraldo. She discovered there were specialists on battered lesbians and transvestite kleptomaniacs, that there existed a veritable army of young girls who had given birth to not one but several children before their thirteenth birthday, and that there were an awful lot of husbands out there who didn't want to make love to their wives. She knew this because here were all these people talking about it, pouring their hearts out to Sally Jessy and Geraldo and Oprah and Phil on national TV. There were no secrets anymore, no such thing as privacy.

She thought of calling the networks. I have a great idea for a show, she would tell them: Women who *don't know* whether they're battered lesbians or transvestite kleptomaniacs, who *don't know* how many children they might have borne by the age of thirteen, who have no idea if their husbands make love to them more than twice a year. *Women who don't know who they are*. Aw, forget it, she could hear the networks reply, there's too many of those around.

Maybe, she concurred. But how many of them have almost ten thousand dollars in their pockets and blood all over their clothes?

Well, why didn't you say so? she heard Phil and Oprah and Sally Jessy and Geraldo coo in excited unison. *Rich, blood-spattered women who don't know who they are!* Now, that's an idea whose time has definitely come!

The talk shows were followed by a spate of game shows, then the soaps. Images of beautiful people dotted the screen, and a deep, masculine voice announced the presence of *The Young and the Restless*. "The Young and the Useless," she heard the young man in the convenience store repeat, as she settled back to watch. Who were all these problem-soaked, beautiful people, and what were they doing so dressed up in the middle of the afternoon?

Reluctantly, she retrieved her own dress from the armoire, examining its blood-covered front as if it were a piece of modern art, perhaps something by Jackson Pollock. But like a piece of abstract art, it told her nothing. She rolled it into a tight ball and flung it against a wall, watching it unravel quietly as it fell to the floor, silently mocking her. She returned to her previous position at the foot of the bed and stared blankly ahead until the angle of the sun through the heavy curtains convinced her it was evening.

The six-thirty news carried with it fresh sets of problems but still nothing about a lone woman with blood on her dress and money in her pockets. Dan Rather was as blithely unaware of her existence as were Tom Brokaw and Peter Jennings.

"Who am I?" she cried, angrily snapping off the television and ordering dinner from room service, marveling at the constancy of her appetite. "What happened to me? Where have I put my life?"

By the start of the next day, she knew she had to find out.

* * *

Copley Place is an impressive combination of offices and retail stores located in Copley Square, the heart of the Back Bay. It is home to a major hotel, several fine restaurants, and over one hundred shops located on two levels, each level the length of one city block. It is nothing if not impressive.

She was not impressed. She was frightened.

Wearing only her underwear beneath her coat, her shoes pinching her bare feet, she headed toward the ultramodern Neiman Marcus department store at the far end of the plaza. In her hand she clutched a plastic laundry bag taken from her hotel room and filled with neat little stacks of hundred-dollar bills. The money covered another plastic laundry bag that contained her bloodstained dress.

"Can I be of some assistance?"

She looked around, discovered she had somehow found her way to the ladies' department, and acknowledged the small birdlike woman at her elbow with a nod of her head. If there was one thing she could use at this moment, it was assistance. "I need some new things," she said in a voice that was misleadingly calm. "I have absolutely nothing to wear."

The saleswoman leaned forward and dropped her hands to her sides. "Are we talking a whole wardrobe here?" she asked, trying hard to keep the excitement out of her voice.

"No, just something for today."

The hope of a large commission drained from the woman's gaunt face. "Would you like to see our dresses or are you more interested in casual wear?" Her tone was tentative, as if she couldn't decide whether or not she was being played with.

"Casual," came the unexpected reply. "Maybe slacks and a light sweater."

"This way." The woman led her to a corner of the store that held a selection of beautiful summer wear. "What size?"

She held her breath, trying to recall the size on the label of her blue dress. "Size eight."

"Really?" The woman eyed her coat suspiciously, as if she could see through it. "I would have guessed a six."

"You might be right. I've probably lost some weight in the last few days."

"Well, good for you! I know how hard that can be. I've never weighed more than ninety-five pounds in my life but my daughter, poor thing, takes after her father's side of the family, and she's always on a diet. So, good for you!"

She felt foolishly proud of herself.

"So, you're buying yourself a treat," the saleswoman continued. "Well, you deserve it, dear, although I don't think I'd lose any more weight, if I were you. After a certain age, I think women look better with a few more pounds on them." She reached over and grabbed a pair of light-brown cotton slacks from one rack and a short-sleeved beige cotton sweater with brown flowers down one side from another. "Do you like this?"

Did she?

"Why don't you try them on for size? Then we'll have a better idea what we're looking for."

She nodded, taking the items from the saleswoman's hands and following her to the fitting rooms.

"I'm right outside if you need me."

She entered the small cubicle and pulled the curtain tightly closed before removing her coat. Then she stepped inside the size six brown slacks, and pulled the beige, short-sleeved, one-size-fits-all sweater with flowers down one side over her head. The pants zipped up with no problem; the sweater fell comfortably from her shoulders. She took a step back and admired herself in the mirror. She didn't look bad at all. The saleswoman had a good eye.

"How are we doing in there?" came the question from the other side of the curtain.

"We're doing just fine," she said, emerging from behind the curtain in her new clothes. "I'll take them. Do you think you could cut the tags off?"

"You mean you're going to wear them right out of the store?"

She nodded. "If that's all right . . ."

The woman shrugged. "It's unusual, but I guess it's not unheard of. How will you be paying for these purchases?"

"Cash."

"I thought that might be your answer." The woman led her toward the appropriate counter and pulled out the necessary sales slip. "It's been so long since anyone paid cash, I hope I remember how to do this." She looked around worriedly. "Oh, dear, I think you must have left your purse in the fitting room. . . ."

"I don't have a purse."

The woman seemed to stop breathing.

"I have money." She tapped the laundry bag, reassuringly. "I just don't have a purse. I need a new one."

The saleswoman tried hard not to stare at the plastic laundry bag. "It seems you're in need of quite a few things."

"Yes, actually I am."

"Well, you're in the right store. Our handbag department is on the main floor next to the cosmetics department. That will be two hundred and thirty-seven dollars and twenty-eight cents."

She slowly reached inside the laundry bag and withdrew three one-hundred-dollar bills. The saleslady stared openly and then averted her eyes, quickly making the appropriate change, and watching the change drop into the plastic bag. She then clipped the tags from the newly purchased clothing without further comment. Whatever was going on, it was clear she had decided she would rather not know.

"Remember, handbags are on the first floor, right beside the cosmetics department," the woman called after her.

She spent the next hour shopping. In rapid succession, she discarded her Charles Jourdan pumps in favor of a pair of canvas open-toed flats, purchased a new bra and panties in the palest of pink silks, a stylish handbag in bone-colored leather, a navy wallet, and a pair of tortoiseshell sunglasses. She was slowed down considerably by the fact that she paid in cash, a practice apparently long since abandoned by most shoppers and almost forgotten by sales help. Then she moved on to the cosmetics department where the eager young salesgirl encouraged her to select a peach-colored blush and matching lipstick, as well as a deep-sable mascara she wouldn't want to do without.

She carted all these items into the washroom where she secreted herself in a stall and removed her new slacks and sweater. Then she replaced her underwear with the pink lace delicacies she had just bought. After stepping back into her new brown pants and beige sweater, she transferred several hundred dollars from the plastic laundry bag into her new leather wallet, which she placed, along with her new sunglasses, inside her new purse. She wrapped her old underwear in her coat, then stepped out of the stall, smiling self-consciously at the blue-haired elderly woman who was adjusting her false teeth in front of the mirror. Then she tossed the whole bundle into the wastepaper bin.

Joining the old woman in front of the mirror, she applied her new peach-colored blush in broad, even strokes across her cheeks, and watched the mascara instantly transform her ordinary lashes into something lush and exotic. The peach-colored lipstick did the same thing for her lips, seeming to draw them forward into a full pout.

"That's a lovely shade," the blue-haired woman beside her stated, snapping her dentures into place once and for all. "What's it called?"

She checked the bottom of the tube. "Just Peachy," she read out loud.

"Isn't it, though?" the woman said, and was gone.

"Isn't it, though," she repeated, thinking not of her lips but her predicament. "Isn't it, though."

It amazed her how well she knew the city. She knew exactly how many blocks away everything was, whether she could walk or take public transport, whether it was worth it to take a cab. She felt at ease in this city, and yet, not once had she spotted a familiar face, not once had someone stopped her on the street, not once had anything she had seen tweaked a nerve or triggered a special response. She felt anonymous and alone, like a lost child who has been waiting days for her negligent parents to claim her.

She passed a newspaper kiosk, knowing, because she had already checked, that there was no mention of her in today's paper. Not only had nobody claimed her, nobody seemed to know she was gone. "Just peachy," she muttered aloud, finding herself in front of the busy Greyhound Bus Terminal.

She went inside, cutting through the numerous bodies to the back of the station, seeking to deposit the laundry bag containing her bloodied dress and the bulk of her cash inside one of the storage lockers. But as she was about to drop the correct change into the designated slot, she noticed a sign announcing that the lockers were cleaned out after twenty-four hours and knew she'd have to find another alternative.

"Excuse me," she said, approaching an older man with wispy white sideburns and a neatly pressed blue uniform. "Is there anywhere I can store something for more than twenty-four hours?"

"Turn right," he said, pointing. "Down the long hall."

She followed his directions, holding the laundry bag slightly away from her body, almost as if it contained bloodied body parts and not just her bloody dress. "I need to store this," she told the bored-looking woman behind the counter.

The woman barely glanced up from the magazine she was reading. "Twenty-dollar deposit."

She slipped a twenty-dollar bill across the counter as the woman reluctantly closed her magazine and wrote out a receipt before coming around to the front of the counter and dropping a key into her palm.

"It takes two keys," she explained, her voice on automatic pilot as she led her toward a wall of lockers. "You get one. We keep the other. You need both to open the locker, so don't lose it. Refund or balance of payment due when you pick up your stuff."

She nodded understanding of the rules and quickly thrust the plastic laundry bag inside the now-open locker, watching her hands shake. Had the woman noticed as well? Would she be quick to report her to the police as soon as she was safely out of sight? Suspicious woman with shaking hands storing suspicious package in locker 362. Proceed with caution. Looks guilty of *something*.

It didn't matter. She had already decided to turn herself in. She'd made the decision this morning when it had finally dawned on her that this condition might be more permanent than she had first imagined. She couldn't spend another day in this self-imposed limbo. If she couldn't figure out who she was on her own, then she'd have to let others do it for her, no matter what might have happened to cause her condition, no matter how her dress came to be covered with blood, no matter who stuffed her pockets with hundred-dollar bills. Whatever had happened, whatever she might be guilty of, it couldn't be worse than this—this not knowing.

But she had also decided that before she handed herself over to the powers that be, before she found out what dreadful deed she might have committed, it would be a good idea not to hand over all the evidence. The police would be distracted by the sight of all that money and blood. And who could blame them? Hadn't she herself been similarly distracted?

No, before she confused the issue by presenting the police with the evidence of her guilt, she first wanted to know what crime she might be guilty of. If she walked into the police station carrying a bagful of money and displaying a dress covered in blood, they would panic, as she had panicked. It was better to keep such knowledge to herself, at least for the time being. First things first. And the first thing she had to find out was who the hell she was.

She waited until the woman was back behind the

counter and reabsorbed in her magazine before removing one new shoe, peeling back its instep liner, and laying the locker key inside. Then she replaced the flap, and slid her foot back inside her shoe. It felt strange, wrong, as secrets often do. It would feel better once she got used to it, as soon as her body adjusted to the lie.

She discarded her receipt in a nearby garage bin and walked briskly out of the terminal, debating whether she should stop somewhere for a quick something to eat, amazed at the persistence of her appetite. Then she saw the boyish-looking police officer standing on the corner of Stuart and Berkeley and her appetite suddenly vanished. ''Excuse me,'' she began tentatively, approaching him with caution. ''I was wondering if you could help me.''

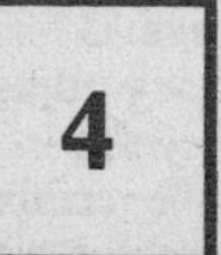

"OKAY, JUST RELAX, THIS ISN'T GOING TO HURT."

"What are you going to do?"

"You're just going to take a little ride. No, lie still. I promise you, you won't feel a thing. Try to relax. It'll be over in about ten minutes."

She was in the Boston City Hospital, a 450-bed hospital that was mostly for charity cases and the poor. The police had brought her here when it was determined that no woman of her description was wanted for anything, nor was she on their current list of missing persons. They had taken her fingerprints, which they intended to send to Washington, and her photograph, which they planned to release to the newspapers, but first they wanted the hospital to run a few tests. They decided on the Boston City Hospital over the posh Massachusetts General when they realized that someone with no identity was unlikely to be carrying any medical insurance.

The police officers left her in the care of a nervous intern who didn't know what to make of her any more than she did. He asked her the same questions as had the police: When did you realize you had no memory? Where exactly were you? Where did you go? Had you been drinking? Could you tell us anything about yourself at all? She answered all their questions except the last one, the one that mattered most.

The intern began his physical examination of her by checking her pupils to see whether they reacted to light. They did, so he moved on to her blood pressure and heartbeat, both of which were good. He checked her urine and felt her head for any signs of external trauma. Everything checked out, so he called the resident, a bearded and resolutely humorless young man who looked as if a smile had never creased his face, and indeed one never did, at least in the half hour he spent examining her.

Dr. Klinger, as he introduced himself solemnly, giving equal weight to each syllable, also checked her pupils, her heartbeat, and her blood pressure, then ordered a battery of blood tests. When she asked what they were for, he explained, with a noticeable trace of impatience, that they were trying to eliminate various physical causes for her amnesia. When she urged him to be more specific, he appeared put out, as if the answers should be self-evident, and told her they were seeking to eliminate alcohol, drugs, AIDS, and tertiary syphilis as possible causes of her condition. Her eyes widened in alarm. Tertiary syphilis was something she'd never even considered.

"Do you really think I might have syphilis?" she couldn't help but ask, finding the idea almost amusing.

"Not really," he replied, sounding as if it were an effort to speak. "I'd consider it more of a possibility if you were black."

Even without knowing who she was, she knew she was offended by the casual cruelty of this remark. I'm a curiosity to them only because I'm white, she thought. If I were black, I'd be dismissed as drunk or stoned or in the final stages of dementia brought on by my rampant promiscuity. She felt her hand form a tight fist underneath her purse, and fought the urge to slam it against the good doctor's face.

"What else are you checking for?"

His voice was dry, disinterested. "We're doing a series of metabolic tests to rule out thyroid, kidney, or liver problems. Also any chemical derangement or vitamin deficiency.''

''How long will that take?''

''We should have the results back in about an hour. In the meantime, we'll do an EEG.''

''That's where you stick a bunch of wires in my head?''

He didn't bother with a reply until the wires had been placed at appropriate intervals in her scalp.

''An EEG records brain waves, lets us see any abnormalities. I don't think we'll find anything in your case.''

''Why do you say that?''

He shrugged, said nothing.

''You think I'm an alcoholic, don't you?''

''I think there's that possibility.''

She was so angry now that it took all her concentrated willpower to keep from leaping off the table and lunging for his throat. Did he treat all his patients with such careless disdain? ''If I were an alcoholic,'' she began slowly, swallowing her rage, ''wouldn't my body be in some stage of withdrawal right now? I mean, I haven't had anything but mineral water to drink in two days, and it hasn't been a problem.''

''There's really little point in speculating. Why don't we just wait until we get the results from the blood tests back?''

Why don't we just stick one of those vials of blood up your tight ass, you patronizing, condescending twirp! she thought but didn't say.

The EEG revealed her brain waves to be perfectly normal. Dr. Klinger pursed his lips into something appropriately smug, his lips curling downward like a Fu Manchu mustache. ''What now?'' she asked as he scribbled a few undoubtedly illegible words on his clipboard.

''We'll wait for the blood tests to come back,'' he said, as he had said, earlier. ''In the meantime, I'll consult with Dr. Meloff about a CAT scan.''

His back was to her and he was already half out of the room as he was speaking, so she didn't hear what exactly they were going to do until Dr. Meloff spoke the same words some time later.

Dr. Meloff, a staff neurologist, was consulted when the blood tests revealed no traces of thyroid, liver, or kidney problems, no chemical derangement, no vitamin deficiency, no hint of alcoholism, drug abuse, AIDS, syphilis or other brain-damaging infections. He was a good-looking man with a full head of dark hair, graying slightly at the temples, and an easy smile that went well with his relaxed manner. "I'm Dr. Meloff," he said, looking over her chart and shaking his head, suppressing a chuckle. "So, you're not quite yourself today, are you?"

She could only laugh in reply.

"That's better," he said, examining her pupils as had the resident and intern before him, then turning her head this way and that. "What's my name?" he asked casually.

"Dr. Meloff," she stated quickly, automatically.

"Good. Follow my finger." He directed her eyes to follow the path he was tracing through the air. "Now, this way." His finger trailed beyond her line of vision. "No, don't move your head. That's it. Good. Very good."

"What's very good?"

"On the surface, there doesn't appear to be anything physically wrong with you. You don't recall any blows to the head? A fall, perhaps?" His fingers were probing her scalp, massaging the back of her neck.

"No, nothing. At least nothing that I can remember."

"What is it, exactly, that you *do* remember?"

She groaned. "Do I have to go through this again? I've already been over everything with the police and the other doctors. I'm sure it's all down on the chart somewhere. . . ."

"Indulge me."

He said it so sweetly that she couldn't resist. Dr. Klinger could take a few pages out of this man's book, she thought, noting that Dr. Klinger had left the room. "I don't remember anything about myself at all," she told

Dr. Meloff plaintively. "All I know is that I found myself at the corner of Cambridge and Bowdoin and I didn't know what I was doing there, how I got there, or who I was. I had no identification; I was alone; I didn't know what to do. So, I walked around for a few hours and then I checked into the Lennox Hotel."

"Under what name?"

"I made one up." She shrugged. "Cindy McDonald. The police have already checked it out. I don't exist."

He smiled. "Oh, you exist all right. A little underweight, perhaps, but you definitely exist. What's my name?"

"Dr. Meloff."

"Good. So, you spent a few nights at the Lennox Hotel and then turned yourself over to the police."

"Yes."

"How did you pay for the hotel?"

"I found some money in my pockets," she said, and almost laughed.

"Why didn't you go to the police immediately?"

She took a deep breath, preparing her body for the lie that was to follow. The police had asked her the same questions. She gave the doctor the exact reply she had given them. "I was confused," she began. "I kept thinking my memory would come back at any minute. I don't *know* why I didn't go to the police right away," she concluded, picturing the neat little stacks of hundred-dollar bills and her blood-spattered dress, knowing full well.

If he doubted her, he gave no such indication. "But you have no trouble remembering the events of the past few days?"

"No trouble at all."

"What about current affairs? You know who's President?"

"I know who's President," she told him, "but I don't know if I voted for him."

"Stand up," he told her, helping her down from the examining table. "Close your eyes and balance on your right leg. Good. Now, the other leg. What's my name?"

"Dr. Meloff. Why do you keep asking me that? I don't have any trouble remembering who anybody *else* is, only who *I* am."

"You can open your eyes now."

She opened her eyes to the unpleasant sight of Dr. Klinger. "The patient's CAT scan is waiting," he said as if she wasn't there, denying even her presence in the room, diminishing what little remained of her sense of self. Dr. Meloff took her arm. "It's all right, Dr. Klinger," he said, guiding her out of the examining room. "I'll accompany Ms. McDonald to X-ray."

Her smile was almost audible as they stepped into the hall.

The X-ray department was located in the hospital's basement. Patients wandered the tired-looking corridors, looking frightened and confused, generally ignored by the staff unless pressed to do otherwise. Everyone appeared distracted, overtired, overworked. They all looked as if they wished they were somewhere—*anywhere*—else.

The room where she was to be tested was dominated by a large tunnellike machine at its center. She was instructed to lie down on a long, narrow table that fed into the machine, to keep her hands at her sides, and lie very still. The technician checked her hair for bobby pins and handed her purse to a nurse.

"What's going to happen?" Her voice carried faint traces of a whine.

"Okay, just relax, this isn't going to hurt."

"What are you going to do?"

"You're just going to take a little ride."

She sat up, about to object.

"No, lie still. I promise you, you won't feel a thing. Try to relax. It'll be over in about ten minutes."

"And then what?" she asked as she felt the table delivering her into the mouth of the machine.

"Lie very still," instructed the technician. "Close your eyes. Have a nice little rest."

"I'll see you in ten minutes," Dr. Meloff called as the darkness covered her like a soft blanket.

Her body vibrated gently to the soft hum of the machine as she inched her way through the tunnel. She wanted to open her eyes and look around but was afraid to. She couldn't remember whether they had told her to keep her eyes closed. She could only hear them repeating to her the importance of lying still.

Don't move, she whispered silently. Don't turn your head. Don't panic. Don't panic. Don't panic. Don't panic. Don't panic. Don't panic.

It's only for ten minutes, she reminded herself, wanting to scream. Only ten minutes and then she'd be out of this damn contraption. Surely, she could hold on for ten minutes. Ten minutes was a very short time in the general scheme of things. Ten minutes wasn't too long to ask of anyone.

Ten minutes was an eternity. It was an endless succession of seconds to be gotten through, to be overcome. She should never have agreed to these tests. She should never have come here in the first place. She should never have turned herself over to the police. She should have stayed in the Lennox Hotel until her money ran out and she had no other choice.

She should have run away when she had the chance. How many people, after all, got the chance for a whole new life? How many people got to wipe the slate clean, or had it wiped clean for them? She'd been handed a chance many people would kill for. *Had* she killed for it?

No, she admonished herself, don't start thinking about that! Not now. She had to stop worrying about who she might be and what she might have done. Wasn't that why she was here? So that *they* could find out for her?

What was so all-fired important about knowing who you were anyway? Look at the number of people in this world who knew exactly who they were and look how miserable they were! No, she'd been given a chance to start again fresh and she'd carelessly, thoughtlessly, thrown it into the garbage along with her coat and her underwear. And now she was stuck. Stuck in the middle of some monstrous machine that was taking pictures of her insides and undoubtedly sneaking peeks into her soul as well. Stuck in the middle of a mystery that would most likely be better left unsolved. Stuck in the middle of a life she had tried to abandon.

Don't panic, a little voice repeated silently in her ear. In another few minutes, it will be all over.

What will be over? she demanded of the voice. What exactly will be over?

Calm down. Calm down. Try not to get excited. Try not to get upset. You know you only get into trouble when you get upset.

What do you mean? What trouble? What trouble do I get into when I get upset?

Relax. Try to stay calm. You know it doesn't do any good to lose your temper.

How do I know that? How do *you* know that? Who are you?

The voice was swallowed by the hum of the machine. She heard nothing further but the stillness, felt herself returned to the womb, as if she were floating in a suspended state, waiting to be born. Behind her closed lids, she saw colors, large splotches of purple and lime green. They formed a kaleidoscope, dancing before her, bursting forward and then retreating into the darkness, only to reappear seconds later. Follow us, they beckoned. We'll guide you through the darkness.

She followed them until they vanished in the glare of a bright sun, and she found herself stranded in what appeared to be a tropical rain forest. Large leaves hung wet from exotic trees as she stumbled through the dense, highly foliated jungle. The earth seemed to be growing up her legs like tall winter boots. Was she sinking? Had she stumbled into quicksand?

A breeze swirled about her head, threatening to wrap itself around her neck like a boa constrictor, then suddenly dissipated, losing its power, and vanishing. It reemerged seconds later as a steady hum, no longer threatening. She felt her body suddenly freed of its narrow constraints.

"There now, that wasn't so awful," a familiar voice reassured her as she opened her eyes.

"Dr. Meloff?"

He smiled. "And I didn't even have to ask you."

She sat up, bewildered. Where was she? More to the point, where had she been? "I must have fallen asleep."

"Good for you. You probably needed the rest."

"I had the strangest dream."

"Judging from what's been happening with the rest of your life, that's not too surprising." He patted her hand. "I'll have the nurse take you back upstairs while I try to figure out the results of your scan. I won't be too long."

He wasn't. Within the hour he returned with the news that her scan was perfectly normal.

"So, what now?"

"I'm not sure," he said and she laughed, appreciating his honesty.

"You never answered my question," she told him, watching him raise one eyebrow. "About why you keep asking me your name."

"Checking for something called the Korsakoff's syndrome," he replied sheepishly.

"Sounds like a book by Robert Ludlum."

He laughed. "Yes, it does. Have you read any?"

"I don't know."

"Just testing."

"And this Korsakoff's syndrome, what exactly is it?"

"It involves a loss of memory. The patient can't recall anything from one minute to the next, so they confabulate constantly."

"Confabulate? You mean lie?" He nodded. "Confabulate," she repeated. "What a lovely word."

"Isn't it?" he agreed. "Anyway, you tell them your name and two minutes later, they can't remember it, so they make something up."

"But why would they do that?"

"People who suffer from amnesia often find it a useful tool not to make others aware of the extent of their condition. That way they're able to gather more facts about themselves with no one being the wiser."

"Sounds like a lot of work."

"Nobody said forgetting who you are was going to be easy."

She smiled. "So you've decided I don't have this Korsakoff's syndrome?"

"I'd say we can forget Mr. Korsakoff. Besides, it's a syndrome usually related to alcohol abuse, and we've definitely eliminated that."

"What haven't you eliminated?"

"My best guess, and that's *all* it is," he stressed, "is that your amnesia is due to some sort of psychological trauma."

"You think I'm crazy?"

"That's not what I said."

"You think it's all in my head," she stated almost angrily, then laughed. "You're trying to tell me the fact that I have nothing in my head is all in my head."

He smiled. "I'm trying to tell you that you may be suffering from an acute nonpsychotic syndrome."

She could feel her body becoming restive, impatient. "Could we speak English here, please, Dr. Meloff?"

He chose his next words slowly, deliberately. "Everyone has a limit to their tolerance of anxiety. When that limit is reached, some people choose escape through the sudden loss of memory. It's called a fugue state and it's most often characterized by flight. When the life situation becomes too stressful, the individual chooses to deal with it by not dealing with it at all, by escaping."

"Come on, Dr. Meloff, people live with great amounts of stress in their lives every day. They don't just go wandering off forgetting who they are."

"Some of them do. Others have nervous breakdowns, beat their kids, have affairs, rob a bank, even commit murder. Hysteria comes in a variety of shapes and sizes."

She looked up at the ceiling, suppressing a few unwanted tears, the image of her bloodied dress dancing before her eyes. "So you think I'm some sort of hysteric?"

"There's a big difference between being a hysteric and suffering from hysterical amnesia. Hysterical amnesia is a coping mechanism, a form of self-preservation, if you will. It involves a loss of memory involving a particular period in a person's life, a period usually associated with great fear, rage, or deep shame and humiliation."

"It sounds like you've been reading up on this."

He grinned. "I stopped and had a few words with one of the staff psychiatrists on my way back here."

"Maybe *I'm* the one who should be talking to the psychiatrist."

He nodded agreement. "I'd like to run a few more tests first. Just to make sure there isn't something we've overlooked."

"Such as?"

"I was thinking of a magnetic resonance scan. It's different from the CAT scan in that it takes an image of the brain using a magnet rather than an X-ray. There's also something called a BEAM test, which stands for Brain Electrical Activity Mapping and is a computerized analysis of brain activity, rather like an EEG. We might also consider a PET-scan, which stands for Positron Emission Tomography, and which tests the metabolism of the brain using radioactive material."

"You're going to nuke me?"

He laughed. "Maybe we'll leave that one out."

"And if all these tests are normal?"

"We could do a spinal tap to look for infections of the nervous system or an arteriogram of the vessels going to the brain."

"Or we could simply send me to the staff psychiatrist," she offered, thinking what an attractive alternative this had suddenly become.

"Or we could simply send you to the staff psychiatrist," he agreed.

"And what could the psychiatrist do? I mean, it's not like I have anything to reveal."

What about the money? What about the blood? she heard a little voice somewhere inside her head demand.

She shook the voice away with a toss of her head.

"She'll probably run a battery of psychological and memory tests," Dr. Meloff answered.

"More tests," she interrupted.

"Hey, it's what we do best."

"How long will all this take?"

"Depending on how fast I can get these things organized, I'd say we're looking at a few days."

She groaned.

"What's the matter? Got a heavy date?"

"I was hoping that this nightmare would be over by then."

He moved to her side and took her hand in his. "It might be." She looked at him expectantly. "Hysterical fugue states, if that's what we're dealing with here, can reverse themselves at any time. And I've never heard of one lasting longer than a couple of months."

"A couple of months?!"

"They usually disappear as quickly as they occur, generally within a few days to a few weeks of their initial onset. But look," he said, placing her hand in her lap and covering it with his own, "let's stop second-guessing ourselves and get some of these tests out of the way." He reached toward a nearby chair and retrieved a magazine someone had left behind. "Relax, catch up on what's happening in the world that you may have forgotten." He checked the date on the front of the magazine. "Well, check up on what was happening a year and a half ago. There'll be a quiz when I return." With that, he was gone.

She sat on the examining table in her newly purchased clothes, clutching her new purse, feeling the key she had secreted under the instep liner of her new shoe pressing against the bottom of her bare foot and wondered if she should tell Dr. Meloff the whole truth. About the money. About the blood. It would certainly go a long way toward supporting his theory about her being in some sort of hysterical fugue state. And then what? Would he run straight to the police or would he be bound by doctor-patient confidentiality? What would confiding everything in the good doctor accomplish aside from making her feel better and possibly sparing her the discomfort of a spinal tap and an arteriogram of the vessels going to her brain?

Wasn't that reason enough?

Taking a deep breath, she determined to tell Dr. Meloff the whole story as soon as he returned. In the meantime, she would do as he suggested and renew her acquaintance with some of the events of the not-too-distant past, testing her powers of recall. She flipped through the well-thumbed pages of the magazine, chuckling at the photograph of Dan Quayle during an early visit to Latin America, losing herself momentarily in the intensity of Tom Cruise's gaze, smiling at the outrageousness of Christian LaCroix's once-fashionable designs. And then she saw the young woman staring at her from the open doorway, and the magazine dropped to the floor.

"I'm sorry," the young woman in the crisp white lab coat apologized, rushing to retrieve the magazine. "I thought I recognized you when I walked by before, but I wasn't sure. You probably don't remember me—"

"Who are you?" Her voice was a shout.

"Dr. Irene Borovoy," came the immediate response. "We met at the Children's Hospital a little over a year ago. I was interning under your husband." She stopped abruptly, her hands flying to her mouth. "You *are* Dr. Whittaker's wife, aren't you? Jane Whittaker? Isn't that right? I'm usually so good at putting names to faces."

"Jane Whittaker," she repeated, fitting her tongue around the unfamiliar name.

"Your husband is such a wonderful man."

"Jane Whittaker," she said again, tasting the sound of it in her mouth.

"Is someone taking care of you, Mrs. Whittaker?" Dr. Borovoy asked, a worried look skewering the evenness of her features. "Are you feeling all right?"

She looked into the young doctor's clear blue eyes. "Jane Whittaker," she said.

5

SHE WAS WAITING FOR THE MAN WHO CLAIMED TO BE her husband to finish conferring with the doctors and the police and confront her.

"Jane Whittaker," she said again, thinking the constant repetition of the name would eventually snake its way into her memory and push her identity out. But the words were hollow, lacking resonance. They merely vibrated inside her head for as long as they took to pronounce, and then vanished, leaving no trace. They brought with them no revelations, no sudden epiphanies. They carried with them no emotional baggage, only a surprising, almost overwhelming, feeling of indifference. "Jane Whittaker," she whispered, drawing out each syllable, feeling nothing. "Jane Whittaker."

It struck her as ironically appropriate that her name should be Jane. Wasn't that always the name they assigned to unidentified female bodies found floating in the Boston Harbor? To unidentified women found murdered in the streets? "Jane Doe," she muttered under her breath.

Or how about Jane Eyre, waiting for the mysterious Mr. Rochester to appear? Would the man now claiming to be her husband make as dramatic an entrance as that gentleman had done, appearing boldly on horseback, only to suffer a fall and sprain his ankle in front of his confused heroine? Would he be similarly dark and strong and stern? And would she fail to recognize him as Jane Eyre had failed to recognize the future great love of her life?

And what of another Jane, Lady Jane Grey, teenage pretender to the throne of England, beheaded when she tried to be someone she was not? Or Jane, wandering through the jungle looking for her Tarzan: "Me Tarzan, You Jane." Did that account for her strange dream during the CAT scan? Was her subconscious using jungle imagery to reawaken her sense of self? *You Jane*. Was it really that simple?

You Jane. Plain Jane. See Jane. See Jane run.

She fought the sudden impulse to leap from her chair and flee the hospital, seek out the safe obscurity of the Lennox Hotel, order room service, and hide under the bed covers from the rest of the world. Spend her days with *The Young and the Restless*, her nights with Johnny Carson and David Letterman. She didn't want to meet the man claiming to be her Mr. Rochester. *Michael Whittaker*, they told her. A doctor, they said with pride, looking at her with fresh respect. A pediatric surgeon, no less. How very lucky she was!

She forced herself to remain in her chair. Where could she run to after all? Weren't the police, the doctors, her husband, huddled together in the next room, dissecting her past and making pertinent decisions about her future? Why should she have expected to be involved in any such decisions when she had so definitively abdicated her responsibilities with regard to her own life? Hadn't she given up on reality and opted for a hysterical fugue?

"Oh, fugue off!" she exclaimed loudly, looking around guiltily to make sure she hadn't been overheard. But she was alone in the room, as she had been since a police officer had announced that Dr. Whittaker was waiting in the lounge, and the doctors had filed out, rendering her nonexistent once again. If a tree falls in the forest and nobody is there to hear it fall, did it make a noise? she found herself wondering. If this man fails to identify me, am I any less real?

What was he like, this Dr. Michael Whittaker, renowned pediatric surgeon, whom everybody seemed to know and admire? The medical staff spoke his name in respectful, no, downright reverential, tones. Even Dr. Klinger's relentlessly impassive face betrayed signs of approval, hovering for several seconds in the vicinity of a smile. And Dr. Meloff had immediately decided to hold off on further testing until he had a chance to meet and confer with his respected colleague.

"Your husband is such a wonderful man," Dr. Irene Borovoy had told her before running off to fetch Dr. Meloff. It seemed to be the consensus of opinion. She was married to a wonderful man. Lucky her!

Why wasn't she wearing his ring?

It stood to reason, she decided, that if she was indeed the wife of renowned pediatric surgeon Michael Whittaker, she would be wearing some proof of this on the third finger of her left hand. There was no such proof. In fact, aside from her watch, she wasn't wearing any jewelry at all. So, in all likelihood, Dr. Michael Whittaker was not her husband. Hadn't he insisted when he was first contacted several hours before, that his wife was visiting her brother in San Diego?

A brother who lived in San Diego, she thought wondrously. Was it possible? Had she been on her way to visit him and been waylaid, savagely attacked in an attempted robbery? Maybe—but that hardly explained how *she* ended up with the money, not to mention someone else's blood covering the front of her dress.

A brother! A brother and a husband! Two for the price of one. At what price? she wondered.

The door opened and Dr. Meloff walked inside, followed by several police officers. They were smiling but looked serious. Seriously smiling, she thought, feeling herself smile in response. So many questions leaped from her brain to her tongue that they stumbled over one another and blocked each other's exit. The result was that when she opened her mouth to speak there was only silence.

"Your name is Jane Whittaker," Dr. Meloff told her gently as tears filled her eyes. "Your husband is waiting in the next room and is very anxious to see you. Do you think you're up for it?"

It took all her strength to push the words from her mouth. Even then, she noticed Dr. Meloff had to lean forward to hear her. "Are you sure? What makes you so sure?"

"He brought photographs, your passport, your marriage license. It's you, Jane. There's no mistake."

"I thought Dr. Whittaker's wife was visiting her brother in San Diego."

"That's what *he* thought. But apparently you never showed up."

"Wouldn't my brother have called him to find out where I was? I mean, if I was supposed to show up in San Diego a few days ago? . . ."

One of the police officers was laughing.

"You'd make a good detective," Dr. Meloff told her. "Officer Emerson asked him the same question."

"To which he obviously had a satisfactory answer," she stated more than asked.

"Apparently you'd planned the visit as a surprise. Your brother didn't know you were supposed to be there until your husband called to find out if you were."

There was a moment's silence. "So, I really am this Jane Whittaker," she said with quiet resignation.

"You're really Jane Whittaker."

"And my husband is waiting in the next room."

"He's most anxious to see you."

"Is he?"

"He's understandably very concerned."

She almost smiled.

"He was so sure you were in San Diego."

"And now he's sure I'm here. Maybe he's wrong this time too."

"He's not wrong."

"What did he say about me?" she asked, seeking to

delay the inevitable confrontation, to arm herself with some much-needed facts.

"Why don't you let him speak for himself?" Dr. Meloff turned toward the door.

"Please," she begged, the urgency in her voice stopping him. "I'm not quite ready."

Dr. Meloff returned to her side and knelt down, forcing her eyes to his. "There's nothing to be afraid of, Jane. He's your husband. He loves you very much."

"But what if I don't recognize him? What if I look into his eyes the way I'm looking at you, and all I see is the face of a stranger? Do you know how terrifying a thought that is for me?"

"Can it be much more frightening than looking in the mirror?" he asked logically, and she had no reply. "Are you ready now, Jane? I don't think it's fair to keep him waiting much longer."

"You'll stay with me? You won't leave us alone!" The second request emerged as a command.

"I'll stay until you ask me to leave." He stood up.

"Dr. Meloff," she called, once again stopping him, this time as his hand reached for the door. "I just wanted to thank you."

"It's been a pleasure." He paused, as if carefully considering his next words. "I'm here if you ever need me."

And then he opened the door and stepped into the hall. She held her breath, hearing voices approach. She stood up, then quickly sat back down, then immediately stood up again, hurrying to the far wall and positioning herself beside the window. The police officers watched her with bemused curiosity from the other side of the room.

"It'll be all right, Mrs. Whittaker," Officer Emerson said. "He seems like a very nice man."

"But what if I don't recognize him?" she repeated, panic filling every pore. "What if I don't know him?"

She didn't.

The man who preceded Dr. Meloff into the room might have been anyone. He was perhaps forty years old, tall, approaching six feet, and slender, with longish, fair hair that had undoubtedly been blond as a child. Even full of anguish, his face was decidedly handsome, with pale-green eyes and full, sensual lips. Indeed, the only thing that marred the otherwise perfect cast of his features was a nose that was slightly off angle. It humanized him, rendered him more accessible, instantly likable. He was not some perfect Ken doll; she would not be expected to be Barbie.

He rushed toward her, an instinctive act. Just as instinctively, she recoiled. Both came to abrupt stops. "I'm sorry," he said quickly, in a voice that was at once gentle and strong. "I'm just so relieved to see you." He paused, his gaze shifting from her frightened face to the floor, biting back tears. "You don't know me, do you?"

It was her turn to apologize. "I want to," she ventured meekly.

"We'll leave you," Officer Emerson stated as he and his partner headed for the door.

"Thank you for everything," she called after them, fixing Dr. Meloff with a look that implored him not to follow their lead.

"If you don't mind," Dr. Meloff began, "I'll stick around for a few minutes."

"I think that Jane would appreciate that," Michael Whittaker said immediately. He tried to smile, and almost succeeded. "Actually, so would I." He took a deep breath. "I seem to be very nervous."

"Why are *you* nervous?" she asked, the thought that he might be as nervous as she was simply not having occurred to her.

"I feel like I'm on a blind date," he answered guilelessly. "And I really want to make a good impression." A laugh caught in his throat. "I thought I was prepared for just about everything," he continued, "but I have to confess that I don't know what to make of this situation." He lifted his eyes from the floor, returning them to his wife's worried face. "I'm not sure how to act."

"So this has never happened to me before," she stated rather than asked.

"God, no."

"Why do you think it's happening now?"

He shook his head, his confusion too expansive for words to contain.

He was dressed casually in gray pants and a blue shirt that was open at the neck. She noticed that his shoulders stooped ever so slightly, probably the result of long hours spent leaning over an operating table. His large hands dangled uncomfortably at his sides, and his long, thin fingers clutched at the air, as if trying to grasp the larger picture of what was happening to their lives and bring it into sharp, clear focus. He had a surgeon's hands, she recognized, noting the carefully kept nails, and imagining those fingers operating with deft precision on a small child. Gentle hands, strong fingers, she thought, suddenly aware of the thin gold wedding band he wore.

"Why aren't I wearing a wedding ring?" she asked, catching everyone, including herself, by surprise. "I mean, you're wearing one and I'm not. It seems a little unusual. . . ." Her voice trailed off, disappearing into the still confusion of the room.

It took him a minute to respond. "You haven't worn one for a while," he said slowly as she looked to him for further clarification. "You had some sort of allergic reaction to the gold. Your finger became very itchy underneath the band and the skin got all flaky and red. You took the ring off one day and never put it on again. We kept saying we'd replace it, get you something with diamonds instead—nobody's allergic to diamonds, we'd laugh—but we never got around to it. To be honest, I'd forgotten all about it." He shook his head, as if amazed he could have forgotten anything so important.

"You'd be amazed at the things you can forget," she said, seeking to reassure him.

He laughed, and suddenly she was laughing as well.

"This might be a good time for me to take my leave," Dr. Meloff volunteered, and she nodded. "Let one of the nurses know when you're ready to go home. I'd like to see you before you check out."

"He seems like a very nice man," Michael Whittaker remarked after Dr. Meloff had left the room.

She smiled. "That's what they all say about you."

He sighed, the air sliding from his mouth in ripples, like a wave. "What can I say that will reassure you? Tell me what I can do to help."

She edged herself gingerly away from the window closer to where he stood, careful to leave a space of at least several feet between them. "How long have we been married?" she asked, feeling infinitely foolish.

"Eleven years," he answered simply, no attempt at embellishment. She liked that.

"What day did we get married? How old was I?"

"We got married on April seventeenth, 1979. You were twenty-three years old."

"That makes me thirty-four?" she asked, although the answer seemed obvious enough.

"You'll be thirty-four on August thirteenth. Would you like to see a copy of our marriage license?"

She nodded, moving closer to his side as he reached into his pocket to pull out their certificate of marriage. "It says we got married in Connecticut," she noted, aware of the warmth emanating from his body.

"That's where you were from. Your mother still lived there."

"And my father?"

"He died when you were thirteen years old."

She felt instantly saddened, not because her father had died when she was still in her formative years, but because she had no recollection of his ever having lived. She felt doubly abandoned. "How did I end up in Boston?"

He grinned. "You married me."

She bit her lip, not ready yet to discuss their life together. She needed to digest more facts about herself first, to come to their marriage with some sense of personal history.

"Would you like to see a copy of your passport?" he asked, offering it forward, as if it were a piece of evidence and this hospital room a court of law.

Her eyes quickly scanned the small booklet, noting that her maiden name was Lawrence, that her physical description matched with what she had discovered about herself, and that the photograph at the bottom, while far from flattering—she had the look of a frightened doe caught in the glare of a car's headlights—was unmistakably a picture of herself. "Do you have more photographs?" she asked, knowing he had.

He drew several snapshots out of his pants pocket. Her body inched closer to his side, so that their arms were touching as he held out the photographs for her to see.

The first picture was of the two of them carousing on a beach. He was tanned; she was just slightly less so. Both wore modestly attractive black bathing suits, and both looked as if they were having trouble keeping their hands off one another.

"Where was this taken?" she asked.

"On the Cape. At my parents' cottage. About five years ago," he continued, knowing this would be her next question. "That was when we still believed that the sun couldn't be anything but good for us. Your hair was a little longer then. I was probably a few pounds thinner."

"You don't look like you've put on any weight." She felt instantly self-conscious, as if she had trespassed onto too personal ground. She quickly turned her attention to the second photograph.

Again the two of them faced the camera smiling, their arms locked tightly around one another's waist. This time, however, they were in more formal attire, he in a dinner jacket and black tie, she in a dark-pink evening dress. "This is more recent," she stated, her mind registering the passage of the years.

"It was taken at Christmas. We were at a hospital dance."

"We look very happy," she marveled.

"We *were* very happy," he said with emphasis, then more softly, less assuredly, "I know we will be again."

She closed her hands over the photographs and returned them to him, along with their marriage certificate and her passport. Then she walked back to the window, staring out at the street below before turning again to the stranger to whom she had been married—apparently very happily—for the past eleven years.

"So I grew up in Connecticut," she said after a long silence.

"You lived there until you went away to college."

"What was my major, do you know?"

He smiled. "Of course I know. It was English. You graduated at the top of your class."

"And after I graduated?"

"Well, you found out that there weren't a whole lot of jobs out there that specifically required a degree in English literature, and you didn't want to teach, so you eventually got a job at Harvard Press."

"In Boston?"

"Cambridge."

"Why didn't I go back to Connecticut, or head for New York?"

"Well, I like to think I had something to do with that decision."

She turned back toward the window, still not ready to discuss their life together. "What about my brother?"

He seemed startled by the question. "Tommy? What about him?"

"How old is he? What does he do? Why is he in San Diego?"

"He's thirty-six," he began, calmly answering her questions in order. "He owns a yacht dealership, and he's been living in San Diego for the past ten years."

"Is he married?"

"Yes. Actually it's his second marriage. His wife's name is Eleanor and I'm not exactly sure how long they've been married."

"Do they have children?"

"Two small boys. I'm embarrassed to admit I don't know how old."

"So I'm an auntie."

"That you are."

"What else am I?" she asked suddenly, the question popping from her mouth before she could stop it.

"I'm not sure I understand."

She swallowed hard, as if she could force the question she had been avoiding back into her gut. "I'm an auntie," she repeated, gathering her strength. "Am I also . . . a mother?"

"Yes," he said, with something approaching eloquence.

"Oh, God!" Her voice was a low moan. How could she forget she had a child? What kind of mother did that make her? "Oh, God." She felt her body folding in on itself, like an accordion. Her arms wrapped around her shaking frame and her head fell forward.

"It's okay. It's okay," he whispered, his voice a salve, coating her, protecting her. She felt his arms guiding her back into an upright stance. She buried her head against the warmth of his chest, hearing his heart beat loudly, understanding he was as frightened as she was.

He let her cry uninterrupted for several minutes, stroking her back as if she were a child. Her cries shuddered to a halt. "How many children do we have?" she asked so quietly that she had to clear her throat and repeat the question.

"Just one. A little girl. Emily."

"Emily," she repeated, savoring the name, as if it were wine on the tip of her tongue. "How old is she?"

"Seven."

"Seven," she whispered wonderingly. "Seven."

"She's with my parents," he said. "I thought it might be wiser, until things got straightened out, that she stay with them."

"Oh, thank you!" Her tears of shame became tears of relief. "I just don't think it would be a good idea for me to see her yet, or for her to see me."

"I understand."

"It would be so awful for her to have to look at her mother knowing that her mother didn't recognize her. I can't imagine anything more frightening for a child."

"It's all taken care of," he assured her. "They've taken her to the cottage. She can stay with them all summer as far as they're concerned."

She cleared her throat again, wiping several stubborn tears away from her cheeks. "When did you arrange all this?"

He shrugged, his hands lifting from his sides, palms up, into the air. "It just sort of worked itself out," he said, as if acknowledging that he had no control over any aspect of his life at the moment. "We'd already planned for Emily to spend the time with my parents while you were in San Diego . . ." His words trailed off, like a windup toy running out of steam.

"Tell me more about myself," she urged.

"What would you like to know?"

"The good things," she said immediately.

He didn't hesitate. "Well, let's see. You're bright, determined, funny . . ."

"I'm funny?"

"You have a wonderful sense of humor."

She smiled gratefully.

"You're a great cook, a terrific companion, a loyal friend."

"I sound too good to be true."

"You couldn't sing on key if your life depended on it," he continued, laughing, "and you *love* to sing."

"That's my worst fault?"

"When you're angry, you turn into the Devil Girl from Mars."

"I have a temper?"

He grinned sheepishly. "You were always very good at understatement. Yes," he agreed, after a pause, "you have a temper."

She digested this piece of information, then went on. "What's my favorite color, my favorite food?"

"Blue," he answered easily. "Anything Italian."

"Do I have a career? You said I worked for a few years in publishing." The questions were coming faster now, one following doggedly on the heels of the question before it.

"You gave up working full-time when Emily was born. I was able to convince you to come and work for me a few days a week only after Emily was in school all day."

"I work for you?"

"Tuesdays and Thursdays. Answering my phone, taking care of my correspondence, occasionally rearranging my files."

"Sounds very fulfilling."

She hadn't meant for the words to carry such a sarcastic edge, so she was grateful when he declined to take offense. "Actually, you took the job primarily as a way for us to spend more time together. I have a very busy practice, and my hours aren't always dependable. We wanted to make sure we didn't lose the closeness we'd always had. This way, we knew we had Tuesdays and Thursdays together. I'm in the operating room the other days."

"Sounds like the perfect marriage."

"Well, nothing's perfect." He paused. "We've had our share of arguments, just like everybody else, but on balance, I think we'd both agree we had something pretty special."

She found herself aching to believe him. "Where do we live? Beacon Hill?"

He smiled. "No, we decided the city wasn't a great place to raise a family. We have a very nice house in Newton."

She recognized Newton as a well-to-do-suburb of Boston, no more than a twenty-minute highway drive away.

"Would you like to go there?" he was asking.

"Now?"

He gently touched the sides of her arms. She felt a current, like an electrical charge, travel along her skin to the base of her brain. "Trust me, Jane," he said gently. "I love you."

She looked into his kind face, saw his commitment to her reflected in his eyes, and longed to tell him she loved him in return, but how could she love someone she didn't know? Instead, she reached up to gently touch his lips, feeling them instantly kiss the tips of her fingers. "I trust you," she said.

6

"SORRY ABOUT THE TRAFFIC," HE APOLOGIZED, AS if he could be held accountable for the line of cars that crawled along Highway 9 at a speed of no more than twenty miles an hour.

"There must be an accident up ahead," Jane said matter-of-factly, not saying what she really felt, that anything that delayed her reentry into her past life, a life she remained totally unaware of, was welcome, indeed preferred. She caught him looking at her strangely. "What?" she asked, feeling frightened, though she wasn't sure why.

"Nothing," he answered quickly.

"No, there's something. I could see it in your eyes."

He paused, pretending to be studying the traffic. "I was just thinking that if this were more normal times," he began self-consciously, "then you'd be reaching across the steering wheel to honk the horn."

"I'd be reaching across the steering wheel to honk the horn when *you* were driving?!" Her tone was incredulous.

"You've done it before."

"I'm that impatient?"

"You always liked to get where you were going as quickly as possible. Traffic was one of those things that drove you crazy,'' he continued, speaking of her in the past tense, as if she were newly deceased.

''Why was I always in such a hurry?''

''That's just the way you are,'' he said simply, returning her to the here and now.

''Tell me about you,'' she said.

''What would you like to know?''

''Everything.''

He smiled, his lips forming an easy, relaxed upward curve. She studied his face as he pondered where to begin. In profile, the wayward slant of his nose was more pronounced, and his forehead was all but hidden by a curtain of hair that fell unmolested into his eyes, creating an impression of casual disregard for his appearance. Still, Dr. Michael Whittaker managed to retain an air of dignified authority, an aura that she knew encouraged respect from others no matter what the occasion or how he was dressed. It was a feat few would be capable of, and one that he performed effortlessly, probably because it was something he was unaware of.

''Well, let's see,'' he began, relaxing back into the black leather of the front seat of his black BMW. ''I was born and raised in Weston, not ten minutes away from where we live now. I had a happy childhood,'' he said, laughing. ''Is this the sort of thing you want?''

''Exactly. Were you an only child?''

''I had a brother.''

''Had?''

''He died when I was in high school. Actually,'' he continued before she could interrupt with more questions, ''I never really knew my brother. He was four years older than I was and was born with a wide variety of congenital deformities. He had to be institutionalized at birth.''

''I'm so sorry,'' she told him, and she was.

''It all happened a very long time ago.'' He shrugged. ''And like I said, he was never really a part of my life. By the time I came along, my parents had pretty much adjusted to his absence, so I grew up completely doted upon—you know, the classic cliché of the only child who has everything."

"Including the total responsibility for his parents' happiness," Jane said, understanding the situation without needing to hear it in so many words.

He regarded her with a mixture of surprise and respect. "It's reassuring to see that in some ways you haven't changed at all."

"Meaning?"

"That's exactly what the old Jane would have said."

"The old Jane," she repeated, and laughed, the nervous laugh of one not sure how else to react. "Tell me about your parents," she encouraged.

"My father was a brilliant scientist." It was his turn to laugh. "Are there any other kind? Anyway, he's retired now, but when I was a child, he was very caught up in his work. I don't remember him being around much, so my mother did a lot of overcompensating." He seemed lost temporarily in images of the past. "My father used to say that if he'd let my mother have her way, she would have nursed me until I was five years old."

"But she didn't."

"Not that I can remember. We did take baths together, however, until I was, oh, in second grade." He grinned, the self-satisfied smile of Alice's Cheshire cat. "I *do* remember that."

"She was probably anxious to keep you a baby for as long as she could," Jane said, thinking out loud. "Because of your brother."

"I guess we were all more affected by his condition than any of us realized. I mean, my brother's undoubtedly the reason I went into medicine, why I specialized in pediatric surgery. Most of what I do in my practice involves kids who are deformed in some way or another, cleft palates, disfigurements of various kinds. Anyway," he continued after a long pause, "I was accepted into Harvard Medical School, which was great because it meant I didn't have to go out of state, and Harvard was expensive enough, even on a partial scholarship." Another wide, unexpected grin flashed across his face. For an instant, he looked and sounded just like a teenager. "This is great. I haven't talked about this stuff in years. It's like we're getting to know each other all over again."

"Tell me about our first date. Tell me how we met."

"We were fixed up."

"By whom?"

"I guess it was a mutual friend. Yeah, it was Marci Tanner. Good old Marci Tanner. I wonder whatever happened to her. She was on her third husband and living somewhere in South America last we heard from her."

"And it was love at first sight?"

"Are you kidding? We hated each other! Hated, loathed, despised!"

She tried, but failed, to keep the surprise out of her face. Instinctively, she moved closer to the window, as if to put greater distance between a man she could have hated, loathed, despised on sight approximately a dozen years ago.

"I had just had my heart broken by some beautiful young thing," he explained, "and you had had your fill of egotistical young doctors. We were both very wary. We went to a party. I even remember what you wore! It was a gray dress with a little pink bow at the collar. I thought you were as cute as hell. But having just had my heart broken by another cute young thing, I wasn't about to rush into another relationship, and I probably made that as clear as I could as fast as I could. 'Hi there, I'm Dr. Michael Whittaker and I have no intention of getting involved at this point in time, so admire me from afar, but don't get your hopes up.'"

She laughed. "Somehow that doesn't sound like you." She relaxed into her former position, lulled by the sound of his voice.

"We couldn't agree on a thing. I liked action movies; you only went to foreign films. I loved beer and salami sandwiches; you preferred wine and cheese. You were into classical music; my thing was rhythm and blues. You liked to spend hours talking literature, and the only book I knew anything about was *Gray's Anatomy*. I was a sports fanatic, and you didn't know the Boston Celtics from the Boston Red Sox."

"Somewhere along the way, we obviously made peace."

"It took a while. We spent most of that first evening waiting for the other to make some huge gaffe, the kind of mistake that could justify the other's storming off the premises. But we didn't. And then we found ourselves dancing together. It was a slow dance, a real oldie, Johnny Mathis singing "The Twelfth of Never," of all things. And I think that's what did it."

"Chemistry over common sense," she noted with a smile.

"Maybe in the beginning. But after a while, I found I got used to subtitles and you discovered that salami sandwiches weren't so bad after all. You even learned to tell the difference between a hockey puck and a basketball, so how could I not love you? And I learned that there was more to literature than the latest medical journal, so how could you resist falling in love with me?"

"And so we got married and lived happily ever after."

"I hope so," he said sincerely, reaching across the seat to take her hand in his, withdrawing it when he felt her body tense. "I'm sorry," he said quickly. "I promise I won't rush you."

"I know that," she agreed. "I'm sorry too. I want so much to remember." She looked out the window at the cars moving freely in the opposite direction. "I wonder what's causing the delay."

"I suspect we'll find out soon enough. I see ambulance lights ahead." He regarded her carefully, as if he were studying her face to see how she might react.

"What?" she asked again, as she had asked earlier when she caught him looking at her in this same way.

He shook his head. "Nothing," he said.

"So, what else can you tell me?"

He tossed his head back across the top of his spine, as if looking to the roof of the car for inspiration. "Well, you're a big one for causes."

"What do you mean? What causes?"

"Lately, you've been very concerned with protecting the environment, and saving the rain forests. That sort of thing. And I don't mean it to sound like you're one of those dilettantes who dabble in whatever cause is the current rage. You're not. Just that when something genuinely concerns you, you become totally committed. You're a great one for righting wrongs," he said with obvious admiration.

Her mind formed an immediate mental image of a blood-splattered blue dress and a laundry bag full of hundred-dollar bills. Had she collected these items while busy "righting wrongs"? Was she some misguided, latter-day Robin Hood, stealing from the rich to give to the homeless, her latest cause of the hour?

"Tell me about the kinds of things we do together," she said, willing the blood-soaked image away with the sound of her voice.

"We play tennis; we go to movies, the theater; you've even gotten me addicted to the Boston Pops. We spend time with friends; we like to travel whenever we get the chance. . . ."

"Where do we go?"

"Well, we haven't had a real holiday in a couple of years, but we did manage a trip to the Orient about four years ago."

"What about the jungle?" she asked, recalling the strange dream she had had while tunneling her way through the CAT scan.

"The jungle?" He sounded surprised.

"You said I was concerned about rain forests. Have we ever visited one?"

"I think you were interested in *preserving* them, not visiting them."

She smiled, marveling at the strange way her past was trying to infiltrate her subconscious. An interest in preserving the rain forests had snaked its way into one of her dreams. If her unconscious self could remember such relatively insignificant details of her life, surely it wouldn't be too long before the rest of her caught up, especially once she was back in her familiar environment.

Should she tell Michael about the money and the blood? she wondered. She had planned to tell Dr. Meloff, but then that other young doctor, Dr. Borovoy, had confused everything by knowing who she was, and the opportunity had passed. Maybe Michael knew something about it. Maybe, as unlikely as it seemed, it was all rather innocent, carrying a relatively straightforward explanation. Maybe he might be able to help her. He was her husband, after all. They shared a life, a child. He loved her. There was absolutely no doubt in her mind about that. So why hadn't she confided the whole story to him? Why was she hesitating, even now?

She knew the answer without having to form the words: self-preservation. Saving the rain forests was one thing; protecting herself was something else again. The rain forests would have to wait. As Michael would have to wait to hear the whole story.

"Don't look," he was saying.

Immediately, like a child who has been told not to stare and can't help herself, she looked in the direction he had told her to avoid. There were three automobiles, several police cars, and an ambulance pulled over to the side of the road. She caught a quick glimpse of twisted metal and broken glass, of a young man crying on the pavement, his head buried in his hands. She saw a stretcher being pushed inside the ambulance, its doors closing before she had a chance to absorb who had been injured and how badly. A policeman was standing beside the young man, trying to coax him into one of the waiting police vehicles.

Traffic came to a complete standstill as the ambulance roared away from the scene, sirens blaring. The young man allowed himself to be helped into the police car, which took off immediately, so that only one police car remained, undoubtedly awaiting the arrival of a tow truck. Everyone else had left the scene. Jane wondered what had caused the accident and how many people had been involved, how many had been injured, and how it would affect the rest of their lives.

"What are you thinking about?" Michael asked,

watching her intently. He looked as if he were afraid that she might bolt from the car.

She told him her thoughts, and he seemed relieved. She was about to ask him why, thought better of it, and asked instead, "Where did we go on our honeymoon?"

If he thought the question a strange one at this particular time, he said nothing, simply answering her question. "The Bahamas," he said, watching the road, waiting for the flow of traffic to resume.

Her imagination immediately brought forth images of white sandy beaches and bright-blue water, of wildly colored fish swimming just beneath the ocean's surface, of attractive low buildings in shades of pink and yellow, of lovers joined at the hip, barely able to keep their hands and lips to themselves as they flirted with the water's edge.

She saw herself, wearing her modest black bathing suit, jump from the photograph Michael had brought with him to the hospital and onto the Nassau beach. She saw Michael beside her, watched them trip over each other's feet as they sought to keep in step while wrapped in each other's arms. She saw them give up the attempt and collapse onto the cool white sand, rolling over one another as if they were waves.

She saw them later in their hotel room, their bathing suits now in a careless heap on the floor. They were a round ball of arms and legs, their bodies shiny with sweat as they arched toward one another, her hands falling to the small of his back, his lips grazing the tips of her breasts. She watched his head move between her legs as she slipped her tongue along the middle crease of his buttocks. She groaned out loud.

"Are you all right?" he asked quickly.

Please don't ask me what I was thinking, her eyes begged his, and he did not. "I'm fine," she reassured him, trying to blink away the stubborn image of their imagined lovemaking. Were they really so good together? Was she really so provocative a lover? Were his hands as gentle as the hands her mind had lent him?

She directed her gaze out the side window and was

surprised to see how quickly they were moving. As if he could read her thoughts, he said, "It should just be another few minutes."

She tried to smile but anxiety seized her lips and kept them resolutely straight. A fresh fear invaded her body like a steady stream of ice water. It traveled from her breast bone to her bowels, and for an instant, she thought she might have to tell him to pull over and stop the car, but the urgency faded, although the fear did not.

"Tell me about our friends," she said, hearing the quaver in her voice.

"Would you like them in descending order of favorites?" He laughed, and she laughed too, thinking this a wonderful idea. "Well, let's see, first on the list would have to be Howard and Peggy Rose, who are spending the summer in the south of France, as they have every summer for the past ten years. Next is probably the Tanenbaums, Peter and Sarah, who we always beat at tennis but who are wonderful sports about it. And then there's the Carneys, David and Susan—they're both doctors, and then probably Ian and Janet Hart, and Eve and Ross McDermott. Do any of these names mean anything to you?"

They meant nothing; she shook her head. "What about girlfriends?" she asked.

"Mine or yours?"

"Let's start with mine," she said, acknowledging his wry smile. "Do I have any?"

"A few. There's Lorraine Appleby—you used to work together way back when—and Diane somebody-or-other, I can never remember her last name."

She thought of the note she had found in her coat pocket, saw the name PAT RUTHERFORD scrawl itself across the car's windshield in invisible ink. She held her breath. "Anyone named Pat?"

He gave the name a few seconds' thought before answering. "I can't think of any Pats," he said finally. "Why? Does the name Pat mean something to you?"

"It's just a name," she lied. A name I found scribbled on a piece of paper stuffed into my coat pocket along with almost ten thousand dollars in hundred-dollar bills. Oh, and did I also neglect to mention that the front of my dress was covered in blood?

He shrugged, as if assuming that someone named Pat was of no further consideration to their lives. Maybe he was right. After all, there was no telling how long that note had been lining her pocket. "There's the cutoff just ahead." He pointed to the sign that announced the city of Newton, a suburb of Boston bordered on three sides by the Charles River. Newton was composed of fourteen diverse villages that managed to blend effortlessly into one another. "We live in the village of Newton Highlands," Michael said, pulling off the highway. "Does anything look familiar?"

She toyed with the idea of pretending that she recognized a particular street, had fond recollections of a certain well-tended garden, but tossed the idea aside with a shake of her head that said, no, nothing looked remotely familiar. Hartford Street had no more meaning for her than did Lincoln or Standish. One garden looked the same as the one beside it. The houses, large, attractive wooden structures, spoke of prosperity and calm. There was no clue as to what kind of disorder might lie just beyond each threshold, no hint of the possible chaos inside. She wondered if she would recognize her own street, whether she would be able to identify the house she lived in. Would these things find some way into her subconscious as the rain forests had done? Would they beckon to her like a kind of second sight?

"This is our street," he told her, putting an end to such speculations. Forest Street, the sign proclaimed, no forest anywhere in sight. The street was as anonymous as the ones preceding it, flanked on both sides by the familiar wooden houses, one painted gray with a large screened-in front porch, another painted blue and almost hidden behind several monstrous oak trees. "There we are," he announced, pointing. "Third house from the corner."

The third house from the corner on the left-hand side of the street was no more, no less, imposing than any of the other homes in the area. It was an inviting, two-story structure, painted white, a double row of red and pink impatiens running along its base, underlining its storybook appeal. There were black shutters around each window and flowerboxes filled with red and pink impatiens below. Several steps led to the large black front door, and a double garage was situated to the left of the house, its doors also black. She noted the presence of a stained-glass window in one of the upstairs rooms.

It looked to be a very comfortable house in a very comfortable neighborhood. She could have done a lot worse than to find herself sitting in a new-model BMW in front of a beautiful home in the tony suburb of Newton, Massachusetts, married to a handsome and sensitive pediatric surgeon.

So why had she chosen to escape into a hysterical fugue? What had driven her out of her comfortable house in this most comfortable of neighborhoods?

"Who's that?" she asked, catching sight of a woman in an old pair of Bermuda shorts watering the front lawn of the house directly across the street from her own. The woman had become so distracted at the sight of Michael's car that she had ceased paying attention to what she was doing and was now diligently hosing down her front door.

Michael raised his hand in what was simultaneously a wave and a signal of reassurance. The gesture acknowledged the woman's presence while communicating that everything was under control. "Her name is Carole. Carole with an *e*. Carole-with-an-*e* Bishop," he enunciated clearly. "She and her family moved here a few years ago from New York. By family I mean a husband, two teenage children, and an elderly widowed father. Unfortunately, the husband moved out again last fall." He pulled into their driveway. "I take it none of this rings a bell."

"Should it?"

"Well, you and Daniel used to go running together a few mornings a week. Daniel is her husband. *Was*," he corrected. "Or soon to be *was*, at any rate."

"I'm a runner?"

"Occasionally. You haven't done much running since Daniel moved out."

"Why was she looking at us like that?"

"Like how?"

"I think you know how. You seemed to signal to her that everything was okay."

He shook his head. "You still don't miss a thing, do you?" His voice carried equal traces of admiration and amazement.

"I take it she knows about my disappearance."

"She knows," he said, clicking the remote-control unit fastened to the sun visor of his car. The double garage door automatically lifted, revealing a silver Honda Prelude. Her concentration shifted from her neighbor to the small automobile inside the garage.

"Is that my car?"

"That it is."

So she hadn't abandoned it on some city street. It was safe and sound at home, the way she should have been. Michael drove slowly into the garage. For a second, she felt as if she were entering a tomb.

"Scared?" he asked.

"Terrified."

His hand reached for hers and this time she didn't pull away. "Just take it slow," he urged. "If you don't recognize anything, and you probably won't, don't worry about it. I'm right beside you and I won't let anything happen to you."

"Do we have to go in yet?"

"We can sit here as long as you like."

They sat in the garage for some minutes in silence, their hands intertwined, their breathing short and irregular, until she said, "This is silly. We can't sit here all day."

"What do you want to do?" he asked.

And she said, "I want to go home."

7

HE PUSHED OPEN THE FRONT DOOR, THEN STOOD BACK to let her step inside. She hung back, half expecting him to scoop her into his arms and carry her over the threshold, as if they were newlyweds making their first entrance into their new home.

In many ways, this was exactly how she felt. Her heart beat with the same kind of nervous apprehension, the excitement at beginning a new life, the trepidation that accompanied that first step into the unknown. Did modern-day grooms still carry their brides across the thresholds? Probably not, she decided, looking to the man who had been her husband for eleven years for one of his reassuring, soft smiles and not being disappointed. The world had grown too sophisticated, too blasé, too jaded, for such simple pleasures. Besides, from everything she had seen and heard on Oprah and Phil and Sally Jessy and Geraldo, today's women didn't want or need to be carried through any symbolic doorways, and today's men were in no condition to support their weight.

"What do you think?" Michael was asking, his apprehension palpable even as he tried to hide it. "Think you want to go inside?"

Jane exhaled a long deep breath of air and forced her eyes to focus on the small front hall, papered in delicate red flowers. There was a central staircase painted white and carpeted in pale green, as was the entire downstairs, altogether an attractive beginning. It was an inviting house, one that beckoned a visitor to enter. She took another deep breath, forced one foot in front of the other, and stepped inside.

Her first impression was one of light. It poured in from everywhere, from the large front windows of the living room on her left, from the equally large front windows of the dining room on her right, from the mammoth skylight that looked down on the central hall from the second floor. The hall narrowed once it passed the stairs, leading to the rooms at the back of the house.

Jane walked slowly into the middle of the hall and stopped, not sure whether her legs would sustain her.

"Would you like the tour?" Michael suggested, not asking whether anything looked familiar. She nodded, following him into the spacious dining room, papered in red-and-white stripes, that somehow managed to be bold and subtle both. The top of the dining room table was a green marble slab; the eight chairs that sat around it were covered in the same red-and-white stripes as the walls. There was a glass cabinet filled with a delicate red-and-white floral china, and a glass server crammed with multicolored bottles of liqueur. Several tall plants rested in Oriental vases by the front window. "Everything's very nice," she said, wondering whether they had picked up the vases on their trip to the Orient, and following Michael across the hall into the living room.

It was a large room running the full length of the house, and papered in a variation of the floral chintz that covered the walls of the hall. A chintz sofa and matching chairs were grouped around a large stone fireplace, on one side of which rested an impressive-looking bookshelf and on the other an elaborate stereo system. On the opposite wall stood an upright piano in shiny ebony. Jane tentatively approached the piano and let her fingers slide across the keyboard, carelessly tracing out a melody by Chopin.

The delicate sound caught her by surprise. She looked

at her fingers, which turned automatically clumsy and forgetful. It seemed her playing was a reflex action that could not withstand close scrutiny.

"Don't worry," Michael said. "It'll come back to you. Just try not to think so hard about what you're doing."

"I didn't realize I played." Her voice was wistful.

"You took lessons as a child. Every now and then you sit down to play that same old piece by Chopin." He laughed. "Actually, it was one of the things I was hoping would stay forgotten." His smile faded almost immediately. "I'm sorry. I didn't mean to sound glib."

"You don't have to apologize." Her eyes were drawn to a cluster of photographs that rested along the top of the piano. Among them were three classroom pictures of young children arranged in neat little rows according to height, looking proud and happy for the photographer. ARLINGTON PRIVATE SCHOOL announced the small blackboard held by one of the boys in the front row. Undoubtedly her daughter was among these children.

"Do you know which one she is?" Michael asked, reading her thoughts, and coming up behind her. She felt his warm breath on the back of her neck.

Jane lifted one of the photographs into her hands, her eyes skipping quickly over the imp-faced little boys to concentrate on the more eager-to-please little girls. Would she recognize her only child?

"She's the second one from the end," Michael said, ending her agony, pointing to a delicate little girl with long light-brown hair and enormous eyes. She was dressed from head to toe in yellow and looked to be about three or four years old. "That was in junior kindergarten," he continued, answering her silent question. "She was four." He picked up the next photograph, pointing to the same little girl, older by one year, wearing pink and white, her long hair swept back into a ponytail. "Senior kindergarten."

"She's tall," Jane remarked, hearing her voice crack.

"Always in the back row, I'm afraid. Things haven't changed a lot since we were in grade school."

She exchanged the first picture for the third and last, quickly locating Emily, now in grade one, wearing black-and-white checks, her hair loose and disappearing down her back, her smile not quite as broad as in previous years, her eyes more self-conscious and shy. My baby, Jane thought, thinking her a beautiful child, but feeling none of the maternal instincts she knew she should. Six-year-old Emily Whittaker was just a pretty face in a crowded class photograph. The realization saddened her, brought tears to her eyes. "Where's this year's picture?" she asked.

"What?" He sounded surprised, almost alarmed.

"Shouldn't there be one more picture?" Mentally, she worked her way through the years. "There's junior kindergarten when she was four, then we have senior kindergarten and grade one, which would make her five and six. But you said she was seven."

"Yes, she just completed grade two." His eyes scanned the top of the piano. "I guess we didn't get a picture this year," he said slowly, giving the matter careful thought. "She must have been away sick or something." He shrugged, lifting a photograph of Emily sitting on Santa Claus's knee into his large sculptured hands, which she noticed were trembling. "This was taken a few years ago. And this one," he continued, handing her a large silver frame, "was taken last June."

Jane found her eyes glued to the faces of the three smiling strangers who were her husband, her daughter, and herself. Her hands shaking, she allowed Michael to take the picture and lead her away from the piano.

"Do you want to lie down?" His voice was as soft as a blanket. She longed to curl up inside it.

Instead she shook her head. "You probably should show me the rest of the house first."

His arm around her waist, he guided her out of the living room down the hall toward the back of the house. They passed a powder room and a row of closets before reaching the kitchen, a large sunny room whose entire south wall was windows. The kitchen, which overlooked a large garden, was decorated almost entirely in white:

a round white table and four chairs; a white ceramic tile floor; white walls. The only color came from the abundance of trees outside and from the backsplash of tiles on the wall above the kitchen counter that contained, at irregular intervals, handpainted tiles of miniature red apples and watermelons.

"It's lovely," she said, moving directly to the floor-to-ceiling windows and peering out at the well-kept yard. She noticed a door on the right wall that led outside, and had to fight the urge to run to it, fling it open, and flee.

"You ain't seen nothing yet," he said, his voice a smile. His arm moving to her shoulder, he led her through the kitchen door on her left toward yet another room: "Madame's sunroom," he announced proudly.

She stepped into a wonderland of glass and greenery. "We added this room about three years ago," he explained as she turned circles in the center of the room.

"I've never seen such a beautiful room," she told him, knowing this was true no matter what else she might have seen and forgotten.

His smile grew so wide that it seemed his entire face was involved. "You say that every time you come in here," he said, sounding almost hopeful.

People in glass houses, she mused, deciding that no stones could ever have been hurled in this room. Nothing bad could have happened in a house with a room as beautiful as this.

The south and west walls were made completely of glass; the floor was covered in a mosaic of tiny white and black tiles; plants and potted trees were everywhere. Along the north wall—a wall that truly was a wall, the other side of which was the living room—was a white wicker sofa-swing with pillows of green and white. It was flanked on either side of similarly patterned low-slung chairs, themselves flanked by a variety of white wicker and glass tables.

Jane approached the swing sofa and sank down, feeling it sway with her weight. She rocked gently back and forth, wondering how she could have forgotten this paradise on earth. "My own private rain forest," she said out loud, watching Michael grin approval.

''It'll all come back to you,'' he told her, collapsing into the chair on her right and stretching his long legs out in front of him. ''Just take your time. Try not to force things.''

''Did Dr. Meloff say anything to you about how long this condition might last?'' She wondered if the good doctor had confided more in her husband than he had in her.

''He said that most cases of hysterical amnesia, if that's what we're dealing with, usually reverse themselves spontaneously, that it could be a matter of hours or days.''

''Or weeks or months.''

''It's unlikely to go on for months, but it's true, there's no set timetable. Conditions like this usually right themselves when they're ready.''

''But what caused this condition in the first place?'' Her eyes shot frantically around the room, the plants and potted trees blocking out unwanted visions of blood and hundred-dollar bills. ''It doesn't make sense. I mean, I seem to be a woman who has everything: a nice house, a loving husband, a beautiful daughter. Why would I suddenly forget it all? What could have happened to make me want to pretend none of this ever existed?''

Michael's eyes closed, the fingers of his right hand massaging the wayward bridge of his nose. When he reopened his eyes, he looked at her as if he were measuring her strength, as if he were wondering how much truth she could stand.

''What?'' she asked. ''What are you thinking about? What aren't you telling me?''

Instantly, he was at her side, his sudden weight rocking the sofa-swing back and forth. ''I'm thinking that it's been a long, hard, puzzling day, and I'm tired. I'm thinking that we should let matters lie until we've both had a good night's sleep. I'm thinking that there'll be plenty of time to talk in the morning.''

''Then there *is* something,'' she persisted.

He patted her hand reassuringly. "No," he told her. "Nothing."

The doorbell rang.

"Who could that be?" Jane asked.

Michael pushed himself off the sofa-swing and stood up. "I think I have an idea."

Jane reluctantly followed him out of the sunroom, back through the kitchen, to the hall. She hung back as he approached the front door, watching from the shadow of the stairway as he opened the door and stepped back.

"How is she?" the woman asked, coming inside.

"Confused," Michael told her, leading her into the living room. "She doesn't remember anything about herself at all."

"My God! Nothing?"

He shook his head.

"Is she lying down?"

"I'm right here," Jane told Carole Bishop, recognizing the woman Michael had identified as their neighbor from across the street. She was still wearing her baggy Bermuda shorts, her dimpled knees peeking out from underneath them.

Carole Bishop looked to be in her mid-forties. She was short, no more than five feet two inches, and probably carrying around twenty unnecessary pounds, but she was one of those women for whom the words *cute* and *perky* were no doubt invented. As soon as she saw Jane, the color drained from her round face, her expression hovering uneasily between worry and fear.

Is she worried about what she should say? Jane wondered. Or frightened by what I might say?

"Michael told me about your amnesia," Carole began, looking to Michael for support.

"I called her from the hospital and explained briefly what was happening," Michael said quickly. "I asked her to drop by." He raised his hands in the air in a gesture of helplessness. "I thought you might feel less threatened with someone else around."

Once again, Jane's eyes filled with tears of gratitude.

"I don't feel threatened," she whispered, wanting him to take her in his arms.

"I guess you must be pretty scared," Carole said.

"I'm more anxious than scared," Jane qualified. "I just wish I knew *why* this was happening." She began pacing, her feet wearing deep prints in the thick green carpeting. "I have a feeling that once I know that, the rest will fall into place."

"You can't remember anything?"

"Nothing."

"Well, maybe I can help you out," Carole offered, drawing Jane toward the sofa and sitting down. "My name is Carole Bishop. That's Carole with an *e*. I've been your neighbor for—how long now?" She looked to Michael, who remained standing. "Three years?"

"About that."

"About three years. When we first moved in, you came running right over with this wonderful chocolate cake you'd baked, said it was your specialty. Best chocolate cake I'd ever eaten, and God knows I've eaten more than my share. You even gave me the recipe, and I can't tell you how many times I've made that cake since then. Every time we had company, I'd make that cake." She swallowed several times, looking into her lap before continuing. "Of course, I don't have a whole lot of company since Daniel moved out. You'd be amazed at how fast some of your so-called friends desert you once your husband leaves. Daniel was my husband," she added, almost as an afterthought. "You used to go running with him a few mornings a week. You don't remember any of this?"

"I'm afraid not."

"I wish *I* could forget the s.o.b. that easily." Carole sighed, a long, deep sigh that caused her ample bosom to shake. "He moved out the end of October. I tried to persuade him to take the kids with him," she joked. "At least take the dog, I begged him. Or my father! But he said if I kept the house, I was responsible for its contents. So there you have it. You're all up-to-date." She ran her fingers through her short, curly blond hair. "Go ahead, ask me anything. Obviously, I'm not shy. I have no secrets.''

Jane studied Carole's hands that were twisting in her lap, noting that the woman still wore her wedding and engagement rings. "I don't know what to ask," she said after a long pause.

Carole looked from Jane to Michael, then back to Jane. "I just want you to know that I'm here for you if you need anything, if you have any questions at all. . . ."

"Thank you."

"You were really more Daniel's friend than mine," she continued, unprompted. "But after he left, you were very supportive. You always had time for me. You let me come over and cry on your shoulder whenever I felt the need. So, if you need anything now, I hope you know I'm here for you."

"Thank you," Jane and Michael replied, a half beat apart.

"I could bring over some dinner," Carole volunteered. "I have lots left over. When in doubt, eat, I always say."

Jane's eyes widened in alarm.

"What?" Carole asked. "Something I said?"

Jane became highly agitated, finding it difficult to sit still. Michael was immediately on his knees in front of her. "What is it, Jane?"

"What you just said," Jane told them, the words tumbling out of her mouth in a mad scramble so that they were barely recognizable, and it became necessary to stop, take a few seconds to reformulate her thoughts, and begin again. "When I was at the Lennox Hotel, and I didn't know what to do with myself, I remember thinking, 'When in doubt, eat!' It was like I heard this little voice prompting me, saying 'When in doubt, eat!' And I wondered where that expression came from."

"My legacy!" Carole said with appropriate irony.

"That's great," Michael told Jane, then gently stroked the side of her head. "It means everything's in there, all locked up for safe-keeping. We just have to find the proper keys."

Jane smiled agreement, feeling light-headed with sudden optimism.

"I'll just run home and put some dinner together," Carole began.

"Not for me," Michael said quickly. "I couldn't eat a thing."

"Me neither," Jane confirmed. Although she felt hungry, she was too excited to eat.

"But thank you," Michael continued. "The offer is greatly appreciated."

"Well, you can always call me if you change your mind. I've got plenty of food." She laughed, a harsh sound totally devoid of mirth. "My kids eat every meal like they've never seen food before, and somebody forgot to tell my father that old people are supposed to lose their appetites, not to mention our dog, who thinks he's human and consequently won't eat anything that he doesn't see us eating, so I cook enough for the entire neighborhood. Oh well, I shouldn't complain. The kids are off to camp soon, and at least everybody's healthy. If you get hungry later, you can always let me know."

"We will," Michael told her, rising to his feet, signaling the end of the conversation by walking to the front door.

Carole Bishop took Jane's hands in her own. Her strong voice became a whisper. "You're in good hands," she confided. "You couldn't ask for a better husband." She fought back the sudden appearance of unexpected tears. "Everything will be all right, Jane. Just let Michael take care of you."

Jane sat perfectly still as Carole joined Michael in the hall.

"You'll call me if you need me?" she heard Carole ask before the front door closed.

"She seems very nice," Jane said as Michael reentered the room.

"Yes, she is."

"It must be very hard for her, having to look after both her father and her children."

"A true member of the sandwich generation," Michael said.

Jane nodded, recalling an episode on *Donahue* that dealt with exactly that—women sandwiched between the demands of their children and the needs of their elderly parents. Was she a member in good standing of this same group?

Her father had died when she was thirteen years old, Michael had told her at the hospital. But what about her mother? Did she still live in Connecticut or had she decided to move to the Boston area to be closer to her only daughter? Or maybe she'd preferred the sunnier shores of California and was busy sandwiching her brother Tommy.

That made more sense, she decided immediately. If her mother lived anywhere in the vicinity, Michael surely would have called her to come over, not Carole. "Does my mother still live in Connecticut?" she asked, watching Michael sink into a nearby chair and stare blankly out the window. "Michael?" she asked again, thinking maybe he hadn't heard her. "Does my mother still live in Connecticut?"

He shook his head, folding his hands together and bringing them toward his mouth.

"Michael?"

He looked directly into her eyes and she understood immediately that her mother was dead. Even so, she found it necessary to say the words. "My mother's dead, isn't she?"

He nodded solemnly. "Yes."

"When?"

"Last year."

"How old was she?"

"Sixty-three."

"That's very young," she remarked, feeling no emotional connection to the woman who had birthed her and was now gone.

"Yes," he agreed simply, saying nothing further.

"How did she die? Cancer? A stroke?"

"No."

"What, then?" She pushed herself to the edge of the sofa, anxiety growing in the pit of her belly.

He hesitated only a few seconds. "She was in an accident."

"What kind of accident?"

"A car accident."

"A car accident," she repeated, thinking of the accident they had seen on their way home, recalling the strange way Michael had looked at her, as if waiting for some sign of recognition on her part, as if weighing her reaction. "Tell me about it."

He took a deep breath before beginning. "Your mother was spending a few weeks with us. Actually, we'd been trying to persuade her to move to Boston, but she kept insisting that her bridge club back in Hartford couldn't get along without her, so that was that. End of discussion. You could never win an argument with your mother." He paused, smiling at the memory. "Anyway, she decided to drive into Boston one afternoon, do some last-minute shopping at Filene's Basement before she went back to Connecticut, and you—" he halted, then began again. "You were busy with Emily that day, some project at her school, I think it was. . . ." He stopped again, began a third time. "So, she took your car. . . ."

"My Honda?" Jane asked, picturing the silver Prelude in the garage, needing details to lend reality to what she was hearing.

"No. You had a Volvo. Dark green," he expanded without further prompting. "Anyway, she borrowed your car and off she went." Again he stopped, temporarily unable, or unwilling, to continue. Jane wasn't sure if he was trying to spare her, or himself, the pain of what was coming next.

"Go on."

"It happened just a few blocks away. She hadn't even reached the highway. Some guy ran a stop sign and plowed into her at sixty miles an hour. She died instantly." He moved from his chair to her side, and she saw his eyes were filled with tears.

Now tears formed in her own eyes. Not tears of grief

but rather tears of frustration. How could she forget anything as profound as the death of her mother? How could she fail to be moved by the awful story her husband had just recounted?

And yet, as when he had told her of her father's death, she felt no more than a modicum of sadness, the kind of sadness one feels upon hearing of the demise of a friend one lost touch with long ago. "Were we close?" she asked.

He nodded. "You were inconsolable after she died."

Suddenly, Jane jumped to her feet. "Damnit! Why can't I remember?!"

"You will, Jane," he reassured her, trying to calm her. "When you're ready. . . ."

"You were afraid to tell me about this," she stated, confronting him. "Why?"

"I was afraid it might upset you."

"No, that's not it. Please, tell me the truth."

He looked toward the front hall, as if hoping Carole Bishop would reappear to help him out. "The accident," he began, "it happened almost exactly a year ago."

"So, what are you saying? That you think the anniversary of my mother's death may have triggered my amnesia?"

"I think there's that possibility, yes. You'd been very agitated; you hadn't been sleeping; you were very upset. It was the reason I suggested you get away for a few days to visit your brother."

She digested this information as best she could. It obviously made sense to Michael. The anniversary of her mother's tragic death was upon them; she was upset, having trouble coping with the memory, ultimately deciding to lose it altogether. Perfect. Except that it didn't explain how her dress came to be spray-painted with blood and her pockets lined with hundred-dollar bills. Still a few loose pieces to the puzzle, she concluded, feeling infinitely weary.

"I think you should get some rest," Michael told her, once again reading her mind and coming to her rescue. "Come on," he urged softly, "let me put you to bed."

8

HE LED HER UP THE STAIRS TOWARD THEIR BEDROOM. Underneath the giant skylight, she stopped and stared up at the still-sunny sky, then checked her watch. It was almost eight o'clock. It would be getting dark soon. The moon, now only a series of pale-white dots against a light-blue background, would fill out and grow bright, exercising its dominion over the night. Where had all the time gone?

"This way," Michael said, directing her toward the bedroom at the left end of the hall.

"What are these other rooms?" She stopped in front of the first doorway to the right of the stairs.

"Why don't we continue the tour in the morning?" His voice was light, but it bore traces of a more serious undertone, as if he felt there had been enough revelations for one night, that any more might adversely affect the delicate balance on which her sanity rested.

"I'd like to do it now," she persisted. "Please."

His voice was gentle. "Whatever you'd like."

They stepped into the medium-sized, pale-green-and-yellow guest bedroom to the right of the stairs. A four-poster double bed was situated opposite a large antique dresser, over which hung a huge antique mirror. Jane patted the obviously old and valuable quilt that lay spread across the bed, avoided looking into the mirror, touching the antique chair in front of it for support as she walked toward the stained-glass window. A white unicorn was kicking up its hooves in the middle of a green-and-red field. Her eyes followed her fingers as they traced the black borders of the cut glass. The unicorn is a mythical beast, she thought, wondering if the same could be said about herself. Jane Whittaker is a mythical beast, she repeated silently, liking the metaphor.

She was pulled from her reverie by the sound of loud squeals. Her eyes traveled from the stained-glass window to the more ordinary window beside it, watching as two youths burst from the front door of Carole Bishop's house in a display of teenage enthusiasm that seemed almost staged for her benefit.

"Andrew and Celine," Michael told her, joining her at the window. "Andrew is fourteen, and I believe Celine will be sixteen in the fall. They used to baby-sit for us."

"Used to?"

"It's getting harder and harder to pin them down. You know teenagers. They think they deserve a life of their own."

Jane smiled, leaning her forehead against the windowpane, feeling it cool against her skin. Just then, an old man in a pair of crumpled striped pajamas stumbled out the door, followed by a large, barking dog. They both jumped directly into the middle of a row of colorful petunias that ran along the side of the front walk. Carole Bishop was right behind them, grabbing at the dog's collar, and pulling on the bottom of the old man's pajama top when he tried to flee. Jane heard the frustration in Carole's voice even through the glass. "Get back inside the house, Dad!" she shouted over the loud barking, while her children watched from the sidewalk, doubled over with laughter.

"He looks like a prisoner trying to escape," Jane commented, her heart going out to the old man.

"That's probably exactly how he feels," Michael said. "It's sad, really. Carole tries so hard. But sometimes, no matter what you do, it's never enough."

Jane wondered in that instant whether Michael was talking about Carole or himself.

"Get back in the house, Dad," Carole was pleading loudly. "Come on, you're ruining my flowers and creating a scene. Does the whole neighborhood have to see you?" As if she had been suddenly apprised of Jane's surveillance, Carole's eyes darted directly toward the second-story window where Jane stood. She immediately pulled back and away, feeling the crunch of Michael's toes beneath her feet, the hardness of his chest at her back.

"I'm sorry," she apologized, feeling his heartbeat against her, wanting to lose herself in his strength, loath to pull away.

"No apologies necessary."

Jane returned to the doorway, carefully avoiding her reflection in the antique mirror as she walked past.

"You don't have to be afraid of mirrors, Jane," Michael said softly, immediately at her side. "You *do* exist. You're not some sort of vampire."

She crossed into the room on the other side of the hall, taking with her the image of her teeth buried inside the skin of an exposed neck, the blood of her hapless victim spilling onto the front of her dress. "Your study?" she asked, trying to concentrate on the heavy oak desk by the window, the green leather sofa across from it, the bookshelves filled with medical texts.

"My office away from the office."

Jane ran her hand across the fine wood grain of his desk. The latest in modern computers sat proudly to one side, its large blank screen staring at her like a face whose features had yet to be filled in, its keyboard all but hidden by sheets of looseleaf paper. A silver ballpoint pen protruded from underneath an opened medical textbook, its top nowhere in sight. "You're working on something?"

"I'm delivering a paper at a medical convention in the fall. I've been trying to get my thoughts in some sort of order."

"And I'm helping you by falling apart."

"You help me by just being here."

She tried to size up his reflection in the blank screen of the computer. "Are you always this nice?"

His image retreated from her line of vision. She felt his arm brush against her own, turned to see him standing beside her, staring out the window at the Bishops' front lawn. "Oh, look. She managed to get him back in the house."

Jane swiveled around in time to see Carole Bishop pushing both the dog and her father through her open front door, then pulling the door closed behind them. Her teenage children remained on the sidewalk, paralyzed into immobility by laughter. "That was a real question," Jane told Michael, amused by the puzzled expression that appeared on his face.

"The question being . . . ?"

"Are you always this nice?" she repeated, and waited for his reply.

His face relaxed into a smile. "I have my moments."

"You seem to have a great many of them."

"You're not a difficult person to be nice to," he said simply.

"I hope that's true."

"Why wouldn't it be?"

She pretended to be caught up in the sight of Andrew and Celine Bishop awaking from their paralysis to run circles around each other down the street. "Where's Emily's room?" she asked after the two had disappeared around a corner.

"Next to ours."

She followed him down the hallway, past a cheery yellow-and-white bathroom toward two more rooms situated to the left of the stairs. "Did we have a decorator?" she asked casually, admiring the tasteful warmth that was everywhere in evidence.

"A great decorator," he confirmed. "Her name is Jane Whittaker."

Jane smiled, feeling foolishly proud of a job well done, even if she couldn't remember having done it.

"This is Emily's room," he said, following her inside, then hanging back, clinging to the doorway.

"It's perfect. A perfect room for a little girl. She must love it."

Jane quickly absorbed the details of the room: the fresh white wallpaper dotted with blue and green flowers; the brass bed with its white lace bedspread; a laundry basket in the shape of a kangaroo, its pouch a basket for dirty clothes; stuffed animals and dolls everywhere; a miniature table and chairs by the window overlooking the backyard; a panel of stained glass similar to the one in the guest bedroom, the floor covered in the same mint-green carpeting as the rest of the house. On the wall opposite the bed, between the green-and-blue flowers of the wallpaper, was a series of Impressionist paintings, framed prints by Monet, Renoir, and Degas.

"And this is our room," Michael said, ushering her so smoothly from their daughter's room to their own that she was almost unaware she had been moved.

Jane stepped gingerly into the room, suddenly careful not to stand too close to the man whose bed she had shared for the past eleven years. The room was a soothing combination of the palest lilacs and greens, dominated by a kingsize canopied bed in the center. One wall was windows; the other was made up entirely of mirrored closets reflecting their backyard, bringing it inside. The illusion was of a room that recognized no boundaries, knew no limits.

Jane found it impossible to be in this room and not see her reflection. While she tried to concentrate on the Chagall lithographs that hung on the wall across from the giant bed, her focus kept returning to the wall of mirrors.

"What do you see?" Michael asked, catching her off guard. She watched herself jump.

"A frightened little girl," she answered, trying to make sense of her reflection, giving up, and pulling open each of the closet doors in turn, ridding herself of her image once and for all.

The clothes of her past life confronted her. She examined the contents of the closet as if each item were a priceless artifact from another era, turning the various fabrics over in her hands, seeking traces of her history in each designer label. There were half a dozen dresses and probably double that number of blouses, as well as a smattering of skirts and slacks. Some of the outfits were very stylish; others looked more suited to an adolescent than to a woman in her thirties. She obviously had her good shopping days and her bad.

A built-in set of drawers divided her clothes from her husband's. She opened each drawer in turn, examining the delicate satin and silk underwear, marveling at the intricate lace of her camisoles and teddies, self-consciously stuffing a black garter belt and stockings to the rear of the drawer before Michael took notice. Did she actually ever wear these things? she wondered, feeling flushed. She'd been wearing panty hose when she discovered herself wandering the streets of Boston. Maybe she preferred garter belts in the privacy of her bedroom. More probably, it was Michael who preferred them.

She dropped her gaze to the floor, counting twelve pair of shoes before feeling strong enough to face him. "I have a lot of nice things," she said.

"I think so," he agreed, "although I don't recognize the clothes you're wearing now."

Jane looked down at the clothes she had purchased just that morning. "Neither do I," she said, and he laughed.

"Are you tired?"

She nodded, wanting desperately to crawl into bed, not sure whether or not she wanted Michael to join her.

"You don't have to worry, Jane," he told her, once again reaching inside her brain to read her errant thoughts. "I'll sleep in the guest room until you tell me otherwise."

"I can sleep in the guest room," she volunteered quickly.

"No," he said forcefully. "This is your room."

"Our room," she corrected.

"It will be. I have faith." He pulled a long white cotton nightgown off a hanger. "Your favorite," he told her, throwing it gently on the bed. "Why don't you get changed? There's a bathroom right through that door." He pointed past the jagged line of open closet doors. "In the meantime, I'll go downstairs and make us some tea."

He was gone before she had time to say, That would be nice.

Slowly she allowed her body to sink onto the bed, one hand gripping the tall post at the foot of the bed, the other reaching for the white cotton nightgown that lay beside her. She examined it closely, wondering how anyone who could prance around in a black garter belt and stockings could also buy anything as antiseptic and virginal as this. Her favorite! "Oh, well," she said out loud, "at least it beats sleeping in my coat."

In the next minute she was out of her clothes and into the floor-length cotton sheath. Removing her new shoes, she checked the sole of her right shoe and was relieved to find the key to her locker safe and secure in its hiding place. She quickly hung her new pants on a hanger, placed her new sweater in a drawer with a stack of others, and secreted her shoes at the very back of the closet, before hurrying into the bathroom to wash her face and brush her teeth.

It wasn't too difficult figuring out which toothbrush was hers—she doubted Michael would favor the pale-pink one—and she brushed her teeth vigorously, then scrubbed her face until it was as pink as her toothbrush. Lifting the hairbrush from the vanity table beside the double set of sinks, she brushed her hair until she felt her scalp tingle, all the while focusing on the large Jacuzzi bathtub, the double-sized shower stall, and the bidet. All the necessary conveniences, she thought, wondering if she really belonged here.

She returned to her bedroom and perched on the edge of the bed, wanting to crawl under the down-filled comforter, not knowing what to do with her hands. They moved restlessly from the stiff white cotton of her nightgown to the night table beside the bed, picking up the alarm clock and needlessly checking the time, pushing the ornate white-and-gold telephone to the rear of the table, then immediately returning it to its original position, rubbing the china base of the small lamp beside it as if she were expecting Aladdin to come popping out.

She thought she heard Michael on the stairs, but when she looked toward the door, she saw no one. She stood up, then sat back down again, returning her attention to the night table beside her. She thought of setting the alarm clock, turning on the lamp, using the phone, eventually settled for pulling open the top drawer of the small table instead, not looking for anything, just something to do with her hands.

She saw it immediately, didn't have to wonder what it was. All telephone-address books looked vaguely alike. This one was medium-sized with a paisley cloth cover. She reached for it slowly, feeling like a nosy houseguest snooping where she didn't belong. She brought it to her lap, where it remained unopened for several seconds before she found the courage to peek inside. Come on, she told herself impatiently. It's yours. Open it. What's the matter with you? What are you so afraid of? It's just the alphabet, for God's sake. Just a bunch of letters, a list of names. Names that mean nothing, she reminded herself, turning to the A's. *Lorraine Appleby*, she read, remembering that Michael had described her as a girlfriend of fairly long standing. *Arlington Private School* was listed right below. Arlington Private School? Of course, the school Emily attended. See, this was easy, she told herself, growing bolder, flipping to the B's, finding the name *Diane Brewster*, deciding that this must be her other friend, the Diane somebody-or-other that Michael had mentioned in the car. She quickly located the other names he had listed: David and Susan Carney; Janet and Ian Hart; Eve and Ross McDermott; Howard and Peggy Rose; Sarah and Peter Tanenbaum. All there in black and white and alphabetical order.

She found the listing for her brother, Tommy Lawrence, on Montgomery Street in San Diego, then felt her hands shake as she flipped back to the R's.

She hadn't seen it the first time, so why would she expect to find it when she looked again? Still, her eyes carefully perused the page from top to bottom, dismissing

Howard and Peggy Rose, who, she remembered, were vacationing in France for the summer, not recognizing any of the other half-dozen names that were scribbled there, rechecking the Q's and the S's to make sure she hadn't listed the name in the wrong place. But no. There was no *Pat Rutherford* anywhere. Whoever this Pat Rutherford was, he/she was no more than a casual acquaintance at best, not significant enough to rate even a mention in her private phone book.

She was still peering through the book when Michael returned.

"Find anything interesting?" he asked, depositing the tray with two cups of tea and some cookies on the small round table by the window.

Jane returned the book to the drawer and joined him at the window, sinking into one of the two round tub chairs that she hadn't even noticed before were there. "Maybe I should call my brother," she began, gratefully accepting a cup of tea from Michael and drawing the hot liquid into her mouth. "He's probably worried."

"I already called him and assured him that everything was under control. Why don't you wait and call him in the morning?" he suggested, and she smiled, grateful because she didn't feel ready to speak to anyone yet. What could she say, after all, to a brother she didn't know, who lived on the other side of the country? "Having a great time—wish you were here?" *Wish I knew who you were*, would be closer to the truth. And wouldn't that only cause him further worry when, she suspected, he'd already worried enough? No, she'd wait to call her brother when she could remember who he was. And if he phoned in the interim, then she'd just pretend to know him. She'd *confabulate*.

"The tea's good," she told him, and watched him smile, thinking how little it took to make him happy.

"Specialty of the house. Here, take this." He handed her a couple of small white pills.

"What's this?"

"A mild sedative."

"A sedative? Why? I haven't had any trouble sleeping."

"It's just to relax you."

Jane studied the two tiny pills, feeling them heavy in the palm of her hand. "Dr. Meloff never said anything about sedatives."

"Dr. Meloff is the one who prescribed them," he told her without a hint of impatience. "They're just to help you relax, Jane. They're very mild, really. You won't feel any aftereffects."

"It's just that pills make me kind of nervous," she said.

His smile was enormous. "They always did. See? You're getting better already. They're working!"

Jane laughed, wondering why she was giving him such a hard time. "I guess I'm just afraid of losing control," she admitted, trying to find a rational explanation for her behavior.

"What control?" he asked, and she laughed again. What control was right! How could a person who didn't know who she was have any hope for control?

She popped the pills into her mouth and swallowed them down with the last of her tea.

"Have a cookie," he offered. "They're delicious. Paula made them on Friday."

"Paula?"

"Paula Marinelli. She comes in a few times a week to do the cleaning and the laundry, a bit of baking. I've asked her to come every day until you're feeling better."

"Until I'm feeling more myself, you mean."

He laughed. "Until you're feeling more yourself."

She took a large bite of the chocolate chip cookie, watching a cascade of crumbs spill to the carpet at her feet. "Oh God, am I always this sloppy?" She bent over to pick up the crumbs and felt her head reel, the room spin. "Whoa!"

He was immediately at her side, helping her to her feet, guiding her toward the bed. "You must be really exhausted," she heard him say as he pulled down the comforter and positioned her underneath the sheets.

''There's no way on earth those pills could work that fast.''

''I *am* tired,'' she agreed, closing her eyes, knowing she had been fighting her fatigue for too long, feeling suddenly overwhelmed.

''Get some rest,'' he said softly, kissing her forehead as if she were a small child. ''Do you want me to sit with you until you fall asleep?''

She smiled, feeling like a pampered little girl. ''I'll be okay. You must have things to do.''

''Nothing that can't wait.''

''You go,'' she said, her voice heavy, distant. ''I'll be fine.''

She felt him rise. ''Remember, if you need anything, just holler. I'll be here in two seconds.''

I know you will, she thought, but was too tired to say. She tried to smile, hoped her lips had managed the appropriate shape, then gave in to the pleasant numbness that was creeping through her limbs toward her brain. She felt Michael smooth her covers, then disappear from her side. Her eyes fluttered briefly open, then immediately closed again. In the next instant, she was asleep.

She dreamed that she was standing in an open field. Behind her was a low building, rather like a motel, but with no sign to identify it. A no-name motel, she thought, hearing music emanate from one of the rooms. And suddenly Michael was beside her. She felt his soothing hands on her bare arms. ''Do you feel like a walk?'' he asked.

She nodded, snuggling against him.

''Oh, no, no,'' came a voice from somewhere behind them. ''You cannot walk.''

''Of course we can walk,'' she said stubbornly, trying to recognize the voice.

''No.''

''But why?'' she demanded, exasperated. ''Why can't we walk?''

There was silence. Then the voice spoke. ''The field is full of cobras,'' it said.

She spun around.

Michael was gone. A giant snake, coiled and ready to strike, lay at her bare feet. She took a step back, falling into the field of waiting cobras. She felt their bodies rise up in unison from between the blades of tall, yellow grass, and sway toward her. She felt their vipers' tongues whip against her legs. She watched the giant snake rise to his full height and lunge toward her. She screamed.

She was screaming.

"Jane!" she heard him calling, but was too terrified to open her eyes. "Jane! Are you all right? Jane, wake up! It's only a dream. You're having a nightmare. Jane, wake up!"

She forced her eyes open, her arms flailing in all directions when he tried to touch her.

"It's me, Michael. I'm here. Everything's okay."

It took her another minute to settle down, to consign the cobras to the netherworld of demons where they belonged, to remember that she wasn't stranded in some unidentifiable motel, but that she was home, in her own bed, safe and sound. "I had the most awful dream," she began, her voice a whimper. "There were snakes everywhere."

"It's all right now," he comforted her, taking her in his arms. "They're gone. I scared them all away."

She clung to him. "It was so real. I was so scared." She realized she was bathed in sweat from head to toe, and pulled out of his arms. "I'm soaking wet."

"Let me get a washcloth. I'll be right back."

She sat in bed, shaking and shivering in turn, until Michael returned. By then, the details of her dream had started to vanish. She made no attempt to hold on to them, wishing them gone as quickly as possible. But she remembered the feeling of stark terror that had violated every pore of her body, the terrifying sensation of falling backward into a pit of poisonous snakes. She shuddered, the revulsion causing her to gag.

"Take deep breaths," Michael was saying, running a cool cloth over her forehead. "That's right. Keep taking deep breaths. Try to relax. Everything's okay now."

"It was so awful."

"I know," he said, talking to her as gently as if she were one of his small patients. "But it's okay now. It's over."

She saw that he was wearing only a pair of jeans, something he had undoubtedly jumped into when he heard her scream. What dreams had she taken *him* from? she wondered, as he laid her back against her pillow. She felt the soothing cool cloth against her arms.

Suddenly she felt something prick the exposed surface of her skin, and thought the cobras had invaded her bed. She gasped, lifting her head in time to see the viper make a hasty retreat.

"It's just a shot of something to help you sleep without the nightmares," Michael told her soothingly, returning the syringe to his side and taking her in his arms again. "You need to sleep, Jane." He kissed a damp hair away from her forehead. "It's the best thing for you."

She nodded, feeling him lower her to the pillow. She studied his face in the near darkness, saw the fear and loneliness he tried so hard to hide, and longed to reach out and touch him, draw him to her, let him hold her through the night. Instead, she felt her eyes start to close. She knew he wouldn't leave her until she was safely asleep, and she fought to stay awake. Through half-closed lids, she saw him lift his hand to his head to push back the hair from his forehead. And she saw the long row of stitches that snaked along the side of his scalp just above the hairline, normally hidden by his hair.

What's that? she tried to ask, but her mouth was too dry to form the necessary words. What happened to your head? she wanted to know, but before she could force the question from her mouth, she was surrounded by darkness, and she fell into the dreamless sleep he had promised.

9

SHE OPENED HER EYES TO THE SUN STREAMING through the shutters. She sat up slowly, propping herself up with her elbows, leaning against the headboard, waiting for her eyes to focus and the buzzing in her ears to stop. She swallowed several times, trying to draw moisture into her mouth, which felt as dry as if a wad of cotton had been stuffed inside it, like a gag. Then she tried to stand up.

The room spun; her head swayed precariously on her shoulders, as if too sudden a move would cause it to tumble to the floor. It seemed a massive weight, too imposing for her fragile body to sustain. Humpty Dumpty sat on a wall, she thought, falling back onto the bed. Humpty Dumpty had a great fall.

She looked toward the mirrors. All the king's horses, she heard a small voice chant, and all the king's men—

"Couldn't put Jane Whittaker together again," she announced to the multiple of images she saw reflected. "Jane Whittaker," she intoned solemnly, wishing her reflection would sit still. "Who the hell *are* you?"

Her reflection wavered, then fell from view as a fresh wave of dizziness pushed her back onto her pillow. "Take it slow," she advised, knowing it was slow or not at all.

She pictured a maze of cobwebs spun from one side of her brain to the other, and watched as her hand reached into the picture to sweep them all away. But they were instantly replaced by more cobwebs, and no matter how many times she attempted to push them aside, the result was the same.

She shook her head, as if this act of defiance might shake the cobwebs free, but it only sent her head reeling, and she was forced to close her eyes to keep from fainting. Her head felt numb, anesthetized, frozen. It felt vast, filled with poisonous gas, in danger of exploding.

With her eyes closed, she tried to bring herself up-to-date: She was in Jane Whittaker's home, sleeping in Jane Whittaker's bed, Jane Whittaker's husband just down the hall, which was fine because she *was* Jane Whittaker. She had documented proof. Michael had produced her passport and their marriage license. She had recognized herself in the family photographs on the piano. She had even played the piano, for God's sake. How much proof did she need?

So, okay, she was Jane Whittaker, and Michael Whittaker, handsome and renowned pediatric surgeon, was her loving and supportive husband. And she had a beautiful daughter and a lovely home, and lots of friends. So why did suddenly knowing all these wonderful things about herself make her feel so depressed? Why did she want to crawl into a hole somewhere and die?

She recalled the vague outline of her nightmare with a shudder. She'd always hated snakes. She rubbed her arm, feeling again the sudden prick of a needle as it pierced her skin, and she opened her eyes, expecting to find Michael at her side, but there was no one.

He'd promised her a sleep devoid of dreams, and he was as good as his word. There'd been no more nightmares. She'd slept soundly, seamlessly. So why did she feel so crummy? Why did her head feel as if it were encased in cement?

Her eyes found the clock on the night table by her bed and managed to bring its numbers into clear focus. "Ten after ten!" she read incredulously. Could it really be after ten o'clock in the morning? Could she really have slept more than twelve hours?!

She brought the clock to within inches of her face. It was definitely ten minutes after ten. God, half the morning was gone, she thought, determining to get out of bed. Why me? she wondered, standing up and watching the floor tilt toward her. Her hand shot out in front of her, stopping on something cold and clear, like an ice pond, she thought, lifting her eyes and coming face-to-face with her own image. The palm of her right hand was pressed into its own reflection, as if the stranger in the mirror had come to her rescue, was holding her up.

Where was Michael? she wondered, staggering toward the bathroom and sinking onto the toilet seat, her head in her hands. She hadn't even bothered to shut the bathroom door. Suppose he walked in right now. Would he be embarrassed? Would she? Were they the kind of people who politely closed the bathroom door on their ablutions, or did they leave the door open for all the world to see? She didn't know; she was too groggy to care. If Michael were to walk in now, she wasn't even sure she'd notice.

Still, she was surprised he hadn't already been around. She'd expected to see him as soon as she opened her eyes. Was she disappointed? Was that the reason for her depression?

Maybe he was downstairs making breakfast. Maybe he was as expert at brewing coffee as he was at making tea. Maybe he was preparing to bring her bacon and eggs in bed. Immediately, her spirits lifted, then sank at the realization of how dependent she was already starting to feel. "Didn't Oprah teach you anything?"

She flushed the toilet. Surely that noise would bring him to her side. Then she washed her hands and face, splashing cold water repeatedly over her eyes. But it was as if they were coated with an invisible film. No matter how many times she rubbed them with the washcloth, she couldn't wash away the fog that seemed to have settled over her eyes like a pair of glasses.

In spite of everything, she was surprised to discover

that she didn't look so bad. Her hair hung shiny and straight around her shoulders; her complexion was clear, if a little pale. Even the bags under her eyes seemed to have shrunk, as if recognizing she had problems enough. She brushed her teeth and debated getting dressed. But she was too tired to drag her nightgown over her head, and what difference would it make anyway? She wasn't going anywhere.

She threw her head back defiantly, trying to rid herself of the lethargy that had seized control of her body, but the motion only sent her head spinning and she barely made it to the bed before she collapsed. "I'll just rest here for a few minutes," she whispered into the pink floral sheets that were the last things she saw before unconsciousness.

When she opened her eyes again, it was almost an hour later. "Jesus," she said, straightening her shoulders, pushing herself out of bed. This time, the floor remained steady beneath her feet. Her dizziness was gone, although a vague sense of depression lingered. She told herself that depression was an improvement over terror. "You're making progress," she said out loud, and watched her reflection smile.

She absently brushed some hair away from her forehead, unconsciously mimicking Michael's gesture of the night before. And then she stopped. "My God," she said, recalling the neat row of stitches that lay just above his hairline. What did it mean? Did it mean anything at all?

Maybe he'd had some sort of minor surgery. Or maybe he'd fallen, cut his head open. Her mind immediately conjured up the image of her bloodied blue dress. Head wounds bled a lot. Was it possible the blood on her dress had been Michael's?

She dismissed the thought as quickly as it had appeared. If this were the case, surely Michael would have said something, although he'd been reluctant to tell her anything that might upset her further.

Maybe there hadn't been any stitches. Maybe the

whole thing was a figment of her perverse imagination. She'd been hysterical over her nightmare; she was confused; it was dark. If her mind could conjure up fields of venomous snakes, then surely it was capable of imagining a simple row of stitches. Surely a mind that was capable of forgetting who she was, was capable of anything.

At any rate, it would be an easy thing to find out. She'd merely take a good look at Michael, and if the stitches were there, she'd ask him how he got them. Simple. Life was really very simple once you got the hang of it.

She walked over to the windows that ran across the back wall, and drew back the shutters, staring into the backyard, wondering why it was taking Michael so long to join her. Was it possible he was still asleep?

She heard her stomach growl, and she laughed, glad to see some things never changed. Oh, well, if Michael wasn't going to bring her breakfast in bed, she'd have to find her way down to the kitchen and fix it herself. Maybe even surprise *him* with breakfast in bed.

She turned to the door and screamed.

The woman who stood in the doorway was young, with an unfashionably deep tan. She was of medium height, maybe five feet four inches tall, with black hair that was pulled away from her face in a neat braid. She was slim, although her legs looked sturdy beneath the dark denim skirt she wore. "I'm sorry," she said in a voice that was surprisingly strong. "I didn't mean to startle you."

Jane stared at the woman, estimating her age as late twenties. Her round face wasn't delicate enough to be regarded as pretty, nor so coarse as to be considered plain. It was a face that would probably be best described as "interesting," one that might, on occasion, possibly even rise to the level of "mysterious." Her eyes were opaque, as dark as her hair, her nose was long and narrow, offsetting a mouth that was wide and red.

"I'm Paula," she began without further prompting. "Paula Marinelli." She waited for her name to register, continued when it didn't. "I clean your house a couple of times a week. Dr. Whittaker was supposed to remind you."

"Yes, he did," Jane assured her, vaguely recalling the conversation. "I'm sorry. I'm having a hard time keeping track of things." She almost laughed at her use of understatement.

Paula Marinelli looked embarrassed. "Dr. Whittaker said that you're suffering from amnesia."

"It's just temporary," Jane offered. "At least that's what they tell me." She cleared her throat, more for something to do than because she felt the need. "Where is Dr. Whittaker anyway? Is he still asleep?"

Paula Marinelli looked genuinely shocked by the idea. "Oh, no. Dr. Whittaker left for work first thing this morning."

"He went to work?"

"Emergency surgery."

Jane nodded. "Of course. I guess that must happen quite a bit."

"Everybody wants Dr. Whittaker. Which isn't surprising," she added, with a faint trace of pride. "He's the best there is." She looked around the room. "Are you hungry? I can bring you some breakfast."

"I think I'd prefer to eat in the kitchen."

Paula regarded her suspiciously. "Dr. Whittaker said he'd like you to get as much rest as possible."

"I think I can manage the trip downstairs," Jane told her, trying not to whine. "Really, I'll be fine."

They went downstairs.

"You just rest while I get things ready," Paula told her, guiding Jane into one of the kitchen chairs.

"I'm sure there must be something I can do to help." Jane felt uncomfortable doing nothing while this young woman, as efficient as she obviously was, was getting everything organized. "I think I can probably remember how to make coffee."

"Coffee's already made," Paula told her, pouring her a cup. "How do you take it?"

"I'm not sure," Jane told her. "I've been taking it black for the past several days."

"Black it is." Paula deposited the steaming cup of black coffee in front of Jane, and waited for further instructions.

"Aren't you going to have any?"

"Maybe later. What else can I get you? Scrambled eggs? French toast? A bowl of cereal?"

"Some toast would be nice," Jane said, not wanting to be a bother. "And some orange juice, if it's not too much trouble."

"Of course it's not too much trouble. It's the reason I'm here."

"To get me orange juice?" Jane hoped the serious young woman would smile, but no smile was forthcoming. I wonder if she's related to Dr. Klinger, Jane mused, recalling the sullen young resident at Boston City Hospital.

"To help you in any way I can."

"What do you normally do when you're here?" Jane asked, taking a long sip of coffee.

Paula was already busy at the kitchen counter, putting two slices of bread in the toaster, pouring out a large glass of orange juice, returning the bottle to the fridge, waiting for the toast to be ready, quickly buttering both slices as soon as they popped out, bringing everything to the table, along with a selection of jams.

"Usually I clean up, do the laundry, the ironing," she answered, standing over Jane until Jane took her first bite of toast. "Aren't you going to take any jam?"

Jane reached for the orange marmalade, thinking it was easier than a prolonged discussion.

"I'll do that." Paula took the knife from Jane's hand and spread a generous helping of marmalade across each piece of toast. Jane watched her with the helpless anger of a small child. I can do that, Mommy, she wanted to say, but thought better of it. The young woman obviously had her instructions, which she was intent on following to the letter. There was no point in upsetting her when she was only trying to help.

"How long have you been working for us?" Jane asked as Paula began wiping up the already spotless kitchen counter.

"A little over a year."

"I wish I could remember."

"There's no reason for you to remember me," Paula told her. "I'm here on Tuesdays and Thursdays, the same days you help Dr. Whittaker at the hospital. I come after you leave in the morning, and I'm gone by the time you get back."

"But I did hire you," Jane stated.

"Actually, it was Dr. Whittaker who hired me."

"My husband hired you?" Even not knowing the details of their relationship, it struck Jane as odd that Michael should be the one interviewing their domestic help.

"I met Dr. Whittaker at the hospital," Paula informed her, no friendlier than she had to be. "He operated on my little girl."

"You have a daughter?"

"Christine. She's almost five now. Thanks to Dr. Whittaker."

"He saved her life?"

"She had a series of spinal aneurysms. One minute she was in the backyard playing with her friends, and the next minute she was screaming that she couldn't walk. I rushed her to the hospital, where they discovered the aneurysms. Dr. Whittaker operated on her for over eight hours, and it was touch-and-go for a few days after that. She would have died without him."

"But she's all right now?"

"She walks with a brace. Probably always will. But that doesn't seem to slow her down any. More toast?"

"I'm sorry?"

"Would you like some more toast?"

Jane looked down at her plate, surprised to see she had eaten both pieces of the marmalade-slathered bread. "Uh, no. That was great, thank you."

"You look like you could stand to gain a few pounds."

Jane stared at her slender body, seeing the outlines of her nipples through the white of her cotton nightgown.

Probably she should have put on a housecoat. "Where is your daughter now?" she asked, looking toward the front hall, half expecting to see her.

"My mother's looking after her."

"So that you can look after me," Jane stated rather than asked.

"I'm happy to do it."

"I'm sure that in a day or two, I'll be able to manage on my own."

"Oh, no. I'm here until everything's back to normal," Paula told her, brooking no further argument.

"So, how was it exactly that my husband came to hire you?" Jane said, returning to the original question.

Paula removed the dishes from the table and began washing them by hand. "Dr. Whittaker," she began, rinsing, then rerinsing, the same dish many times over, "is very sensitive to other people's problems. He knew I could never afford to pay for Christine's surgery, so he arranged for one of those charities he's involved with to foot most of the bill. Then, he offered me a job."

"Where was your husband through all this?" Jane asked, understanding instinctively that Paula was in love with Michael, and understanding why. She also knew in her gut that Michael was totally unaware of Paula's feelings.

"I never had a husband." Paula Marinelli began vigorously drying the dishes she had just washed. "The man I was involved with decided his involvement didn't include marriage and a baby. With my Catholic upbringing, abortion was out of the question. So I went ahead and had the baby on my own, and that's pretty much the way it's been ever since." She paused, her eyes checking Jane's for any signs of disapproval. "I never went very far in school, so my job prospects were never that great to begin with. After Christine, I couldn't find work at all. I was on welfare when Christine had to have her surgery. Most doctors wouldn't even have looked at her. They'd be too busy trying to line their pockets."

Jane thought immediately of the hundred-dollar bills she had found lining her own pockets, and frowned.

"Sorry," Paula immediately apologized. "I guess you've got a lot of friends who are doctors."

"No apology necessary."

"I was just trying to tell you how great your husband has been to me. He saved my little girl, then he saved me. Got me enrolled in night school, got Christine enrolled in some special school for handicapped kids. Got my name right to the top of the list." She returned the dishes to the cupboards. "At first, I kept waiting for the other shoe to drop. You know, I kept thinking, nobody's *this* nice. What does he want, *really*? But there wasn't another shoe. He just wanted to help. He said he believed in this Oriental philosophy, that once you saved someone's life, you were responsible for them from then on." She took a long, deep breath. "The man can do no wrong, as far as I'm concerned. I'd do anything in the world for him."

"Do you know what happened to his forehead?" Jane heard herself ask.

"You mean the stitches?"

Jane nodded.

"Some kid threw something at him," Paula said, shaking her head. "He keeps all these toys in his office. Dolls and trucks and things, you know, so the kids will feel more relaxed. Didn't work, I guess. One of them threw a jet plane at him. One of those ones with the real sharp noses. He said he saw it coming but couldn't get out of the way fast enough. Can you imagine? He needed almost forty stitches to close it up."

"Sounds awful."

"Well, you know Dr. Whittaker. He's not one to complain a whole lot."

Jane smiled, hoping Paula would continue, tell her more about the man to whom she was married. She liked hearing good things about her husband, not only because it was nice to find herself married to such a man, but because it implicitly implied that, if a man like Michael could love her, she couldn't be so bad. So why the hysterical fugue?

"Would you like to go back up to bed now?" Paula asked, moving to her side.

Jane shook her head. "I think I'd like to sit in the sunroom for a while."

Paula helped her through the kitchen door, and although Jane was feeling strong enough to make it on her own, she knew it would be pointless to protest.

The room was every bit as glorious as she remembered, her very own wonderland. Immediately the sun rushed over to welcome and embrace her, to warm her bare arms. Paula directed her toward the sofa-swing, depositing her on the cushions as if she were a breakable piece of china. "I'll get you a blanket," she said, and was gone before Jane could tell her not to bother. She had a baby-sitter whether she liked it or not. She was going to be cared for, whether she cared for it or not. They were going to see that she got better, so she'd better get used to it, the sooner the better. You'd better believe it!

This is silly, she thought and giggled. I'm being silly. I'm acting like one of Michael's patients, the one who tried to land his toy plane on Michael's forehead. Just because the woman is in love with my husband is no reason not to like her. I'm just a big, ungrateful kid who doesn't know when she's well off, who can't remember how to behave when people are being nice to her, who doesn't know when people are only trying to help. I don't know what's good for me, she shouted wordlessly. I don't know what's expected of me. I don't know why this is happening to me. I don't know anything. Goddamnit! I don't know anything!

She burst into a fit of uncontrollable laughter, then watched helplessly as the laughter dissolved into a barrage of tears. Paula was instantly at her side, covering her with a soft yellow blanket. "Take these." She extended her hands, displaying two tiny white pills in one palm, a glass of water in the other.

"I don't need any pills," Jane told her, wiping at her nose with the back of her hand, like a child.

"Dr. Whittaker said you're to take them."

"But I don't need them."

"You wouldn't want to upset the doctor," Paula said simply, speaking the unthinkable. Jane understood that there was no point in arguing. She knew, and she knew Paula knew, that sooner or later, she was going to swallow those two little white pills, so why make life difficult for this young woman whose life was already difficult enough?

She took the two little pills from Paula's hand, dropped them onto the tip of her tongue, and swallowed them.

10

IN HER DREAM, JANE SAW HERSELF WALKING DOWN A dark street she didn't recognize beside a woman whose face she couldn't quite recall.

They were talking, laughing over a line from the movie they had just seen, arguing over who had been the first to discover Kevin Costner, and therefore who had the greater proprietary right to him, should they ever meet him face-to-face and he was forced to choose.

"I've already had the towels monogrammed," the woman proclaimed, shaking her mane of red curly hair.

"You're nuts, Diane," Jane laughed.

So, the woman's name was Diane, a voice whispered from somewhere far away. Diane somebody-or-other, she heard Michael say. DIANE BREWSTER, she'd seen printed in her telephone-address book.

Jane put her hand through the other woman's arm, and together they prepared to cross the street. "Here comes some guy who doesn't have his headlights on." She waved at the dark-haired young man behind the wheel of a bright red Trans Am. "Excuse me, your lights aren't on," she said as he rolled down his window.

His response caught her with the force of a surprise slap to the face. "You fucking bitch! What the fuck do you want?"

"Let's get out of here," Diane whispered, pulling at Jane's arm.

Jane stubbornly held her ground. Surely, the young man had misunderstood her. "I was simply trying to point out that your headlights aren't on," she repeated as pleasantly as she could.

"You fucking bitch! Fuck you!"

Something clicked in Jane's mind. Her response was automatic. "Fuck yourself, asshole!" she said.

"Oh, Jesus," Diane moaned.

The young man's eyes bulged so violently that they looked as if they might burst from his head. Waving his middle finger wildly in her direction, he took off down the street.

"Thank God," Diane sighed.

"He's coming back!" Jane exclaimed, watching, transfixed, as the red Trans Am came to a screeching halt in the middle of the street, then reversed, gaining speed and momentum as it careened backward toward them, its driver leaning so far out his window that he was almost standing, screaming obscenities. "You fucking bitch! I'll kill you!"

Jane grabbed Diane's hand and ran, hearing his angry words chase after them. She turned to see the young man in pursuit, his short legs gaining speed, closing the distance between them, his car abandoned on the sidewalk.

"Where is everyone?" Diane yelled, her eyes frantically scanning the empty street.

"Help!" Jane screamed. "Somebody help!"

And suddenly a giant was standing before them, a man of astonishing proportions, at least six feet six inches tall, with a broad chest and enormous neck. And the dark-haired young man with the short legs and dirty mouth was scurrying back to his red Trans Am, waving his fists in the air as he made his ignominious retreat.

"I think you ladies could use a drink." The giant led them inside the dimly lit restaurant from where he had emerged. "Rick, give these two damsels in distress a drink. On the house." A phone began ringing somewhere in the background. "I better answer that. I'll be right back."

"That's Keith Jarvis, the football player!" Diane squealed as soon as he was out of earshot. "I can't believe it. You almost get us killed by some maniac, and then you get us rescued by Keith Jarvis! I wonder if he's married."

"Why doesn't he answer the phone?" Jane wondered, hearing its persistent ring.

Suddenly the ringing stopped. "Hello," a voice said quietly, not the voice of a giant at all, but rather that of a young woman. "No, I'm sorry. She's not in. She's gone to visit her brother for a few weeks."

Jane opened her eyes, her dream fading as she came fully awake. She took immediate stock of her surroundings, trying to reorient herself as quickly as possible. She was half-sitting, half-lying on the green-and-white-floral sofa-swing, her body covered by the soft yellow blanket, the sun having temporarily disappeared behind a voluminous cloud. How long had she been sleeping? And who was writing these strange dreams of hers?

"Yes, it was very spur-of-the-moment," she heard Paula say, recognizing her voice as the one she had heard at the end of her dream. "No, everything's fine. She just felt like surprising him."

Jane pushed herself off the sofa-swing as quietly as she could, steadying it with her hands so that it wouldn't make any noise, then tiptoed toward the kitchen. She pushed open the door dividing the two rooms and listened.

"I'm sure she'll call you as soon as she gets back," Paula was saying into the phone, her back to Jane, unaware of her existence. "Have a nice day. Good-bye." She replaced the receiver, took a deep breath, and turned around.

If she was startled by Jane's unexpected appearance, she recovered quickly. "I thought you were still asleep," she said.

"Who was that?" Jane indicated the phone.

Paula looked embarrassed. "I forgot to ask."

"Why did you say that I was visiting my brother?"

Now Paula looked sheepish, uncertain. "Dr. Whittaker thinks it would be better if you weren't disturbed by phone calls. At least for the time being. Until you get your strength back."

"I'm plenty strong," Jane replied testily, feeling just the opposite. "My problem isn't my strength. It's my memory."

"What's the point of talking to someone you can't remember?"

The very logic behind Paula's question made Jane angry. "The point is that I might remember something."

"And you might not. And then you'd only be more upset. Now, are you ready for some lunch?"

"Didn't I just have breakfast?"

"That was hours ago. Come on, you need to . . ."

"Get my strength back, I know."

Jane sat down at the kitchen table and waited while Paula prepared her lunch.

She found the photograph albums on the bottom bookshelf in the living room.

Jane went through each of the six leather-bound books in turn, watching her life unfold in a series of sometimes silly, mostly ordinary, occasionally remarkable, photographs. Her hair was long one year, short the next, curly, straight, worn up or down to match current hemlines. There were bell-bottoms and stretch jeans, open-toed sandals and thigh-high boots, leather jackets and oversized sweaters. The only constant was her smile. She was always smiling.

There were lots of pictures of her and Michael: their courtship; their wedding; their trip to the Orient. With others. Alone. And always their arms around each other's waist, their eyes reflecting their love.

There was a photograph of Michael flanked by an elderly couple Jane supposed were his parents. They were a handsome pair, tall and imposing, his father's gray hair thinning, his mother's a stubborn blond helmet. On another page were photographs of Jane hugging a woman who could only be her mother. Jane felt her heart lurch toward this woman. ''Forgive me, Mother,'' she whispered, tracing the woman's outline with her fingers. ''I want so much to remember you.''

Jane snapped the album shut, feeling tears rush to her eyes, refusing to let them fall. ''Damnit, I *will* remember.'' She reopened the book. ''Of course I remember you, Mother,'' she told the smiling photograph, happy to note that her mother looked suitably pleased. ''And of course I remember my brother, Tommy. How are you, Tommy?''

A young man with fair hair and a slight gap between his two front teeth grinned back. He stood between the young woman who was Jane and the older woman who was her mother, his arms around both, looking proudly possessive. And yet, the next picture showed another young man, this one dark haired and closemouthed, in a similar pose, looking equally possessive of the women on either side of him. So, maybe this was Tommy.

She tore open another album, and found herself staring with wonder at a monstrously pregnant woman in a striped shirt and blue jeans, her hair pulled back to reveal an almost pudgy face, her jeans rolled up to expose a pair of hugely swollen ankles.

Instinctively, Jane stroked her stomach. There she was, the very picture of expectant motherhood, and here she was now, and she couldn't recall a single minute of it. And there was Emily, pink faced and beautiful, with wisps of blond hair and little chipmunk cheeks, peeking out from beneath her baby blanket. Jane watched her daughter grow up before her eyes, one minute a baby cooing on the living room floor, the next a little girl diving fearlessly into a lake.

''You're a beautiful little thing,'' Jane whispered, quickly skimming the last album, chuckling with the realization that her daughter had obviously replaced her as her husband's favorite model. Had she resented it? Had she been jealous of her only child?

She rubbed her forehead, feeling the threat of a headache behind her eyes. Please don't turn out to be one of those awful, insecure mothers who hate their children. "Don't do that to me," she said, hearing the rumble of a vacuum cleaner above her head.

Paula was certainly a busy little lady. If she wasn't cooking, she was cleaning. If she wasn't cleaning, she was watering the plants. If she wasn't watering the plants, she was making the beds. Or telling Jane it was time to take a nap. Or time to take her pills. Time to take a hike, Jane wanted to tell her, feeling encumbered by the woman's efficiency. God, is that the kind of person I am? she wondered. Jealous even of the housekeeper? Scornful of her dedication and concern?

"No wonder I'm depressed," she said. "I'm a miserable rotten person."

Jane tried to picture the young woman pulling the long coil of the central vacuuming system from room to room. Judging from the hum, she was most likely in Michael's study now, carefully seeing to his things.

How long had she known that Paula was in love with Michael? And how much had it bothered her? Could she really have held it against her? Wasn't it only natural to be at least a little in love with the doctor who saved your child's life, especially when the doctor was as easy to love as Michael?

Still, the woman made her feel uncomfortable. Could Paula have had anything to do with her amnesia? she wondered.

Sure, Jane thought. You tried to kill her and she's getting her revenge by cleaning your house from top to bottom. The woman was devious, all right.

Jane returned the albums to their proper place on the bottom bookshelf, then wondered what to do. She could watch television, catch up on the doings of "The Young and the Useless," but she was already feeling useless enough, so she decided against it. She could read, she thought, perusing the rows of hardcover books, wondering which books she had already read, curious as to whether she preferred fiction to biographies, romance to suspense. Michael had told her she'd majored in English, then worked in publishing. What exactly had she done? What kind of position had she held?

She wished Michael would get home so that she could ask him these questions, ask him whether he thought she should consult a psychiatrist, possibly even a hypnotherapist if he thought that might help. She wanted him to come home so that she could inquire about his day, tell him about hers. So that they could pretend to be living a normal life. Did he really have to be gone all day on this her first day back?

"Back from what?"

She wandered into the sunroom, understanding that it was to this room she came whenever she needed to think things through. She obviously had a wonderful life. What possibly could have taken place to make her want to throw it all away, to pretend it had never happened?

Her fingers grazed the leaves of the numerous plants, her eyes automatically checking to make sure they had enough water. Of course they did. Paula had seen to that.

I should be ashamed, she thought, sinking into one of the chairs and staring at nothing in particular. Here is this young woman with an illegitimate handicapped daughter, no money and few prospects, and she's busy upstairs cleaning *my* house—she's *coping*—while I sit here with a wonderful husband and a healthy child, up to my eyeballs in self-pity, *not* coping. Except hadn't Dr. Meloff explained that hysterical amnesia was, in fact, a coping mechanism? A way of dealing with an intolerable situation brought on by great fear or rage or humiliation?

What could it be? she demanded silently, banging her fist against the side of the chair. How long was this going to go on? Surely, whatever intolerable situation she had run away from couldn't be more intolerable than this!

"What is it?" she heard Michael ask from the doorway, and she jumped. "Are you all right? You're not in any pain . . . ?"

"I'm fine," she told him quickly, the sight of him bringing her to her feet. "I'm so glad to see you." In the next instant she was in his arms. "I missed you," she whispered sheepishly. She was almost foolishly happy to see him.

"I'm glad," he told her, kissing her forehead. "I was hoping you'd feel that way." He pulled back, scrutinizing her from arm's length, although he didn't let go of her. "What's the matter? Did something happen? Hasn't Paula been taking good care of you?"

"It's not that," Jane said, wondering just what it was. "I guess maybe I was expecting too much. I don't know. I guess I thought that once I got home, my memory would come back."

"It will. Give it time."

"How was your day?" she asked, and laughed self-consciously.

Once again, he folded her into his arms. "Busy. Very busy." His hands smoothed the hair at the back of her neck. "I'm so sorry I had to run out of here this morning. I hadn't planned to go to work at all today, but it was one emergency after another, and every time I phoned, Paula said you were asleep."

The sound that escaped Jane's mouth was halfway between a laugh and a snort. "I did a lot of sleeping today. I think it must be those pills."

"The pills shouldn't make you *that* sleepy," he told her. "More likely you're just more exhausted than you know."

"I had such strange dreams."

"More snakes?"

"No, thank God. This time it was only maniacs in red cars trying to run me down."

He looked startled. "Tell me about it."

She recounted the details of her dream, still as vivid as when she had first conjured them up.

"That wasn't a dream," he said softly when she was finished.

"What?"

"That really happened. About two years ago, I think it was."

"Some lunatic tried to kill me because I told him his headlights weren't on?"

"Some lunatic tried to kill you because you told him to fuck off." He laughed in spite of himself. "You have quite a temper," he told her, shaking his head in amazement. "We always said that one day it would get you into a lot of trouble."

"It really happened," she repeated, offering no resistance as he settled her into the sofa-swing and tucked the blanket around her.

"Don't you see what this means, Jane? You're starting to remember. Just give yourself time. Don't get discouraged. Everything will work itself out. In the meantime, why don't you rest a bit before dinner? Maybe something else will come back to you."

Maybe something else will come back to me, she repeated wordlessly, seeing the red Trans Am racing backward toward her from behind closed lids. "You have quite a temper," Michael had stated. "We always said that one day it would get you into a lot of trouble."

11

"WELL, HI! HOW ARE YOU?"

"Can I come in?"

Carole Bishop immediately backed into her front hall to let Jane enter. "Of course you can. Come in and have some coffee. How are you feeling?"

"Not bad," Jane lied, feeling lousy. She followed Carole to her kitchen, situated, as was Jane's, at the back of the house.

"I haven't called because I didn't want to bother you. Michael said he'd phone if there was anything you needed. . . ."

"There's nothing I need." Except my sanity, Jane thought. "I'm being very well looked after." I'm being held prisoner in my own home, she wanted to say, but didn't, knowing how melodramatic it would sound, how unfair a statement it was. In truth, she *was* being very well looked after. Michael couldn't have been more solicitous, more caring. And Paula was busy cooking, cleaning, managing the household, seeing to Jane's every desire. Except what Jane really desired was to be left alone, and this Paula wouldn't do.

Almost a week had passed since Michael had brought her home from the hospital. In that time, she had done little but eat and sleep. When she wasn't sleeping, she had to fight to stay awake, and when she was awake, she had to fight to keep from being depressed. The longer she stayed awake, the more depressed she became. The only way to escape her depression was to fall asleep. She'd even managed to sleep through an appointment Michael had set up for her with a leading Boston psychiatrist. Out of professional courtesy, Michael's colleague had specifically cleared his calendar to make room for her, but when Michael had arrived home to pick her up—after rearranging his own schedule—he'd been unable to rouse her. Another appointment was set up for six weeks down the road, the psychiatrist unwilling to put himself out a second time. Surely in six weeks' time, Jane prayed, she would no longer require his services. This nightmare would be over.

She'd had no more dreams. No more memories. She existed, if she existed at all, and she was beginning to doubt even this, in a complete void.

"I forget how you take your coffee," Carole was saying.

"Black. And thank you for not remembering."

Carole laughed. "Wait till you get to be my age. You'll see that your condition is not unique. A little extreme, maybe. But not unique. There are days I can't remember a damn thing. I have to write everything down. I have a million lists." She walked to a small desk by the far wall and produced half a dozen slips of paper. "I have a list for everything. If I don't write it down, I forget it." She returned to the counter and poured Jane a steaming mug of hot coffee. "I make a huge pot in the morning," she explained, indicating the coffee maker, "and just leave it on all day. It's decaffeinated, so it doesn't keep me up at night. Of course, they say it gives you cancer, but then, what the hell, so does everything else. Cheers," she said, lifting her mug toward Jane's and clicking it against hers, as if they were drinking champagne. She pulled up a chair and sat facing Jane. For several seconds neither woman spoke, taking the time to let their thoughts settle and their questions form.

Jane allowed herself the opportunity to casually take in the room. It was approximately the same size kitchen as her own, but it was in desperate need of a fresh coat of paint, and she noticed that there were several burn marks scarring the countertops. The cane seats of the kitchen chairs were fraying, verging on collapse, and the linoleum floor was strewn with forgotten crumbs. In the background, she recognized the country twang of Dolly Parton emanating from the radio on the wall by the phone.

"You like country music?" Jane asked absently.

"I love it," came the immediate reply. "How can you not love music that gives you songs like 'I'm Going to Hire a Wino to Decorate Our Home'?"

Jane heard laughter, and was glad to realize it was her own. It had been days since she'd laughed out loud. Michael was gone most of the time, and Paula wasn't exactly a joke a minute. Jane looked out the window to the backyard, saw the Bishops' large dog chasing a squirrel, and half expected to see Paula lurking somewhere in the overgrown bushes.

It was almost two o'clock, usually a time for her to be napping. But she'd pretended to be asleep when Paula had come in to give her her medication, then snuck out of the house when Paula was in the bathroom, feeling like a naughty child. How long before Paula realized she was missing?

Carole's house suddenly shook with the sound of footsteps cascading down the stairs. "I'm out of here," a voice yelled from the hallway.

Carole was immediately on her feet. "Andrew, just a minute. Andrew, come in here."

A teenage boy, all arms and legs and restless twitches, appeared in the doorway. He swayed, he bounced, he all but vibrated. There was not a muscle in his skinny frame that seemed to stay still. "What is it, Mom? I'm running late."

"Don't you say hello?" His mother indicated their guest.

"Oh, hi, Mrs. Whittaker. How ya doing?"

"Fine, thank you."

"Okay, Mom, gotta go."

He was halfway into the hall before Carole's voice stopped him. "Wait a minute. You were supposed to take your grandfather out for a walk."

"Celine'll do it."

Jane heard the front door open and close.

Carole's shoulders slumped in defeat. "Sure. Celine will do it. And do we see Celine anywhere? No, Celine is at the mall and will no doubt be too worn out from shopping to take her grandfather for a walk, if and when she finally deigns to honor us with her presence. Do I sound bitter to you?" The question was only partly rhetorical.

"You sound tired," Jane told her.

Carole smiled, returning to her seat. "I'll take that as a compliment."

"Carole?" An old voice cut into the moment's silence, like fingernails scratching against a blackboard. "Carole, where are you?"

Carole's eyes closed, her head falling back. "Another quarter heard from. I'm in the kitchen, Dad."

A frail, bent figure appeared in the doorway. Jane recognized the old gentleman, who managed to retain a certain dignity in spite of his stained shirt and oversized gray flannel pants, as the man she saw trying to escape from this house on her first night home. Her heart went out to him. She knew exactly how he felt.

"I'm hungry," he said. "Where's my lunch?"

"You just had lunch, Dad," Carole reminded him patiently.

"No," he insisted, "I didn't have lunch. You didn't give me my lunch." He glanced suspiciously at Jane, as if *she* might have eaten his lunch. "Who are you?"

"Dad, this is Jane Whittaker. She lives across the street. She used to go running with Daniel. You remember her, don't you?"

"If I remembered her, would I ask who she is?"

It seemed a logical question, and Jane found herself smiling. She liked Carole's father, if for no other reason than they seemed to have a lot in common.

"Please excuse him," Carole apologized. "He's not always this rude."

"Did you say something?" Carole's father stamped his foot angrily, reminding Jane of Rumpelstiltskin. "If you're going to talk about me, I'd appreciate it if you'd speak up."

"If you want to hear the conversation, Dad, you should wear your hearing aid."

"I don't need my hearing aid. What I need is lunch!"

"You had lunch." Carole gestured toward the front of his stained shirt. "There it is. And there. I thought I told you to go upstairs and change."

"What's the matter with what I've got on?"

Carole lifted her hands into the air as if a gun were being held to her back and she had decided to give in without a struggle. "Not a thing. Heavy winter pants and mustard-covered shirts are all the rage in Boston this summer. Don't you agree, Jane?"

Jane tried to smile. Mustard was preferable to blood, she thought, trying not to stare at the eerie grayness of the old man's skin, which made him look as if he were covered in a thin layer of dust.

Carole's father began nodding his head up and down as if he were taking part in a conversation only he could hear. Absently, he manipulated his dentures with his tongue, pushing them forward, then pulling them back, thrusting them in and out of his mouth in time to the country music on the radio, Glen Campbell wailing about somebody being gone, gone, gone.

"Just keep your teeth in your mouth, will you, Dad?" Carole looked at Jane. "He does it to annoy me."

"Where's my lunch?" the old man bellowed.

Carole took a deep breath and walked to the fridge. "What would you like?"

"A steak sandwich."

"We don't have any steaks. I can make you a salami sandwich. How's that?"

"What did you say?"

"Sit down, Dad."

Carole's father pulled out a chair and sat down. "Make

one for her too,'' he said, his thumb directed at Jane. ''She's too thin.''

''No, thank you,'' Jane said quickly, checking herself over. Like Carole, she was dressed for comfort in culottes and a T-shirt. ''I'm not hungry.''

''He ate less than two hours ago,'' Carole said, spreading mustard across two pieces of bread and cutting a salami into thin slices. She put the sandwich on a small plate and deposited it in front of her father.

''What's this?''

''Your sandwich.''

''That's not a steak sandwich.'' He pushed the plate away from him like a spoiled child.

''No, Dad. It's salami. I told you we didn't have any steak. You'll be having supper in a few hours anyway. Right now you'll have to settle for salami.''

''I don't want salami.'' He shook his head in dismay. ''Don't get old,'' he said to Jane, rising from his seat and shuffling proudly out of the kitchen. She heard his weighted footsteps on the stairs, then directly overhead, as he slammed the door to his room shut.

''How long has he been like this?'' Jane asked, not sure for whom she felt more sorry.

''It gets worse every year. He can't hear, not that he listens. He's rude, argumentative. I never know what he's going to say or do next. The other night I woke up about three o'clock—I haven't been sleeping that well since Daniel left—so I thought I'd check on him. I found him standing in the front hall, staring at the door. When I asked him what he was doing, he said he was waiting for the morning paper, and why wasn't his breakfast ready? When I told him we didn't usually eat breakfast in the middle of the night, he said that if I wouldn't get it for him, he'd make it himself. So what does he do? He puts a bunch of eggs in the microwave and turns it to High. A few minutes later, I hear this explosion. I come running in. The place is a mess. The microwave looks like it's been hit by a bomb. It's three A.M., and I'm cleaning eggs off the fucking ceiling. It would be funny if it weren't so damn pathetic.'' She shook her head, the same gesture as her father's. "Can you believe it? You're having problems I can't even imagine, and here I sit bitching about mine!"

"How long has he lived with you?"

"Since my mother died. Six years now, I guess."

"How did your mother die?"

Carole's voice was soft, barely audible. "What else?—cancer. It started in her stomach, then it kind of branched out everywhere."

"I'm sorry."

"It was hard." She paused, her eyes filling with tears. "I remember going to visit her in the hospital a few days before she died, and she was in a lot of pain, even with all the drugs. I asked her what she thought about all day, lying there staring up at the ceiling, and she said, 'I don't think about anything. I just want it to be over.'"

"I wish I could remember my mother," Jane said, noting the look of surprise that overtook the sadness in Carole's face. "Michael told me about the accident."

"He did?"

"Not a lot. Just that she died instantly, and that it happened about a year ago."

"A year ago, already," Carole muttered. "God, time goes so fast. You have no memories of her at all?"

Jane shook her head. "I look at pictures of her, and they mean nothing to me. I feel so . . . disloyal."

"I know all about feeling disloyal." Carole pulled her chair so close to Jane's that their knees were touching. She leaned forward, whispering conspiratorially. "I love my father. But sometimes, lately, it's like I'm just putting in time, waiting for him to die. Oh God, I'm so awful. You don't even know me, and you must think I'm the most awful person alive."

"I don't think you're awful. I think you're human."

Carole's face broke into a grateful smile. "That's why I was always on your doorstep after Daniel left. You always managed to find something to say that would cheer me up."

"Tell me about Daniel. That is, if you don't mind talking about him."

"Are you kidding? I live to talk about Daniel! I have no friends anymore because they got so bored with listening to me go on and on about Daniel. They think I should stop talking and get on with my life, but I'm still not ready to give up the ghost. Not after fifteen years together. There's still too much I want to say."

"Say it to me. Please," Jane urged. "Maybe if people would start treating me the way they always did," she continued, putting her thoughts of the past few days into words for the first time, "then I'd get the hang of my life that much quicker. Right now, everybody's so busy being solicitous, tiptoeing around me, doing things for me, and making sure I get my rest, that I feel like I'm living in some kind of glass bubble. Please," she said again, "tell me about Daniel."

"Well, just don't say I didn't warn you." Carole waited for Jane's nod of assurance. "We got married when I was twenty-eight. I was *really* ready to get married, let me tell you. Here I was, a little overweight, not the prettiest girl on the block, all my friends were already married. I was getting desperate. My parents had all but given up hope. You're about ten years younger than I am, so you probably can't relate to that kind of desperation, but this was just before it became fashionable to say you could get along without a man. So here comes Daniel Bishop. He's a dentist. He's good-looking. He's a few years younger than I am, but so what? It was only five years. I fell head over heels."

"So, you got married," Jane prompted.

"Actually, I got pregnant first. Then we got married. We had Celine, and then a few years later, we had Andrew. It was a strain at first, but the marriage seemed to be getting better as the years went on. Daniel's practice was flourishing. Everyone was healthy. The money was rolling in.

"And then things started to go wrong. Daniel discovered one of his partners was robbing him blind, and that was a whole mess, they had to go to court. And then my mother got sick, and that put a real strain on things. And then, of course, my father came to live with us after she died. I think it all got to be too much for Daniel. I tried to get him to talk about it, but he was never much of a talker. He liked to get rid of his tensions athletically, which kind of left me out in the cold, since I've never been very good at sports. He took up running, and he became a fanatic about it. He had to run every day. At first, he tried to get me to run with him, but I kept telling him I was too old, I'd leave the running to the young guys. Mistake, right?

"Then he had this good offer to go into practice with some guy he'd gone to school with, and he wanted to take it. It meant moving to the Boston area, but we both thought it would be a new beginning for us. At least that's what we tried to tell ourselves.

"We bought this house; we bought a dog. The kids started school. Everybody seemed happy. Daniel loved his new partners, adored his practice. He joined a tennis club and a golf club, and he started running again every day. Sometimes he'd take the dog, which is how he met you."

"Tell me," Jane said eagerly.

"Well, the way I remember it is that he came home after work one day and decided that J.R. needed some exercise. J.R. after that fellow on *Dallas*, right? And so he took the dog out with him one morning. Just before they really got going, J.R. heard the call of nature, and decided to answer it. And of course, Daniel hadn't bargained on that and didn't have his pooper scooper with him, so he was just standing there, jogging in place, while the dog did his business on your lawn. Suddenly, he heard a scream. Actually, the whole neighborhood heard a scream."

"Me?" Jane asked, already intuiting the answer.

" 'Get that shit off my lawn!' you yelled. Oh, it was glorious. 'Hey, you, get that shit off my lawn!' And you came flying out your front door, waving your arms. Daniel said later he thought you were going to hit him."

"Oh, no."

"Oh, yes. You were beautiful. So angry. So indignant. 'I have a little girl who plays on this lawn,' you shouted at him in no uncertain terms. I was standing at the front door, and I thought, 'Oh, great, she'll never make me one of those fabulous chocolate cakes again.' So Daniel dutifully returned to the house and got a plastic bag and went back to your lawn and picked the poop up. And next thing I knew, the two of you were fast friends and running together whenever you could work it into your schedules."

"It seems I have quite a temper."

Carole's face grew grave. "Yes, I'd say you do."

"When did Daniel move out?"

"October twenty-third. There was no big fight, no major disagreement, nothing you could point to directly and say, 'This is what led to that.' He'd just had enough, I guess. He was tired of my father, tired of having two teenagers, and tired of me. He decided he was still young enough to play the swinging bachelor. So, he bought himself a condominium on the waterfront in downtown Boston, paid over a million dollars for it, and now he jogs along the Freedom Trail every morning instead of the less exciting streets of Newton Highlands, and he walks to work, and he gets to see the kids whenever he feels like it, and his life is just the way he wants it. Isn't that peachy?"

"Just peachy." Jane thought of the lipstick she had purchased, then neglected. She decided to put some on when she got home.

"How do they work it?" Carole demanded, getting to her feet and walking over to the counter, where she poured herself another cup of coffee and helped herself to some oatmeal and raisin cookies from a chipped ceramic cookie jar. "You want some?"

Jane shook her head.

"I mean, how do they manage to stay little boys all their lives? How come they get to throw away a lifetime of responsibilities and date blondes, and we get to sit here and watch our pubic hair turn gray? I mean, I ask you, is it fair?" She finished one cookie, then started another. "What would you know of any of this? You're married to the perfect man."

"He does seem very nice," Jane agreed, feeling like an idiot. Could she really be describing her husband of eleven years in this way? *He does seem very nice*?

She turned to Carole and found the other woman staring at her, as if there was something she wanted to say, something she wanted to tell her. "What?" she asked.

Carole was startled into a flurry of useless activity. She returned to the table and sat down, lifted her coffee to her mouth, then deposited the mug back on the table without taking a sip, then repeated the same action with her cookie. "What?" she said, parroting Jane. "What do you mean?"

"You looked like you had something you wanted to tell me."

Carole shook her head. "No. Nothing."

"Please, tell me. Was it something about Michael? Something about our relationship?"

Carole brought the coffee to her lips and, this time, took a long sip. "I think if you have any questions about your relationship with Michael, he's the one you should ask. Really, I don't know anything."

"Would you tell me if you did?"

There was a long pause as Jane watched Carole trying to measure out her response. The radio was playing k.d. lang in a duet with Roy Orbison. "Isn't Roy Orbison dead?" Carole asked suddenly.

"I think so," Jane told her, feeling suddenly out of sync with the conversation. "Didn't he die a few years back?"

"I can't remember. See? That's what I mean about getting older and forgetting everything. I always *used* to know who was dead."

From outside in the backyard came the sound of loud barking.

"Oh, shut up, J.R.," Carole barked in return through the closed window. The dog went immediately silent. "I wish everybody was that easy to control," she sighed. "Hey, I've got a joke for you."

Jane waited, understanding that their real conversation was over.

"This woman finds a magic lamp, and she rubs it, and out pops a genie. And the genie tells her that he'll grant her any wish her heart desires. So she thinks for a minute and then she says, 'I wish for thin thighs!' And the genie looks at her and says, 'That's it? That's your wish? I tell you I'll grant you anything your heart desires, and you wish for thin thighs! There are people out there starving; wars are raging, disease and poverty are everywhere. And you, who could wish for anything, you wish for thin thighs!' And of course, this poor woman is very embarrassed, so she thinks for a minute, and then she says, 'Oh, all right. Thin thighs for everyone!' " Carole burst into great gales of laughter. Jane managed a few chuckles. "Oh, what would you know?" Carole asked. "Your thighs are like matchsticks. My father was right. You're too thin. Have a cookie."

Jane was about to accept when she heard a frantic knocking at the front door.

"Carole," her father shouted from upstairs, "someone's at the door."

Carole was already on her feet. "It's either Andrew, who's forgotten something, or Celine, who's so loaded down with parcels that she can't find her keys."

Jane knew even before Carole reached the front door that it was neither Andrew nor Celine. "Is Jane here?" she heard Paula ask, her voice just shy of hysteria.

"Yes, she is," Carole said calmly. "We were just having some coffee. Would you like a cup?"

"I've been frantic," Paula said, rushing into the kitchen and confronting Jane. "Why didn't you tell me you were going out?"

"I didn't think it was necessary," Jane lied. "You were busy. I didn't want to bother you."

"I went to see if you needed anything, and you weren't in your room. I searched the whole house, the backyard, the garage. I ran up and down the street twice before I thought of coming here. I was at my wits' end. I thought you might have run off again." She was on the verge of tears.

"I'm sorry if I frightened you," Jane told her, and

she was. It had been very irresponsible of her to leave the house without at least telling Paula where she'd be. Why hadn't she? "I just wanted to get out of the house for a while."

"Well, I can understand that," Paula told her, catching Jane by surprise. She hadn't expected Paula to be sympathetic. "Just that next time, I wish you'd tell me first."

"Next time I will."

"And meantime," Paula said, checking her watch, "we really should get home. You should have a nap before Dr. Whittaker gets back, and—"

"I know," Jane said. "It's time for my pills."

12

SHE WOKE UP WITH A HEADACHE.

The dull throbbing emanated from the base of her neck and stretched into her skull, like a tree in winter, spindly and bereft of adornment, its bare branches catching on delicate nerve endings. Even her teeth ached.

Just another day in Paradise, she thought, trying to swing her legs out of bed. They felt heavy, as if someone had attached lead weights to them while she slept. She checked. Her bare toes wiggled back at her from beneath her white cotton nightgown. No lead weights that she could see, she thought, standing up and leaning against the bedpost for support. Only the ones in her head.

She sighed, fighting the urge to climb back into bed. What point was there in getting up? She felt lousy. She'd only feel lousier as the day progressed. In a few minutes, Paula would be in to check on her, to feed her more pills, and offer her breakfast. And then she'd sleep some more, and when she wasn't sleeping, she'd go back over the photograph books trying to remember who all these strange people were, even though Michael had gone over every photograph with her at least half a dozen times until she knew each person's name by heart, and would undoubtedly recognize each and every one of them should she ever run into any of them on the street, which was unlikely, since she rarely left the house.

She looked toward her bedroom door, expecting to see her jailer's face, but there was no one. "You're not being fair," she said to her reflection in the mirror. "Paula is not your jailer. *You* are."

She stared at the stranger in the mirror, watching the woman pull at the front of her white nightgown in disgust. "Whoever you are, you have lousy taste," the woman told her. "This thing has about as much sex appeal as a straitjacket." Which would probably be more appropriate attire, she added silently.

So why do you keep putting it on? her eyes demanded of their mirror image.

Because every time I throw it in the hamper, you-know-who washes it and lays it back across my pillow. And it's easier to wear it than to fight about it. And it's safe, she realized. She didn't have to worry about it stirring anything in her husband that she wasn't yet prepared to deal with. She could probably wear this number in front of Warren Beatty and not get any response.

She ran her hands along her body, her fingers grazing the tips of her breasts, the slight curve of her stomach, the soft mound of her pubis. She felt a gentle stirring. How often did she and Michael make love? she wondered. And what kind of lover was he?

She dropped her hands to her sides. These were not questions she was prepared to deal with. What was the point in activating these impulses if she wasn't ready to act on them?

Was she ready to act on them? Was she ready to make love to a man she didn't know just because he was her husband?

"Are you?" she asked the woman in the mirror.

The woman shrugged.

"Slut," Jane said, and laughed, then spun around, expecting to see Paula's disapproving face in the doorway.

Then she remembered it was Saturday. Paula had weekends off. It would just be her and Michael. Lots of time to act on these desires should she make that choice.

Could that really be what she wanted? Could it be as simple as that?

Maybe her enforced celibacy was the cause of her headaches. Or the reason for her continued depression. Maybe she just wasn't used to going this long without sex!

And what would be the harm in going to bed with the man? She found him enormously appealing. And he was her husband, after all. She'd been sleeping with him for eleven years. It wasn't as if they'd just been introduced. It wasn't as if she'd just met him and agreed to come home with him.

Except that was exactly how it was.

And she didn't know him any better now than she had a week ago. Oh, she knew *about* him. She knew the details of his life, of their life together. She knew that he was kind and sensitive and patient, and everything she could have wished for in a husband.

Maybe that was all she had to know.

So what if she didn't remember him? Was that really necessary? She'd known him for just over a week now. People often hopped into bed together after knowing one another far less time than that. And she liked him. Even in her confused, depressed state, she found him attractive. She understood why she had been drawn to him some eleven years ago. So what would be the harm in inviting him into her bed? Clearly, he was waiting for an invitation, though he had never said a word. They were consenting adults. What's more, they were legally married consenting adults. Who would they be offending? Maybe if they slept together, it would help her to remember. And even if it didn't help her to remember, it just might make her feel better. And what would be so wrong about that?

"I don't know," she whispered, opening one of the closets and fishing through her top drawer for her black lace garters. She held them up for her reflection to see, was satisfied by the expression of shock they elicited. "These would probably get him going."

Is that what you want? her reflection asked silently.

Do you really want to get him going? You better be damn sure before you start anything.

"I don't know. I don't know what I want," Jane said angrily, returning the garters to the drawer and slamming the closet door shut. "I can't think clearly. My head feels like someone has stuffed it full of rocks." She brought her hands to the back of her skull and dug her nails into her scalp, feeling it tingle. "My head hurts," she cried. "My head hurts and I can't think clearly, and I'm tired all the time. Goddammit, what's the matter with me?"

It had to be the pills she was taking. Despite Michael's assurances that they were very mild, obviously they were too strong for her. She probably wasn't used to any kind of prolonged medication. The pills were responsible for her disorientation and depression, for her constant fatigue and sense of hopelessness. Yet every time she questioned Michael about them, every time she asked him whether they were really necessary, he told her that Dr. Meloff had specifically prescribed them, with instructions that she continue to take them for at least several more weeks.

Had those been Dr. Meloff's instructions?

"Now, what does that mean?" she demanded of her reflection, wondering from what perverse corner of her brain this strange thought had sprung. "What are you trying to say? That Michael is lying to you? That Dr. Meloff never prescribed any medication? That Michael, with Paula's assistance, is deliberately trying to keep you drugged and dopey and depressed? Why? And how can you be having such thoughts about a man you were, only moments ago, ready to hop into bed with?"

"Because I'm obviously going crazy," came the immediate response. "Who else but a crazy person would argue with her own reflection?"

There's an easy way to find out, the woman in the mirror informed her, silently passing the message through the glass. Call Dr. Meloff.

"What?"

Call the good doctor. He told you to feel free to phone

him any time. Call him and ask him whether he prescribed any drugs for you.

How can I do that?

Easy. Just pick up the phone and dial.

Jane's head spun toward the phone on the bedside table. Was it really that easy? Was that all she had to do? Pick up the phone and dial?

Her hand reached for the phone, then stopped. What if Michael were to walk in? Where was he anyway? It was after nine o'clock. Was it possible he was still asleep?

She walked purposefully out of her room into the hall, careful not to make any noise. If he was sleeping, she didn't want to disturb him. If he was busy in some other part of the house, she didn't want to bring him rushing to her aid. At least not yet. She tiptoed down the hall, peeking first into Emily's room, then the bathroom, the guest room and finally Michael's office. But the bed in the guest room had been made, and he wasn't working at his computer. She heard barking and so she approached the window, glancing outside.

Michael was talking to Carole Bishop on her front lawn. J. R. barked impatiently and pulled on his leash, his walk obviously having been interrupted. From where Jane stood, their conversation looked serious. Both had their heads bowed, their eyes directed at the grass at their feet. She watched Carole nod her head and Michael pat Carole's arm solicitously. She's probably going on about Daniel, Jane thought. Or her father. Michael was just being his usual caring self. Could she really doubt him?

She returned to her bedroom, feeling angry and ashamed. Had the man done anything, one single thing, to make her question him? To make her suspect he might be feeding her unnecessary drugs? No! He'd done nothing but look out for her, look after her. And feed her pills around the clock. Jane looked at the telephone beside her bed. "Pick up the phone and dial," she said out loud.

Tentatively, she reached over and lifted up the receiver. There was no dial tone. Her eyes followed the phone cord to its socket on the wall. The socket was empty. The cord lay coiled on the floor directly underneath it like a sleeping snake. Michael must have pulled the cord out of the wall in case the phone rang while she was sleeping. He didn't want her to be disturbed. He was only thinking of her welfare, as he had proven every day since her return home. And she was about to repay his kindness by checking up on him.

She bent over, steadying herself against the bed, fighting the sudden wave of dizziness that swept over her, and reconnected the phone. The dial tone droned loudly in her ear, rebuking her. "What now?"

Now, you call information, she instructed herself, sitting down on the bed, punching out 411.

"What city please?" came the almost instant response.

"Boston," she said equally quickly. "The Boston City Hospital."

There was a pause during which the human voice was replaced by a machine. It repeated the number twice while she fished in the drawer of the night table for her telephone-address book. "Just a minute," she urged the machine. "I want to write this down. Where's my book?" She distinctly remembered having gone through the paisley-covered book page by page when she came home from the hospital. And now it was gone. "I'm sorry, could you repeat that?" she asked, giving up the search and trying to concentrate on the numbers the automatic operator was relaying. "Great, now you're talking to machines."

She immediately dialed what she hoped was the correct number.

"Boston City Hospital," announced the voice on the other end of the line.

"Could I speak to Dr. Meloff, please."

"I'm sorry. Could you speak up, please. Which doctor did you wish to speak to?"

"Dr. Meloff," Jane repeated louder.

"I don't think Dr. Meloff is in today. But if you hold on a minute, I'll try his extension."

"Of course, it's Saturday! He won't be there on Saturday.'' Jane was about to hang up when she heard his voice. ''Dr. Meloff?''

''Speaking. May I help you?''

''It's Jane Whittaker.''

There was no response.

''Jane Whittaker? Dr. Michael Whittaker's wife.''

''Oh, of course, *Jane,*'' he said, giving an emphasis to her name that suggested he was glad to hear from her. ''I'm usually not in today, so I wasn't expecting any calls. How are you?''

''I'm so sorry to bother you . . .''

''Don't be sorry. I'm delighted to hear from you. Is everything all right?''

''I'm not sure.''

''I've spoken to your husband a few times. He told me that he'd had to reschedule your appointment with the psychiatrist but that he felt you were making progress, that you'd remembered an incident from your past.''

''Yes,'' she confirmed, trying not to sound as confused as she felt. ''I didn't realize you'd been speaking to him.''

''Well, I hope you don't mind my being curious, and your husband, of course, is very concerned. So, we thought we should keep in touch. What can I do for you?''

''It's these pills you prescribed for me, Dr. Meloff,'' she began, half expecting him to burst in with an indignant, What pills?! I've prescribed no pills! But he said nothing. ''I was wondering what exactly they were.''

''I believe I prescribed Ativan. Just give me half a second and I'll check my files.'' There were several seconds of intense silence. So, Dr. Meloff had prescribed medication for her after all. Michael was simply following doctor's orders. ''Yes, Ativan,'' Dr. Meloff stated, coming back on the line. ''Its main ingredient is something called lorazepam. I don't know if that means anything to you or not, but essentially, it's just a very mild tranquilizer, not unlike Valium, but not addictive in the same way.''

''But why do I need to be taking anything at all?''

"A mild sedation usually works very well in cases of hysterical amnesia." He paused, and Jane could almost hear him smile. "Look, you're in a very stressful situation: You don't remember who you are; you're married to a man you don't know; you're surrounded by a bunch of strangers. That has to be producing a great deal of anxiety which will only get in the way of your memory coming back. The Ativan is supposed to counteract that anxiety, let your memory find its way back home."

"But I'm so tired all the time, and depressed. . . ."

"That's not out of keeping with the situation. You're bound to get more depressed the longer this thing drags on. That's why the Ativan is so important. And as for your fatigue, well, I'd say your body is trying to tell you something. Namely, that you need sleep. Don't fight it, Jane. Listen to what your body is telling you."

"So, you don't think it's the medication that's making me feel this way? . . ." Why was she asking him that? Hadn't he just told her that Ativan was a very mild tranquilizer? That he considered it essential for her recovery?

"There's nothing in Ativan to cause depression. I suppose it's possible that it could make you sleepy, considering you're a little underweight, but that should stop once your body gets used to it."

"It's just that I feel so helpless, like I have no control. . . ." She stopped, suddenly aware of Michael's footsteps on the stairs. "I should go," she said quickly. "I've bothered you enough."

"I'm just glad I was here when you called. Listen, if your husband is there, I'd like to talk to him for a minute."

Michael stood in the doorway.

"He's right here," she said into the phone, then stretched the receiver toward her husband. "Dr. Meloff," she told him, her heart pounding wildly. "He wants to talk to you."

Michael looked appropriately puzzled as he took the receiver from her hand. He looks as confused as I feel, Jane thought, wondering again what had prompted her phone call to Dr. Meloff. Had she really suspected her husband might be feeding her unnecessary medication? Why? The man had been nothing but good to her. He'd been patient and supportive and wonderful. Was she allergic to wonderful men? Was that her problem? She couldn't cope with being so happily married, so she'd escaped into some sort of temporary insanity, and now she couldn't cope with his continued love and devotion, so she tried to convince herself he must be plotting against her. That made a lot of sense.

When was the last time anything had made sense? Did it make sense that she should find herself walking the streets of Boston without a clue as to who she was? That she should have pockets filled with hundred-dollar bills and a dress that was streaked with blood? That she couldn't remember her daughter's birth or her mother's death? That she should be so distrustful of, and hateful to, the people who were only trying to help her? That the mildest of tranquilizers could turn her into a zombie? That she was growing so paranoid she felt like a prisoner in her own home?

Did it make sense that her back ached and her head throbbed and it hurt her to swallow? That she couldn't accomplish the simplest of tasks? That she distinctly remembered returning her telephone-address book to the drawer of her night table, and now it was gone? Did any of that make sense? And how could anyone who couldn't remember her own name claim to distinctly remember anything?

"Where's my telephone-address book?" she asked as Michael replaced the receiver. He's hurt, she recognized, trying to avoid his eyes. He doesn't understand why I called Dr. Meloff. And what can I tell him when I don't understand myself? "It was here." She pulled open the top drawer of the night table for emphasis. "And now it's gone."

"I don't know where it is," he said simply.

"It was here when I got home from the hospital." Why was she persisting? Why was she making an issue of something where none existed? Because the best defense was a good offense. Because that way she didn't have to explain her call to Dr. Meloff.

"Then it must still be there," he was saying.

"It isn't. Look for yourself!"

"I don't need to look. If you tell me it's not there, then I believe you."

Jane translated this to mean, If you told me that Dr. Meloff had prescribed medication for me, then I wouldn't dream of checking up on you. It fueled her anger. "Paula must have moved it," she shouted, pacing back and forth in front of the bed.

"Why would she move it?"

"I don't know. But it was here last week and it's not here now. So, somebody had to move it."

"I'll check with Paula on Monday," he said, clearly upset by her behavior, but fighting to keep calm. "I don't understand what you want with the book anyway."

"Maybe I want to call one of my friends," she shot back, sounding irrational even to herself. "Maybe I want to start picking up the pieces of my life. Maybe I get tired of being cooped up here all day, watched over by that Nazi. . . ."

"Nazi?! Paula?! My God, what's she done?"

"Nothing!" Jane shouted, all pretense of sanity gone. Nothing could prevent the torrent of words from rushing from her mouth, as if they, too, had been kept prisoner for too long and were now hell-bent on escaping. "She does everything exactly right. She's a goddamn machine. She watches over me like Big Brother. I can't go to the bathroom without her checking up on me. She doesn't let me answer the phone. She tells my friends I'm out of town. Why won't she let me speak to my friends?"

"What would you say to them?" he asked plaintively. "Do you really want your friends to see you like this?"

"What are friends for?" she demanded.

The color drained slowly from Michael's face, as if someone were adjusting the tint on a color TV. He sank onto the bed, his face in his hands. "It's my fault. I told Paula not to let you take any calls. I thought I was helping you, keeping you away from stressful situations. I thought it would be best if not too many people knew about what was happening. You've always been a very private person, and I didn't think you'd appreciate having everyone know . . . I'm sorry. I'm sorry," he repeated, his voice drifting off, disappearing into the space between them.

She sat down beside him, her anger suddenly vanquished. "No, *I'm* sorry. You obviously know me better than I do." She hoped he would smile and was gratified when he did.

"If you want to speak to your friends, just say the word. I'll call them right now if you want, tell them to come over."

Jane thought for an instant, the idea of speaking to virtual strangers, let alone facing them in person, causing her heart to race. He was right—it would undoubtedly prove too stressful. Whom would she call? What would she say? "No, not now," she told him, then, "Please forgive me. I'm just very confused."

"Is that why you called Dr. Meloff?"

"I don't know why I called Dr. Meloff."

"Don't you think you can talk to me?" She saw tears forming in his eyes, saw him struggling to contain them. "Don't you know that there isn't anything in this world I wouldn't do for you? That if you have any questions, any doubts, any fears, that you can talk to me about them? If you don't like Paula, we'll get rid of her. If you want to get out of the house more, I'll take you wherever you want to go, or you can go by yourself, if that's what you want. You can come to the office with me, if you'd like. Or you don't have to go anywhere with me at all." He stopped, his chest caving in as if he'd been punched, hard, in the stomach. "Is that it, Jane? Am I the problem? Because if it's me, if I'm the one you don't want around, then just say the word. I'm out of here. I'll pack some things and move into a hotel until this nightmare is over."

"No, that's not what I want. You're not the problem. I'm the problem."

"I just want what's best for you, Jane. What's best

for us.'' He was crying openly now, not bothering to hold anything back. ''I love you so much. I've always loved you. I don't know why this awful thing is happening to us, but I'll do whatever I can to make it go away as quickly as possible, even if it means giving you up.''

Now she was crying too. ''I don't want you to go away. I want you to stay with me. Please don't leave me. Please.''

She felt his arms surround her as she laid her head against his chest, and they both cried. And then they weren't crying any more, and her eyes were seeking his, and his mouth was covering hers, and they were kissing, and it felt good, no, more than good, it felt wonderful. It felt, for the first time, as if she really had come home, as if she really did belong here.

''Oh, God, Jane, you're so beautiful,'' he said, kissing her again and again, his hands finding her breasts, pushing her nightgown aside so that he could stroke her legs. And then suddenly, he was pulling away, retreating, burying his gentle hands beneath the covers of the bed. ''I'm sorry. Please forgive me. I shouldn't have done that.''

''Why not?'' Jane asked, well aware of the answer.

''You're confused now; you're not sure. . . .''

''I'm very sure.''

He stared at her for several long seconds, then bent his head forward to kiss her nose. ''I've always loved you in that stupid nightgown,'' he said, and she laughed.

''Make love to me, Michael. Please.''

He looked carefully into her eyes, as if trying to crawl inside her head.

''It's what I want,'' she told him, and there were no further protestations.

13

THE FOLLOWING WEEK, JANE HAD ANOTHER DREAM.

She was standing with a little girl she recognized as her daughter at the edge of a small skating rink in Newton Center. They stood side by side, Emily in her pink snowsuit and new white skates, Jane in a hooded parka and heavy winter boots, about to step onto the ice when they were halted by a stern male voice.

"Excuse me, but you can't go on the ice without skates."

Jane's gaze dropped to her feet, then back to the ruddy-cheeked young man before her. "But I'm only going to lead my daughter around the rink."

"You have to be wearing skates. I'm sorry, but it's the rule."

Jane felt her hackles rise. "Look, I don't want to argue with you. Can't we work something out? There's no one else on the ice, and I don't see what harm it would do. . . ."

"You can't go on the ice without skates, lady. It's that simple."

Jane felt every muscle in her body tense at the word *lady*.

"Come on," Jane urged the young man, hiding her clenched fist inside the pocket of her warm jacket. "You don't want to disappoint my little girl. She's been looking forward to this all week."

The young man shrugged indifference. "Look, lady, rules are rules. Take it or leave it." He turned on his heel and started to walk away.

"Asshole," Jane muttered, not quite under her breath.

"What did you say?"

Everything after that happened very quickly: the young man spinning around, marching back, his hand grabbing hold of the front of her collar, lifting her into the air, spewing invective at her; Emily screaming at her side, people rushing to the scene; the young man hurriedly letting her go, her feet returning gratefully to the ground; "I'm sorry, I lost my cool"; "I understand, rules are rules"; retreating to a nearby bench, her legs shaking; Emily making her way onto the ice alone, managing quite well by herself; Michael trying to reason with her later that night, "God, Jane, why do you do these things? One day some guy's liable to kill you!" "I'm sorry, Michael, he just made me so mad!"

"Are you okay?"

"What?"

Jane fought her way through the fog of her memories toward Michael's face. "I was just going over what happened at the skating rink again."

"Did you remember anything else?"

She shook her head, wondering briefly what day it was, how many days had passed since the incident at the skating rink had come back to her.

"I have to go to the hospital now. Paula's downstairs if you need her."

"What time is it?"

"Almost eight o'clock."

"In the morning?"

He kissed her forehead. "In the morning."

"I wish you didn't have to go," she said, contemptuous of the whine in her voice. "I feel so alone when you're not here. I get so scared."

"There's nothing to be scared of, Jane. You're home

now. And you're remembering more things. That's good news, not something to be scared of."

"But I feel so panicky inside. I feel so disoriented, so weak. . . ."

"Maybe you should try to get out today," Michael offered, pulling away from her, looking down at her from the side of the bed. "Why don't you get Paula to take you for a walk this morning?"

"I don't think I'd get very far."

"A drive, then. The fresh air will do you some good."

"I just don't understand why I'm so tired all the time."

"I really have to go, honey. I see my first patient in less than an hour."

"Maybe I should see Dr. Meloff again. Maybe there is something wrong with my brain."

"Why don't we talk about it when I get home? All right?" He kissed her again, then walked toward their bedroom door. "I'll have Paula bring up some breakfast."

"I'm not very hungry."

"You have to eat something, Jane. You want to get better, don't you?"

Don't you? Don't you? Don't you? Don't you? The words followed her like an echo as she stumbled out of bed toward the bathroom. She needed all her concentration just to put one foot in front of the other, and once in the bathroom, she couldn't remember what it was she had wanted to do. "What's wrong with me?" she asked her reflection in the mirror above the sink, noting the presence of drool dribbling from the side of her mouth, and angrily wiping it away. And was it her imagination or had her features acquired an eerie, almost masklike cast?

She tried to straighten up, feeling the muscles in her back go into one of their increasingly frequent spasms. Was it possible she had suffered some kind of a stroke? Certainly that would explain her loss of memory, the lethargy that had become her constant companion, the variety of physical ailments that plagued her. And yet, surely evidence of a stroke would have surfaced in at least one of the tests she had been administered at the Boston City Hospital. Unless she'd suffered the stroke since she'd come home! Was it possible to have a stroke and not be aware of it?

"Something is very definitely wrong with you," she informed her passive reflection. "You're a very sick girl."

Jane splashed some cold water on her face, not bothering to dry it, then returned to her bed, crawling inside and hugging her pillow to her wet cheek, smelling Michael though she knew he was gone.

She pictured him lying beside her in bed, his arms snaked around hers, their bodies fitting together like spoons, the calm of his breathing steadying hers. They slept in the same bed now, though they hadn't made love since that first time together, how long ago now? A few days? A week? She was always so tired. She hadn't the strength. He made no demands, simply snuggling in peacefully beside her, seemingly content with whatever scraps she threw his way. Could a week really have passed?

Jane flipped onto her back, calling forth fresh spasms. She took deep breaths, trying to will the spasms away, understanding that their will was stronger than hers. She tried to concentrate on other things: the sound of Michael's voice as he whispered words of love; the soft wetness of his tongue as it danced along the slender curves of her flesh; the way the muscles of his arms tightened when he pushed into her; the grateful way he collapsed beside her when their lovemaking was done.

She looked up, half expecting to find his nude body looming above hers, saw instead Paula's earnest face staring down at her. Jane gasped, immediately feeling the muscles in her lower back knot in protest. Her gasp turned into a cry of pain.

"Your back bothering you again?"

Paula was obviously used to her spasms, Jane thought, nodding affirmation, barely able to lift her head off the pillow.

"Turn over on your side," Paula instructed. "I'll massage it for you."

Jane obeyed without hesitation. How many times during the past week had this ritual been repeated? She felt Paula's hands at the small of her back, applying gentle pressure.

"Here?" Paula asked, her fingers drawing invisible circles on the surface of the white cotton nightdress.

"A little higher. Yes, there. Thank you."

"Try to direct your breathing into the area," Jane heard Paula say, and wondered what the hell she meant. How could she direct her breathing anywhere? "Concentrate," Paula said, and Jane tried to do what she was told, failing miserably. How could she concentrate her breathing when she could barely concentrate at all?

What was happening to her? When had she crossed the line from hysteric to invalid?

"How's that now?" Paula asked, her hands withdrawing.

"Better, thank you."

"You should try to get up, do a little exercise."

The thought of exercise made Jane want to throw up. "I don't think that would be a very good idea."

"Dr. Whittaker thinks we should get out of the house today. He said I should take you for a walk."

"Or a ride in the car," Jane said, remembering the second, much preferable, alternative.

"He said you didn't feel like breakfast."

"I don't think I could keep anything down." Jane's eyes flashed hopefully to Paula's. "Do you think I have the flu or something?" she asked, wondering if her amnesia might have confused everyone into ignoring other obvious physical reasons for her present condition. Suppose one thing had absolutely nothing to do with the other. Suppose she just happened to be sick.

Paula's hand was immediately on Jane's forehead. "You do feel a little warm," she admitted, "but then so would anyone who stayed in bed all day." The words carried traces of reproach. Jane felt as if she were a little girl being reprimanded by her nanny.

"I'll try to get up."

"You better take these first." Two small white pills materialized in the palm of Paula's hand, followed by a glass of water.

She must moonlight as a magician, Jane thought, slowly transferring the pills into her own hand, and staring at them with an intensity that suggested she expected them to speak.

"Take them," Paula instructed as the phone rang in the other room, Michael having removed the phone from their bedroom sometime earlier in the week. "I'll be right back." Paula put the glass of water on the night table and walked briskly from the room.

"If it's for me, I'd really like to talk to whoever it is," Jane called after her, receiving no acknowledgment that her words had been heard. "Fat chance," she said to her reflection in the mirrors across from her bed, pushing her hair away from her face and trying to force the muscles at her mouth into a smile. Her mouth refused to move. "I'll force you to smile," she announced, bringing her fingers to her lips, trying to manipulate the sides of her mouth upward, as if her skin were clay. The white pills fell from her hand onto the mint-green carpet at her feet. "Oh, God, I forgot all about you guys." Jane collapsed onto her hands and knees, retrieving the pills and then lifting her head, staring at herself in the wall of mirrors. Woman as Dog, she thought with amazement, wondering what had reduced her to this state.

Concentrate, she heard Paula repeat silently. Concentrate. You were feeling fine when you were wandering the streets of downtown Boston, you were feeling okay at the Lennox Hotel. You were all right at the police station and the hospital, and when Michael first brought you home. It's only after you started taking these stupid little white pills that are supposed to be so helpful and mild that it became an effort to get out of bed, that you developed this disgusting drool, that you lost your appetite. "It doesn't make any sense," she said out loud. "Even when I lost my memory, I never lost my appetite!"

She studied the two small, round, uncoated, bi-concave white pills with the beveled edges for several seconds before pulling open her closet door and thrusting them into the toes of a pair of black shoes, briefly wondering whether other people's shoes were as interesting as hers were rapidly becoming. Then she forced herself to her feet and over to her night table, where she quickly swallowed the glass of water just as Paula reentered the room.

"That was my mother," Paula announced without prompting.

"Is everything all right?"

"Christine got it into her head that she wanted to wear a certain outfit and my mother couldn't find it. She wanted to know if I knew where it was."

"And did you?" Jane was reluctant to let go of the conversation, grateful as she was to anything that made her feel even vaguely human.

Paula shrugged. "Christine outgrew that dress years ago. I don't know where she gets these things in her head." She frowned. "She's got a million crazy ideas these days. I guess it's part of being five years old."

Jane nodded, trying to recall Emily at five years of age, immediately conjuring up the image of a little girl in a pink snowsuit clinging tightly to her hand at the edge of a small, oval-shaped skating rink. Michael said that incident had happened about a year and a half ago, so Emily would have been five. What million crazy ideas had been going on in *her* five-year-old head? What crazy ideas must be going on in her head right now?

Does she think about me? Jane wondered. Does she wonder why a few days with her grandparents has stretched into a few weeks? Why I don't phone her to say hello? Does she think that I've abandoned her? By the time I remember who she is, will she still remember me?

"I'd like to call my daughter," Jane announced suddenly.

"You'll have to discuss that with Dr. Whittaker when he gets home."

"I don't need my husband's permission to call my daughter."

"I don't think it would be wise, in your present condition, to do anything that might upset both you and your daughter."

"How would talking to her own mother upset her?"

Paula hesitated. "Well, you're not exactly the mother she remembers, are you?"

Jane felt her resolve crumble. There was no denying the validity of Paula's last utterance. Besides, she couldn't very well insist on calling her daughter when she didn't know exactly where the child was or the phone number where she could be reached.

"Paula," she said abruptly, as Paula was bending over to make her bed. She watched Paula's shoulders tense, her arms coming to rest at her sides. "Where did you put my telephone-address book?"

Paula glanced at her from over her shoulder, her position unchanged. "I didn't put it anywhere."

"It was in my night table and now it's gone."

"I've never seen it," Paula informed her, "let alone touched it."

"It was in the night table and now it's gone," Jane repeated, stubbornly.

"You'll have to ask Dr. Whittaker about it when he gets home," Paula said again, just as stubbornly.

"I should make a list of all the things I have to ask him." Jane didn't bother trying to disguise the sarcasm in her voice.

"Feeling a little feisty this morning, aren't we?" Paula remarked. "Maybe that's a good sign." She finished making the bed. "Why don't you get dressed and we'll go for that drive."

It was more demand than request and Jane decided not to argue. Paula could be very obstinate. Besides, Jane really wanted to get out of the house. Hadn't she been begging Michael and Paula for just that opportunity? When had she stopped wanting to get out more? And why? What had stopped her?

She peered inside her closet, pretending to be concerned with what clothes to select for her outing, but in reality, her eyes were directed to the floor, focused on the toes of a pair of black patent leather shoes.

"Come on, damn you. Don't give me a hard time."

Jane held her breath and waited for Paula's anger to subside. It was the second such outburst in the course of their ten-minute-old excursion.

"Damnit!" Paula's hand slapped against the steering wheel, accidentally triggering the horn. The car behind them immediately honked back. Paula waved her apologies into the rearview mirror, then returned her attention to the problem at hand. "Damnit, don't die on me now!"

"Maybe if you turn the engine off for half a second," Jane suggested.

"No, that won't work. It's been stalling like this for about a month now. I know its pattern. It won't start again until it's good and ready."

"You need to take it in."

"I need a new car is what I need."

Jane said nothing. What was there to add? Paula's car was indeed old, had probably been old when she bought it. It was definitely on its last legs, a fact Jane found strangely appropriate in that it made her feel less alone. I shouldn't be the only one on her last legs around here, she thought, deciding against sharing such thoughts with her companion.

Paula made another attempt to get the car moving, but the old Buick only sputtered momentarily before wheezing into unconsciousness. Paula looked suspiciously at Jane, and, for an instant, Jane felt Paula might be holding her responsible. "Was it Dr. Whittaker who told you to turn off the engine?"

"I don't remember," Jane said, thinking it an odd question. "I guess so."

That was good enough for Paula. She immediately turned off the ignition.

The car behind them honked his indignation. "Just what would you like us to do?" Jane called out. "Pick up the damn thing and carry it?'' She gave the man an indignant finger.

''Jane, for God's sake, what are you doing?''

Jane guiltily brought her hands back into her lap. ''Sorry. Force of habit, I guess.''

''So I understand.''

''What do you mean?''

Paula ignored the question, focusing her concentration on the car's ignition. With fresh determination, she reached over and turned the key. The car hiccuped, coughed, then belched into action. ''Thank God,'' Paula whispered, waving to the driver behind them and continuing northwest along Woodward Street.

''What did you mean, 'So I understand'?''

''Dr. Whittaker's told me about your famous temper.'' Paula stared resolutely at the road ahead, so that Jane was unable to draw any further inferences from Paula's expression.

''What exactly has he told you?'' Jane heard the testiness in her voice that she recognized as a precursor to anger, and wondered what she was feeling so angry about. Had she not expected Michael to discuss her with the woman who was being paid to look after her?

''Just that you have a temper.''

There was more, but Jane understood from the stiffness in Paula's shoulders that that was all she was going to tell her. ''He told me that I used to honk the horn of his car when he was driving,'' she volunteered, hoping that Paula might be tempted by this tidbit to offer further revelations of her own.

''Try that with me and you'll lose an arm.''

Jane found herself hugging her arms to her sides. She decided against further attempts at conversation, and instead directed her attention to the rows of fine old Victorian homes that lined the streets. She was feeling slightly perkier than she had when she first woke up. Did the fact that she hadn't taken her morning medication account for her clearer head, or was it simply a question of mind over matter? Wasn't her whole life these days a question of mind over matter? And did it matter at all? Never mind.

She found herself chuckling.

"Something funny?" For the first time since they had crawled into the messy front seat of Paula's gray Buick, Paula looked directly into Jane's eyes.

It was Jane's turn to look the other way. "I was just thinking about how ridiculous this whole thing is."

"It's very hard on Dr. Whittaker."

Oh, screw Dr. Whittaker! she almost yelled, biting down hard on her bottom lip to keep the words from escaping. She felt a trail of drool run quickly from her mouth to her chin, and she reached up with the back of her hand to wipe it away.

"There's some tissues in the glove compartment."

"I don't need any tissues." Jane felt an unwanted quiver in her voice, and realized she was close to tears. How could she move so fast between two such extremes? One minute she was laughing, the next she was crying. I'm acting like a child because I'm being treated like one, she told herself, staring out the side window, watching, as if on cue, a group of perhaps twelve children, their miniature fists clenching a common rope, marched along the sidewalk, bracketed on either end by several determinedly enthusiastic young women wearing T-shirts proclaiming their allegiance to the Highlands Day Camp.

The children were about six or seven years old, the girls outnumbering the boys by a margin of approximately two to one. If this were a more normal summer, would Emily be part of this smiling menagerie?

Jane felt an ache deep within the pit of her stomach. I may not be able to remember you, sweetheart, she thought, turning away from the children, but I know that I need you, and I think that you need me. She decided that she would definitely ask Michael to bring their daughter home.

Paula turned left onto Beacon Street. Another Beacon Street, Jane thought. Boston was full of them. "Stop!" she cried suddenly, and Paula's foot jammed hard on the brake. The car sputtered its reproach, then lapsed into a noisy, quivering coma.

"What the hell . . . ?"

"It's Emily's school!" Jane jumped out of the car and ran toward the simple two-story structure that was Arlington Private School.

"Get back in the car, Jane."

Jane came to an abrupt halt at the sound of Paula's voice but made no effort to return to the car. Indeed, she couldn't have moved had she tried. Her legs were rooted to the concrete; her whole body was shaking. Something was racing toward her, gathering strength, like an enormous tidal wave, and she could neither retreat from it nor leap out of its path to avoid being swept away. She stood paralyzed, more with wonder than with fear, as another memory flooded over her.

14

"OKAY, DOES EVERYBODY HAVE THEIR TICKETS ready?"

Jane listened as the teacher's shrill voice forced its way into her consciousness. She saw herself on the upper level of the South Station standing in the middle of a large gathering of children, their teachers, and a handful of parent volunteers, everybody tired after a full afternoon at the Children's Museum in downtown Boston. She quickly counted the heads of the eight children, including Emily, who had been assigned to her care.

"Remember that the transit system is for everybody," the teacher continued, "so no pushing or roughhousing, and keep the noise level down. Are we ready?"

And then, suddenly, a man—short, squat, his balding head jutting forward, his gaze directed toward the floor—was charging through the children, a disgruntled Moses parting the Red Sea, his hands shooting from his sides to push the children out of his way. One of the little girls fell against another child and both started to cry; a little boy narrowly missed being struck in the eye. The man, unrepentent, unforgiving, livid at the invasion of what he obviously considered his space, continued burrowing his way through the now-terrified children, while their teachers and parents watched in helpless fury. He was almost at the exit when Jane's voice caught up to him.

"Hey, you!" she yelled, chasing after the man, swinging her large heavy purse into the air like a baseball bat and aiming it directly at the back of his head, hearing the two surfaces connect.

Absolute silence filled the area as Jane's eyes scanned the hushed crowd. The teachers and other parent volunteers stood, mouths opened and eyes wide with shock; the children stared at her with something approaching awe. Or perhaps it was fear, Jane thought, experiencing the same sensation as the man spun around to confront her.

Oh shit, Jane thought. He's going to kill me.

Instead, the man, about fifty, muscular, ugly in his rage, began shouting, "What's the matter with you? Are you crazy?" before running off.

Am I crazy? Jane wondered. Why is it always me doing these things? I didn't see anyone else charging after him, rushing to the children's defense. Her eyes sought out the eyes of the other adults present, but each pair of eyes merely stared back at her, as if afraid to do or say anything that might set her off again. Only one woman, a mother whose hand was draped protectively across a little girl's shoulders, stared back at her with anything approaching approval. Even Emily hung back, as if she felt somehow responsible for her mother's outrageous behavior.

"What is it?" a voice asked, coming up behind her.

"What?"

The tidal wave vanished, leaving Jane high and dry, coated with the bitter residue of her memories. She turned to see Paula's worried gaze, the same look that had shaped the faces of the parents and teachers of Arlington Private School.

"Do you think I'm crazy?" Jane asked Paula, watching her take an automatic step back.

"You're going through a very hard time."

"That's not what I asked you."

"It's the only way I know how to answer." Each

woman avoided looking directly at the other. "Come on, Jane. Get in the car. We'll go home."

"I don't want to go home." The adamancy in Jane's voice caught both women by surprise. Paula winced as if she half-expected Jane to strike her. Well, isn't that my usual routine? Jane asked herself silently. Lose my temper and endanger my life? It's a wonder I'm still alive. It's a wonder my husband hasn't had me institutionalized. I'm obviously certifiable. Why else are my memories nothing more than a collection of temper tantrums?

Unless these memories are trying to tell me something. Unless there is some significance to what my subconscious is choosing to reveal. Or worse. Perhaps these memories are simply the hors d'oeuvre, leading up to the main course, laying the groundwork for the final pièce de résistance, the specialty of the house, the ultimate act of indiscretion that netted me almost ten thousand dollars, a bloody dress, and an empty head. Am I really as crazy as my subconscious would have me believe? Why these memories, and not others?

"I want to see Michael."

"You'll see Dr. Whittaker at dinner."

"Now."

Paula was trying to usher Jane toward the open car door. "Dr. Whittaker is a very busy man. You wouldn't want to barge in on him when he's seeing patients."

"That's exactly what I want to do."

"I don't think it would be a good idea."

"Take me to see my husband," Jane commanded. "Now." She climbed into the car and slammed the door after her.

"You're being unreasonable." Paula resumed her position behind the wheel, and began struggling with the car's ignition.

Jane was unapologetic. "It's what I do best."

"I'm afraid you can't go in there. Oh, Jane! Is that you? My God, I didn't recognize you."

The receptionist stared at Jane through large, cumbersome glasses. But even the glasses failed to keep the alarm from registering on her otherwise nondescript face. Do I look that awful? Jane wondered, trying to catch a glimpse of herself in the glass of the painting behind the receptionist's desk, appropriately a Renoir of two young girls embracing beside a piano.

"Rosie," she began, taking note of the woman's name tag, and pretending to remember her, "I really need to see my husband."

"Can it wait a few minutes? He's busy with a patient at the moment. Is he expecting you?" There was a worried cast to her mouth that suggested she already knew the answer.

"I tried to tell you, Jane," came a voice from somewhere beside her. Christ, was Paula still here? Did the woman never take a break?

"He's not expecting me, but I'm sure he'll see me if you just tell him that I'm here. And that I'm very anxious to talk to him."

The receptionist, whose name tag fully identified her as Rosie Fitzgibbons, knocked gingerly on the door to Dr. Whittaker's inner office and then stepped inside, angling her body in such a way that none of the inner office was visible to anyone in the outer reception area.

"We shouldn't have come. Dr. Whittaker will be very upset with me."

"Oh, go take a hike," Jane muttered under her breath, rubbing her head, thinking it clearer than it had been in days.

A sharp cough drew her gaze to the row of chairs across from the receptionist's desk. A forlorn-looking woman sat with her small daughter on her lap, the child pale and fidgety, refusing to play with any of the toys that lay scattered at her feet like discarded tissues. She alternated between coughing fits and whimpering. Her mother checked her watch, more, Jane suspected, to avoid Jane's scrutiny than because she needed to know the time. A large Mickey Mouse clock stared down at the woman from the wall beside the door. Directly underneath the clock sat a middle-aged man and a young boy with a pronounced harelip, who could either have been his son or his grandson. You never knew these days. The young boy was totally involved with several model airplanes, using his father's (grandfather's?) crossed feet as a makeshift runway. Had one of those toy planes been the culprit that took off part of Michael's skull? "Excuse me," she said, kneeling down and joining the boy at his father's (grandfather's?) feet. "Could I see that jet plane for a minute?"

The boy regarded her suspiciously, clutching the toy close to his small chest.

"I'll give it right back. I promise."

"Let the lady see the plane, Stuart." The voice of male authority. Stuart immediately handed over the plane.

Jane felt the weight of it in the palm of her hand. Or rather, its lack of weight. How could anything this light have resulted in a wound that required almost forty stitches to close? She shut her eyes, tried to picture the toy plane flying through the air at a speed fast enough to tear the skin off a grown man's forehead. How strong would a small child have to be to throw something this light that fast, and do that much damage?

"Jane?" Michael was suddenly beside her, helping her to her feet. The little boy, Stuart, immediately grabbed the toy airplane out of Jane's hands.

"I'm so sorry, Dr. Whittaker. She insisted that we come."

"That's all right, Paula. You did the right thing. Jane, are you all right?"

"I need to talk to you, Michael," Jane heard herself say.

"Then we'll talk," he said easily. "Come on in my office." He guided her gently toward the proper door just as a young woman and her small son were making their exit.

"Thank you so much, Dr. Whittaker. For everything you've done," the woman whispered, shaking his hand repeatedly.

"My pleasure. Just take good care of the little guy,

and drop me a line now and then to let me know how he's coming along."

"You don't have to see him again?" The woman sounded almost disappointed.

"Not unless something unexpected happens. Of course you can always call me if you're at all worried about anything."

The woman smiled her appreciation, and shook Michael's hand again before she left.

"Paula, why don't you get yourself a coffee and relax for a few minutes?" Michael suggested, and Jane wanted to hug him on the spot.

She followed him into his office, which looked very much like his study at home, a variation of the same green leather furniture, a large oak desk, walls lined with books. She was quick to note the presence of her photograph prominently displayed on his desk, as well as a large smiling picture of their daughter, minus one of her front teeth.

"I want to see Emily," she announced as he was closing the door.

"You will see her."

"Soon. Now."

"Soon," he confirmed. "Not now. Jane," he continued, before she could protest, "we agreed that she'd be better off with my parents until your memory came back."

"It's coming back." She quickly apprised him of her latest recollection.

"Jane," he said softly, carefully weighing his words, "don't get me wrong. I think it's great that you're starting to remember things, but it's just the beginning. You still have a very long way to go. You've had a few dreams, recalled a couple of highly dramatic incidents, but not the stuff of everyday life, and I think it would be counterproductive, maybe even harmful, both to Emily and yourself, to bring her back into your life at this particular point in time."

"But I think that if I could just see her . . ."

"What? That everything would come back to you?"

Jane nodded lamely. Is that what she really thought?

"It's unlikely to happen that way," Michael informed her. "If your memory were going to come back all in one swoop, the odds are it would have happened by now. You seem to be recalling things in fits and starts, a little bit at a time. Now, I'm not saying you aren't going to eventually get your memory back, I'm just saying that it might take a little longer until all the pieces fit together."

"And if that takes months? . . ." She wouldn't admit to the possibility that it might take even longer.

"Then that's how long we'll have to wait."

"But what about Emily?"

"Jane, do you really think it would be a good idea for her to see you in your present condition?"

Jane sank into the small leather sofa by the wall across from his desk, not having to check her appearance to know what he meant. "I'm feeling a little better this morning. I didn't take my pills, and I think that—"

"You didn't take your pills? Why? Did Paula forget to give them to you?"

"No. She gave them to me. I just didn't take them. I hid them when she went out of the room."

"You hid them? Jane, is that the act of a woman who wants to get better?"

"They were making me feel worse!"

Michael began pacing the room in frustration.

"Really, Michael. I've been feeling so crummy lately, and the only thing I could figure out was that I'd either had a stroke . . ."

"A stroke?" Now he was looking at her as if she had taken complete leave of her senses.

"Or that it was the medication that was making me feel so awful. Maybe I'm allergic to it, I don't know. I only know that I didn't take the pills this morning, and I feel a lot better. My head doesn't feel as if it's encased in cement. I don't feel like I'm talking to you from the middle of a tunnel. Please don't be angry with me."

He collapsed into the seat beside her. "Jane, Jane," he began, taking her hands in his, "how could I be angry with you? Of course I'm not angry at you. I'm as frustrated and confused as you are. All I want is for you to get better. I want my wife back. I want my family back. Don't you think I miss my daughter? Don't you think I'd give anything to have us all together again?"

"That's what I want—us all together again."

"Then you have to follow Dr. Meloff's instructions. You have to take your medication."

"Can't I just try it for a while without it? If I'm no better in a few days, then I'll start taking it again. I promise."

"That's a few more precious days wasted."

She had no reply. What were a few more precious days, one way or the other?

"I'm sorry," he was saying. "I don't mean to give you a hard time. If you think the medication is making you feel sick, then I'll speak to Dr. Meloff. Maybe he can prescribe something else. And I think that now might be the time to try hypnosis. I'll see if I can set something up."

There was a timid knocking at the door.

"Yes?" Michael answered.

Rosie Fitzgibbons angled her head inside the door. "Mr. Beattie asked me to tell you that he has to be back at work in twenty minutes, and that if you can't see Stuart now, he'll have to reschedule the appointment."

"That won't be necessary." Michael stood up, straightening his white lab jacket. "I can see him now. You don't mind, do you, Jane?"

Jane quickly rose to her feet. "You want me to leave?"

"Of course not. Look, why don't I try to get home for lunch? We can talk some more then." He ushered her back into the waiting area. Paula had yet to return from her coffee break. "Rosie, will you look after my wife until Ms. Marinelli returns?"

"Happy to, Dr. Whittaker."

"See you soon," Michael whispered, kissing Jane on the cheek, then retreating into his office with Mr. Beattie and his son (grandson?), Stuart.

"You want a cup of coffee or anything?"

"No, thank you."

Jane watched as Rosie Fitzgibbons resumed her position behind her desk.

"Why don't you sit down and make yourself comfortable?"

Jane sat. "You don't have to entertain me. You look pretty busy. . . ."

"Well, I'm always busy. You know what this place is like! We really miss you around here. When are you coming back?"

How much did this woman know? Jane wondered. "I'm not sure."

"Michael said you had some kind of peculiar virus. . . ."

"They're not sure what it is exactly."

"That's what he said."

"I must look awful."

"Well, I've seen you look better, I don't mind telling you that." The phone rang. Rosie picked it up. "Dr. Whittaker's office. No, I'm sorry. He's in with a patient right now. I can take your name and number and have him call you later. A little slower, please. Could you spell that? *T-h-r-e-t-h-e-w-y*? Threthewy? Got it. And the number? Yes, I have it. He'll get back to you as soon as he can. Thank you." She hung up, turning back to Jane when the phone rang again. "It never stops."

"I remember," Jane lied. No, she wasn't lying—she was *confabulating*.

"Dr. Whittaker's office. No, I'm sorry, he's with a patient right now. Oh, yes, hello, Mrs. Sommerville. What seems to be the problem?"

Jane turned her attention from the farsighted receptionist to the little girl who sat whimpering on her mother's lap.

"It'll be all right, Lisa," the child's mother was saying. "Dr. Whittaker just has to check and make sure everything's all right. He isn't going to hurt you."

"I don't want to go." The child's voice gathered strength with each word.

"We'll be in and out in five minutes. No needles, I

promise you. Here, why don't you play with the building blocks for a while?" She reached into the large toy box beside her and pulled out a stack of wooden blocks. They promptly fell to the floor and scattered in all directions. Lisa squealed and jumped from her mother's lap to retrieve them.

The woman became aware of Jane's steady gaze. "She doesn't like anything to do with doctors. The other day my husband said he wanted to take a few pictures, and she started screaming. We finally figured out that she thought he was going to take X-rays! I mean, that's what we always said when she had to go for X-rays, that she just had to have a few pictures taken, so she naturally started equating the two. Once we explained that they were two different things, we had no problem at all. She turned into a regular Cindy Crawford."

CINDY CRAWFORD.

Jane looked at her hands, recalling the beautiful, confident face that had smiled up at her from the cover of the magazine moments before she discovered the front of her dress covered with blood.

The memory caused Jane to leap from her chair. She bolted for the door without any thought as to where she might be going. It was only when she felt a sharp stab at her ankle that she stopped, looking down to see the wing of the toy airplane that had struck at her leg, like a snake in the grass. She reached down to pick it up, hearing voices rush to surround her.

"Jane, are you all right? Where were you going?"

"I'm sorry. Did I say something to upset you?"

"I'm sure Ms. Marinelli will be back any second."

"Mommy, I want to go home."

Jane looked from the toy airplane in her hands to little Lisa on the floor, to the child's mother, half-in, half-out of her chair, to Rosie Fitzgibbons, standing behind her desk, the phone still in her hands. "Maybe you should get rid of these things," Jane said, indicating the model plane, thinking of what had happened to Michael. "They're a menace."

"You have to be very careful where you walk around

here,'' Rosie agreed, returning the phone to its carriage, and sitting back down.

Jane's eyes traveled across the well-worn carpet. ''You certainly did a good job of cleaning up the blood.''

''Blood?''

''Mommy!'' Lisa quickly retreated to her mother's lap at the mention of the word.

''When that little boy threw the plane at Michael's head. There must have been a great deal of blood to have required so many stitches.''

Rosie Fitzgibbons looked totally perplexed. ''I'm not sure I'm following you. . . .''

The door to Michael's inner office opened and Stuart and his father (grandfather?) emerged. Almost simultaneously, Paula strode into the reception area, and Michael appeared at her side.

''I'll get home as soon as I can,'' he whispered, then winked. ''We'll do lunch.''

Jane smiled, her eyes lifting to his forehead, imagining the row of stitches hidden by his hair, convinced that in addition to her memory, she was now losing her mind.

15

OF COURSE IT WAS POSSIBLE THAT THE INCIDENT hadn't occurred in the outer office at all, Jane told herself, vaguely mindful of the scenery rushing past. Paula was driving very quickly, as if to minimize the time wherein anything might go wrong with her car. Jane was anxious to get out of the aged automobile. Its sputtering made her nervous, her heart lurching in time with the engine. She would have preferred to get out and walk the rest of the way, but she knew Paula would never agree, even though they couldn't be more than a few miles from her home. Maybe when they were safely back in her driveway, Paula would consent to a stroll around the neighborhood before lunch. She was feeling stronger. It was conceivable that her legs could carry her a few blocks.

The more Jane thought about it, the more she was convinced that the fresh air would do her good—clear away the remaining cobwebs, give her thoughts, as well as her legs, some needed room to stretch. Right now, a million disparate ideas were crowding against the edges of her brain, straining against one another, pushing this way and that without ever really connecting, like children fighting in a playground. She needed to open the gates, let her thoughts run free, give some of these crazy theories the room they required to express themselves and then be gone.

And just what were some of these theories? That her husband had lied when he told Paula he'd been hit in the head by a model airplane? That Paula had made the whole story up to protect Michael? That it was some sort of elaborate conspiracy? Or maybe Michael really had been struck in the head by a model airplane, exactly as he had said, except that the incident hadn't taken place in his office, at least not the outer office—had he ever said it happened in the outer office—but somewhere else.

Where else? The outer office was where he kept his toy box. Of course one of the children could have carried the model plane into his inner office, let it loose in there. Except that there'd been no bloodstains on that carpet either. She would have noticed. She'd noticed everything else: the furniture; the books; the photographs. True, she hadn't been thinking about his head wound at the time, but surely she would have noticed something as identifiable as a bloodstain. She was getting very good at recognizing blood.

Or maybe the incident hadn't taken place at all.

Rosie Fitzgibbons didn't seem to know anything about it. Her eyes had grown as wide as her glasses when Jane had brought the subject up. "I'm not following you," she had said. Obviously, she knew nothing about any such incident. Unless, of course, she'd been away from her desk at the time. Or away that day. There was always that possibility. God knew, there were endless possibilities.

And the worst of all possibilities—that she really *was* going crazy. That she had misinterpreted everything: the stitches, Paula's explanation, Rosie's response. It didn't make sense. Nothing about her life made sense anymore. Had it ever?

Why would Michael lie? What would be the point? Her mind raced in frantic circles searching for answers. There was only one possible explanation: If Michael had lied, he had lied to protect her. He knew what had happened, what she had done, and it was something so awful, so unforgivable, that she had to be protected from it. Had he been there? Tried to stop her? Was she the one responsible for the deep gash across his forehead that required almost forty stitches to close? Had it been Michael's blood covering the front of her blue dress?

She gasped, her body crumpling.

"What's the matter? Are you going to be sick?" The sound of Paula's voice caused the unpleasant images to scatter.

"What? Oh, no. No." Jane pushed herself back into a more appropriate position, looking out the side window as the car turned onto Forest Street. "I was just stretching, trying to get some exercise." She wasn't lying, she told herself. She was *confabulating*. "Maybe we could go for a walk."

"I think you've done enough for one day."

"Just a short one."

Paula pulled the car into the driveway. "We really don't have time. I have to make something special for lunch if Dr. Whittaker's coming home."

"You don't have to come with me. I'm sure I can manage."

"Just this morning you could barely make it out of bed."

"But I'm feeling much stronger now, and besides, I'll only go around the block."

"And not be here when your husband comes all the way home for lunch just to be with you?"

"I'd only be a few minutes," Jane began, then stopped, recognizing a lost cause as easily as she recognized blood. She opened the car door and climbed out.

She was heading for the front door when a strong male voice stopped her. "Jane!"

She turned, expecting to see Michael, determined to run to him, plead with him to tell her the truth. All this second-guessing was making her crazy. She would tell him everything, about the money and the blood, as she should have done in the first place, and beg him to do the same. I don't need protection, she would tell him. I need to know what really happened. But instead of Michael, she saw a nice-looking stranger with dark-brown hair and an easy smile waving to her from Carole's front lawn. Was he someone she was supposed to know?

Before Paula could stop her, Jane burst from her side and ran across the road, leaving Paula to stare helplessly after her. "Hi," Jane called as the smiling figure advanced to greet her.

"It's nice to see you," he said, getting closer, his smile freezing, his voice growing dark. "Are you all right? You don't look very well."

Jane was grateful for his use of understatement, whoever he was. "I've been sick. But I'm getting better."

"I hope nothing serious." His eyes told her he was afraid it was.

"Just one of those mystery viruses," Jane told him, remembering what Michael had told his receptionist. "I'm on the mend." Who was she talking to? Who was this man and why did he care *how* she felt?

"I guess you haven't been doing much running lately."

"Running? No, I certainly haven't felt much like running." Running *away*, maybe, she thought, but didn't say. "This is the first day in over a week that I've been up and around."

"Well, then I'm doubly lucky to have been here today. Actually, I haven't been doing much running either," he confessed, obviously trying to prolong the conversation. "Although I'm starting to get back into it again." He looked at his feet. "I guess it's always hard beginning again."

At last a statement with which she could identify!

So, this must be her former jogging partner, Carole's ex-husband, Daniel, she realized, looking at him with fresh perspective. Not just some charming stranger inquiring as to her health, but the man who had abandoned his wife and teenage children, not to mention his father-in-law and dog, for a permanent jog down the old Freedom Trail. A man with the courage to succeed where she had failed, the courage to create a whole new life.

"So, how is everything working out for you . . . Daniel?"

"Oh, no, you're not going to go formal on me, are you?" He sounded almost despondent.

"What?"

"Well, I know that Carole prefers *Daniel*, and you've probably been talking to Carole a lot these days, but does that mean you have to call me Daniel too? Couldn't you just call me Danny, like always?"

Jane swallowed her mistake, then smiled. "Danny," she repeated.

"That's better. I heard *Daniel* come out of your mouth, and I was afraid you'd started to hate me."

"I could never hate you." Was that true? Somehow, she knew it was.

"Well, I tell you, divorce sure lets you know who your friends are. I can't tell you how many of our so-called friends totally deserted me after the split. People I thought I could count on, people I thought could somehow manage to find room in their lives for both Carole and me, but I guess I was expecting too much."

"It's hard." Was it?

"I've felt very guilty about you, though," he said, and Jane found herself trying to crawl inside his opaque blue eyes. "At the very least, I should have called to say good-bye."

Jane said nothing, afraid she would reveal her ignorance should she voice any opinion at all. Obviously, Carole had said nothing to him about her condition. She wondered if she should tell him.

"I started to call you at least half a dozen times," he continued without prompting, taking her silence as a sign to continue. "But I guess I felt we'd already said our good-byes. All those mornings where I poured my heart out to you. All those times you listened to me moan about my life. You knew what I was going through." He was silent for a moment. "And I knew you had a pretty good idea how I felt about you." Another second's silence. "What more was there to say?" He put his hands in the pockets of his casual pants, then immediately pulled them out again, reaching toward her, connecting, running his hands up and down her bare arms. "Still, I don't think I ever told you how much you meant to me, how much you helped me. I know you didn't approve of the way I ultimately handled things but at least you never judged me. And I appreciated that. And I still do." He paused, as if carefully selecting what he was about to say next. "I've missed you," he began. "I think about you a lot. I used to wonder if you still went running without me." He looked at her closely, his face filling with concern. "I'm really sorry to hear that you haven't been well."

"Actually, it's a little bit more than that."

"What do you mean?"

Jane shrugged, wondering where to begin, when out of the corner of her eye she saw the front door to Carole's house open and Daniel's son, Andrew, emerge from the house, one arm around a large rolled sleeping bag, the other weighted down with a large canvas overnight bag. Jane shook her head, deciding now was not the best time for true confessions. "Are you going somewhere with Andrew?" she asked instead.

"I'm driving him to camp." They both watched as Carole followed her son out the front door, then surrounded him with her body, pinning his arms helplessly to his sides.

"She spends all day yelling at him, and then she can't bear to let him go," Daniel remarked, and Jane wasn't sure whether he was talking about Andrew or himself.

"What about Celine?"

"She left on Saturday."

"They don't go to the same camp?"

"No. Celine goes to Manitou. Don't you remember? You're the one who recommended it."

Jane felt her body break into a sweat. "Of course. I don't know what I was thinking about."

Daniel's dark-blue eyes narrowed in concern, his hand returning to stroke her bare arm. "Are you all right? You went white as a ghost. Maybe you should get back into bed."

"No, I'm fine." The last thing Jane wanted was to get back into bed. "I guess I'm still a little weak, that's all." She had to learn to say as little as possible during these encounters with strangers from her past. The quieter she was, the more they revealed, the more she learned, the fewer mistakes she could make.

"Where should I put this stuff, Dad?" Andrew was already at his father's car. "Hi, Mrs. Whittaker."

"Hello, Andrew," Jane said softly.

"I think there's some room in the trunk. If not, lay them on the backseat."

"That's your new philosophy on life, isn't it?" Carole asked, joining Jane and Daniel on the lawn, her voice as sharp as a straight razor. "Laying them on the back seat?"

Jane turned away, feeling embarrassed and even a little guilty, though she wasn't sure why. She watched Andrew open the trunk and deposit his bags inside, his arms and legs in constant motion, as if he were more animated cartoon than real boy. Were all teenage boys so *busy?*

"Do you think we could lay off the sarcasm for a few minutes?" Daniel's voice was quieter than Carole's, though no less angry.

Jane had no wish to find herself in the middle of a family squabble. Maybe now was the right time to retreat. Maybe she *could* use a little rest before Michael came home. "I probably should get going. . . ."

"You're not going to let a little spousal tension scare you away, are you?" Carole's voice was a challenge.

"Well, I'm still feeling a little weak . . ."

"I know. You've been through so much." There was a nasty undertone to Carole's voice that Jane had never heard before. It was as if her anger at Daniel extended to anything, and anyone, in the immediate vicinity. "It was so thoughtful of you to climb out of your sickbed to say hello. I bet you've been watching from the bedroom window all week, waiting for Daniel to turn up."

"Jane was just getting home as I was coming out the door," Daniel explained.

"How wonderfully convenient. But then, you've always managed to suit things to your convenience, haven't you?''

Jane wasn't sure whether the question was directed at her or at Daniel.

''Carole, is this really necessary?''

''Oh, I'm just getting started. Stick around.''

''Sounds delightful, but I have to drive our son to camp.''

''Isn't it nice always having somewhere to run off to?''

''Look, Carole, I don't know what set you off, but in another minute, I'll be out of your hair, and you won't have to see me again till the fall.''

''Just as long as I see my monthly check.''

Daniel's shoulders slumped forward in defeat. Jane could feel the conflicting urges—to respond, to let it lie, to strike back, to smooth things over—vibrating through his body. He was about to speak when Andrew interrupted from the side of the car.

''Come on, Dad, let's get out of here.''

''The voice of reason,'' Daniel remarked, turning to Jane. ''Take care of yourself.''

''Oh, go on and kiss her, for God's sake. Don't let me inhibit you,'' Carole spit out, pushing past them toward the car, where she locked her squirming son in one last embrace.

''Call me if you need . . . anything,'' Daniel said instead.

''Thank you,'' Jane began. ''I might do that.''

''I'm sure she will,'' Carole interrupted, stepping away from the car. ''Jane's very needy these days, aren't you, dear?''

''Come on, Dad!''

''Have a good time at camp, Andrew,'' Jane called toward the young boy who sat fidgeting in the front seat. ''Drive carefully,'' she said to Daniel.

Daniel nodded without speaking, and climbed behind the wheel of his car. Jane watched them back out of the driveway onto the street, Daniel waving one last time. Jane stared after the car until it disappeared, and even then, she was reluctant to turn around. She felt Carole's eyes, as intense as lasers, searing into her back, hostility covering her like a layer of acid, burning away her skin. Why?

"Is something wrong?" Jane asked, finding the courage to face the woman she had hoped was her friend.

Carole's response was a harsh, bitter laugh. "You must think I'm an idiot."

"I don't think any such thing. I don't know what you're talking about."

"Oh, yes, I forgot—you forget! How convenient!"

"Please, won't you tell me what's bothering you? You seem so angry at me."

"What possible reason could I have for being angry at you?"

"I don't know."

"You don't know."

"No, I don't. You weren't angry at me the last time we talked. At least I didn't think you were."

"Can't you remember?"

"I remember that I thought we were friends."

"Funny about that. That's what *I* thought."

"Then what happened? Did it upset you to see me talking to Daniel?"

"Why should that upset me?"

"I don't know. Maybe you felt a certain sense of betrayal."

"*Betrayal*. An interesting choice of words, don't you think?"

"I don't know what to think. I wish you'd stop talking to me in riddles."

"You don't like riddles? That's odd. I thought people who enjoyed playing games usually liked riddles. It just goes to show you, I guess, that you never really know anybody as well as you think you do."

"Please tell me what you think I've done."

"Oh, I don't just think. And believe me, I'd like nothing better than to tell you. Just that I made a promise, and unlike some people I could name, my vows mean something to me."

"You made a promise to whom? About what?"

"Carole! Carole, come in here," an old voice called out in terror. Carole's father appeared in the doorway of their home, gesticulating wildly. "There's a fire. There's a fire in the kitchen!"

"Oh, my God!" Carole raced toward the house, almost tripping on the dog, which had run outside and was barking furiously. "Move it, J.R.!" she screamed, disappearing inside the front door as the smoke detector began to sound.

Jane reacted instinctively, running into the house after Carole. If there was a fire, then maybe she could be of help. Paula obviously felt the same way because she was right behind Jane, both women following the path of billowing gray smoke into the kitchen.

Carole was already at the stove, trying to smother the flames shooting out of the frying pan with the small fire extinguisher that rested on the side of the counter, but not having much luck. Jane reached for the lid of the frying pan and dropped it onto the top of the pan. The flames shot up from the sides of the pan in one last gasp of protest, and then died.

"Jesus Christ, Dad, what are you trying to do? Burn us down?"

"I wanted some scrambled eggs."

"Just because your brains are scrambled doesn't mean you can make scrambled eggs! Haven't you done enough damage around here without having to blacken the ceiling? Look at this!" she yelled, pointing to various stains on the counter. "All these mementos of your vast culinary artistry! If you wanted scrambled eggs, why didn't you ask me?"

"Because you'd tell me I just ate, that's why!" the old man shot back clearly over the loud barking of the dog and the continuing scream of the alarm.

"I could make him some scrambled eggs," Jane volunteered.

"You're very kind," said the old man, pitifully grateful.

"You'll do no such thing." The phone rang, interrupting Carole's angry words. "Yes, hello," she snapped into it. "No, there's no fire. It's all been taken care of. Just my father trying to add a few more gray hairs to my collection. Thanks for calling." Carole replaced the receiver. "Good thing the monitoring service checks before sending out the fire department." She stared at Jane, ignoring her father, Paula, the barking dog, and the screaming alarm. "You can go home now. Show's over."

"Please tell me what I've done that has you so upset."

"Go home, Jane," Carole repeated. "I don't want to do anything I'll regret."

"Like what?"

"Like tell you what I really think of you." Carole's anger flared then suddenly dissolved. "I thought you were my friend, for God's sake."

"I thought so too."

Carole began pacing the smoke-filled room, the dog and her father both scurrying out of the way of her angry steps. "I feel like such an idiot. I guess that's the worst part. That I never even suspected. That I never had the slightest clue."

"Clue to what?"

"Oh, cut the innocent shit with me, okay? I know all about your affair with my husband! I know everything."

"My affair with your husband?! What are you talking about?" Jane could barely believe her ears. Surely she had heard wrong. "No!" It couldn't be possible.

"All that time I was crying on your shoulder, all those mornings I spent pouring my heart out to you, and you were laughing at me. Tell me, did you and Daniel have a good chuckle about it later?"

"None of this makes any sense," Jane pleaded, looking to Paula for support, seeing only disgust in her expression.

"On the contrary, it's all very clear to me."

"I think we should go now," Paula said. "Dr. Whittaker will be home shortly."

Could it be true? Had she been having an affair with her neighbor's husband? Daniel had hinted at his feelings for her out there on the lawn. Was it possible that she had returned those feelings? That they had acted upon them? Had his conscience tricked him into confessing the whole nasty affair to his wife? Had he just finished divulging the sordid details when she and Paula arrived home? Was that the reason for Carole's sudden change in attitude toward her?

Could it be that Daniel was the source of all her problems? That Michael had found out about the affair? That he had discovered them together? Had there been a fight? Had she lashed out at him? Struck him across the head with whatever object was handy? Had she tried to kill her husband because she was having an affair with another man? Was the affair real or the product of Carole's overripe imagination?

What was real and what wasn't, for God's sake?

Was she really standing in the middle of a smoke-filled kitchen with a siren screeching around her, a dog barking at her feet, an old man beside her pleading for some scrambled eggs, an outraged housekeeper to her right, silently damning her to hell, and a half-crazed neighbor in front of her, who had just accused her of sleeping with her husband, an affair she couldn't remember with a man with whom she had just spent the better part of ten minutes in pleasant conversation? On her neighbor's very own front lawn with his son waiting in the car! Was that her reality? Jane Whittaker—*this is your life*! No wonder she had run away. No wonder she wanted no part of it.

"How do you know?" Jane heard herself ask.

"I know." Carole sank into one of the kitchen chairs. "Michael knows too."

"Oh, my God."

"He made me promise not to say anything to you until you were better." She shook her head in mock amazement. "I don't know how you do it. One day you'll have to tell me your secret. You treat men like shit, and they fall all over themselves trying to make sure you're okay. It must be a special talent. Maybe one day you'll write a book."

"I'm so sorry," Jane mumbled. "Please believe me

when I tell you I don't remember any of it."

"Oh, I believe you. Daniel's lovemaking was far from memorable. If you'd asked me, I'd have spared you the time and trouble. Now, I'd really like you to get out of my house before I seriously try to kill you."

Jane bit down hard on her bottom lip to keep from screaming, letting Paula lead her out of the house. As the front door closed behind them, Jane heard Carole's father asking when it was time for lunch.

"No!" Jane was screaming as she raced up the stairs to her bedroom. "No, it can't be!"

"Try to settle down before Dr. Whittaker gets home," Paula pleaded, running after her.

"What kind of person am I? What kind of person cheats on a man like Michael with her neighbor's husband?" Jane waited for Paula to provide her with some sort of answer, and when none was forthcoming—did she really expect Paula to have any answers?—she ran into her bedroom and began pounding her fists against her mirror image. "Who are you, goddamnit? What kind of mess have you made with your life? Who else have you been fooling around with? How many other affairs have there been? How many other men does Michael know about? Jesus Christ, look at you! You're a goddamn mess. Why don't you answer me, damn you!"

"I'll get your medication."

"I don't want any medication. I just want to get out of here!" Jane glared at her reflection. "I don't want to know who you are anymore!" Jane slammed the palm of her hand against her startled image. "I don't want to remember anything about you. I just want to get as far away from you as I possibly can, like I tried to do before. Only this time, I'll do it properly." She threw open her closet doors as Paula hurried downstairs. "I have to get out of here. I have to get away from this. I have to get away."

She tore frantically, and without reason, at the clothes in the closet, tugging them off their hangers, scattering them about the room. One after another, blouses were pulled off their hangers, then ripped and discarded, then the skirts and dresses, next her slacks. She opened all the drawers and emptied each one, hurling scarves and nightgowns across the floor, deliberately treading on her underwear, kicking at delicate items with her feet. "God-damn you!" she was shouting, grabbing her white cotton nightgown, trying to tear it to bits. "None of this is mine! None of this is who I am!"

In the next instant, she was on her hands and knees, reaching into the far corners of the closet, scrambling among her shoes, reaching up to yank what few clothes remained off their hangers. "Goddamn you," she cried. "Goddamn you to hell, whoever you are! Do you hear me? I don't want anything more to do with you. You're crazy! Nothing but a goddamn lunatic!" She kicked at her shoes, watching them bounce into the air, as if kicking back. Then she was suddenly on her feet again, stretching toward the high shelf that ran along the top of the closet, a shelf filled with old hats and sweatshirts, travel cases, and boxes. Her hand swept across the shelf in one fluid motion, sending each item crashing to the floor. "This is how crazy people clean house," she cackled as a box hit her head and bounced to the floor. She watched it spill open, a navy purse tumbling out and landing at her feet.

Everything stopped. As frantic as she had been only seconds earlier, she was equally still now. With deliberate slowness, Jane lowered herself to her knees and scooped the abandoned purse into her hands. Holding her breath, though she wasn't sure why, she snapped open the handbag and withdrew some old tissues, a set of car keys, house keys, and a maroon-colored wallet. Jane pulled open the wallet and checked inside.

Everything was there: her driver's license; her social security number; her charge cards. Her identity. Hidden in a box at the top of her closet. Why? If she'd been planning to visit her brother in San Diego, wouldn't she have taken these things with her? Did it make sense that she would be flying to California without any identification? That she would have left the house without her purse?

Unless she'd never been planning to visit her brother at all. But then why would Michael claim she had? Why would he give that story to the doctors and the police? Why would he lie? Was he still trying to protect her?

Or himself.

"Now I know you're crazy," she whispered, unable to come to terms with these sudden suspicions. "You've totally flipped out."

She looked toward the door to see Michael and Paula, side by side, their faces a mixture of fear and concern. "What's going on here, Michael?" she asked, displaying the contents of her purse.

"Hold still," Michael told her as Paula gripped her arm and held it straight.

"No, please—" Jane cried, but it was too late. The needle had already pierced her skin and the medication was rushing through her veins.

16

JANE AWAKENED FROM A DREAM, WHEREIN SHE HELD a group of Nazi skinheads at bay with one of her daughter's stuffed animals, feeling sweaty and sick. Her arm ached, and for several minutes, her eyes refused to open. She finally forced her lids apart, then had to close them again when she saw the room spinning around her.

Don't panic, she cried silently, panicking nonetheless. It'll be all right. Wasn't she safe at home in her own bed? Wasn't she being looked after by the world's greatest husband?

Could she really have cheated on him?

"No," she groaned out loud. "I didn't. I couldn't." I may not know who I am, but I know I didn't have an affair. I may be capable of murder, but I am not capable of cheating on my husband. Christ, listen to me. What deranged mind thought up this perverted value system? I'll kill but I won't sleep around; I'll save rain forests but I'll destroy marriages.

Did any of this make sense?

Did it make sense that Carole would lie? What possible motive would she have?

Even with her eyes tightly closed, Jane could feel her head spinning. She was convinced Carole's rage had been genuine. Her anger had been too real to be fake. Still, how well did Jane know Carole? And wasn't it Carole who had remarked that we never really know anyone?

She can't be that good an actress, Jane thought, convinced that Carole truly believed her to be guilty of an affair with her husband. Yet on both Carole's initial visit to Jane's house and Jane's subsequent visit to her home, Carole had been friendly and open and eager to be of help. She had been neither resentful nor angry. Certainly not hostile. That meant she had to have arrived at the knowledge of Jane's duplicity only recently. Either Daniel had confessed their affair out of some misguided sense of fair play, or someone else had told her. Who?

Jane knew the answer without having to form the word or say the name. Carole had told her that Michael knew about the affair, that he had asked her not to confront Jane until after she had fully recovered. It stood to reason that Michael had also been the one to tell Carole of the affair in the first place.

Jane fought through the fog that had enveloped her head to recall when this might have transpired. Hadn't she seen Michael and Carole together one morning? Hadn't she watched from the window as they whispered together on Carole's front lawn, J.R. straining on his leash beside her? Oh God, Jane moaned, rolling over on her side, then returning to her back when her arm started to pulsate. Why would Michael tell Carole anything so potentially destructive?

Maybe he'd just gotten tired of bearing the entire burden alone. Maybe he'd needed someone to confide in. Or maybe his motivation was to drive a wedge between the two women. Maybe his intent was to keep them apart. But why? What could Carole tell her that Michael didn't want her to know?

And if Michael *had* been the one to tell Carole about Jane and Daniel's supposed affair, then that meant one of two things: that Michael was telling the truth, or that he was lying. *Ask me no secrets, I'll tell you no lies.* What secrets? Jane wondered. How many lies?

Jane's eyes opened wide with fear. There was another possibility, she realized, watching the Chagall lithographs on the far wall come alive and dance toward her, the upside-down fiddlers suddenly righting themselves, brides and grooms swaying back and forth to music only they could hear: the possibility that Michael and Paula and Carole were part of some larger plot, that they were all in this together. Oh, great, a conspiracy, Jane thought, rubbing her sore arm, feeling stupid and melodramatic. Where was Robert Ludlum when you needed him?

The truth was undoubtedly much simpler: She was as crazy as a loon.

The inside of her left arm began to throb and Jane forced her eyes to the source of the pain. The skin at the crook of her arm was bruised a bluish-purple. Her fingers drew gentle circles around the area of discoloration, but even such timid ministrations were painful. She lifted her arm closer to her line of vision, recalling the prick of the needle as Paula held her arm straight while Michael administered the sedative. How many times had the needle pricked her arm since then? How many days had passed? How long had they been keeping her sedated?

She forced herself to her feet, fighting the urge to throw up, clinging to the bedposts as she crept to the bedroom door. Paula's voice wafted up the staircase toward her from the kitchen. Was she talking to Michael? Jane strained to make out pieces of the conversation, but as Paula's was the only voice she heard, she concluded that Paula must be speaking on the telephone. Unless she was talking to herself, Jane thought and almost laughed. Maybe it was the house that was driving them all insane. Maybe it hadn't been properly insulated, and asbestos poisoning was making them all nuts.

Hanging on to the railing, feeling the sun pressing down on her back from the skylight above, Jane continued toward Michael's study, wondering only briefly what she was doing as she sank into the chair behind his desk and gingerly picked up the phone, bringing it slowly to her ear.

"... having these nightmares for a few weeks now," Paula was saying. "What? Are you trying to tell me I never had nightmares as a kid?"

The woman on the other end of the phone muttered something in Italian.

The silence that followed was so full of hostility that Jane found herself holding her breath. "Okay, so you were the perfect mother and I'm not," Paula conceded bitterly. "But I can't afford to sit home all day and look after her. Her nightmares are bound to stop sooner or later. She's a kid, for God's sake. Kids have nightmares."

More Italian.

"Mom, do what you want, okay? You want to put her in bed for a few hours, fine. Do it. So, she won't want to go to sleep at night. At least she won't be having nightmares. Right? Okay, listen, I've got to go. I have to start getting dinner ready."

Dinner? Jane glanced at the clock on Michael's desk, carefully returning the receiver to its carriage. It was after four o'clock. Of what day? How many days had she missed?

She stared at the phone, hearing Paula busy in the kitchen. How many of her friends had tried to call her in the past few weeks? How many had been told she was off in San Diego visiting her brother?

Her brother! she thought, jumping to her feet, banging her knees against the bottom of the desk, hearing an involuntary cry escape her lips, then standing very still. Had Paula heard? Jane clutched at the sides of the desk to keep from falling over, her heart pounding with such ferocity that she feared she might faint. Her brother, she repeated, supporting herself against the wall as she slid back toward her bedroom, suddenly remembering how she had trashed her closet, how she had stumbled on her purse, found her driver's license and her charge cards, all the items she would have surely taken with her on any long-distance trip.

She staggered into her room, half-expecting to see the mess she had made, to find her clothing strewn all about, but the room was clean and tidy. There wasn't a trace of her earlier tantrum. She approached the closet and silently pulled open the mirrored doors.

Her clothes hung neatly and all in their proper place. Nothing looked as if it had been disturbed. Shoes she remembered flinging hither and yon stood primly side by side; sweaters she had thrown across the room were stacked smoothly one on top of the other. The drawers she had emptied were well filled and carefully arranged. Old hats and sweatshirts lined the shelf above her head. The only thing missing was the box that had fallen during her tirade, the box that had opened to reveal her purse, which in turn had disgorged her charge cards and her driver's license. Had such a box ever existed? Was it possible that she had imagined the whole episode?

Or was it possible that Michael had been lying to her all along?

Michael had told the police that the reason he hadn't reported his wife's disappearance was that he thought she was visiting her brother in San Diego. He told Jane she had planned the visit as a surprise, and that was why her brother hadn't been alarmed when she hadn't shown up. He claimed to have called her brother after bringing her home from the hospital to assure him that everything was all right. But could her brother really have been reassured by a few well-chosen words? Hysterical fugue states couldn't be that common an occurrence, even in California. Did it make sense that her only brother would be so blasé about something as serious as a total loss of memory? That he wouldn't insist on flying in to see her? At the very least, you'd think he would be sufficiently concerned to insist on talking to her himself. And if he had called, if he'd been told repeatedly that she was sleeping or sickly or unable to answer the phone, wouldn't that have made him all the more concerned?

There was an easy way to find out, she realized, looking back toward the hall, hearing the sound of Paula's footsteps on the stairs. All she had to do was call him.

She crawled back into bed and closed her eyes, feigning sleep, just as Paula reached the door. Just check on me and leave, Jane urged silently, feeling the young woman approach her bed. You see, I'm asleep. Safe and snug as a bug in a rug. Isn't that how the rhyme goes?

Isn't that how you want me—all docile and unconscious? Just fix my covers and leave. I have things to do, people to call. Just straighten my blankets and go get dinner ready. That's a good girl. No, what are you doing? What are you doing?

Jane felt her sore arm being pulled out from beneath its covers, then laid out flat, its inside exposed. She smelled rubbing alcohol, felt something cold and wet against her already bruised veins, and opened her eyes in protest. ''No, please, don't,'' she cried, feeling the needle make contact.

''There, there,'' Paula said, as if talking to her little girl. ''It's for your own good.''

''Why are you doing this?'' Jane pleaded, determined not to give in to sleep.

''You need to rest, Jane,'' she heard Paula say, her voice retreating even though she was standing still.

''But I don't want to rest,'' Jane said, feeling her eyes close, not sure whether she had said anything at all.

She woke up to the sound of a dish breaking.

''Oh God, I'm sorry, Dr. Whittaker. I'll replace it.''

''Don't worry about it. It's only a plate. You didn't cut yourself, did you?''

''No, I'm fine. Here, let me clean it up.''

Jane forced herself out of bed toward the top of the stairs, carrying her nausea like a child on her shoulders. She strained to make out the conversation below, then struggled to retain it.

''I don't know what's the matter with me today. I'm dropping everything. I guess I'm just tired.''

''It's not easy looking after someone in my wife's condition.''

''Oh, Mrs. Whittaker isn't the problem.''

Jane imagined Michael's eyebrows arching in concern.

''Between my daughter's nightmares and my mother's nagging, I'm not getting much rest these days.''

''You want to talk about it?''

''I think you have more than enough on your mind

these days without concerning yourself with my problems."

"Why don't you leave the rest of the dishes for a few minutes and tell me about them," Michael offered, and Jane pictured him pulling out a kitchen chair for Paula to sit down.

Jane fought the urge to lay her head against the carpet and go back to sleep. She couldn't risk lying down, not even for a minute. She had to use the phone. She had to call her brother in San Diego. She had to do it now while Michael was caught up in Paula's problems. Before it was time to administer her next injection.

She pulled herself silently along the railing at the top of the stairs to Michael's study, pausing for a second at the doorway, trying to decide whether it was riskier to close the door or leave it open. If she closed it, there was less chance of her being overheard. But there was also less chance of her hearing them, should they decide to come upstairs. She decided to leave it open.

Sitting behind Michael's desk, she reached for the phone, hearing each action magnified a thousandfold. She pressed the phone to her ear, and was immediately greeted by the deafening blast of the dial tone. Surely they had heard it downstairs. She buried the receiver against her chest and waited for the sound of footsteps on the stairs, but there was nothing. Slowly, awkwardly, her fingers unsure of their destination, her aim unsteady, she punched out 411.

"What city please?" the woman all but screamed into the phone. Jane pressed the receiver tighter against her ear. She mustn't allow any sounds to sneak through.

Her own voice was barely a whisper. "I need the number of Tommy Lawrence in San Diego."

"I'm sorry. You'll have to speak up."

Jane bowed her head as if in prayer and spoke into her chest. "I need the number of Tommy Lawrence in San Diego."

"San Diego? Did you say San Diego?"

"Yes." Goddamnit, yes!

"You'll have to call the long-distance operator for that information."

"How?" The word was as much sigh as question.

"One—two-one-three—five-five-five—one-two-one-two," the operator told her and clicked off.

Jane fumbled for the button at the top of the phone, received another dial tone, then pressed the appropriate numbers.

"Operator. What city, please?"

"San Diego." Jane felt the words reverberate throughout the study as if in an echo chamber.

"Yes?"

"I need the number of Tommy Lawrence."

"Address?"

"I don't know."

"One minute please."

Hurry. Please hurry, Jane begged silently.

"I show a listing for a Thomas Lawrence at One fifty-five South County Road and a Tom Lawrence at Eighteen hundred Montgomery Street."

"I don't know." Oh, God, I don't know. Think, a little voice dictated. Try to remember the address that was listed in your little book. Try to see the name. Jane closed her eyes and held her breath, calling up the image of her telephone-address book, turning to the proper page, seeing her brother's name, his address just below. "I can't see . . ."

"I can't hear you."

"Eighteen hundred Montgomery Street!" she exclaimed louder than she had intended. "I think it's Eighteen hundred Montgomery Street."

But the operator was already gone, replaced by the familiar machine. Jane scribbled down the number as it was relayed to her, her eyes locked on the open doorway, hearing faint laughter from downstairs. Keep laughing, she urged. Laugh so I can hear you.

Jane pressed out the number, realized she had forgotten to include the area code, and had to begin again. She wanted desperately to lay her head down along the top of the desk. All she needed was a few more seconds of sleep and then she'd be ready. Her head angled toward the desktop, stopping only when confronted with her image in the blank computer screen.

The woman who stared back at her through half-closed lids looked only vaguely human, her face distorted and gray. Was this the same woman whose face she had first confronted in the washroom of the convenience store on Charles Street? The woman the ponytailed proprietor had described as "kind of pretty"? Good God, what are they doing to me? she asked, forcing her body into an upright position.

Somewhere a phone was ringing, a voice was saying hello.

"Hello," Jane said back, covering her mouth with her hand. "Hello. Who is this?"

"Since you're the one who called," a woman was saying, "suppose you tell me."

"It's Jane."

"Who? I can hardly hear you."

"Jane," Jane repeated louder.

"Jane? Tommy's sister?"

"Yes!" She was starting to cry.

"My God, I didn't recognize your voice. Do you have a cold or something?"

"I haven't been feeling very well," Jane began. This woman must be Tommy's wife, Eleanor.

"You sound awful. What is it, the flu?"

"No. One of those mystery viruses," Jane told her, a sinking feeling in the pit of her stomach. "How have you guys been?"

"Oh, the same as usual. Jeremy just got over a cold and Lance has a permanent runny nose, and your brother keeps complaining about his back, and I'm going crazy trying to figure out what to pack . . ."

"You're going away?"

"Our trip to Spain, remember? Finally. At last. God, how could you forget? We've been planning it for years. I assumed that's why you were calling, to wish us bon voyage."

"Eleanor, I need to talk to my brother!" Jane wondered if her voice was as loud as she imagined.

"Eleanor? You know I prefer Ellie. And your brother's at work. He won't be home for another hour."

Jane checked the clock on Michael's desk. It was almost seven o'clock. "He's working late?"

"It's only four o'clock. Jane, did you forget the time difference?"

Jane swallowed the urge to vomit, speaking clearly into the phone. "Eleanor . . . Ellie, you have to tell me the truth."

"The truth? Why would I lie about your brother being at work?"

"Have you been speaking to Michael lately?"

"Michael? Well, no, I haven't—"

"Has Tommy?"

"I don't think so. At least he hasn't said anything to me."

"He didn't say anything about Michael calling and asking if I was there."

"Why would Michael ask if you were here?"

"Because that's what he told the police."

"That's what who told the police? Jane, what are you talking about?"

Jane could hardly speak over the rapid pounding of her heart. She thought she heard voices, footsteps on the stairs, but when she looked, there was nothing. "You've got to listen to me, Eleanor . . . Ellie. Ellie, you have to listen to me."

"I'm listening."

Her head was spinning; her mind was racing. She heard the voices drawing closer, then nothing. Her eyes focused on the door. Still nothing. She had so much to say, so little time to say it. "Something has happened to me."

"What? What's happened?"

"I don't know. I can't explain it. I can't remember who I am."

"Jane, you're not making any sense."

"Please, listen. Don't interrupt. It's very hard for me to concentrate. They keep giving me drugs—"

"Drugs? Who's giving you drugs?"

"Michael and Paula."

"Paula? Who's Paula?"

"They were supposed to help me, help me remember. But they only make me feel worse, and now they're giving me injections—"

"Jane, is Michael there? Can I speak to him?"

"No!" Jane knew she had spoken too loud. "Listen to me. Michael has been lying to me. He told the police that I was visiting my brother in San Diego. He told me it was supposed to be a surprise. But then I found my purse with all my identification, and how could I go to San Diego without any identification? So, he was lying about why he didn't call the police after I disappeared—"

"Jane, slow down. You disappeared? I don't understand. Can you start from the beginning?"

"No, goddamnit. There isn't time. They'll be up in a minute to give me another shot. Please, Ellie, you have to help me. You have to tell my brother. He has to come and get me."

"Ellie," a male voice cut in on the extension as Jane watched Paula step into the room. "Ellie, it's Michael."

"Michael, what's going on?"

Jane listened absently to the conversation, knowing it was pointless to say anything else. Paula was walking toward her, syringe in hand.

"I'm sorry you had to get involved," Michael was saying. "I didn't want to worry you."

"What the hell is happening over there?"

"I wish I knew."

Was Michael crying?

"I get this crazy call; I don't even recognize her voice; she's telling me some nutty story about disappearing, losing her memory, being given drugs . . ."

"We *are* giving her drugs," Michael explained. "We're supposed to be keeping her calm. That's what her doctor advised."

"Her doctor?"

"Jane is having some sort of breakdown. I think it's all related to the accident. . . ."

"My God. What can we do?"

"There's nothing anybody can do except wait. The doctor is confident it won't last much longer. He calls it a hysterical fugue state. Apparently, they usually don't last longer than a couple of weeks."

"A hysterical what?"

"It's not important. What's important is for you not to worry."

"We're supposed to be leaving for Spain in a few days," Jane heard Eleanor sputter as Paula reached her side.

"Go," Michael urged. "You've been planning this trip forever. There's nothing you can do. I wouldn't even tell Tommy about this. There's really not a damn thing you can do to help, and the whole episode will probably be over and done with by the time you get back."

"I've been really looking forward to this trip" was the last thing Janc heard her sister-in-law say before Paula took the phone out of her hand.

I bet I never liked that woman, Jane thought, giving her arm to Paula without a struggle.

17

"CAN I GET YOU ANYTHING?" PAULA ASKED.

"What?" Jane was no longer sure when she was hearing things and when she wasn't.

"I said, can I get you anything? Some more orange juice? Some toast?"

"How about some coffee?"

"Sure."

"Real coffee, not that decaffeinated shit."

"Jane. . . ."

"Paula. . . ."

"If you're going to be difficult, I'll have to take you back to your room."

"Please let me stay here. I love this room." Jane opened her eyes briefly to make sure the sunroom was still there.

"If you want privileges, you have to behave."

"Privileges are what you give to children."

"When you act like a child, you get treated like one," Paula told her.

"I don't mean to. It's just that I feel so awful, and I get so confused."

"You have to follow your doctor's instructions."

"I'm trying."

"You have to try harder."

"I will. Thank you for letting me come downstairs."
"The sunroom was Dr. Whittaker's idea."
"I'm grateful," Jane said, and she was.
"Do you want some coffee?"
"No."
"Suit yourself."

"How's your daughter?" Jane asked, thinking that Paula looked tired.
"She's fine."
"What's her name again? Caroline?"
"Christine."
"Your mother's looking after her?"
"Temporarily."
"I bet you didn't think you'd be here this long."
"It shouldn't be much longer."
"Why? Why do you say that?" Jane pushed herself up on the sofa-swing.
"Don't get all worked up. It was just something to say."
"But you sounded like you knew something."
"All I know is what Dr. Whittaker tells me."
"What did he tell you?" Jane asked.
"That it shouldn't be much longer," Paula answered.

"Has Michael been talking to Emily?"
"I don't know." Paula was watering the plants.
"He must miss her."
"I'm sure he does."
"Does he ever talk about her?"
"No."
"What does he talk about?"
"He doesn't say much."
"But I hear you talking," Jane persisted. "There are some nights when I'm in bed and I can hear the two of you talking in the kitchen."
"I ask him about his day. He tells me if anything particularly interesting happened."
"I should be doing that."
"Yes, you should."

"Does he ever talk about me?"

"Sometimes."

"What does he say?"

"That he loves you. That he wishes he could help you. Sometimes he cries."

"It's time for your pills." Paula held out the pills for Jane to take.

"Do I have to?"

"You're not going to give me a hard time, are you, Jane?"

"It's just that they don't seem to be working."

"Dr. Whittaker thinks they are."

"But I just sit here all day, like a zombie."

"That's all you're supposed to do. You're giving your subconscious a chance to work things out." Paula's balance shifted from one foot to the other.

"But I can't think clearly. My head doesn't stop spinning. I can barely move."

"You're not supposed to move."

"How long has it been now?"

"How long has what been?"

"How long have I been back from the hospital?"

"A little over three weeks."

"And I just sit here all day." Jane could hear the amazement in her voice.

"You're getting your strength back."

"But it wasn't my strength that I lost."

"We're not going to have an argument, are we, Jane?"

"I don't want to argue. I just want to understand . . ."

"Understand that if you don't take your pills, Dr. Whittaker will put you back on injections."

"He said I didn't have to have any more needles."

"Not as long as you take your pills. Now, what's it going to be?"

"Maybe we could go for a walk today," Jane said.

"Maybe."

"You always say that."

"Do I?"

"Yes. And then we never go."

"Maybe today we will." Paula shrugged, then returned to her dusting.

"Are you afraid I'd try to run away?"

"No."

"I haven't the strength to run away. You don't have to worry."

"I'm not worried."

"You don't fool me, you know," Jane told her.

"I'm not trying to fool you."

"I know the real reason you let me stay in the sunroom."

"And what's that?"

"So you can keep an eye on me."

"You don't like me very much, do you?" Jane stated.

"That's not true."

"What is true?"

"Don't ask me." Paula approached the back window of the sunroom and stared outside.

"Do you think I cheated on Michael?"

"I don't know."

"Cheated on him with my neighbor's husband?"

"I don't know."

"My neighbor certainly thinks so."

"Yes, she does."

"Do you think she was lying?" Jane asked.

"No."

"Would you let me call Daniel?"

"What?!" Paula made no attempt to contain her amazement.

"That way I could ask him."

"You want to call your neighbor's ex-husband and ask him whether or not you slept together? Jane, do you have any idea how crazy that would sound?"

Jane closed her eyes in defeat, knowing that Paula was right. "I just want to know the truth," she whispered.

"Are you sure?" Paula asked.

* * *

"Who was that on the phone?" Jane wondered aloud as Paula came back into the room.

"Just someone trying to sell you a subscription for the Boston Pops."

"You're lying."

"Jane . . ."

"I can always tell when you're lying because you get this funny little expression on your face, like you've got a mouthful of pits you want to spit out."

"That's ridiculous," Paula protested.

"Also I heard you say I was still in San Diego."

"Didn't anyone ever tell you it's not nice to eavesdrop?"

"I don't know. I don't remember."

"This isn't funny, Jane."

"I want to know how long you think you can keep me from speaking to my friends."

"Hopefully until you can remember who your friends are."

"What would be so awful about my speaking to them now?" Jane demanded.

"Because it would probably upset you and it would definitely upset them."

"Why would it upset them?"

"For openers, you slur your words," Paula told her, straightening the throw cushion behind Jane's head.

"Do I? I wasn't sure. . . ."

"And they'd get very worried, and probably insist on seeing you . . ."

"So?"

"So, have you looked in the mirror lately?"

"You think I'm an awful person, don't you?" Jane stared at Paula, not sure whether she wanted an answer.

"I think you're a difficult person."

"You don't understand how a man like Michael can stay married to a woman like me."

"I think that when a man like Dr. Whittaker makes a commitment, he stands by it," Paula said.

"Through thick and through thin—"

"Through the good times and the bad—"
"For richer or poorer—"
"Till death do you part." Paula smiled.

"What are you baking?" Jane stood in the doorway between the kitchen and the sunroom, watching Paula at the counter.

Paula spun around. "What are you doing in the kitchen?"

"It's *my* kitchen."

Paula shrugged. "Then you might as well pull up a chair."

"Can I do anything to help?"

"You can sit quietly and let me concentrate. I don't want to slice my finger off because I'm busy talking to you."

"What are you slicing?"

"Apples."

"Are you making an apple pie?"

"I thought that Michael could stand a little something to cheer him up."

"So it's *Michael* now," Jane observed.

The phone rang.

Jane's head spun toward the sound, then continued spinning. She gripped the sides of the table, focusing on the small vase of summer flowers that sat at its center.

"Damnit, why does the phone always ring when your hands are full of guck?" Paula reached for a towel hanging on a hook beneath the sink.

Without stopping to consider her actions, Jane propelled herself into a standing position and lunged toward the phone.

"Don't answer that!"

"Why not? It's *my* phone!" She grabbed the receiver off the wall. "Hello?"

Paula dropped the dish towel and grabbed for the phone cord, yanking at it and almost succeeding in tearing it from Jane's hands. Jane immediately and repeatedly wrapped the long cord around her, using her body like a giant ball of yarn, leaving only her hands free to keep an increasingly frantic Paula at bay. "Get back," Jane hissed.

"Hello? Hello? Jane, are you there?"

"Hi," Jane shouted into the receiver.

"Jane, is that you?"

"Yes, it's me."

"Well, great. I wasn't sure what the story was. Susan said she called the other day and your new housekeeper, or whoever it was, said you were still in San Diego and she wasn't sure when you'd be back in the city."

"I got back last night." Jane almost laughed.

"Oh, well, if this is a bad time, you can call me later."

"No! This is a great time. I've missed you."

Who the hell was she talking to?

"I've missed you too. I couldn't believe you spent almost a month with Gargamella."

"Who?"

"Your sister-in-law."

"Gargamella?" Wasn't the woman's name Eleanor?

"Well, isn't that what you always call her? You said she reminds you of Gargamel, the evil villain who's always chasing those poor little Smurfs. Why am I telling you this? You're the one who explained it to me."

"She's evil?"

"Well, no, you just never had much use for her. Jane, is something wrong? This is a very strange conversation we're having, in case you hadn't noticed."

"Everything's fine. How've you been?" Jane watched as Paula began moving in slow circles toward her. "Stay away from me!"

"What?"

"Not you."

"What do you mean, Stay away from you?"

"There's a big spider in the kitchen." Jane decided this was as good a description of Paula as any. "You know how I hate spiders."

"Well, no, actually, I didn't know that."

Paula began swaying back and forth, forcing Jane's eyes to follow her, playing to her dizziness.

"Stay still, damn you!"

"Jane, just ignore the damn thing. It's more afraid of you than you are of it."

"Give me the phone, Jane." Paula voice was low, soothing, almost hypnotic.

"Stay away from me!"

"Jane, why don't you just call me back."

"No!"

Paula leaped toward her, grabbing at the phone. Jane vaulted out of her reach, wrapping the phone even tighter around her body, hugging the receiver against her ear with her shoulder, flailing out with her free arm, knocking Paula slightly off balance as she dived for the knife that rested on the counter beside the bowl of sliced apples, brandishing it at Paula, who froze, obviously terrified, then sank into one of the kitchen chairs, admitting her defeat.

"Jesus Christ, Jane. That must be some spider. What's going on there?"

Jane watched Paula watching her. She waved the knife, seeing Paula flinch, her chest heaving, her eyes wild. What was she planning? Jane wondered, silently debating whether or not to tell whoever this woman was on the other end of the receiver exactly what was going on.

And what would she say? Help, I'm being held prisoner in my very own kitchen by a woman who, only moments ago, was making me an apple pie? My husband and this woman are keeping me drugged and away from my friends, whom I can't remember anyway because I've lost my memory. Lost my mind is more what she'll believe, which is probably a damn sight closer to the truth.

Unless I can get her over here, unless she can see me for herself, unless I can find the necessary time to really talk to her, to explain to her in person everything that's happened.

"I'd love to see you," Jane ventured, seeing Paula's teeth clench, though she sat very still. "When are we going to get together?"

"Well, that's the main reason I called. To see if we're still on for tonight."

"Tonight?"

"You *did* forget. I knew it. I said to Peter, I bet she's forgotten all about it. I mean, we made these plans so long ago."

"Of course I haven't forgotten."

"Dinner's still on?"

"Of course."

"Are you sure? I mean, you just got back from California. You probably have a million things to do. . . ."

"Why do you think I came back?"

"Oh, yeah? Well, I'm very flattered. But you're sure you're up for entertaining? I mean, we could just as easily go to a restaurant."

"I wouldn't hear of it."

What was going on? What was happening? She had to think fast, which was hard to do when your head was spinning and your heart was pounding and you were holding a knife on someone. She needed a minute to put everything together. Who was she speaking to? And who was this man, this Peter, whom she had mentioned? Probably her husband. And they were coming for dinner. Tonight.

Peter, she thought, repeating the name in her mind, tightening her grip on the knife when she saw Paula move. But Paula only crossed one leg over the other, seemingly resigned to her fate. She's waiting, Jane thought, like a cat observing its prey. As soon as I present her with the opportunity, she'll pounce. In the meantime, I have to figure out who belongs to this voice on the telephone.

I could always ask her, Jane thought, and almost laughed. Oh, sure, be here at seven, and by the way, who are you? No, don't be silly. Think, she admonished herself. Don't get giddy. You have to work this out. She's obviously a friend, probably even a good friend. And she's given you a clue. Her husband's name. Peter.

Peter who? Peter Cottontail. Peter Rabbit. Peter Finch. Peter, Paul, and Mary. Peter Peter Pumpkin Eater. The

Peter Principle. Salt-peter. Saint Peter. Peter Piper picked a peck of pickled peppers. Peter. Peter-if-you're-a-friend-then-your-name-would-have-been-in-my-little-paisley-covered-book!

She tried to recall the pages of her telephone-address book, mentally flipping through the pages: Lorraine Appleby; Diane Brewster; David and Susan Carney; Janet and Ian Hart; Eve and Ross McDermott; Howard and Peggy Rose; Sarah and Peter Tanenbaum.

Sarah and Peter Tanenbaum. Yes! Who else could it be? How many close friends could she have whose husbands were named Peter? The woman to whom she was speaking had to be Sarah Tanenbaum. Jane bit her tongue to keep from saying the name out loud.

"So, what time would you like us?"

"Any time. The sooner the better."

"I guess you probably want to make it an early night."

"Not at all. I'm really very anxious to talk to you."

"Oh, yeah, me too. I had another run-in with the Gestapo."

"What?"

"You know—my neighbor. I'll tell you all about it when I see you. You would have been proud of me. So, what time? Seven o'clock?"

"That sounds great."

"Can I bring anything? Dessert?"

"Oh, no," Jane said quickly, a smile creeping onto her lips. "Actually, I was just baking an apple pie."

Paula rolled her eyes toward the ceiling. If looks could kill, Jane thought.

"Sounds wonderful. I can hardly wait."

"Me too. Oh, and if anyone should call you," Jane added, "and say that dinner's off, don't listen, okay? Come anyway. Promise?"

"Who would call me and say something like that?"

"I don't know. Someone. As a joke. Maybe even Michael."

"Michael?"

"As a joke."

"Jane, is something going on that I don't know about?"

"You'd be surprised."

"Nothing you do surprises me anymore."

"Promise me you'll come, no matter what."

"Jane, you're making me nervous. . . ."

"Promise."

"Okay. I promise. Now, are you going to tell me what's going on?"

"Tonight. Don't be late."

Jane heard the phone click. She lowered it to her chest and smiled, relaxing her grip on the knife and letting it drop to the counter. Paula was on her feet immediately, sweeping the knife out of Jane's reach and clutching it to her side.

"You're crazy, you know that! You could have hurt yourself."

Jane calmly and methodically separated herself from the telephone cord although she felt anything but calm. She felt elated. Alive. Even all the drugs in her system couldn't diminish her excitement. She extricated her body from the last of the cord and replaced the receiver on its hook, then sat down at the kitchen table, the smile never leaving her lips. "Guess who's coming to dinner," she said.

18

"WOULD YOU LIKE SOMETHING TO DRINK?"

"Do you think that's a good idea?"

"I don't mean anything alcoholic. I was thinking along the lines of a Coke or a ginger ale."

"Ginger ale would be fine." Why was he being so nice to her? Jane watched as Michael rose to get her a drink. "I'll pour it," she volunteered, hastily joining him at the coffee table where Paula had carefully arranged a number of glasses and a selection of beverages.

"Do you really think I'm going to put something in your drink?" His voice resonated hurt feelings.

"Of course not." That was exactly what Jane thought. Was she overreacting?

Michael had been concerned, even alarmed, when Paula had summoned him home to recount the afternoon's events, but he'd admitted to Jane privately when he was helping her dress for dinner that he could understand her level of frustration, that he hadn't understood how eager she was to speak to her friends. Certainly Paula should never have tried to wrest the phone away from her. If Jane really felt she was up to entertaining, then he was only too delighted to play the host. Could she at least tell him who they were expecting?

No, she told him. She couldn't—wouldn't—do that.

All right, he had said. He could understand even that. She refused her medication and he didn't insist. "I'll let you decide about that, too, from now on," he told her, asking only that Paula be the one to cook and serve dinner. Jane readily agreed, determining to eat only what everyone else ate, thereby ensuring that no drugs could be added to her food. She needed to be awake; it was vital that she stay alert, although what exactly she was planning to say to Sarah (assuming it was Sarah who was coming to dinner), she wasn't altogether sure.

Jane uncapped the fresh bottle, breaking the seal, and poured herself a tall ginger ale, watching the bubbles dance in the glass. She took a small sip, then retreated to her chair by the fireplace, studying Michael as he fixed himself a gin and tonic. He looked at her and smiled, and she smiled in return, though it took some effort. In truth, she wasn't feeling either particularly strong or particularly well. Only particularly determined, she thought, her teeth chattering behind trembling lips.

"Are you okay, sweetheart?"

"Fine."

"They won't be here for another ten minutes. You could go upstairs and lie down. . . ."

"I'm fine."

"You look lovely," he said, and managed to sound sincere.

Did she look lovely? She doubted it. Presentable was about all she could hope for these days. Still, she had tried, applying makeup for the first time since her return home, allowing Michael to steady her hand when it faltered, brushing on perhaps a trace too much blush in an effort to give her face some necessary color. Michael had even combed her hair, securing it into a girlish ponytail with one of Emily's pink bows. It matched the soft pink sweater he had suggested she wear. Why was he being so helpful? Why was he being so damned nice to her when she was being so damned difficult?

Why did you lie to the doctors and to the police? she wanted to demand, realizing that she was still desperately trying to believe that he hadn't lied, that he could somehow provide her with all the right answers, tie the loose ends together, make everything all right again. Was it possible? Please explain all the lies, Michael. Tell me there's a logical explanation for all my suspicions. Make the lies go away.

She couldn't ask him. She couldn't risk incurring his wrath. Not now, not when her friends were almost at the door. Not when with a single injection, he could render her as helpless as a baby.

"You're sure you're up for this?" he was asking.

She nodded silently, suddenly understanding that her decision not to question him on these matters had less to do with the fear that he couldn't come up with satisfactory answers than with the fear that he might.

Because if he could present her with satisfactory explanations, it meant that she really *was* in the middle of some kind of nervous breakdown, that her stubborn refusal to continue with her medication was only contributing to her deterioration, that she alone was responsible for her plight, that it might go on indefinitely, that she might feel this way for the rest of her life, that she had lost her real self out there somewhere, and this was what had wandered home, and was here to stay.

She took a long sip of her drink, trying to decide which alternative she preferred: Either she was a very sick girl and her husband was only trying to help her; or her husband had sinister reasons of his own for trying to turn her into a very sick girl.

Does the contestant choose Alternative Number One or Alternative Number Two? Stay tuned for today's episode of "The Young and the Psychotic."

The doorbell rang.

"I'll get it," Jane insisted loudly, her voice stopping Paula as she was headed for the door.

"It's all right," Michael assured the morose young woman, who instantly retreated to the kitchen.

Jane's hands were shaking visibly, ginger ale spilling from the glass to the floor. She carefully lowered the glass to the small table beside her chair and took several deep breaths, hoping her legs were steadier than her hands.

"You can do it," Michael encouraged her, rising from his seat on the sofa.

Jane forced one foot in front of the other, hearing the doorbell ring a second time before she was able to actually move.

"Easy does it," she heard Michael say as she reached the front door and pulled it open.

Two attractive strangers stood before her, the woman carrying a bunch of summer flowers, the man a bottle of white wine in a fish-shaped green bottle. "Welcome home!" the woman shouted, drawing Jane into a hearty embrace. "How dare you go away for so long and not tell anybody!" She stepped back to take a good look at Jane, giving Jane the opportunity to do the same.

The woman was tall and slender, with streaks of blond running through chin-length straight brown hair. She was wearing navy pants and a pale-blue silk shirt decorated with a rhinestone pin spelling out the word SMACK above a pair of silver lips. Her earrings were a series of colorful stars that reached almost to her shoulders, and her lips were bright red. Jane's first impression of Sarah Tanenbaum was that she was a very sophisticated and vivacious woman. She wondered what on earth they had in common.

The woman was staring at Jane as if she were wondering the same thing. "What have you done?" she asked, pulling out of their embrace.

Jane's hands immediately moved to her face, wanting to hide behind her trembling fingers. "What do you mean?"

"What have you done to your face?" The woman turned Jane's head around in her hand, paying particular attention to the skin around her hairline. "You didn't have some kind of botched face-lift while you were out in California, did you?"

"What the hell kind of a question is that?" the man standing beside her asked, closing the front door and handing the bottle of wine to Michael, who had come forward to greet him. "Good to see you, Michael. How've you been?"

"Not bad, Peter. And you?"

"Great. I'm always great once tax season is over."

"Sarah," Michael acknowledged warmly, kissing the woman on both cheeks, and directing them all into the living room.

"What's the matter with Jane?" Jane heard Sarah whisper, and saw Michael respond with a shake of his head. "What have you done to yourself?" Sarah persisted, absently handing the flowers to Paula, who had materialized with a plate of pâté and crackers. Paula took the flowers, deposited the tray, and left the room. "Who *was* that?" Sarah asked, totally confused. "What's going on here?"

"Sarah, for God's sake, you just walked in the door," Peter admonished his wife.

"That was Paula," Michael explained as Jane felt Sarah's eyes boring into her face. "She used to clean for us twice a week, but when Jane took her extended holiday, I asked her if she'd consider working full time, and she agreed. At least for the summer."

"Lucky you," Sarah said, continuing to stare at Jane. "I think."

"I haven't had a face-lift," Jane felt compelled to explain. "Really. Maybe it's my makeup. Or my hair."

"No, it's nothing so superficial."

"And my wife's an expert on superficial, aren't you, darling? Have some of this pâté, girls, it's delicious." Peter stuffed one cracker into his mouth and was spreading pâté on another.

"I think she looks wonderful," Michael said, rushing to his wife's defense, kissing her on one overly rouged cheek. "What can I get everyone to drink?" he asked.

"Bloody Mary," Peter was quick to respond.

"Is that a gin and tonic?" Sarah indicated the drink in Michael's hand.

"That it is."

"Looks good. What about you, Jane?"

Jane picked up her glass and raised it in the air in a

mock toast. "I think I'll stick with ginger ale."

"Now I know something's wrong," Sarah said. "Since when did you start drinking ginger ale?"

"My stomach's been a bit upset," Jane lied, sensing it was not the right time to get into the larger issues. "Probably the flight."

"Well, why didn't you just cancel? We could have made this for another night."

"No, I'm fine. Really."

"You don't look fine."

"Sarah!"

"Don't *Sarah* me, Peter. I have a right to be concerned."

"Concerned, maybe, but not rude."

"And speaking of rude," Michael interrupted, "I don't believe we thanked you for the bottle of wine or the lovely flowers."

"Our pleasure."

"Just what's wrong with the way I look?" Jane whispered to Sarah.

Sarah hesitated. "How can I say this without it sounding too awful?" She shook her head in defeat. "I can't." She swallowed, exhaling a deep breath of air. "I don't know. It's almost like you've been embalmed, like you're not real. I can't put my finger on it. Maybe it is your makeup. Maybe it's the sweater. Maybe you're just so . . . pink."

"I've always loved Jane in pink," Michael stated, putting his arm around his wife while simultaneously handing Sarah her gin and tonic.

"No, blue's her color." Sarah lifted her glass in a toast. "Well, cheers, everybody. Health and wealth." They all drank, Jane emptying her glass.

"Would you like another?" Michael asked solicitously.

"I'll get it," Jane said.

"Allow me," Peter offered, quickly refilling Jane's glass.

"Why don't we all sit down?"

"Good idea. How about some of that pâté you've been stuffing your face with, Peter?"

"God, women!" Peter groused, fixing his wife a cracker heaped with pâté. "I suppose now you'll want one too," he asked Jane, who was trying to decide whether he was serious. Peter Tanenbaum struck her as a big, handsome kid. Like his wife, he was tall and slim, his brown hair peppered with gray. But there was something mischievous, definitely childlike, about his gold-flecked brown eyes. You couldn't be sure whether he meant what he said or whether he ever really said what he meant. Could you ever be sure of anyone? "Don't look so serious," he was saying. "You don't have to eat it if you don't want it."

Jane took the cracker from Peter's outstretched hand and swallowed it in one bite.

"Oh, sure. Now you're going to tell me you want another one."

"So, tell us about San Diego," Sarah urged. "What did you do there for so long?"

"What are you talking about? San Diego's a great place," Peter said.

"For a week, it's a great place," his wife told him. "For almost a month . . . I mean, how many times can you visit the zoo?"

"Jane's always loved the San Diego Zoo," Michael said.

"And she can barely tolerate her sister-in-law. You always said she had shit for brains," Sarah reminded her.

"Obviously, she's changed," Michael volunteered.

"She must have changed a great deal."

"People do."

"Yeah? Since when?"

"My wife, the cynic."

"My husband, the know-it-all."

"Ah, young love, ain't it grand."

"So, okay," Sarah continued, not about to be put off so easily, "you went to the zoo and you went to the marine museum, and you took a few boat rides, and then what?"

"What is this?" Peter asked. "An inquisition? What does anybody do when they go on holiday? They visit their friends and relatives; they sightsee; they try to relax."

"Did you go to L.A.?"

"For a few days," Jane lied, starting to feel a bit dizzy and wondering if all this *confabulating* was the reason. "It was great."

"Now I'm really confused. I thought you hated L.A."

"Well, sometimes I do."

"But not this time?"

"This time it was great," Peter answered for Jane, finishing off his Bloody Mary. "So, Michael, how's the world of medicine?"

"Busy."

"Too busy to get away with your wife?" Sarah asked.

"I flew out a few weekends."

"That was nice."

"And the world of accounting?" Michael asked as Jane watched his face divide into two halves and then reunite. What was happening to her?

"Well, summer's always a good time. The pressure's off. You can relax a little, cultivate a few new clients. Oh, did I tell you who I brought into the firm?"

"Jane, are you all right?" Sarah was leaning forward in her chair.

"I felt a little dizzy for a minute."

"Jane, what is it? Are you okay?"

Jane stared into Michael's worried face. "I'll be fine." Could Paula have slipped something into the pâté? As if responding to her unvoiced accusation, Michael fixed himself a cracker heaped with the stuff, popping it into his mouth while Peter leaned forward to make himself another. So, it couldn't be the pâté that was making her feel this woozy. What, then? The ginger ale? Was it possible for Michael to have slipped something into her drink after all?

Oh, please don't come unglued now, she wailed silently. You felt okay this afternoon. Well, not okay maybe, but not this awful sick feeling, this feeling where you have no control, where the room dances circles around you, and people's voices drift in and out. Please stay with it at least until after dinner, until you've had the chance to explain everything to Sarah.

How would Sarah react? She was already spooked enough by Jane's appearance, by Jane's prolonged stay in San Diego with a woman she obviously despised. I knew I didn't like that woman, Jane thought, recalling her sister-in-law's voice on the telephone when she'd tried to convince her she needed help. It's nice to know some of my instincts are still intact.

So, what do your instincts tell you about Sarah Tanenbaum? How will she accept the story of your amnesia? Your version of your confinement? Will she have the same trouble digesting the information as your sister-in-law? Will she react the same way, opting to believe Michael? And how can you expect her to believe that Michael has been lying to you when *you're* not even convinced he's lying? Although he lies so easily, she thought. ("I flew out a few weekends," she heard him tell Sarah. Why had he said that?) Will she think you've gone crazy, react as Eleanor had, convinced you were in the middle of an emotional collapse?

And how much are you planning to reveal? Are you going to tell Sarah about the ten thousand dollars? About the blood on your blue dress? Blue's definitely your color, Sarah had said.

"So, I told him, Frank, do yourself a favor and get rid of the jerk. I mean, I know he's a local celebrity, and it's always nice being able to say 'I do so-and-so's taxes,' but the man's giving you ulcers, and it's not worth it. I mean, the guy actually called Frank up in the middle of the night to discuss a dream he'd had about tax shelters. A dream! Can you believe it. And Frank listens. So of course the guy's going to keep calling. It's cheaper than going to a shrink, which, frankly, I think Frank could use."

"So, who's this bigshot celebrity?"

"You can't breathe a word of what I told you. . . ."

"He's already told half the city," Sarah deadpanned.

"It's Charlie McMillan."

"Who's Charlie McMillan?"

"The weatherman on channel six! For Christ's sake, Michael. You're no fun. You never know anybody. You know who I mean, don't you, Jane? Jane?"

Jane fought to bring Peter's face into focus. Why doesn't he sit still? she thought, trying to recall what he had asked. But how could she be expected to hear him when he kept lowering his voice, so that he sounded like a bad telephone connection? "I'm sorry. I didn't hear you."

"Jane, what's wrong?"

"Maybe you'd like to go upstairs and lie down for a few minutes."

"We could do this another time."

"No! I'm fine. Really, I'm fine. I mean, what is this? Why are you all jumping on me because I didn't hear something?"

"You looked like you were going to fall over," Sarah told her, hovering close by.

Jane shook her head. "I'm fine. Probably just hungry." She looked at Michael, who pointed to the side of his mouth with his finger, a signal to her that there was something at the side of her own mouth. Jane raised her hands to her lips and wiped away a trail of drool, wanting to take a sip of ginger ale, but deciding against it. Where was Paula with the dinner anyway? She hadn't eaten anything since lunch. She was probably just weak from hunger. She'd be fine once she got a little food in her system.

"How much weight have you lost?" Sarah was asking, as if reading her thoughts.

"Have I lost any weight?" Jane asked in return, strangely grateful to see Paula tiptoe into the room.

"Dinner's ready whenever you are," Paula announced.

Jane jumped to her feet, then had to grab hold of Sarah's arm to keep from falling.

"This is silly, Jane. We should leave. You should be in bed."

"I'm fine," Jane insisted, allowing Peter to guide her toward the dining room. "It's probably just jet lag."

"Michael, what's the real story?" she heard Sarah ask softly, trying to keep Michael back.

"Come on, everybody, let's sit down," Jane called, not allowing Michael a chance to respond, taking her seat at the head of the table. Michael and Sarah followed.

"This looks wonderful," Sarah said, surveying the dinner that Paula was laying out on the table, forcing some cheeriness into her voice.

"Help yourselves," Jane directed, carefully watching as her husband and their guests piled their plates with food. She did the same, then waited until everyone else had sampled Paula's cooking before lifting a forkful of chicken to her mouth.

"This is delicious," Sarah said. "This woman is a gem. Don't ever let her go."

Jane forced the food into her mouth, knowing all eyes were on her. She chewed with deliberate slowness, concentrating on every motion, pushing one mouthful of food down her throat with another. If the chicken tasted any different from the green beans or the wild rice, Jane was unaware of it. It all blended together on her tongue. She only prayed it would stay in her stomach until after they had left the table.

"What happened to your wedding ring?" Sarah asked, trying to sound casual.

Jane stared at the unadorned ring finger of her left hand, unable to recall Michael's explanation.

"I'm buying Jane a new one. I thought she'd look nice in diamonds. What do you think?"

"I think you're a good man," Sarah told him, and patted his hand.

"So, you haven't asked my wife about Hitler," Peter said suddenly, obviously unhappy with the subject of diamonds.

"What?" Jane tried to lay her fork across her plate, but she missed, and the fork fell to the floor. She ignored it, concentrating on Peter. Had he really mentioned Hitler?

"Our neighbor! Mr. Intimidation," Sarah said impatiently. "The one who breaks into a goose step whenever he sees me. The Gestapo—I told you on the phone. You would have been very proud of me. I really let him have it."

"She asked him to pretty please not put his garbage in front of our house anymore."

"I did not! I told him that if he ever left his garbage can in front of our house again, he'd find it all over his front lawn the next morning!"

"Good for you," Michael said.

"Of course, it's not quite in Jane's league. . . ."

"What do you mean?" Jane asked, gripping the sides of the dining room table, seeing two Sarahs instead of one.

"You would have called him a Nazi asshole and emptied the trashcan over his head," Peter told her, as Sarah and Michael laughed in agreement.

Jane heard their laughter as if she were underwater and they were on a distant shore. She tried to swim toward them, to find the top of the water, to break through to its surface, to breathe some air into her lungs. But her efforts only carried her farther down into the abyss. She was drowning, and no one knew. No one could save her.

What could be making her feel this way? She had eaten only what everyone else had eaten. She had opened the bottle of ginger ale herself, had poured her own glass. She had never let the glass out of her hand except when Peter refilled it for her, and even then, she had watched him closely.

No, that was incorrect, she realized with a start. She had put the glass down when she went to answer the door! Michael would have had just enough time to put something in her drink when she was saying hello to Sarah and Peter. Had he? Dear God, had he?

"Sarah, you have to help me . . ." Jane heard the words as if they were coming from someone else's mouth, watched herself collapse on the floor, Michael and Paula and Sarah and Peter rushing to her side, Michael lifting her up and carrying her up the stairs to her room, Sarah and Peter right behind.

"Goddamnit, Michael, are you going to tell me what's going on?" Sarah demanded.

Jane tried to open her eyes, but it was almost as if they had been glued shut. She fought to remain conscious, heard the sound of crying, recognized the pain as Michael's. "I wish to God I knew," he was sobbing softly. "You have no idea what's been going on around here. . . ."

"Tell us."

"Jane is having some kind of breakdown." His voice was hoarse, incredulous.

"That's impossible."

Even with her eyes closed, Jane knew everyone was looking at her.

"She doesn't remember who she is; she says she can't remember anything about our life together. . . ."

"But that's absurd. She remembered us!" Peter sputtered.

"Well, no, not really," Sarah corrected him. "I mean, she didn't remember anything about Hitler. You could see that. At least I could."

What else can you see? Jane asked, pleading through closed lids for Sarah to come to her rescue.

"She was very strange on the phone this afternoon. And I said she didn't look right the minute we walked in the door. Is she on some sort of medication?"

"Her doctor prescribed a mild tranquilizer, but she's refusing to take it. She says she doesn't like the way it makes her feel. I don't know what to do anymore," Michael continued. "You don't know what it's been like. Her behavior has been so erratic. One minute she's up, the next minute, she's down. She's as docile as a kitten in the morning, and by afternoon, she's a raving lunatic, pulling everything out of her closet and stomping on it. I never know what she's going to do or say next."

"How long has this been going on?"

"At least a month."

"She was like this in California?"

"She never went to California."

Jane heard Sarah gasp.

"Actually, it's been going on a lot longer than a month. She's never really been the same since the accident. I guess it was too much to hope for. . . ."

"But she seemed to be doing very well. There were never any signs—"

"In public, no. When we'd go out, she'd make an effort. I don't know. Maybe the effort got to be too much. Suddenly, she just walked away from everything. The doctors are calling it a hysterical fugue state."

"I don't believe this."

"She'll get better again, won't she?"

"They thought she'd be better by now, but she's only getting worse. This afternoon, she pulled a knife on Paula."

"A knife!"

"Good God!"

"I don't know what to do. What happens if the next time she does something like that, she actually hurts someone? What happens if she hurts herself?"

"She wouldn't do that."

"Can I take that chance?"

"What are you saying?"

"I don't know. I don't know what I'm saying anymore. I don't know if I'm coming or going anymore. She gets so depressed, and she won't let me help her. And I'm scared because every time I go out the door I worry that she might not be here when I get back, that she might try to . . . I don't even want to say it."

"Jane is not the kind of person to kill herself," Sarah said forcefully, giving voice to Michael's concerns.

"Was that Jane at dinner tonight?" he asked simply.

The question silenced her, brought stillness to the room.

"If she doesn't get better soon," Michael began, his breathing heavy, his voice low, "then I might have to think about having her committed."

"Michael, no!"

"What other choice do I have? Tell me, Sarah. You tell me what to do and I'll do it. I'm at my wits' end. I've tried everything I know how. I don't know what else to do. I just don't know what other choice I have."

Oh, God, Jane thought, as darkness crept through her, somebody please help me.

19

SHE DREAMED THAT EMILY HAD PHONED AND ASKED to meet her at Boston Harbor. But when she got there, Emily had already left, and so Jane ran feverishly along the Charles River, past the rows of sightseeing boats and the New England Aquarium, the wharfs and the Coast Guard piers, across the Charlestown Bridge, past the tour groups gathered around the U.S.S. *Constitution*, toward the Boston Navy Yard. She raced toward the dock just as Emily's ship was pulling out. "Emily! Emily!"

"I'm afraid you're not with this tour," a young woman said, her voice full of reproach. "You'll have to pick up another tour at the Boston Common. Emily will meet you there."

"Emily!" Jane called, tripping over the grave of Mother Goose in the old Granary Burying Ground. "Emily, where are you?"

"You just missed her," someone said. "She left with Gargamella."

"Oh, no."

"She said she'd wait at Faneuil Hall until four o'clock."

Jane jumped into a waiting automobile and sped off, honking and giving the finger to anyone who slowed her down.

"Temper, temper," Michael cautioned from the backseat. "You don't want to have an accident, do you?"

And suddenly she saw the dark-green Volvo careening out of control toward her. She tried turning the wheel, but it stubbornly locked into place as her foot pumped on the brakes in a vain effort to stop the inevitable.

"No!" Jane screamed, sitting up with such force that she almost tumbled out of bed, her eyes darting frantically about the room, registering quickly that she was in her own bed, in her own house.

She looked toward the night table by her bed, seeing the space where the telephone used to sit before Michael removed it, understanding that Emily hadn't tried to reach her. Or had she? Maybe she had been calling out to her, one frightened soul to another.

She heard distant whispers echoing inside her head—I don't know what to do anymore. You don't know what it's been like. Her behavior has been so erratic.

Michael?

She's never really been the same since the accident.

Why are you saying these things? Is there something about the accident that you haven't told me?

If she doesn't get better soon, I might have to think about having her committed.

Committed? Oh, my God. Surely she had dreamed this as well.

What other choice do I have?

Committed. Michael had said he might actually have to have her committed. He had tricked her, drugged her, then tearfully confided in one of her closest friends that he might have no choice but to have her committed. No dream. This nightmare was real.

She had to get out of here.

Jane fought her way free of her covers, discovering that she was still wearing her clothes from the night before, which was good, because she doubted she had the strength to change. Only her feet were bare, something she could remedy with a few quick steps to the closet.

Her toes touched the carpet and she felt the familiar

dizziness return. Just hold on, she cautioned. Concentrate on what you have to do. Concentrate on getting out of here while you still have the chance.

And what are you planning to do once you're out of here? her reflection asked, a bemused expression on its masklike face.

I'll worry about that later. First things first. And the first thing I have to do is get out of this house.

Jane pulled open the closet door and slid into her black patent shoes, feeling something, like loose pebbles, at her toes.

"What are you doing?"

Jane froze at the sound of Paula's voice.

"I have to go to the bathroom," Jane lied, fighting to remain calm, to stay vertical.

"Well, you're not going to find it in there." Jane felt Paula's hands on her shoulders, guiding her in the right direction, gently pushing her along. "That's right. Straight ahead." She gave Jane a final little push, the way one might do with a child just learning how to walk, then let go.

"I think I need some help," Jane told her, wavering, bringing the other woman instantly to her side. "My God, what's that?" Jane cried, pointing toward the Jacuzzi.

"What?" Paula leaned toward the tub as Jane threw her weight against her. Paula stumbled forward, her hands shooting from her sides to block her fall, ending up half in and half out of the large tub, crying out, more from shock than from pain, as Jane bolted from the room, slamming the door behind her, dragging the night table, lamp and all, from beside her bed over to block the doorway, recognizing that Paula would have little trouble climbing over it to come after her, but hoping it would slow her down long enough to let Jane make her escape.

Jane all but flew down the stairs, losing her balance, falling the last few steps, hearing Paula break free of her temporary prison, running out the front door as Paula reached the top of the stairs.

"Jane, Jesus Christ, what are you doing? Where do you think you're going?"

Jane slammed the door, seeing Carole's car parked across the street, praying it would be unlocked. She pulled at the door to the back seat, almost bursting into tears of gratitude when it opened, and jumped inside, closing the door quietly after her, crouching on the floor of the car, squished against the back of the front seat, her heart pounding wildly, her stomach cramping so badly that she thought she might be sick. She heard Paula calling her name, pictured her searching up and down the street, walking around the side of the house, ultimately throwing her hands into the air in frustration. What now? Would Paula go back into the house? Put in yet another call to Michael? How much time do I have? Jane wondered. And what am I going to do?

She knew without having to look up that someone was peering through the car window at her. Game over, she thought, refusing for several seconds to look up, to give Paula the satisfaction of her capture. Capture, she thought, hearing the door jiggle, like I'm some kind of criminal. She immediately pictured her blood-covered dress and the almost ten thousand dollars in cash she had found in her coat pockets. Maybe that's exactly what I am. Maybe I'm getting exactly what I deserve. Isn't it time you gave up the fight? a part of her urged, the part that was tired and wanted only to get back into bed. Taking a deep breath, steadying herself against the frayed leather of the back seat, Jane forced her gaze to the car window.

Carole's father was smiling down at her, observing her as if she were an exotic bird in a glass cage. Jane became aware of footsteps, heard Carole's voice through the car door. "Dad, what are you doing out here?"

Jane brought her fingers to her lips in a gesture that begged the old man to keep silent. His response was a wide, dentureless grin.

"Dad, I'm not ready to take you for a ride yet. Come back inside. You haven't finished your breakfast. You know how you hate cold toast."

Carole's father stood up very straight, his face growing quite serious at the thought of cold toast. Then he turned and started back toward the house.

"Carole!" Jane heard Paula's voice cry out, drawing closer with each word. "Have you seen Jane?"

"Jane? No. Why—is she missing again?"

"She pushed me into the bathtub and ran out of the house. I almost broke my wrist blocking my fall."

"Good Christ, sounds like she's really flipped out this time."

"Well, if you see her or she comes knocking, will you call me right away?"

"You bet."

"Thanks."

"Dad, get back in the house."

Jane heard a door shut. A moment later, in the distance, she heard another one. Were they both gone? Slowly, she pulled herself up, allowing her eyes to peak over the bottom of the window. No one was there. The lawn in front of Carole's house was empty. Likewise, her own front yard. Of course, someone might be watching from a window. She'd have to be very careful. With great care, she pushed open the car door and crawled outside, mindful to keep her head down, out of sight.

And now what? Where did she think she was going? She had no money, having neglected to grab a purse on her way out. Par for the course, she thought. Once again, I'm to be wandering the streets with no purse or identification. Except that this time, *I know* who I am, even if I don't remember. I'm Jane Whittaker. See Jane run, she thought, scrambling down the street in a crouching position, her fingers grazing the pavement, as if she were more primate than human being.

She turned north on Walnut Street, refusing to stop running even to catch her breath. Instinctively, she recognized that if she stopped, even for a few seconds, she might collapse, curl up right there on somebody's front lawn and fall asleep. She couldn't afford to lose her momentum. A woman could only afford to lose so much.

She heard several cars drive past and gave passing

thought to flagging one down. Would anyone stop? She doubted it, she decided, catching a worried look on the face of a woman who drove past. I must look like quite a sight, running apelike down the street, dressed in pretty pink party clothes, dripping with nervous perspiration, desperately trying to keep my eyes open. What I need is a taxi, she thought, feeling her toes curl around whatever the hell was jiggling in the bottom of her shoes. Except that, unlike my last great escape, I neglected to bring along any money. She reached into her pants pockets. Nothing. Not a hundred-dollar bill in sight.

She came to an abrupt halt. If she was going to have to walk, she was going to be comfortable. Relatively speaking, of course, she thought, pulling off her right shoe, watching as two small white pills fell to the ground. Her medication, she realized, the pills Michael and Paula had been feeding her, the pills she had hidden. She bent over and scooped them up, steadying herself against the sidewalk until she felt strong enough to stand up again. Then she transferred the pills to her pocket and continued her walk, realizing that Paula might have decided to come looking for her in her car. She immediately took shelter behind a row of trees.

Several blocks away, she saw what looked to be a main street. If she could get there . . . what? What was she planning to do? Go to the police? And tell them what? That she was running away because her husband was planning to have her committed?

Your husband? That notorious do-gooder, Saint Michael?

He's not as saintly as he seems.

If something looks like a saint and acts like a saint—

But he's been lying to me, to everyone.

Saints don't lie.

He's been giving me drugs.

Saints don't do drugs.

I've tried not to take them. . . .

Just say no!

"No!" Jane shouted, reaching the ubiquitous Beacon Street, catching the eye of a nearby pedestrian who promptly crossed the street to avoid her. No, I can't go to the police. Look at me. I'm a mess. They'd never believe me.

There was nothing to believe.

What evidence did she have that anyone was plotting against her? She didn't even remember who she was! That would go over very big with the brass. The word of an hysterical amnesiac over that of a renowned saint? Get real. Get lost.

I tried that. It didn't work.

She was staring at the sign for several minutes before it registered on her mind exactly what it meant. BEACON PHARMACY, the large letters proclaimed in blue and gold. Jane's feet propelled her toward the door. She had to step out of the way to allow a customer to exit before she went in. Once inside, she felt the cold rush of the air-conditioning immediately on her skin, freezing the droplets of perspiration that trailed down her neck and arms. She felt clammy and light-headed, and prayed she could make it to the prescription counter at the rear of the store without passing out.

"Can I help you?" the man behind the raised counter asked, peering down at her over the top of a pair of reading glasses. "My God, are you all right?"

"Is there a chair? . . ."

In the next instant, she was on the floor, her legs stretched fully out in front of her, her arms hanging limply at her sides, her back supported by a display of cold remedies. The pharmacist was on his knees beside her, tapping her hand, calling to his assistant for a glass of water.

"Take this," he urged, pressing the glass to her lips.

She allowed the water to trickle into her mouth, fighting to keep her eyes open. The kindly pharmacist, a man of maybe sixty, with a bushy mustache and sideburns that were last fashionable in the early seventies, began patting at her forehead with a handkerchief. "I guess the heat got me," she said, not sure whether she had spoken loudly enough to be heard.

"Well, if you don't mind my saying so, you're dressed

a little warmly for a day like today. The weatherman said it might hit a hundred! Do you think you can stand up?''

Jane shook her head. ''I'd rather not.''

''I've got a chair just behind the counter. We can't have you sitting on the floor. Come on, you can keep me company for a few minutes till you get your strength back.'' He used both arms to help pull her to her feet.

Jane felt someone come up behind her, pushing her from behind. Jane turned to see Paula smiling politely, her hand wedged securely into her back. ''No!''

''I'm sorry. Did I hurt you?'' the startled young girl asked. Not Paula at all, Jane realized, allowing the pharmacist to lead her to the chair behind the counter.

''Are you ill?'' the man asked, his voice full of concern.

Jane felt tears forming, beginning to fall. She collapsed into the chair, her shaking hand reaching into the pocket of her pants to pull out the two little white pills. ''Is there some way you can tell me what these are? I mean without having to send them away for analysis.''

The pharmacist took the pills from her extended palm, turning them over several times and examining them carefully. ''Where did you get these?''

''Do you know what they are?''

''I know what I think they are.''

''Ativan?''

''Ativan? Oh, no, these aren't Ativan. Ativan are skinny and oblong in shape. Who told you these were Ativan?''

Jane felt her heart starting to race. ''They're not Ativan?''

''No, these look more like Haldol.''

''What's that?''

''Something you don't want to mess with.'' His eyes grew narrow. ''You haven't been taking these, have you? I mean, without a prescription?''

She nodded guiltily. ''I was having trouble sleeping and a friend said these would help.''

''First get rid of the pills, then get rid of the friend.

Friends like that are dangerous." He grunted in disgust. "No wonder you almost fainted. How many of these did you take?"

"Only a couple."

"Jesus."

"You're sure it's . . . Haldol?"

"Almost positive. But I'll look it up just to be sure." He disappeared for a few minutes behind a row of files and returned with a heavy blue book. "This has everything." He opened it. "See? Even pictures."

Jane's eyes scanned the glossy pages, perusing the list of medications, accompanied by pictures of the pills themselves. The pharmacist located the H's, quickly finding Haldol. He laid the small pill on the page next to the photograph. "See? They're the same size and color. They both have these beveled edges. They're scored, uncoated. These are definitely Haldol."

"And they're not good for insomnia."

"You got insomnia? I've got a million over-the-counter remedies. You got a major psychosis, you take Haldol."

"Psychosis?"

"Haldol is essentially a drug of last resort. You give it to someone who's suffering from severe depression. If you give it to someone who *isn't* suffering from a severe depression, odds are you're going to induce one."

"So someone who wasn't depressed to begin with is going to get depressed?"

"You take Haldol long enough without good reason, you'll turn into a real zombie. Not to mention, physically it can produce all the symptoms of Parkinson's disease."

"Which are?"

"Difficulty swallowing, spasms, shuffling—"

"Drooling?"

He nodded. "You'd run the gamut of psycho impairment. Trust me, these are not pills to blithely hand over to your friends when they're having trouble sleeping. You'll have to speak to your friend. Warn this idiot that he or she is playing with people's lives. Someone could get seriously hurt." He shook his head in amazement.

"You were lucky you only took a couple. You could have been one very sick young lady." He stopped, studying her carefully. "You're sure that's all you took?"

She smiled, feeling something close to relief. So, she wasn't going crazy after all. The pills Michael had been giving her weren't the pills Dr. Meloff had prescribed. The pills she'd been taking, far from being a mild tranquilizer, were "essentially a drug of last resort," whose prolonged use could turn her into a "zombie." No wonder she felt so damned depressed all the time. No wonder she could barely get out of bed in the mornings. No wonder she could hardly move. She had drug-induced Parkinson's disease! She was "running the gamut of psycho impairment!"

"I need my pills back," she told the druggist almost calmly. "And I have to get to the Boston City Hospital. Do you think you could lend me some money for a cab?"

"Maybe it would be a better idea if I called for an ambulance."

"I don't need an ambulance. I just need to speak to someone at the Boston City Hospital. Please, won't you help me?"

20

"I NEED TO SEE DR. MELOFF."

Jane stared down at the black-haired young woman who sat guard in front of Dr. Meloff's office pretending to be working at her computer. The woman, whose blue eyes were as pale as her hair was dark, regarded Jane with a mixture of boredom and uncertainty. She's not quite sure what to make of me, Jane realized, smoothing the wrinkles from her white slacks, adjusting the bottom of her long-sleeved pink sweater, feeling the lingering dampness on her fingertips.

The young woman, whose name plate identified her as Vicki Lewis and who was elegantly dressed beneath her white lab coat, studied the inappropriateness of Jane's attire for several seconds before responding. "I'm afraid that's not possible."

"I know I don't have an appointment, but I'm prepared to wait." Her eyes scanned the empty office. No one else was waiting to see him.

"That's not the issue."

"I'm sure he'll want to see me when he knows who it is. Please tell him that Jane Whittaker is here."

"But I'm afraid Dr. Meloff isn't."

"I beg your pardon?" Jane checked her watch. It was a little early for lunch. Maybe he was on a coffee break.

Maybe she could find him in the cafeteria.

"Dr. Meloff is on vacation. He won't be back for several weeks."

"Vacation?"

"He's white-water rafting, or whatever they call it. To each his own." Vicki Lewis shrugged. "If you'd care to make an appointment for when he gets back. . . ."

"No. This really can't wait."

"Well, you could see Dr. Turner or one of the residents."

"No, it has to be Dr. Meloff."

Vicki Lewis peered uneasily into the screen of her computer. "Then there's really nothing I can do for you unless you make an appointment to see him when he gets back."

"I can't wait till then." Jane heard the sudden injection of shrillness into her voice, noted the look of concern that flashed across Vicki Lewis's ghostlike eyes, and knew she had to sit down and think things through before she said anything more, before she did anything stupid. "Do you mind if I sit down for a while?"

Again Vicki Lewis shrugged. Jane lowered herself into an uncomfortable orange chair against the far wall and took several deep breaths, mindful of Vicki Lewis's suspicious gaze. She doesn't know what to make of me, what to do about me. Am I someone she should risk offending? Perhaps a personal friend of the good doctor? Am I in genuine need of medical care? Or am I some lunatic off the street, a former patient with a deranged fan's obsession? Do I carry a concealed weapon underneath my baby-pink sweater? Is it the heat or my neurosis that is responsible for my wet skin and shaky hands?

"Are you a patient of Dr. Meloff's?" the young woman asked, obviously eager to see Jane out of her office.

"He examined me about a month ago." Had it been a month? She was no longer sure. She'd lost all track of time. "What day is it?"

"Thursday. July twenty-sixth, 1990," Vicki Lewis told her, dividing the date into three distinct sentences.

"Thank you."

"Maybe I should call one of the residents. I think Dr. Klinger might be available."

"No!"

The sudden outburst caused Vicki Lewis to jump. Her hand reached reflexively for the telephone.

"I don't want to see Dr. Klinger." Dr. Klinger with his blank eyes and unsmiling mouth, his lack of humor and zero sense of compassion. What would he make of the story she had to tell? "I just need to sit here for a few minutes until I decide what to do. Please."

Another shrug, and Vicki Lewis returned her attention to her computer screen.

So what do I do now? Jane wondered, fighting back tears. She'd had everything so nicely worked out. In the taxi, she'd rehearsed her speech to Dr. Meloff until it was letter perfect. She'd prepared herself for his every possible reply, known exactly how she would answer each incredulous question. She had decided to lead him into her nightmare gently, the experienced guide directing the wary visitor toward significant points of interest: I know you're going to find this very difficult to believe, Dr. Meloff, and it's possible there's a logical explanation for everything, but I haven't been able to figure it out. Maybe you can.

And what seems to be the problem, Jane?

Well, you know how you said my memory would probably return in a few weeks. . . .

That wasn't a promise, Jane. The mind has its own agenda.

I know that. That's not why I'm here. I'm here because strange things have been happening to me since I went home. . . .

What kind of things?

I've been very sick, Dr. Meloff. Depressed and lethargic. Some days I can barely get out of bed.

We discussed this on the phone, Jane. I told you that it's not uncommon to be depressed under the circumstances.

I know, but it's more than that. You see, I think my

husband has been altering my medication.

What makes you think that?

You told me that you prescribed Ativan, but I took a few of the pills Michael's been giving me to the druggist. He said they're not Ativan. They're something called Haldol.

Haldol? You must be mistaken. Do you have them with you?

Yes. Here.

These are definitely not the pills I prescribed. Are you sure these are the pills he's been giving you?

Yes. And they make me feel awful. They make me dizzy and dopey and sick.

That's not surprising. This is very potent medication. But why would your husband give you incorrect medication? He's a very respected doctor. He knows better. It doesn't make any sense.

I haven't told you the whole story, Dr. Meloff.

Which is?

When I found myself walking the streets of Boston, I discovered something else, something that I didn't tell anyone.

Not even the police?

I was afraid to tell the police. You see, the pockets of my trench coat were filled with almost ten thousand dollars in hundred-dollar bills.

What?

And the front of my dress was covered in blood.

Blood?

I was going to tell you. And then that doctor recognized me, and after that, everything happened so fast that I didn't tell anyone.

Not even Michael.

No.

Whose blood was it?

At first I had no idea. But now I know that Michael lied about the scar on his forehead.

I see.

What do you see?

You think it was Michael's blood covering the front of your dress.

Yes! I think he knows something he's not telling me, that something might have happened between us, that I might have hit him.

And you think he's been giving you Haldol in order to keep you from remembering what provoked the outburst?

He's been talking about having me committed. That would certainly get me out of the way. Silence me forever.

But what about the money?

The money?

The ten thousand dollars you found in your pockets. Where did that come from?

I don't know. I don't know how it got there.

These are very serious charges you're making against a man whose reputation is above reproach.

I know that. That's why I came to you. If I went straight to the police, they'd never believe me. They'd never take my word against his. But with you helping me, at least I have a chance. Please say you'll help me, Dr. Meloff. Say you'll come with me when I talk to the police.

I'll come with you, Jane.

You believe me, then. You don't think I'm crazy.

I'm not sure what I think. I only know that these are not the pills I prescribed.

Oh, thank you, Dr. Meloff. Thank you.

"Is something funny?" Vicki Lewis's voice interrupted Jane's reverie. "You were laughing."

Jane shook her head, knowing she had definitely overstayed her welcome, but not sure what her next move should be. She could go to the police without Dr. Meloff, but where would that get her? Even if she were to confide in them all her suspicions, even if she were to tell them about the pills, even if she were to lead them to her locker at the Greyhound Bus Terminal and actually present them with her bloodied dress and the stacks of hundred-dollar bills, she would be regarded with skepticism and outright disbelief. She had lied, after all, had neglected to inform them of the money and the blood the first time she had appealed for their help. And who were they more likely to believe now—some crazy dame who still didn't know who she was, or the renowned pediatric surgeon who was her husband and who would undoubtedly have a logical answer to all their queries? And then she'd be back where she started. Only worse. Because now Michael would have all the proof he needed to have her put away for good.

No, she couldn't go to the police. Not yet. She'd have to wait—maybe disappear again—until Dr. Meloff returned from his holiday. Except that she no longer had the financial resources to make disappearing a viable alternative. The key to her locker was in the sole of a shoe at the rear of a closet in a house to which she couldn't risk returning. Maybe if she explained to the officials at the Greyhound Bus Terminal that she had lost the key, they'd open the locker for her. No, they'd never do that, especially since she had no money or identification. She'd have to think of something else.

There *was* nothing else. She had nowhere to go, no place to hide. She had exactly two choices: She could either return home and confront Michael directly or she could turn herself in to the police and let *them* confront him. "I guess that's it, then," she said out loud.

"What's it?" Vicki Lewis asked reluctantly.

Unless she could somehow force herself to remember. Unless she could arm herself with enough facts about her condition to give her subconscious the boost it needed to recall exactly what had gone on between her and Michael. *Then* she could go to the police. *Then* she might stand a chance. "Is there a medical library in the building?" she asked.

"I beg your pardon?" Obviously not a question Vicki Lewis had been expecting.

"Does the hospital have a medical library?"

"On the third floor," Vicki Lewis answered, "but it's off limits to anyone except staff."

"Thank you." Jane stood up and teetered out of the

office, steadying herself against the wall for support, aware of Vicki Lewis's eyes on her back.

She followed the gray line that ran along the side of the wall to the elevators, waiting beside an elderly black lady for one to arrive.

"You must be very warm," the woman said as they stepped inside, the other passengers trying to maintain as much distance as they could between themselves and Jane's pink wool sweater.

"I didn't know it was going to be so hot," Jane said, then directed her eyes to the buttons on the wall panel when she realized no one was interested. She sniffed at the fetid air in the confined space, and instantly became aware of unpleasant body odors, understanding that she was the one responsible. The elevator stopped at every floor, letting people off, picking others up, prolonging the agony, until Jane found herself pushed to the very back of the elevator, and then it was the third floor, her turn to get off. "Excuse me," she said, pushing her way back to the front, getting off just before the doors closed, hearing the sighs of relief from those who remained inside. She tried to focus on the various signs on the walls, arrows and directions which presumably told her all she needed to know, but the letters swam in and out of her consciousness and she ultimately gave up trying to force her eyes to cooperate. "Excuse me," she asked a passing intern, "could you please tell me where the medical library is located?"

He pointed in the proper direction, but not before telling her that the library was off limits to all but hospital personnel. Jane thanked him, then waited until he was out of sight before proceeding. If the medical library was off limits to all but hospital personnel, she'd just have to see to it that she was gainfully employed. "Hello," she told the middle-aged woman she assumed was the librarian. "I'm Vicki Lewis, Dr. Meloff's secretary. The doctor asked me to look up some information for him while he's away."

"Go right ahead."

Jane exhaled a deep breath of air. If the woman was

at all suspicious, she was doing a very good job of hiding it. If only everything else should prove so easy, Jane prayed, wondering how to go about locating the information she was seeking. "I was wondering if you could help me," she ventured.

The librarian smiled. "That's why I'm here."

"I'm looking for a comprehensive book on psychiatry."

"We have many." The woman, who was short and remarkably round, rose from her desk and led Jane past several aisles of books toward a shelf along the back wall. "These are all the psychiatry texts. As I'm sure you know," she added, as if it had just occurred to her that the secretary of a neurologist should be familiar with such things. She pointed to a particularly large and cumbersome text. "This one probably has all that you'll need."

"Thank you." Jane gathered the heavy tome into her arms, then looked around for somewhere to take it.

"Over there." The woman pointed toward several long tables and chairs. She fanned at the air with her fingers as she headed back to her desk, then stopped. "What did you say your name was?"

"Vicki Lewis." Jane's voice was barely a whisper. "Dr. Meloff's secretary."

"Of course. He's on vacation, I understand."

"White-water rafting," Jane confirmed, fighting dizziness.

"How adventurous."

"To each his own," Jane heard herself say, shrugging her shoulders. Maybe she really *was* Vicki Lewis.

She dropped the heavy book on the table with a crash that attracted the attention of a nearby intern, who smiled up at her briefly before returning to his studies. The librarian glanced toward her, then opened the top drawer of her desk, removing what looked to be some sort of list. Is she checking to see whether Dr. Meloff has a secretary named Vicki Lewis? Jane wondered, burying her head in the psychiatry text when the woman looked back in her direction.

Get to work, Jane commanded herself, locating *Amnesia* under the A's. At least it hasn't forgotten where it's supposed to be, she thought and had to stifle a laugh. She snuck a peek at the librarian, but the woman was on the phone and hadn't heard her. Concentrate, she told herself, wishing the words on the pages would stay in a straight line.

Amnesia was described as the partial or total inability to recall past experiences and was the result of either organic brain disease or emotional problems. If the amnesia was based on a disturbance of purely emotional origin, it tended to fulfill specific emotional needs and generally subsided when these needs were no longer operative.

Just as Dr. Meloff had told her, hysterical amnesia was defined as a loss of memory for a particular period of past life or for certain situations associated with great fear or rage. *It could cause severe depression*. Did that mean that her depression might simply be the result of her condition, the way Michael kept insisting? That it had nothing to do with the pills she had been taking?

She flipped to *Hysterical Fugue State* and quickly confirmed that it was a dissociative reaction that set in following a severe emotional trauma. So tell me something I don't know, she thought, her eyes skimming the rest of the paragraph, feeling let down and increasingly anxious. It didn't look as if she'd find anything to help her here.

And then she saw it: *A momentary loss of impulse control that nearly leads to the murder of a loved one may be followed by a complete loss of memory concerning all personal identifying data*.

Was it possible she had actually tried to kill Michael?

She immediately recalled her initial confusion at the Lennox Hotel when she was frantically trying to piece together what might have happened to her. She remembered the horror that had swept through her when she realized that she might have been able to kill someone, that such an act *felt possible*. Everything she had learned about herself in the past month had confirmed she had a very nasty temper that exploded at the slightest provocation. So, she might very well have tried to kill her doting husband of eleven years. But why? Because he had found out about her affair with Daniel Bishop? Was his turning her into a vegetable his way of getting back at her for her betrayal?

The text went on to say that this type of loss of memory was readily recoverable with hypnosis or strong suggestion, particularly when offered in a setting that promised extended relief or actual physical separation from the traumatic life situation. Perhaps her being at home, the probable scene of a possible crime, had been largely responsible for her memory failing to return.

Sleep had conveniently kept her from her first appointment with a psychiatrist, and Michael hadn't rescheduled another visit until six weeks later. His recent talk about taking her to a hypnotherapist had been just that. Jane shook her head, lowering it momentarily against the open pages of the book, feeling the coolness of the printed word against her cheek. It was very possible she'd never know the truth.

Maybe she'd ask the police to hypnotize her, she decided, lifting her head in time to see the familiar scowl of Dr. Klinger walking toward her.

"Mrs. Whittaker," he acknowledged, pulling up the chair across from her and sitting down.

"Dr. Klinger." She wondered if he could see her heart racing beneath her pink sweater.

"You remember me. I'm flattered."

"Even hysterical amnesiacs have to remember somebody." She found his failure to smile somehow reassuring. "And you don't have to tell me that only hospital personnel are permitted to use the facilities. I know that. I just chose to ignore it."

"Obviously you had something important you hoped to accomplish."

"There were some things I wanted to know."

"About your condition?" He turned over the front cover of the book and examined its title.

"No, about the Library of Congress cataloging system."

For a minute it looked as if Dr. Klinger was seriously considering her response. "Oh, I see," he remarked, "a little sarcasm."

"Amnesiacs are very good at sarcasm. It says so on page one thirty-three."

"What else have you learned?"

She shrugged, modeling the careless flip of her shoulders after Vicki Lewis. "Who told you I was down here?"

"Mrs. Pape," he said, indicating the librarian, "called Dr. Meloff's office to check on Vicki Lewis and found out that's who she was speaking to, and Ms. Lewis had a pretty good idea who might be impersonating her, so she got hold of me."

"And what exactly did she tell you?"

"That you came in wanting to see Dr. Meloff, that you seemed upset, distracted—"

"Overdressed?"

"She said it looked like you'd been sleeping in your clothes."

"Ms. Lewis is obviously more observant than I gave her credit for. Tell me, Dr. Klinger, aren't you curious?"

"About what?"

"About *why* I would be sleeping in my clothes."

"Do you want to tell me?"

Jane took a deep breath. What the hell, she thought. "We had guests last night for dinner and my husband slipped something into my drink, knocked me right out, and then had to put me to bed. I guess he couldn't be bothered getting me undressed any more than I could be bothered changing after I pushed the housekeeper into the bathroom this morning and tried to blockade the door. Why is it that doors always open inward, Dr. Klinger? It certainly makes life difficult when you're trying to escape." She studied Dr. Klinger's face for a reaction, received none.

"Why were you trying to escape?"

"It seemed like a good idea at the time." She laughed

loudly. "Flight *does* seem to be my typical reaction to stressful circumstances, doesn't it?" She tapped the cover of the textbook on the table in front of her. "Escape, after all, is the hallmark of acute nonpsychotic syndrome."

"You're obviously a very bright woman, Mrs. Whittaker. You don't seem like the type who would run away from her problems."

This observation and the softness of its delivery caused Jane to look at Dr. Klinger from a somewhat different perspective. Was it possible he was more sensitive than he first appeared? That he could be trusted? Should she use him as a sounding-board, try to enlist his aid? "Would you believe me if I told you that my husband was trying to harm me, that he's been overmedicating me, and keeping me a prisoner in my own home?"

The expression on his face said it all. "I believe that's what you *think* is happening."

Jane looked toward the ceiling, then back at Dr. Klinger. "In that case, could you possibly lend me a few hundred dollars?"

"I beg your pardon?"

"Just enough to tide me over until Dr. Meloff gets off his raft."

"You're joking, right?"

"Does that mean you won't lend me the money?" Jane pushed back her chair and attempted to stand up, succeeding on her second try.

"Wait a minute." Dr. Klinger also jumped to his feet.

"What for? I can see we're not getting anywhere, and I really shouldn't be in here, not being on staff and all."

"Maybe I *can* help you," Dr. Klinger stammered, reaching into his pockets.

"You'll lend me some money?"

"I don't have a lot." He withdrew his wallet and slowly pulled out a handful of cash. "Let's see what I've got here."

"Why would you help me when you think I'm crazy."

"I never said I thought you were crazy."

"You didn't have to."

"Let's just say I don't want you heading back to the streets. Dr. Meloff would never forgive me." He began counting out the few dollars in his wallet. "Let's see, twenty, thirty, thirty-five, forty-five, forty-seven . . . forty-seven dollars and twenty-two cents. Not much."

"It's great," she told him. "I really appreciate it." She reached for the money, only to watch it fall from his hands to the floor.

"Jesus, that was stupid of me." He was immediately on his knees, gathering up the money.

Could he move any slower? Jane wondered, realizing in that instant that Michael had already been notified and that Dr. Klinger was only trying to stall her until Michael arrived. "Never mind the money," she told him, trying to push past him, blocked by his stubborn bulk.

She felt his hands on her arms, watched his mouth form words of protest. And then his arms dropped to his sides and his mouth relaxed into a broad smile. In that instant, even before she saw Michael walking steadily toward her, she knew she was lost.

21

"DON'T COME NEAR ME," JANE WARNED, GRABBING the heavy psychiatric textbook off the table and brandishing it before her like a weapon.

Michael's voice was tremulous, barely audible. "I didn't come here to hurt you, Jane."

"No, you just came to give me my medication, right?"

"I came to bring you home."

"You can forget that idea." Jane laughed, her eyes traveling warily between her husband and Dr. Klinger. "Stay back!" she hollered, though no one had moved. She waved the book in her hands as if it were a gun, knowing how ridiculous she must look. CRAZED AMNESIAC HOLDS HOSPITAL LIBRARY STAFF HOSTAGE WITH WEIGHTY PSYCHIATRIC TOME! she saw scrawled across the imaginary headlines of tomorrow's *Boston Globe*. "Just leave me alone."

"I can't do that."

"Why not? What are you afraid of?"

"I'm not afraid. I'm concerned."

"About what?"

"About you."

"Bullshit!" Jane spotted movement out of the corner of her eye and spun sideways, watching the young intern creeping toward her. "Stay where you are!"

"Jane, this is ridiculous."

Jane stared imploringly at the young intern, then shifted her gaze to the librarian. "You don't know what this man's been doing to me," she began, then stopped as Dr. Klinger motioned both the intern and the librarian toward him.

"This is Jane Whittaker," he said, and Jane fought the urge to answer, Pleased to meet you. "She's suffering from a form of hysterical amnesia. Her husband, Dr. Michael Whittaker, is a pediatric surgeon at the Children's Hospital," he continued, nodding toward Michael, "and has been treating her with mild sedatives prescribed by Dr. Meloff."

"No, he hasn't!" Jane shouted. "Dr. Meloff prescribed Ativan. Michael has been giving me Haldol. He's been keeping me drugged and imprisoned; he won't let me see our friends; he won't let me even talk to our daughter."

"Jane, please—"

"No! I know you have them all fooled. I know they think you're some kind of god because you're this great surgeon and everyone thinks you're so wonderful, and who am I, after all, but some crazy woman who can't remember who she is, but it's not that simple. I may not know who I am, but I know that I'm not crazy, at least I wasn't before this whole horrible mess started. And I wasn't sick, not the way I am now. So, the question is, how did I get this way? What is this wonderful man doing to me that is making me so sick? What has he been giving me?" Jane stopped, abruptly reaching into her pants pocket and pulling out the two little white pills she had shown the druggist, holding them toward Dr. Klinger and the young intern. "Tell me these are Ativan!"

"Where did you get those?" Michael was asking, surprise in every word. "Did you take them out of my bag?"

Jane was almost speechless. "Did I take them? . . . Are you trying to say that you haven't been feeding me these pills?"

"Jane, can we just go home and try to talk this over calmly?"

"You didn't answer my question. Are you trying to tell me that you haven't been feeding me these pills?"

"Of course I haven't."

"You're lying!" Again, she glanced toward the others. "Please believe me. He's lying."

"Why would he lie, Mrs. Whittaker?" Dr. Klinger asked logically.

"Because something happened that he doesn't want me to remember. Because it's in his best interests to keep me in a near-vegetative state. Because he wants everyone to believe I'm crazy so that he can have me locked away in some institution where I'll never remember what happened, and even if I do, no one will believe me."

"Jane, please," Michael pleaded, "don't you realize how insane this sounds?"

"What am I supposed to do?" she begged the intern. "How can I convince you that I'm telling the truth, that I'm not crazy?"

"You're embarrassing him, Jane," Michael told her softly, and Jane could tell by the pink flush that was washing across the young doctor's face that this was true. "Can't we keep this matter between the two of us, at least until Dr. Meloff comes back?"

"It'll be too late by the time Dr. Meloff comes back!" Jane began rocking back and forth on her heels. "Look, why don't you just go away and leave me alone?"

"I can't do that, Jane. I love you."

Despite all her suspicions, Jane somehow knew that this was true. "Then why are you doing this to me?" she pleaded.

"I'm trying to help you."

"You're trying to destroy me!"

"Jane. . . ."

"What happened between us, Michael? What were we fighting about that day I disappeared?"

The look that passed through Michael's eyes convinced Jane she was right: Something *had* happened; they *had* been fighting.

"Please, can we talk about this at home?"

Jane lowered the heavy psychiatric text to the table. "It says in this book that a hysterical fugue state can result from a momentary loss. . . ." She struggled to remember the precise wording: " ' . . . the momentary loss of impulse control that nearly leads to the murder of a loved one.' See? There's nothing wrong with my memory. Tell me the truth, Michael," she urged, seeing that the others present were now equally curious. "What were we fighting about?"

"There was no fight," he told her.

"Liar!"

"Jane. . . ."

"If there was no fight, how did you get that gash on your forehead?"

"It was an accident. A kid threw a toy plane at my head. . . ."

"Bullshit!"

"Dr. Whittaker," the librarian broke in, "would you like me to call hospital security?"

"No!" Jane shouted.

"No," Michael concurred. "Not yet. I think Jane can be persuaded to listen to reason."

"I'm crazy," Jane shot back. "Why would you think I'd listen to reason?"

"Because I know you. Because I love you."

"Then why did I try to kill you?"

"You didn't."

"We didn't argue? You didn't grab me? Maybe shake me? I didn't grab something sharp? Hit you over the head with it?"

Michael was too stunned to speak.

"Tell me, then," Jane began, hesitated, then decided to go all the way, "how did my dress get covered with blood?"

"Blood?" the librarian gasped. "My God."

"It was your blood, wasn't it, Michael?"

Michael said nothing.

"And what about the money, Michael? The almost ten thousand dollars that was stuffed inside my coat pockets. How did it get there? Where did it come from? Tell me, Michael. I can see from the look on your face that you know what I'm talking about."

There was a long pause during which no one seemed to breathe. "Why didn't you mention any of this before?" he asked quietly.

Jane shrugged, feeling an enormous weight fall from her shoulders. There, she'd done it. Her secret was no longer something she had to cart around inside her like a malformed fetus. It was out in the open and they'd all heard it. Now what was Michael going to do about it?

"Could you leave us alone for a few minutes, please?" Michael asked the others. "I really need to talk to my wife in private."

"Why can't you talk in front of them?" Jane asked, suddenly filled with the uncomfortable sensation that she wasn't going to like what she was about to hear.

"I could," Michael agreed. "But I think that what I have to say should be confined to the two of us. At least for now. If you don't feel that way when I'm finished, you can tell them everything yourself. In fact, you can tell whomever you'd like, including the police, if that's what you decide. I've probably made a mistake trying to protect you. I've obviously protected you too long as it is."

"I'll send someone from security to stand outside the door," Dr. Klinger offered, and neither Jane nor Michael refused.

"I'm sorry to usurp your space this way," Michael told the librarian.

"Time for my coffee break anyway."

"Thank you."

"I'd appreciate it if you'd get in touch with me later," Dr. Klinger said, shaking Michael's hand.

Jane watched as the dour resident reluctantly took his departure, followed by the young intern and the middle-aged librarian. "Don't come near me," Jane cautioned as the door closed behind them and Michael took a step toward her.

"What is it you think I'm going to do, Jane?"

"I don't know. You're very slick. I can never see it coming. Like last night."

"Last night? Oh, yes. You think I tampered with your drink."

"Didn't you?"

"No."

"I just suddenly started to feel woozy and sick, and had to be carried up to bed?"

"It's not the first time it's happened."

"So?"

"So, you've been a very sick girl. The day was nothing if not dramatic: You pulled a knife on our housekeeper, for God's sake; you invited a couple of people you couldn't even remember over for dinner; you had to get dressed, made up; you had to lie. You don't think that required a great deal of effort? You don't think that maybe your body is just completely run down and that the strain of yesterday's events might not have taken its toll?"

Jane shook her head. No, she didn't believe it. Did she? "You're so damn convincing," she said.

"If I'm convincing, it's because it's the truth. I didn't put anything in your drink, Jane. I swear to you, I didn't."

Jane bit down on her lower lip until she felt the skin split and she tasted blood. "Tell me about what happened the day I disappeared. Tell me about the money. Tell me about the blood."

"Maybe you should sit down."

"I don't want to sit down." Another lie, she realized as soon as it was out of her mouth. She wanted desperately to sit down. She wasn't sure how long she could remain standing.

"Please, let me help you." Michael took a step toward her, and she stumbled back, out of his reach, the backs of her legs hitting the side of a chair and sending her to her knees. Michael was immediately at her side on the floor, his arms on hers, trying to guide her into a sitting position.

"No, don't touch me!"

"Jane, for God's sake. Do you think I have a syringe up my sleeve?"

"It wouldn't be the first time it's happened," she said, parroting his earlier words.

He stood up and quickly pulled all his pockets inside out. "There. See? Nothing." He removed his jacket, throwing it over the closest chair, revealing his short-sleeved shirt. "Nothing up my sleeves. What now? I'll take off all my clothes if that will satisfy you."

"I just want you to tell me the truth."

There was a long pause during which Jane allowed her body to sink into the waiting chair. "Please believe me, Jane, when I tell you that the only reason I haven't been completely honest with you is that I believed I was acting in your best interests. If I'd known you knew anything about the money and the blood, I might have handled this whole thing differently. God," he whispered, shaking his head. "No wonder you've been so frightened, so paranoid. So many things fall into place now, why you've been so suspicious of me." His fingers absently traced the line of the scar above his hairline.

"You admit you've been lying to me?"

Michael pulled out the chair opposite hers and sat down, his eyes never leaving her face. "I didn't want to cause you any more grief. I kept hoping that your memory would come back on its own when you were ready to face reality. I just didn't want to be the one to have to remind you. Trust me, Jane. I didn't want to hurt you any more than you've been hurt already."

"Tell me."

"I'm not sure I know how to start."

"Is it really so complicated?"

He nodded. "More."

"Tell me," she persisted, her voice a mixture of impatience and fear.

"I guess I have to go back at least a year," he began, then stopped. "To the accident that killed your mother."

Jane found herself holding her breath.

"You and your mother," he began again, "were very close. You couldn't accept what happened. You were angry and very bitter. You'd always had a temper, as you've been remembering, but after the accident, you were even more prone to violent outbursts. Nothing serious," he rushed to assure her. "You'd break things, smash dishes, hurl hairbrushes across the room, that kind of thing. I tried to talk you into seeing a therapist but you weren't interested. You insisted you could handle your grief privately, so I decided to be patient, see what happened. And sure enough, after a while, you seemed to be coping better. We resumed our normal lives. We started socializing again, went out with our friends. For about six months, everything looked like it was going to be okay again."

"And then what happened?"

Michael swallowed, his fingers massaging the bridge of his nose, moving down to hide his mouth, now pursed with worry. "As the first anniversary of the accident approached, you started getting more and more agitated. You were obsessing on the accident all the time, repeating the terrible details over and over again, making yourself crazy. It was almost as if the accident had just happened. You talked about nothing else. You couldn't sleep. When you did, you had nightmares. You couldn't concentrate. You felt guilty. Survivor's guilt, I guess the books would call it." He looked around the room, as if deliberating how to continue, what to say next.

"What do you mean, *survivor's guilt?*"

"You decided to visit the cemetery," he said, avoiding her question, his eyes slowly returning to hers. "I tried to talk you out of it. It was an unseasonably cold day, and I didn't think it was a very good idea, especially in the mood you'd been in. You hadn't slept at all that night; you hadn't eaten in days; you were this close to breaking down altogether." His fingers indicated a space of perhaps a quarter of an inch. "I asked you to at least wait for the weekend, that way I could go with you, you wouldn't have to be alone. But you were insistent, said you preferred to be alone, that you didn't want to wait for the weekend, that this was the anniversary of your mother's death, and you had to go that day. Period. No further discussion. I should leave you 'the hell alone,' I believe is how you put it. I offered to cancel my appointments, but that only enraged you. 'I can do it on my own,' you shouted. 'I'm not a little girl you have to take by the hand.' So what could I do? I went to work. I didn't want to, but I felt I had no choice. I went to the hospital and you went to the cemetery.

"I called a few times that morning to see if you'd gotten home all right, but there was never any answer. I started to get worried. Then Carole phoned."

"Carole Bishop?"

"Yes. She was very upset, said she'd seen you pull into the driveway and had gone over to ask you something, and that you were frantic. You wouldn't talk to her. In fact, she said it was almost as if you *couldn't* talk, you were so upset. She tried to calm you down, and you just pushed her out of the way and ran into the house. Naturally, she was very concerned about your behavior, and she decided to call me at the hospital. I rushed right home.

"When I got there, and I drove like hell, it couldn't have taken more than fifteen minutes, you were in our bedroom, throwing a bunch of your clothes into a bag. You hadn't even taken off your coat. You looked wild-eyed, possessed. I tried to talk to you, to ask you what had happened that morning, but you wouldn't tell me. You were hysterical, screaming at me, then lashing out at me. I grabbed you; I might even have shaken you. I don't remember. I just remember trying to find out what happened.

"But you were like a crazy person. You were screaming, telling me you had to leave, that it was for my own good, that you were like an albatross around my neck, that you would only bring me down, that you'd end up destroying me, like everything else you'd ever loved."

Michael shook his head, as if unable to digest the meaning of his words even now.

"But why would I say those things?"

Michael stared at the floor.

"Michael . . ."

"Maybe we could just stick to *what* happened for the time being, save the *whys* till later," he offered softly.

"Why would I say I'd end up destroying you, like everything else I'd ever loved?" Jane persisted.

Michael's jaw stiffened. His words, when they finally emerged, sounded choked, hoarse. "After the accident, you were overwhelmed with your grief for a long time. Paralyzed. You did things that were totally out of character. I don't mean the tantrums or the throwing dishes across the room," he added, then fell silent.

"What *do* you mean?"

He paused, his hands forming unconscious fists against the top of the table. "You used to go running with Daniel Bishop a few times a week." Another pause. "Suddenly you were out running every morning. At first I thought that was great, just what you needed, something to get rid of all that frustration and anger. But somewhere along the way, I guess you decided that running wasn't enough. You and Daniel . . ."

"We had an affair," Jane acknowledged, finishing his sentence. "How did you find out?"

Michael made a sound that was halfway between a laugh and a gasp. "You told me! Mentioned it casually one night when we were in bed." He shook his head. "I really don't want to go into all that now."

"What did you do?"

"I really don't recall." He laughed. "You see, you're not the only one who blocks out things they'd rather not remember."

"I obviously hurt you very much."

"Yes, but you really weren't yourself. I understood that. At least that's what I told myself. That was when I first suggested counseling, but you wouldn't hear of it. So, I just decided to wait things out. What else could I do? I loved you. I didn't want to lose you."

"So, I was packing to leave you when you came home. . . ."

"I tried to reason with you, to get you to sit still long enough for me to talk some sense into you, but you were beyond that. You raced downstairs and into the sunroom.

I followed you. You were running around in circles, flailing about. You started hitting me, telling me that I was a fool to hang on to you, that I was worse than a fool if I thought Daniel Bishop was the only man you'd been involved with, that there had been others since Daniel, that you'd just come from the latest one's bed.''

Pat Rutherford, Jane thought, feeling sick to her stomach, recalling the name on the note she'd found in her pocket. *Pat Rutherford, R. 31, 12:30.* Was it possible she had visited her mother's gravesite, then met with Pat Rutherford in room 31 of some shady motel, an encounter that had so shaken her she had come away convinced she had to leave her husband, more for his sake than her own?

''I guess at that point, I just lost control,'' Michael was saying. ''I started shaking you. We got into a kind of scuffle, pushing at each other blindly. And then, suddenly, I felt this flash of intense pain, like someone had lifted the top of my scalp right off, and the next thing I knew I was stumbling toward you, bleeding—God, there was so much blood—and I fell against you, and then I guess I blacked out. When I woke up a few minutes later, I was lying in my own blood next to the sofa-swing, and you were gone. You'd left the suitcase, your purse, everything. Later on, I discovered that you'd already cleaned out our joint checking account. Something in the vicinity of ten thousand dollars.''

There were several seconds of intense silence. ''Why didn't you report my disappearance to the police?''

He shook his head, almost laughed. ''Frankly, I didn't realize you'd disappeared. I thought you'd run off with this other guy. You've got to remember that I wasn't thinking too clearly myself at this point. And I was hurt and angry. I thought maybe the best thing to do was to do nothing until I heard from you.''

Jane struggled to keep control of all the facts. ''But when the police first phoned you, you lied. You said I was visiting my brother.''

''I really can't explain that. I don't know what I was thinking about other than that I was embarrassed; I didn't feel like getting into the whole sordid mess with a bunch of strangers. As you've discovered, I *do* have a reputation in the community. But when they told me you were in the hospital and couldn't remember who you were, I realized just how far things had deteriorated, and I knew that I had to do everything that I could to help you."

"And the drugs?"

Jane saw Michael try to turn from the intensity of her gaze, understood that he couldn't. "In the months following the accident, you suffered from severe depression. Your doctor prescribed Haldol. I talked to Dr. Meloff about it. When the Ativan didn't seem to be working, and you were slipping back into a deep depression, he suggested we try the Haldol again, see if that might help."

Jane began pacing back and forth, frequently banging into the side of the table, ignoring Michael's offers of support. "Something is wrong. Something is missing," she muttered, stopping, standing very still. "What aren't you telling me?"

"Believe me, Jane, I've told you everything."

"No, you haven't. I know you well enough to know when you're keeping something from me. Tell me."

"Jane, please, I've said enough."

"Tell me, Michael!" Her voice was a shout. "You said that after my mother died, I suffered from survivor's guilt. But that doesn't make sense. Why would I suffer from survivor's guilt unless I was in the car too? Unless I survived the accident and she didn't?" The shout became a whisper. "Is that it, Michael? Was I in the car?"

Michael lowered his head until his chin almost disappeared into his chest. "You were driving."

Jane felt her knees buckle. In the next instant, she was a crumpled heap on the floor, Michael on his knees before her. "I was driving? I was responsible for the accident that killed my mother?"

Michael spoke slowly, choosing his words carefully. "You'd promised to take her shopping that morning. But you were supposed to attend a meeting at Emily's school that afternoon, and I guess you were running a bit late.

Anyway, maybe you were going a little faster than you should have been, maybe you rushed a turn, I don't know exactly how it happened. According to witnesses, you made a left-hand turn without signaling, and some car was speeding along in the opposite direction and rammed into the passenger side of your car." Michael moved to her side and took her in his arms, holding her tightly against him. "Your mother was killed instantly."

"Oh, my God. Oh, my good God."

"You blamed yourself, of course. Even after the police determined that the other driver was the one at fault, you berated yourself constantly. 'I shouldn't have tried for that turn,' you kept saying. 'I shouldn't have been in such a hurry.' You wouldn't let anyone comfort you." His eyes searched the room, as if he were searching for possible solutions. "But it's gone on for too long, Jane, and you have to stop blaming yourself. It was an accident. Tragic, yes, but it happened, and it's over. And life goes on. I know you don't want to accept that, but you have to or it will be too late for all of us."

Jane became aware of his tears on her cheek, and she quickly pulled out of his embrace. "There's more, isn't there?" she demanded, watching his expression carefully. "There's more that you're still not telling me."

"No."

"Yes! Don't lie to me, Michael. You have to stop lying to me!"

"Please," he begged. "Can't the rest wait until you're stronger? There's only so much your mind can handle, Jane. We know that now."

"What haven't you told me?"

Michael struggled for several seconds before he was able to say the word, and when it finally emerged, it came out in ripples. "Emily," he said, his eyes glazing over, filling with tears.

Jane clutched her stomach, feeling her daughter's name form a fist and ram into her gut. "No. Oh, no!"

"She was in the backseat behind your mother. Apparently, she'd taken off her seat belt. The force of the collision. . . ." His voice trailed off, then returned. "She died in your arms while you were waiting for the ambulance. When they were finally able to pry her away from you, the entire front of your dress was covered in her blood.''

Jane gasped.

''You just went kind of crazy after that. The next year was hell, the violent outbursts, the other men, basically what I've already told you. Nobody else knew how bad it had become. It was like you were Jekyll and Hyde, one way with our friends and neighbors, another way at home with me. I kept hoping it would get better, that you'd eventually come out of it, that you'd come back to me.'' He stifled a loud sob. ''You were all I had left. I couldn't bear the thought of losing you too.'' He wiped at his eyes with the back of his hand. ''But it just got to be too much, even for me, I'm ashamed to admit.'' He pushed himself to his feet. ''When I came home and found you packing, I tried to reason with you, stop you, and in the struggle, you hit me with the vase. It was one we'd bought in the Orient. It was brass and it had all these weird protuberances sticking out of it, and it caught me at some weird angle and damn near scalped me. I collapsed against you and it must have seemed like the accident all over again. I guess the sight of all that blood on your dress was just too much for your sanity to take. You decided you couldn't deal with your life anymore. So you just walked away from it. I really can't say that I blame you.''

''Our daughter is dead?'' Jane half-asked, half-confirmed.

''You still can't remember any of this?''

Jane shook her head. ''I killed my mother and my daughter,'' she mumbled.

''It was an accident, Jane. The police absolved you of any blame. It wasn't your fault.''

''But they're both dead.''

''Yes.''

''And I was driving.''

''Yes. But it wasn't your fault.''

''Impatient and in a hurry, isn't that what you said?''

"That's what *you* said after the accident."

"And I'm the one who would know. I'm the one who lived to tell the tale."

"Did you?" Michael asked. "How many lives is this accident going to claim, Jane? How many people are you going to let it destroy?"

Jane stared at her husband's tear-streaked face, felt the kindness in his eyes, the tenderness of his touch. She said nothing.

22

"SHE'S IN THE SUNROOM."

"How is she?"

"Not good."

"I don't understand. How long has this been going on?"

"It started about the middle of June. She's been getting progressively sicker ever since."

"The middle of June? That's over a month ago. For God's sake, Michael, why did your housekeeper tell me that she was in San Diego visiting her brother?"

"We thought it was the best way to handle the situation. Please understand, Diane, that no one, not me, not her doctors, ever anticipated that her condition would last this long, that it would get worse."

"She has no idea who she is at all?"

"We've told her who she is," Michael explained. "She just doesn't remember. She knows all the details of her life. She just can't recall having lived it."

"My God, I don't believe it. Do you have any idea what brought this on?"

"The accident," he said simply.

"But that's over a year ago. She seemed to be over the worst of it."

"I don't think we've seen the worst of it."

Jane heard their voices as if they were surrounded by static. The words wafted toward her, starting strong, only to fade out prematurely, pushing painfully against her eardrums, only to pull away before she managed to interpret their meaning. They were talking about her, she knew. They were always talking about her. Did it matter what they were saying?

She was lying on her beloved sofa-swing, blankets covering her from her chin to the bottoms of her feet despite the fact that she was sweating. Was it sweat or drool? she wondered, not bothering to wipe the dribble away from the side of her slightly parted lips. She let them do that—her guests, the multitudes that Michael had been reintroducing into their lives ever since he brought her back from the hospital. How long ago? A few days? A week?

She smiled, grateful that time was once again slipping away from her. To think that she had railed against this feeling just a short time ago, that she had been resentful and angry because the drugs they were giving her made one day blend into the next, like chocolates melting in the sunlight, forming one unrecognizable blob. To think that she had tried to fight against the delicious oblivion to which she had finally succumbed, and for what? So that she might remember the sordid details of a wasted life, a life she clung to even after she had sacrificed those of her mother and child?

Michael had brought her home after her outburst at the hospital. She recalled the doctors and nurses being very solicitous, remembered Michael explaining to Dr. Klinger that he had everything under control, telling him he'd be in touch with Dr. Meloff when Dr. Meloff returned from vacation, saying he thought the best thing for Jane at the moment was plenty of rest.

She hadn't offered even a hint of protest. The idea of seeking refuge in her bed suddenly held great appeal. She wanted to crawl under its down comforter and disappear forever. She wanted to die, she realized in that moment, and felt her body shrug.

She no longer fought against her medication, accepting

whatever they gave her, feeling the familiar numbness return to her body, reaching into her fingertips and toes, filling her pores, ultimately settling somewhere behind her eyes, creating a buffer zone between her brain and the outside world. This time she welcomed each unpleasant side effect, almost enjoying the muscle spasms that plagued her because they seemed a fitting punishment for all the pain she had caused, wearing her drool like an expensive piece of jewelry.

It all made sense now.

The money. The blood. *Pat Rutherford*. The logic of his name appearing on a note in her pocket and not in her telephone-address book where Michael might see it. At first she wondered whether he had tried to contact her, was at all curious as to what had happened to her. Had they been planning to run off together? Or had he chosen that morning to end their affair?

The questions disappeared with the restarting of her medication. She felt relieved. What was the point of fixating on questions she couldn't answer? Even Michael couldn't tell her what had happened prior to their fight, before she had flipped out and tried to kill him with an Oriental brass vase. That she had tried to kill her husband no longer seemed a shocking idea. Hadn't she already killed her mother and her daughter?

Jane tried to put a face to death, recalling the many images of the little girl she had watched grow up between the plastic covers of her photograph albums, the beautiful child with the shy smile and curious eyes, wearing one red shoe and one blue, sniffing a low branch of a lilac tree, holding her father's hand, clinging tightly to her mother's side. Emily is a memory now, she thought, except that she wasn't even that.

How many times in the past few days had she gone over the details of the last month? Sitting here in the sunroom, watching the mornings slice across the floor like narrow pieces of pie, growing in size until it grew dark again, she daily retraced her steps, beginning with the first time Michael had brought her home after she had lost her memory. She remembered crossing the threshold into her old life, wondering what exactly was in store for her, then scoffed, feeling the constriction in her throat. In her wildest dreams, in her worst nightmares, she could not have envisioned a scenario so bizarre, so hopeless. No wonder she had been so desperate to escape.

She saw herself cross into the living room, approach the piano, heard her fingers stumble across an old tune from Chopin, watched those same fingers lift several photographs toward her face, among them three class pictures of young children arranged in neat little rows according to height. A little boy in the front row held up a small blackboard identifying them as the children of Arlington Private School. Jane had smiled at the delicate little girl with long, light-brown hair and enormous eyes, dressed all in yellow, standing proudly in the last row, at the same little girl, older by one year, clad in pink and white, her hair in a ponytail, still tall and proud, at the same little girl, her hair flowing free, dressed in black-and-white checks, her smile somewhat less assured, more circumspect. Junior kindergarten, senior kindergarten, grade one. Grade two missing. "I guess we didn't get a picture this year," Michael had told her. "She must have been away sick."

Why hadn't it seemed strange to her that the most recent pictures of Emily were at least a year old? In a family that had carefully recorded and framed its every move, why hadn't she found it peculiar that there were no photographic reminders of the past year? Because she hadn't wanted to, she realized. Because she wasn't ready to confront the mess she had made of her life, to face the havoc she had wreaked, to come to terms with the lives she had destroyed.

I'm the one who should be destroyed, she thought. Put to sleep like a dog gone bad. Lethal injection, she decided, rubbing her arm under the blanket, feeling the spot where Michael had given her another shot just this morning.

She recalled her growing suspicions of Michael, her conviction that he was plotting against her, deliberately trying to rob her of her sanity when all he'd been doing was trying to help her find it.

And now he was bringing someone to see her. After weeks of denying her access to even her closest friends, he had now decided it was time to make them aware of the hell he had been living. First, he had called Sarah and Peter Tanenbaum, and they had come at once, Sarah bursting into tears at the very sight of Jane, Peter averting his head, talking to Michael instead.

She had wanted to reach out and comfort them, to tell them it was all right, that it was better this way, that she had chosen insanity, that it suited her, that they shouldn't worry about her. But somehow her arms wouldn't move and her voice refused to squeeze past the lump in her throat. She stared at them, her eyes clouded, like a camera lens that has been rubbed with Vaseline, and said nothing, wishing only that they would go away and leave her to her fate. It was no less than she deserved, after all. She had tried to run away but she had been recaptured and brought back to face her execution.

There had been other visitors as well. In the past few days, Michael had rallied most of their friends to her side, although he allowed them to stay only a few short minutes. Janet and Ian Hart, Lorraine Appleby, David and Susan Carney, Eve McDermott—Ross was away fishing, she heard Eve explain—they all filed into her sunroom, studying her as if she were one of Madame Tussaud's famous wax dummies. "Don't mention Emily," Michael cautioned each one, and no one did, for which she was grateful.

"Don't mention Emily," she heard him whisper now, from the other side of the door, and in the next minute Diane Brewster was kneeling before her, her eyes immediately filling with tears.

"My God," Diane moaned just loud enough to be heard, her body swaying as if she might faint.

"It's all right," Michael assured her, reaching down to pat her shoulder. "She's not in any pain."

"Can she hear me?"

"Yes," Michael answered, coming to Jane's side and

stroking her hair. "Diane's here, sweetheart. Can you say hello to Diane?"

Jane tried to force her lips into the appropriate shape, to get her tongue around the uncooperative name, but the result was only a few wayward twitches, and so she stopped trying. What was the point, after all?

Diane rose angrily to her feet. "I don't understand this, Michael. I don't understand what's happened to her. I know you told me what to expect. I know she suffered a major trauma . . ."

"Diane," he cautioned, and Diane took several deep breaths, trying to calm herself down.

"Damnit, Michael, this is my oldest friend. She was always so enthusiastic, so definite about everything. I just can't believe this is the same person."

Michael said nothing, merely nodding his head in agreement.

"Can't the doctors do anything?"

"We're doing everything we can."

"But she's lost so much weight."

"She won't eat."

Diane slapped her hands against her sides, then returned to her knees in front of Jane. "You're going to be all right, Janey. You're going to pull out of this real soon. We're going to see to that. Michael and me and all your friends. We're going to make sure that you get better again."

"Why don't you read this to her?" Michael suggested, slipping a brightly colored card into Diane's trembling hand.

"It's a postcard from Howard and Peggy Rose," Diane announced, forcing an upbeat inflection into her voice that made her sound vaguely hysterical. "From France." She displayed the front of the card, a little café by the side of an aquamarine sea. "Let's see, it's hard to make out the handwriting, it's so small, but here goes: 'Well, here we are in the south of France, predictable old us. But we love it and we're having a great time—" She stumbled. ". . . like I'm sure you are back in boring old Boston. Why don't you drop everything and pay us a surprise visit? We love surprises. And we love you. Hope all is well. Like the old song says, See you in September. Howard and Peggy.' That was nice,'' Diane said, her enthusiasm vanishing into a flood of tears.

A surprise visit, Jane thought, remembering the surprise visit she was supposed to have paid her brother. She tried to picture him off somewhere in Spain, but failed to bring him into sharp focus, managed a clearer image of her sister-in-law. Gargamella, she thought and laughed out loud.

''My God, Michael!'' Diane exclaimed, her hand reaching over to caress Jane's face. ''What kind of sound was that? It didn't sound human.''

''Are you all right, Jane?''

I'm fine, Jane responded silently. I just want everybody to go away and leave me alone so that I can die in peace.

''Do you want a drink of ginger ale?'' Michael asked solicitously. ''Or something to eat? Paula made a wonderful blueberry pie.''

I prefer Paula's apple pie, Jane thought, remembering the time she had held Paula at bay with the knife she had been using to chop apples. The good old days, Jane thought, wishing now that she had plunged the knife into her stomach and twisted it up through her heart.

Maybe it wasn't too late. Maybe it was still worth a try. Maybe she could indicate to her husband and her oldest friend that she would indeed like a piece of Paula's blueberry pie but that she'd prefer to eat it in the kitchen. Then, once they were all comfortably seated around the table, lulled into a false sense of security, she'd make a lunge toward the counter, eviscerating herself neatly with her own knife, the blood staining the front of her dress. Her own blood. As it should have been all along. Full circle.

But she said nothing, only watched them stare at her through frightened, confused eyes. It would have been better for all concerned if she had simply disappeared, if no one had ever found her, recognized her, brought her home. Michael would have eventually divorced her—

God knew he had enough grounds. Her friends would have talked about her for a while, then moved on to other, more interesting topics. After a little while, she would be like Emily, little more than a memory. A suitable irony for an amnesiac, she thought, and laughed again.

This time her laugh emerged as a truncated sigh. Diane clutched her hand in support. "You're sure she's not in any pain, Michael?"

"I'm sure."

"I feel so helpless. . . ."

"We all do."

Jane wanted to take her friend's face between her hands and kiss her gently on both cheeks, to reassure her that everything was going to work out for the best. But she knew that if she said or did anything, even something as insignificant as stroking her friend's hair, she would be sending her incorrect signals, giving out false hope. And there was no hope. She knew that now. There was no hope, and there was no point in trying to pretend there was.

She no longer prayed for her memory to return. In fact, she went to bed every night desperately hoping it would never come back. She knew as much about herself as she needed to know. If there was a God, and if he was a merciful God, she told herself, he wouldn't force her to relive the death of everything she once held dear. He'd let her bury herself alive in her drug-induced cocoon until she disappeared again, this time for good.

"I saw this terrible movie the other night," Diane suddenly exclaimed in what Jane understood was another attempt to elicit a response. "Supposed to be very sexy. You know how I like sexy movies. I mean, even if they're bad, they're good, right? Well, forget it. This one had a lot of bare boobs and tushies, and plenty of grunting, but the dialogue was so awful that the audience was actually laughing out loud. Tracy wanted to walk out. You remember my friend, Tracy Ketchum, the one who thought she was pregnant last year only it turned out to be early menopause? Can you imagine? At forty?" She looked to Jane for any reaction, continued when she received none. "Anyway, we were sitting there trying to decide whether or not to leave this turkey, when suddenly one of the guys in the audience starts yelling things at the screen, and he was so much fun that we had to stay and listen. I mean, at one point, this woman, played by Arlene Bates—God knows where she's been hiding out all these years and why she chose to come back in this horrible thing, but she looks great, I think she must have had a face-lift, I mean, there wasn't a line anywhere on that woman's face, although her neck, let me tell you, hers was not a young neck. I don't know why these women do it. And the men too. They have all these lifts and tucks, so that they all look vaguely Oriental, you know like Jack Nicholson and Richard Chamberlain, and even Burt Reynolds, but they have this old skin. Tracy says it gets worse after you hit forty. She says there are all these things that start falling apart. I told her that happened to me at thirty, but she said there's no comparison. She said that the first thing to go is your eyesight. Suddenly, you can't read the back of cereal boxes anymore, and you start holding books farther and farther away, unless you're near-sighted and then it kind of evens out. So, suddenly you're wearing reading glasses, looking like your least-favorite aunt. Then your ass drops. Tracy said that what surprised her the most wasn't that it dropped, but the *way* it dropped. She said she always assumed that when it dropped, it would stay the same shape, only lower. She didn't realize that it dropped because it flattened out. Can you imagine? A flat behind? Like Jack Lemmon's in that movie, what was it, *That's Life?*

"Anyway, back to Arlene Bates and that guy in the audience. Well, Arlene says to this doe-eyed former-fashion-model-turned-excruciatingly-bad-actress, I can't even remember her name. . . ."

Cindy Crawford? Jane wondered, thinking of the famous cover girl, feeling her eyes heavy, wanting to close.

"Pamela Emm!" Diane exclaimed. "That was the poor thing's name. Can you imagine, an initial for a last name? She claims it's genuine. Well, who knows? It's a name I don't think we'll be hearing a great deal of in the future. Yes, sir, it's back to the silent pages of *Vogue* and *Bazaar* for Pamela."

Michael coughed, cutting into Diane's monologue. "Jane's starting to look very tired, Diane. Maybe you could finish this another time."

"Oh, please, Michael. Just a few more minutes. I just have this feeling that I'll be able to reach her."

Jane watched Michael nod and walk toward the back window to stare out at the yard. How can he stand it? Jane wondered. How can he stand being here? Taking care of me? How can he even bear looking at me after everything I've done to him? Oh, I'm a prize package all right. I'm one for the books. One for the silver screen.

"Anyway," Diane was continuing, a growing urgency to her voice, "Arlene, who's playing this bitchy real estate tycoon, says to Pamela, who's in the market for a new house, and judges the livability of each room by making love on the hardwood floors, that she should ask the paperboy to help her out in this regard, since her husband, who's a senator—what else?—is too busy trying to feed the starving multitudes of Ethiopia. And here she is starving at home, right? So, Arlene, who's hiding a pair of opera glasses in her Hermès purse, so we know she's a major voyeur, right?—she says to Pamela, 'Tell him to come in here.' And Pamela floats over to the window slower than it would take me to cross the Atlantic Ocean in a canoe, and stares out at this adolescent who's hurling papers off his bicycle, for God's sake, and she opens her mouth in this little half pout, afraid to speak until Arlene prompts her again, saying, 'Tell him.' And this guy in the audience yells out, 'Tell him *quickly*!' We all cracked up. And I thought of you. I even said to Tracy, 'That's something my friend Jane would do.' God, do you remember the time you almost got us run over by that maniac in the red Trans Am?"

"Diane," Michael interrupted, this time allowing a hint of impatience to creep into his voice, "I don't think now's the time to go into that."

Diane was instantly apologetic. "I just thought that maybe I might be able to jar her memory. . . ."

"Don't you think we've been trying to do that night and day for the past month? I don't know. Maybe we've been putting too much pressure on her to remember. I think the kindest thing we can do for her now is to leave her alone and just let her work through it."

"But look at her, Michael. Do you think she'll be able to work through it on her own?"

Michael stared at the floor. "I don't know. I really don't know what to do anymore. I'm not even sure it's a good idea to go on treating her at home."

"What are you saying?"

"Come on," Michael said, ignoring the question and helping Diane to her feet. "Paula made a fresh pot of coffee and she'll be insulted if you don't at least have a taste of her blueberry pie."

"Michael, what are you saying?"

"I've been doing some investigating, making some preliminary inquiries. . . ."

"About what?"

"About putting Jane in a psychiatric hospital."

"Oh, my God, Michael. Jane, institutionalized?!"

"It's not like *The Snake Pit*, for Christ's sake. Goddamnit, Diane. Are you trying to make me feel guilty? Don't you think that I've tried everything else? That I wouldn't even be considering this if I weren't so concerned, so frustrated. Look at her, for God's sake! She's no better than a vegetable. And she's deteriorating every day."

"Maybe it's the medication she's receiving. . . ."

"Without the medication, she's violent and delusional. At least this way she's not doing herself, or anybody else, any harm. Her mind has a chance to rest and hopefully recover. Look, these places aren't like in the movies, there's no Nurse Ratched hiding under the beds. There are many fine institutions where Jane would get the help she needs."

"I understand what you're saying, Michael. It's just

that I'm having a hard time coming to grips with all this."

Diane stared down at Jane, as if trying to will her to her feet. Jane read the expression in her face. Get up, it said. Get up and defend yourself. Show this man that you are all right, that you don't need to be committed to any institution. Get up, damn you! Diane's eyes screamed.

Jane felt a tingling sensation in her legs, pinpricks at the bottom of her feet, and knew that she wanted to comply, that she wanted to jump to her feet and hug this woman who was her friend, even though the past they shared was gone, and tell her that she would get better, that everything would be all right again.

Except that how could anything ever be all right again? She had caused the deaths of her mother and child, cheated on her husband, almost killed him, betrayed her neighbor, and maybe even some of her friends. She was getting exactly what she deserved.

"I'll come back again, Jane," Diane was saying, leaning forward to wipe a line of drool from Jane's mouth, then kissing her cheek. "You were going to fix me up with that guy you met at one of your environmental meetings, remember? I'm counting on you, Jane. My *mother* is counting on you." She paused, tears dropping from her eyes onto Jane's blanket. "I love you."

Jane felt herself enveloped in Diane's arms. She made no move to either return her embrace or to push her away. I don't deserve your love, she thought, watching Michael lead Diane through the door to the kitchen, imagining Paula pouring them each a cup of coffee as they settled in comfortably around the kitchen table, admiring Paula's fresh blueberry pie.

Life would go on quite nicely without her, she knew, immediately conjuring up many such domestic scenes. Maybe Michael would eventually marry Diane, make Diane's mother *really* happy, or maybe Michael would marry Paula, move her and her small handicapped daughter into the house, an instant family to replace the one he had lost, the one she had taken from him. And Michael would be happy again. And Jane would be—what? In an institution or in the ground. What difference would it make? Ultimately it amounted to the same thing.

23

THEY WERE SITTING IN MICHAEL'S CAR IN A PARKING lot on St. James Avenue, around the corner from the Greyhound Bus Terminal. "Are you all right, Jane? Are you sure you're strong enough to do this?"

Why was he asking her that? It hadn't been her idea to get out of bed and drive into Boston on some stupid treasure hunt. It was Michael's plan. It was Michael who had inquired casually as he was tucking her into bed the previous night—had it been last night or some other night?—as to what had happened to the ten thousand dollars she had taken from their joint checking account.

At first she could barely remember what he was talking about—it all seemed to have happened to someone else a very long time ago—but after some careful prodding, she managed to spit out where she had sequestered the money. He smiled at her ingenuity, especially when she told him that she had hidden the key to the locker inside the sole of one of her shoes. She couldn't remember which pair and so he had taken them all apart.

She hadn't expected to have to accompany him, but then she hadn't realized it was Saturday and Paula had weekends off. Both Sarah and Diane had phoned that morning and suggested dropping over, and he had told them both the same thing, that he was taking Jane into

Boston to finally buy her that diamond wedding band he'd been talking about for so long, and yes, he was hoping that would cheer her up, he'd call them later and tell them Jane's reaction. He didn't mention anything about the Greyhound Bus Terminal, which, she supposed, wasn't too surprising. What could he say? That he was going to retrieve the money she had stolen from their account just before she'd lost her mind? There was only so much even good friends wanted to hear.

"Can I just wait in the car?" Jane asked Michael, the sound of each word alien, as if she were speaking an unfamiliar tongue. Where was she finding the strength to speak at all? she wondered, wanting only to curl into the soft leather of the car seat and go to sleep.

"You need some exercise," Michael was saying. "Come on, Jane. The walk will be good for you. You can't just sit around all day, day after day. You have to get out more. You have to start doing things again."

Why? she wondered but didn't bother to ask. It was ironic that when she had wanted to be taken out, Michael had refused, and now, when she wanted only to be left alone in her bed, he insisted on taking her for walks and rides in the car. When she had been desperate to see her friends, talk to them on the phone, he had told her it wasn't a good idea, and yet in the past few days, when she was too weak and sick to even look at them, she was on constant display. Where was the fairness in that? Where was the logic?

"Come on," he said again, this time getting out of the car and coming around to her side, pulling open her door. She knew that he wouldn't leave her alone in the car because he was afraid she might bolt, run off again and leave him. Why couldn't he understand that this was undoubtedly the best solution to all their problems?

So, here she was, being helped—no, pulled—from her husband's car, clad in a pair of navy trousers and a white middy blouse that looked like something you'd put on a twelve-year-old, and her hair had been neatly brushed and secured in a high ponytail, and Michael was smiling at her and coaxing her onto the sidewalk, telling her that she could do it, he knew she could do it, and they were walking, actually walking, although she had no sensation of her feet actually touching the ground, around the corner toward the Greyhound Bus Terminal.

The sun was shining. The temperature was a pleasant seventy-eight degrees, if you believed the man on the radio. She didn't. It seemed hotter. Definitely stickier. She felt the sun beating down on the top of her head, like the neighborhood bully holding a kid's head under water, and she wanted to scream, thrash her hands wildly about, dislodge and discount its power over her. But the sun only tightened its grip, extended its grasp, and she knew that to protest would be a waste of valuable energy. She opened her mouth gingerly, like a fish, trying to transmit oxygen to her lungs, but swallowed only heat, as if she had been standing over a steaming kettle. She felt her tongue burn and her eyes sting.

"Are you all right? Do you want to stop and rest a few minutes?"

She shook her head. What was the point in stopping to rest? They'd only have to start up again. The whole escapade would take that much longer. No, the sooner they retrieved the money she had hidden, the sooner they'd be able to return to the car, the sooner they'd get back to the house, her bed, her medication, those blessed drugs that provided her with the fog of oblivion that carried her through each day. To think that she had once fought against them.

"Careful now. Watch your step."

Jane lowered her head to her feet, watching one foot cross in front of the other through the terminal's front doors. She was immediately surrounded by a crowd of people, some rushing for buses, others thrilled to have been released, as oblivious to her presence as they had been the first time she had come here. The invisible woman, she thought, feeling Michael pull her along beside him.

In the next instant, she was leaning against several rows of lockers, sweating profusely, and watching absently as Michael and the station employee fitted their respective keys into the appropriate locks. She watched Michael pull open the locker door, his smile widening as he reached inside for the plastic laundry bag from the Lennox Hotel. As the employee returned to her place behind the counter to work out the balance owed, Michael peeked inside the bag, and Jane caught the look of dismay that crept across his face when he saw her crumpled, blood-stained blue dress. In that second, she decided that in addition to all her other psychological problems, she was something of a fashion schizophrenic. How could the same woman wear sophisticated Anne Klein dresses one minute and coy little sailor suits the next?

How could she even be thinking such inane—insane?—thoughts? she wondered, watching as Michael paid the balance owing, and then carefully removed the dress from the bag and, pulling her along beside him, dropped it into the nearest trashcan. He then folded the bag filled with the thousands of dollars she had stolen from him into a neat package, which he placed casually under his arm, as if he were used to transporting large amounts of cash this way. And then they were politely pushing their way through the crowds again, Michael nodding at various passersby, smiling at a policeman who wandered past, holding the door open for an elderly woman weighted down with suitcases.

Once out on the street, she assumed that Michael would guide them back toward the parking lot, locate their car with the same ease with which he seemed to accomplish everything, and then drive her home. But instead of turning onto St. James Avenue, he continued past Boylston and onto Newbury.

"Where are we going?" she asked, trying to keep up with his pace.

"I promised to take my wife shopping."

"Oh, Michael, I don't think I can."

If he heard her, he pretended not to, and minutes later, she found herself shuffling along the fashionable downtown street, Michael whistling a tune beside her, seemingly oblivious to her discomfort, although she knew he was not, that he was only trying to cajole her out of her lethargy. "I'm really not in the mood to shop," she said, wondering at the absurdity of the situation as they walked briskly past the dizzying array of expensive shops.

The street was busy with people, many of whom were already loaded down with shopping bags. Jane wondered if any of the bags were filled with hundred-dollar bills, and looked toward Michael, who was waving at a woman across the street. The woman returned his greeting, before crossing over to say hello.

"Michael, how are you?"

"Just great. How have you been?"

"Wonderful. Couldn't be happier actually. Give me private practice any day."

The woman glanced at Jane, and Jane recognized the look of someone who has seen something unpleasant but is loath to acknowledge it.

"Forgive me," Michael said immediately. "Thea Reynolds, this is my wife, Jane."

"Pleased to meet you," Thea Reynolds said. Jane said nothing, wondering if her lips had formed the smile she'd intended.

"Thea is a specialist in eating disorders. She left the hospital last year to open her own clinic."

Jane nodded, but they had already turned their attention back to one another and no more of her was required. That was good, Jane thought, balancing first on one leg, then the other, pulling at Michael's arm to keep from tipping over like a child whose feet are tired and needs to be supported. She found Thea Reynolds intimidating, with her perfect black hair elegantly coiffed and oblivious to the heat, her broad confident smile filled with teeth, her crisp way of dressing, every accessory perfectly chosen, her nails manicured, the skin around her cuticles smooth and unbitten. Thea Reynolds spoke with authority, with the kind of self-assurance that went hand in hand with a deep sense of self, a sense of security Jane wondered if she had ever possessed. Had she always found women like Thea Reynolds intimidating? Or had she once possessed this kind of effortless confidence herself?

She must have had some of it, she reasoned, remembering that her quick temper and unhesitancy to shoot her mouth off had almost gotten her into a lot of trouble on numerous occasions. So where had all that self-confidence gone?

It was dead, she realized, catching the eye of a woman passerby. Mangled beyond all recognition in a two-car collision, another casualty of her carelessness.

The woman passerby continued to stare at her as she walked past. Jane turned slightly to watch her as the woman continued down the street. There she stopped, hesitated, then went on her way. She probably wanted to compliment me on my wardrobe, Jane thought, watching Thea Reynolds lean forward to kiss Michael's cheek. More likely, it was Michael she was looking at, Michael she thought she recognized for that was the look Jane realized she had caught in the woman's eyes, a look that said I think I know you, but I'm not sure, help me out.

"It's been nice meeting you," Thea Reynolds was saying, not even bothering to sound sincere, so Jane knew she was speaking to her.

"You too," Jane mumbled, focusing on the woman's bright-red lips. Jane watched her recross the street and disappear into the American Bar and Grill. Her walk was as definite as the rest of her, the kind where the shoulders mimic the movement of the feet, sometimes preceding them.

"She's a nice woman," Michael said, resuming their walk, pulling Jane along beside him.

The remark required no comment, and Jane offered none.

"And an excellent doctor," he added, obviously not needing her participation in the conversation. "She started taking eating disorders seriously when most doctors were dismissing them as just another female indulgence."

Just another female indulgence, Jane thought, smarting at the phrase, realizing they had stopped again.

"I thought we'd go in here for a few minutes," Michael was saying.

Jane looked up a large flight of stairs to a curved expanse of floor-to-ceiling windows, trying to zero in on the large black lettering that identified the name of the store. OLIVER'S, the letters proclaimed, then in smaller print she was barely able to make out because it kept jumping up and down, FINE JEWELERS FOR OVER FIFTY YEARS. What the hell were they doing here? "Michael, I can't." She felt his hand on her arm, pulling her up the stairs. "I'm too tired. I can't do it. I just want to lie down."

"Just a few more steps."

"I don't think I can make it."

"We're almost at the top. Atta girl."

Her feet found the top of the final step, although the muscles in her legs continued their climb, cramping and uncramping to the rhythm he had established. "What are we doing here?" she asked, too tired to separate the words, so that they emerged as one—wharewedoinher?

"I told your friends I was going to buy you a new wedding band, and that's just what I'm going to do," he said, tapping the bag of money under his arm. "I just happen to have a few dollars with me."

"Michael, no, you shouldn't. It's not right," she protested, wondering why he didn't just simply divorce her and be done with it.

"I promised you diamonds, and I always keep my promises."

"Diamonds?" What possible use had she for diamonds? Hadn't he been talking, as recently as last night, about putting her in an institution? And hadn't she been giving serious thought as to sparing him the trouble?

Suicide, she thought, hearing the word echo in her brain. Suicidesuicidesuicidesuicidesuicide. When had the thought first occurred to her? When had it begun to feel like the obvious solution to all their problems?

It was becoming increasingly clear to her that Michael would never abandon her. Even if he had her committed, he would continue to visit her regularly, continue to call her his wife. Even now, he was directing her toward the jeweler's counter, determined to buy her a new wedding band, as if reinforcing his commitment to her. Was it fair that they should both be committed? she wondered, and almost laughed.

No, as long as she remained alive, Michael would never be free of her. He would still live in hope that one day she would recover, that their marriage would be saved. The only way he would be free, the only way he would be forced to go on with his life would be if she were dead. It was that simple. It was the least she could do.

It would be easy enough. She knew where he kept the medication. All she had to do was take a few too many of those lovely white pills. If that failed, there was always her friendly neighborhood kitchen knife. Or she could throw herself through one of the stained-glass windows on the second floor of their home, impale herself on the unicorn's horn. Oh, she had plenty of alternatives. Where there's a will, there's a way, after all, she remembered, the expression reaching out to her from another life.

"Jane." Michael beckoned her toward the counter, drawing her tightly to his side. "Do you see anything that you like?"

"Michael, I don't need . . ."

"Do it for me," he said, and the man behind the counter laughed. When he laughed, his wavy blond hair and large tortoiseshell glasses bounced along with the sound.

"First time I've heard that one," he said, glancing at Jane sideways in a way that suggested it was painful to greet her head-on. "Most wives drag their husbands in here kicking and screaming. Is there anything specific I might be able to show you?" the man, who introduced himself as Joseph, asked.

"We're looking at wedding bands," Michael told him.

"A wedding. How lovely."

Jane could see Joseph mentally questioning the wisdom of Michael's choice of brides.

"We have a large selection of wedding bands. Perhaps you have something specific in mind . . ."

"Diamonds," Michael said simply.

"Diamonds," the jeweler repeated almost reverently. "A lovely word, don't you think?" He laughed, causing his hair and glasses to bob up and down, and Michael joined in the gaiety. Jane didn't laugh, or even smile. No sense of humor, she knew Joseph was thinking. Why is this good-looking, obviously intelligent man hitching himself to this humorless drone who wears midi blouses and has no appreciation for the finer things in life? "Were you thinking of a diamond solitaire or an eternity band?"

Eternity, Jane thought. Eternityeternityeternityeternity.

"Well, since we've already been married for eleven years," Michael was saying, as the jeweler nodded his condolences, "I think an eternity band sounds just the thing. What do you think, honey?"

Jane thought: eternity. Eternityeternityeternityeternity.

"Can we have a look at some?"

"Of course." Joseph unlocked the glass case in front of him and deposited a trayful of diamond wedding bands on the counter in front of them. "Would you care to sit down?" he asked, snapping his fingers for his assistant, who promptly produced a chair for Jane, into which she immediately fell. "Is your wife all right, Mr.? . . ."

"Whittaker. Dr. Whittaker, actually. Jane's been a bit under the weather lately," he elaborated, "but she's getting better now."

"I'm sorry to hear she's been ill," the jeweler announced, "and happy to hear you're on the mend," he continued, suddenly addressing Jane, who was busy silently repeating the phrase "under the weather," thinking it a wonderful expression, wondering where it had originated.

"What do you think of any of these, Jane?"

Jane forced herself to look over the hope-filled black velvet tray. The diamonds twinkled back at her like a series of miniature stars, trapped and securely fastened in bands of platinum and gold. Some had no bands at all, their stars invisibly melded to one another as if by magic. She was past the wonders of magic. She was undeserving of stars and eternity.

"They're very nice," she muttered.

"I should hope so," Joseph said, clearly flustered by her attitude. "These are all first-quality gems."

"What about this one?" Michael asked, lifting a band of medium-sized round diamonds from its slot. "I rather like this one."

"An excellent choice," the jeweler concurred. "One of our finest."

"Try it on," Michael urged Jane.

"I don't think so, Michael."

"Perhaps she might like this one better," Joseph offered, holding out a ring whose diamonds were in the shape of tiny hearts.

"Which do you prefer, Jane?"

Jane said nothing. What was the point? She merely offered her hand for Michael to slip the ring on her finger. What difference did it make which ring he chose? It was all the same thing. Would he bury the ring along with her?

"It's a little big," Michael said, slipping the ring back and forth along her finger.

"We can easily fix that. Here, why don't I size her finger?"

He took her hand and measured her finger for the appropriate size. "A five and a half!" Joseph exclaimed. "A bit on the thin side." He looked over his stock of eternity bands. "I don't seem to have anything made up in that size, at least not in the size of diamonds you're looking at. We *do* have something where the diamonds are a little smaller . . ."

"I like the larger size," Michael told him, "assuming they're of good quality."

"We only sell good-quality gems, Dr. Whittaker, I assure you."

"Well, I think it's between these two, don't you, darling?" Michael held both diamond rings in front of her eyes. "Which one do you prefer?"

Jane closed her eyes, turned her head.

"Maybe your wife would prefer something in another stone. I have some beautiful emeralds or rubies . . ."

"No, diamonds," Michael told him. "I think we'll go with the hearts, as you suggested. Only in the correct size."

"We can do that easily."

"How soon can we have it?"

"Say one week from today?"

"Sounds great. What do you think, honey? A week from today okay with you?"

"I think I need some fresh air," Jane whispered, although, in truth, it was much more comfortable in the air-conditioned store than it was outside. But she needed to get out of this place, away from the gray carpeted walls and black tiled floors, away from the wavy blond hair and tortoiseshell glasses, away from the high-quality gems, trapped like fireflies in a jar.

"Why don't you wait at the top of the steps?" Michael suggested, and Jane understood he knew that she lacked the strength to run away. "I can finish up in here."

"My assistant will help you," Joseph offered, as a long-haired young man ushered Jane toward the door. "I'll have him keep an eye on her," she heard him say as she stepped outside. Then, "I'll need a deposit."

"No problem," Michael said as the door closed behind her.

Jane immediately lowered herself to the concrete step, her head in her hands. Poor Michael, she thought. Poor, sweet Michael. Always trying to cheer her up, always trying to make things right again. Using the money she had stolen from their joint checking account to buy her a diamond eternity band! The ring would be ready next week. By that time, she'd hopefully have no need of a diamond eternity; she'd be in an eternity of her own making. An eternity she deserved. Would she be reunited with her mother and daughter in such an eternity? Or had special space been reserved for murderers like herself?

She looked up to find a woman staring at her from the bottom of the stairs. It was the same woman she had seen earlier, the one who had looked at her with unsure eyes when they had passed each other on the street.

"I'm sorry," the woman said immediately, climbing up a few steps and stopping. "Aren't you Mrs. Whittaker? Emily's mother?"

The name elicited a gasp from Jane's mouth.

"I'm sorry," the woman repeated, "I didn't mean to startle you. I thought I recognized you before, but I wasn't sure. You look a little different. Are you Mrs. Whittaker?"

Jane nodded without speaking.

"I'm Anne Halloren-Gimblet," the woman said, introducing herself, as Jane tried to see the name in her mind. "You probably don't remember me, but our daughters were in the same class together. I was on that field trip where you slugged that old geezer with your purse."

Halloren-Gimblet, Jane repeated silently, wondering where people got such names.

"Anyway, I always meant to call you and tell you how much I admired you. I felt so guilty at the time. I mean, I just stood there while that man pushed into our kids, and I didn't have the guts to do anything—well, none of us did, except you. And then we all just sort of stood around and did nothing. I wanted to phone you, but I never seemed to get around to it. You know how it is, you mean to do something, but if you don't do it right away, it doesn't get done." She paused, as if waiting for Jane to absolve her.

But Jane said nothing. Halloren-Gimblet, she thought.

"So," the woman continued, stretching forward to shake Jane's limp hand, "I'm telling you now that I thought you were wonderful, and if anything like that ever happens again, I won't let another six months go by before I get in touch." She let go of Jane's hand and backed down the steps onto the street. "Bye," she said, hesitating for a few seconds at the bottom, then walking away as Michael stepped out of the shop.

"Who was that?" he asked.

"Some woman with a funny name who thought she knew me," Jane answered, her voice a monotone.

"And did she?"

Jane shrugged as Michael helped her to her feet and led her down to the street. Something the woman had said gnawed at the base of her brain like a mouse chewing on a piece of rope, but she knew that it would require all her concentration to recover the conversation, and she was too tired. Ultimately, what difference would it make? Instead she devoted her energy to putting one foot in front of the other, the woman's name repeating silently inside her head with each step, like the sound of a train chugging along a track. Anne Halloren-Gimblet it said. Anne Halloren-Gimblet. Anne Halloren-Gimblet. Anne Halloren-Gimblet.

Annehallorengimbletannehallorengimbletannehallo-rengimblet.

24

JANE AWOKE WITH A START FROM A DREAM IN WHICH she had been chasing Emily through a never-ending maze of bushes. Michael stirred beside her but didn't wake up, so Jane laid her head back on the pillow and waited for sleep to reclaim her, soon feeling the familiar tug of unconsciousness creeping through her muscles.

In the next instant, she was in a large department store, Emily at her side. Together they approached the counter, Jane holding a plastic laundry bag containing a dress she wished to return. "This dress is stained," she informed the clerk, who wore a baby-pink ribbon in her flaming-red hair.

"We don't accept bloodstains," the young woman told her, rubbing her fingers against the blue fabric. "Besides, you bought this dress six months ago."

"There's a lifetime guarantee."

"There are no guarantees."

Jane looked around for her daughter and discovered she had disappeared. "Emily," she called, "where are you?"

And suddenly she was standing in front of an open grave, peering down through the darkness at Emily. The child sat paralyzed with fear as bright-colored cobras danced before her, their hoods extended, their fangs exposed. Seeing them poised, about to strike, Jane threw herself into the snake pit on top of them.

"No!" Jane screamed, lurching up in bed, waking Michael, who immediately wrapped her in his arms and began rocking her gently back and forth.

"It's okay," he was saying rhythmically. "It's okay. It was just a dream."

Jane said nothing. Michael's gentle rocking reinforcing the image of snakes swaying in the pit.

"Do you want to talk about it?"

Jane shook her head. What was there to talk about? She'd lost her daughter only to find her in a grave filled with vipers. But there was more, Jane realized, leaning forward and resting her arms against her knees. Something more.

"I'll get your medication," Michael said, pushing himself out of bed and heading for the bathroom.

Something more. What?

Jane sought to recapture her dream before it faded away, starting in the department store, going over her conversation with the saleswoman, hearing her protest that six months had passed. Six months, Jane thought. What was so significant about six months?

And then she remembered the woman on the steps by the jewelry store on Newbury Street. Anne Halloren-Gimblet, she repeated silently, almost by rote. Anne Halloren-Gimblet had said something about six months. What?

"Here. Take these." Michael's hand held out two white pills, slightly different in shape from the Haldol she was used to taking. When had he changed her medication? She took the pills from his hand, examining the slight varnish of their coating. If not Haldol, then what? Thorazine? What difference did it make? she asked herself, her answer for everything these days. With her other hand, she accepted the glass of water he held toward her.

What exactly had Anne Halloren-Gimblet said to her? Something about being on the field trip where Jane had slugged the man with her purse, that she thought Jane was terrific, feeling guilty that she hadn't told her sooner.

"If anything like that ever happens again, I won't let another six months go by before I get in touch." Yes, that was it. "I won't let another six months go by before I get in touch." Six months? What did she mean? Did she mean anything, or was it just an expression?

"Take the pills, Jane. We can still get a few hours' sleep before we have to get up."

She needed more time. If she took the pills, she'd be a vegetable in minutes, and she needed those minutes to think this through. Her subconscious was desperately trying to tell her something. It had fought through her medication, snaked its way into her dreams, because it had something important to tell her. She just needed time to figure out what it was.

Jane popped the pills onto the top of her tongue, then raised the glass to her mouth. But as the water neared her lips, she tilted the glass forward, watching the water spill out across the front of her nightgown, feeling the wet cotton plaster itself against her breasts.

"Jesus, Jane, look what you're doing." Michael grabbed the glass from her hand and wiped at her wet nightgown with the end of the bed sheet. "It's okay," he told her, returning to the bathroom as she numbly surveyed the mess she had made. "I'll get you some more."

The second he was gone, Jane spit the pills from the tip of her tongue into the palm of her hand, then buried them under the mattress. "I won't let another six months go by before I get in touch."

Six months.

Michael returned with a fresh glass of water, which Jane brought carefully to her lips, throwing her head back to mimic the swallowing of pills and then carefully downing the contents of the glass. Michael deposited the now-empty glass on the table beside her, crawled back into bed, and fitted himself around her protectively.

Jane lay awake, trying to steady the beating of her heart. What did everything mean? What had Anne Halloren-Gimblet meant when she said that next time she wouldn't let another six months go by? If only six months had passed since their last meeting, then the field trip she was referring to, the field trip where Jane had slugged some ignoramus with her purse, had taken place within the past school year. But that was impossible if Emily had been killed in a car accident over a year ago.

Unless Emily hadn't been killed. Unless she was still alive.

Jane felt her body twitch with excitement, felt Michael's hands tighten their grip around her waist. But if Emily hadn't been killed, if she was still alive somewhere, why had Michael told her she was dead? If Emily was alive, that meant that *everything* Michael had told her was a lie.

There was one way to find out, she decided. "Michael," she whispered, sliding out of his embrace, "when we get up, I'd like to visit the cemetery."

The cemetery was located a short distance away in that section of Newton known as Oak Hill. Michael had protested that he saw no purpose in going there, that it would undoubtedly only upset her further, but she had been adamant, and in the end, he had given in. What difference did it make? she could almost read in his expression.

A big difference, she had answered silently. All the difference in the world. The difference between letting herself be buried alive in a pit of vipers or starting to fight back, to find out what the hell was going on, to getting her daughter back.

Michael pulled the car into the open gates of the Mount Pleasant Cemetery, and brought it to a halt in the small, unpaved parking lot. He turned off the ignition and sat for a minute, studying her. Jane lowered her head, feigning great fatigue. It wouldn't do to arouse his suspicions at this point, although, truth to tell, she *was* tired, could have slipped easily, carelessly, into sleep. "Are you sure you can manage this?"

"It's something I have to do," she told him honestly.

"Okay. If it gets too tough, tell me. We'll come right back to the car." He opened his door and got out, coming around to her side and helping her out, leading her up the proper pathway, his slow steps mimicking her own.

Why *was* she doing this? she suddenly asked herself, fighting the urge to run back to the car. Michael was cooperating; he obviously had nothing to hide. So what was the point of the exercise? Anne Halloren-Gimblet had a careless way with words, that was all. Six months was nothing more than a figure of speech. She could just as easily have said six years.

"It's down this way," Michael said, pointing across the neat rows of tombstones, each surrounded by half moons of summer flowers. Jane walked carefully between the rows, her eyes scanning the unfamiliar names, absently noting the years of birth and the dates of death. BELOVED WIFE; LOVING FATHER; TO KNOW HIM IS TO LOVE HIM; A STRONG SPIRIT, A GENTLE HEART; LOVED BY ALL WHO KNEW HER; A LOVING SON, TAKEN TOO SOON; a simple WE MISS YOU.

Michael came to a stop in front of a tombstone carved out of rose-colored granite. "Here it is."

Jane held her breath, looked toward it. EVELYN LAWRENCE, the inscription read. LOVING WIFE, BELOVED MOTHER AND GRANDMOTHER. BORN MARCH 16, 1926. DIED JUNE 12, 1989. IN OUR HEARTS, YOU LIVE FOREVER.

So her mother really *was* dead, she thought, kneeling down and running her fingers against the chiseled stone. Dead at age sixty-three. Jane's fingers probed the deep lines of the letters. She closed her eyes and leaned her head against the headstone, cool despite the morning heat, longing for her mother to reach up from beneath the grave and draw her down beside her, comfort and reassure her, never let her go.

DIED JUNE 12, 1989, Jane thought, opening her eyes, and staring at the letters, making sure she was reading them correctly. But she had found herself walking the streets of Boston on June the eighteenth, a week later than the one-year anniversary. What did that mean?

Michael had said she was very insistent about visiting the cemetery on the exact anniversary of her mother's death, that she wouldn't even wait for the weekend so that he might join her. That meant either that she had disappeared a full week earlier than Michael had claimed or that he had simply been using her mother's tragic death as a convenient springboard for the rest of his lies.

Jane looked toward the grave on her right, holding her breath, releasing it only after she absorbed the stranger's name: KAREN LANDELLA. BELOVED WIFE AND MOTHER, LOVING GRANDMOTHER AND GREAT-GRANDMOTHER. BORN FEBRUARY 17, 1900. DIED APRIL 27, 1989. LOVED BY ALL WHO KNEW HER. Uttering a silent prayer, Jane slowly turned her head to her left, her eyes digesting the words inscribed: WILLIAM BESTER, LOVING HUSBAND, BELOVED FATHER, GRANDFATHER AND BROTHER. BORN JULY 22, 1921, DIED JUNE 5, 1989. SORELY MISSED.

"Where's Emily?" she asked, barely able to speak.

Michael helped Jane to her feet. He was silent for several seconds, then turned, walking quickly among the rows of silent tombs. Jane had to force herself to follow him, afraid to look in either direction, terrified that she might see her daughter's name carved into one of these cold pieces of stone. Was it possible that all her suspicions were mere delusions, that Emily was really here?

"Michael?" she asked, stopping, supporting her weight against a tall gray monument, her knees knocking together more from fear than fatigue. Her eyes finished the question: Where is she? How much farther to go?

"Emily's not here," he said after a lengthy pause, and Jane had to grab the top of the tombstone with both hands to keep from collapsing.

"Not here?"

"We had her cremated."

"Cremated?"

"You couldn't bear the thought of putting her in the ground," he said, and his voice broke, making it impossible for him to continue for several seconds. "You were very adamant about it. So, we had her cremated, then scattered her ashes in the harbor at Woods Hole."

"Woods Hole?"

"By my parents' cottage." He looked into the sun, then down at his feet. "Emily always loved it there."

Jane allowed herself to be drawn into Michael's arms, feeling the steady rhythm of his heart, wondering whether he could sense the urgency beating in hers. Was he telling her the truth? Was it possible for anyone to lie this easily, this callously? Could he arrange his emotions as easily as he could rearrange facts? What kind of monster was she embracing?

She remembered the nightmare she had had on her first night back home: She and Michael poised at the edge of a large open field filled with poisonous snakes. She had turned to him for help only to find he had been replaced by a giant cobra. She shivered, felt Michael tighten his embrace.

Someone is walking over my grave, she thought.

"I think you should lie down for a while," he said, assisting her up the stairs.

"Is it time for my medication yet?" Jane asked, following him into their bedroom and sitting at the edge of the bed.

Michael checked his watch. "Half an hour. Why?"

"I thought maybe I could have it now. I'm feeling very low and I don't think I'll be able to sleep."

He bent over and kissed her forehead. "I don't think half an hour would do any harm." He pulled his shirt, sweat-stained from the heat, over his head, and dropped it in the clothes hamper on the way to his study. Jane watched his slender torso disappear down the hall, trying to corral her thoughts into a definite plan. Whatever she intended to do, she had better do it fast. She wouldn't have a lot of time.

Think, she admonished her addled brain. What are you going to do?

The first thing she had to do, she realized, hearing Michael going through his doctor's bag, was get in touch with Anne Halloren-Gimblet. Jane looked at the antique white-and-gold phone on the night table beside their bed. Sometime in the past few weeks, Michael had grown secure enough to return it to its rightful place. Whatever she did, she had to make sure that he stayed secure, that she did nothing to arouse his suspicions. Going to the cemetery had been risky enough. But she had played her part beautifully on the drive home, pretending not to have noticed the discrepancy in dates, bemoaning the fate of their beautiful child, crying on cue, blaming herself over and over, apologizing for the mess she had made of their lives, permitting him to shine in his starring role of understanding saint.

She watched Michael emerge from his study and walk toward her, his chest bare, shoulders slightly stooped. Could this handsome man, this revered mender of little children, really be so diabolical as to try to rob her of both her daughter and her sanity? Was it possible? Why? What did she know? Goddamnit, what had she found out, only to block out?

"Here," he said, coming back into the room and standing over her. She took the pills from the palm of his hand and popped them into her mouth while he went to get her a glass of water.

As soon as he left her side, she spit the pills into her hand and dropped them into the breast pocket of the white T-shirt she was wearing. Michael was back at her side almost immediately, standing so that his hips were level with her head. Taking the glass from his hand, she mimed swallowing the pills, then returned the glass to him, expecting his retreat. But instead, he stayed where he was, swaying slightly in front of her. Suddenly his hand was in her hair and he was pulling her head gently toward him, so that the side of her mouth brushed against the front of his pants. He groaned.

"Oh, Michael," she whispered, "I don't think I can. I'm so tired."

"It's okay," he was saying. "It'll be okay." His hands moved to the bottom of her T-shirt.

"No," she protested weakly as he pulled it over her head.

"It's okay, Jane," he repeated. "Everything will be all right." He tossed her shirt to the floor, lowering himself to his knees and kissing her bare breasts. A small cry escaped Jane's lips as she saw one of the pills tumble out of the pocket of her T-shirt and roll to a stop a short distance away from Michael's feet. "It's okay, darling," he whispered, mistaking her cry for passion, and easing her back so that she was lying down and he was lying beside her.

This can't be happening, Jane thought as he removed the rest of her clothing, then his, guiding her hand where he wanted it to go. She felt him stiffen beneath her touch. "That's right," he was saying, "touch me there. That's right. You're doing just fine." Jane felt him prod her legs apart, felt him enter her, move gently back and forth inside her. This isn't happening, she thought, denying the weight of his body on hers. This isn't happening.

He kissed the sides of her face, her eyes, her mouth, her neck, the tops of her breasts, all the while pushing back and forth into her. His strokes gradually grew more insistent, less gentle, almost harsh. He began pounding into her, his body slapping angrily against hers. And then she felt his hand at her head again, except that this time any pretense of gentleness was gone. His fist yanked at her hair so hard that her head was lifted off the pillow, forcing her eyes open. He was staring at her with a look of pure rage. "Damn you," he cursed, as his body shuddered to a climax. "Damn you for what you've done."

Jane's first thought was that he had seen the pills tumble out of her pocket, knew she had deliberately deceived him, but he pulled out of her and disappeared into the bathroom without once looking at the floor. She immediately catapulted off the bed and flung the pills beneath it, then fell back against her pillow, gasping for air. Her head spun; the room danced. It was several seconds before everything settled and she heard the shower running in the bathroom.

"Now!" she said out loud, needing to hear her voice, to reassure herself that what was happening was real, not some awful nightmare, not another insane flash from the past. She grabbed the phone and quickly dialed 411, waiting for the operator's voice.

"What city please?"

"Newton," Jane whispered, hearing Michael in the

shower. She'd try Newton first. It stood to reason that if Anne Halloren-Gimblet's daughter attended Arlington Private School, she probably lived in the area.

"Name, please."

"Halloren-Gimblet. With a hyphen." Jane pronounced the name carefully, then spelled it, all the while keeping her eyes glued to the bathroom door, her ears tuned to the sound of the shower.

"Do you have an address?"

"No. But there can't be very many."

"I have no listing for anyone of that name."

"You have to."

"I can try the new listings, if you'd like."

"All right. Wait—wait—"

"Yes?"

"Try Gimblet," Jane suggested.

"Do you have a first initial?"

"No." Damn this woman, Jane thought, then heard Michael's voice, "Damn you," he had said. "Damn you for what you've done." What did he mean? If her daughter was still alive, then what exactly had she done?

"I have that number for you," the operator said before being replaced by the automatic voice of a computer.

"The number is five five five—six one one seven," the computer told her in cheery, even tones, then repeated the information as Jane committed the numbers to memory.

She concentrated all her energy on dialing the correct number, ignoring the stickiness between her legs, the throbbing at the side of her temple where Michael had grabbed a fistful of her hair. Why had he chosen now, of all times, to make love to her? He hadn't touched her in weeks. Why now? Had his grief overwhelmed his better judgment? Had he simply needed to be with her? Was he as confused as she was?

Was he saying good-bye?

The phone was ringing. She held it tight against her ear, convinced that Michael would be able to hear it above the running of the water.

"Please answer," she whispered into the receiver. "Please answer quickly."

The phone kept ringing. Three rings, four, then five.

"Anne Halloren-Gimblet, please be home."

But if she was home, she wasn't answering her phone. Seven rings, eight, then nine. On the tenth ring, Jane dropped the receiver into its carriage, conceding defeat. She'd have to try again later.

Suddenly, she lunged forward, almost knocking the phone from the table in the process, and grabbing the receiver to her ear, redialing 411.

"What city, please."

"Newton. The name is Gimblet. G-i-m-b-l-e-t. Can you tell me if the correct address is Fifteen Forest Street?"

"I show no one by that name on Forest Street," the operator told her, as Jane had known she would. Fifteen Forest Street was the address of Michael and Jane Whittaker. "I have a Gimblet at One twelve Roundwood."

"That's it. Thank you." Jane almost kissed the receiver before dropping it back into its carriage. Her hand was still on the phone when she became aware the water from the shower had stopped running. How long ago? Had Michael come out of the shower in time to hear her on the phone, overhear what she had said?

Her hand jumped from the phone as if she had just touched something hot. She quickly crawled beneath the covers and gathered the comforter around her, closing her eyes as the bathroom door opened and Michael emerged.

She felt him approach the side of the bed, his body still damp as he leaned forward and pushed some stray hairs away from her forehead. "Sleep well, darling," he said.

25

JANE LAY AWAKE ALL NIGHT, COUNTING THE HOURS till morning. When Michael got out of bed at six-thirty, she feigned sleep, debating whether to try Anne Halloren-Gimblet's number again while he was in the shower, then rejecting the idea as being unnecessarily risky. She had the woman's address. After Michael left, she would somehow escape Paula's watchful eye and make her way over to Roundwood. She'd worry about exactly how when the time came.

"Jane," Michael was saying, and she realized with a mixture of dismay and alarm that she must have dozed off. "I'm going to the hospital now. Paula's downstairs. She'll bring you your breakfast and your medication in a few minutes."

She nodded, pretending to be too sleepy to open her eyes, peering at him through mere slits.

"I'm in surgery all day," he was telling her, "but I've made an appointment for us to see a Dr. Louis Gurney at the Edward Gurney Institute at five-thirty this afternoon. Jane, can you hear me?"

She mumbled something she hoped was sufficiently incoherent, but her heart was racing. The Edward Gurney Institute was a private psychiatric hospital a good two-hour drive away.

"I've asked Paula to help you pack some things, in case Dr. Gurney wants you to stay a few days. Jane, do you hear me?"

"I'm supposed to pack," she muttered, not lifting her head from the pillow.

"No, Paula will do the packing. You might just want to suggest what you'd like to take." He bent over and kissed the side of her cheek. "I've scheduled my surgery back-to-back so that I can be home early to take you there myself."

"Have a good day," Jane told him with exaggerated awkwardness, following him with her eyes as he walked to the bedroom door. Hell, she thought, two can play this game. "I love you," she called weakly after him, watching him come to an abrupt halt.

What are you feeling right now? she demanded silently. How does it make you feel when the woman you've turned into a zombie with your drugs and your lies, the woman you're planning to lock away in some private psychiatric hospital miles away from anywhere and anyone, tells you that she loves you? Does it make you feel sad or does it make you feel smug? Does it make you feel anything at all?

Michael turned around, returning to the bed and resting on one knee, burying his head against the tangles of her hair. "I love you, too," he said, and Jane felt his tears drop against her cheek. "I've always loved you."

In the next instant, he was gone, and Paula was at her side.

"Ready for your breakfast?"

Jane propped herself up in bed, staring at the dour young woman and wondering what exactly her role was in all this. Was she an unwitting dupe or a willing accomplice? Jane opted for the unwitting dupe, sensing that the girl simply believed whatever Michael told her, did whatever he asked. In that way, Paula was really no different from anyone else. Whenever Michael spoke, everyone listened. Everyone believed. He was the man, after all; she, the little woman. He was the respected surgeon; she was his hot-tempered wife, forever chasing causes, unhinged by a tragic accident that had taken place over a year ago, not yet recovered. Poor Jane. Poor Michael. It would be better for everyone concerned if she were placed in the Gurney Institute, where she'd no doubt get the care she deserved.

Would she? Would she get what she deserved? Or would Michael?

"I'm not very hungry," Jane told Paula. "I'll just have coffee."

"Michael said no coffee today."

"Why not?"

"He said orange juice is better for you."

"All right. Orange juice," Jane agreed, her mind already on other things. "I was wondering if you could bring in a straight-backed chair from the other room. My back's been killing me."

"I guess that can be arranged."

Paula swiveled on her heel and left the room, her beige skirt spinning after her, her long braid bouncing as she walked. Jane swung her feet out of bed, noted she was wearing one of Michael's old shirts, vaguely recalling Michael having slipped it over her shoulders sometime last night. It frightened her that even though she hadn't taken any medication in twenty-four hours, it was obviously still very much present in her system, that she had to wage a constant battle against the lethargy that threatened to overtake her, that she could still drop off to sleep without any warning. Please let me stay awake. Please let me get out of here and over to Anne Halloren-Gimblet's in one coherent piece.

Paula returned carrying the high-backed antique chair from the guest bedroom. "Any special place you want it?"

"Right there is fine," Jane told her. Paula deposited the chair in front of the mirror-covered closets, then hurried downstairs to pour Jane's orange juice. When she returned, Jane was sitting in the tall, straight-backed chair.

"Well, you're very ambitious today."

"Michael thought I should get out of bed."

"Yes, he told me I should get you out today, that you needed a little exercise."

"To tire me out."

"What?"

"As long as I don't get too tired out," Jane said, correcting herself.

"Here." Paula handed Jane the orange juice and three little white pills.

"Three?"

"That's what Michael said."

Jane put the three pills on the tip of her tongue, then waited for Paula to turn away. She didn't.

"Michael said to make sure you took them."

Jane felt the pills beginning to dissolve in the natural moisture of her tongue. Had she aroused Michael's suspicions or was he simply taking no chances? Surreptitiously, she slipped the pills to the side of her mouth, then brought the juice to her lips.

"Uh uh," Paula said, stopping Jane's mouth with her hand, forcing her jaws apart, and peering inside. "Swallow the pills, Jane. No fooling around."

Jane had no choice. She swallowed the pills. Afterward, Paula checked her mouth.

"Good girl."

Jane felt herself panicking. Three pills, for God's sake. And she had swallowed them. How long before they started to work? At best, she probably had only a few minutes left of clear thought. She had to get out of here. She had to get these pills out of her system before they started to work. "I don't feel well!" she shouted with an urgency that brought Paula immediately to her side.

"Do you think you're going to throw up?" Paula asked, helping Jane off the chair and guiding her toward the bathroom.

"Oh, God, what's happening?" Jane cried. "You have to help me. You have to help me. Please—don't leave me."

"I'm right here."

Jane waited until Paula was leaning over the toilet bowl beside her before suddenly shifting her weight and heaving Paula sideways against the Jacuzzi, watching her lose her balance and tumble backward inside.

"Jesus Christ, not again!" Paula shouted as Jane bounded out of the bathroom, slamming the door after her, and grabbing the straight-backed chair she had secured for exactly this purpose. Carefully she lodged it underneath the door handle, preventing Paula's escape. "What the hell do you think you're doing?" Paula demanded, banging on the door. "This is crazy, Jane. Where do you think you're going?"

Paula's protests followed Jane down the hall toward the guest bathroom where Jane hurled herself against the toilet bowl and immediately thrust her fingers down her throat. She retched, feeling her body convulse in a series of mostly dry heaves, her eyes stinging and her throat burning with the acrid taste of freshly squeezed orange juice. Had she managed to throw up the pills? Had she gotten them all out of her system? She couldn't be sure. She'd have to move fast.

Returning to her room, she pulled a pair of dark green walking shorts over Michael's pale blue shirt, ignoring Paula's loud demands to be released, and fled the room, racing down the steps and into the kitchen, looking for Paula's purse. She finally located it in the front hall closet, and opened it, grabbing the keys to Paula's car. Then she stuffed the few dollars Paula's wallet contained inside one of her pockets and ran toward the rusty gray Buick that sat parked in her driveway.

The car was unlocked, and Jane scrambled behind the wheel, hitting her knee against the dashboard as she stuck the key in the ignition. She groaned with a mixture of pain and relief when she heard the engine turn over, then backed expertly out of the driveway onto the street, not sure whether to turn left or right, choosing right, then searching through the glove compartment for a street map when she came to the first stop sign.

Like everything else about the old car, the map was falling apart. It was torn and dirty and missing one of its panels, but Jane was able to scan the list of street names and locate section C3 where Roundwood was supposedly located. The street proved more elusive to find, existing as it did among a plethora of little red and blue lines, black letters, and a variety of strange symbols that the legend at the bottom of the map informed her stood for such things as county lines, city limits, aqueducts, and transportation systems. By the time she found the small curve marked ROUNDWOOD, the letters were beginning to blur and her mouth was becoming dry. She told herself it was only her nerves, and stepped harder on the gas, feeling the car jerk forward, sputter, and die. "No!" she screamed, restarting the engine, once again hearing it turn over. "Thank you," she whispered, realizing she had to proceed with caution.

Roundwood was in the other direction, in the village of Newton Upper Falls, a few miles away. Following the map, Jane took Columbus Street to Hartford, turned west on Boylston to Hickory Cliff Road, then turned left at the first street. ROUNDWOOD, she read with relief, wishing the street sign would hold still, knowing it wasn't moving. She proceeded slowly down the street, her eyes peeled for the right number. "There it is!" she shouted, inadvertently slamming on the brakes. The car bounced, made a weird choking noise, then stopped. "Fine," Jane said, not bothering to restart the engine or bring it closer to the curb, propelling herself out of the car toward the white Victorian-style house that was not unlike her own. Anne Halloren-Gimblet, please be home.

She stumbled up the front walk, tripping over her feet not once, but twice, before reaching the front door, leaning against it, praying silently for strength. She waited for several minutes before realizing she had forgotten to ring the bell, then rang it several times in rapid succession, simultaneously banging her fists against the wood.

"Just a minute," came a woman's voice from inside. "Hold your horses."

The white door opened several inches. Anne Halloren-Gimblet peeked out. "Yes?"

"Anne Halloren-Gimblet?" Jane asked, unable to separate the words, feeling like a police lieutenant.

"Yes." The woman's voice was trepid, as if she wasn't sure.

"It's Jane Whittaker. We talked the other day on Newbury Street. Our daughters were in the same class?" She stated this as a question, sensing the woman's reluctance to let her inside. "I wonder if I could come in and talk to you for a few minutes."

"My God, I didn't recognize you!" Anne Halloren-Gimblet exclaimed, backing into her front hall and motioning for Jane to enter.

"I was in a hurry to get out this morning," Jane said, realizing how disheveled she must have looked, trying to tuck Michael's outsized shirt inside her walking shorts. The cuffs of his sleeves dangled below her fingertips, and Jane realized for the first time that she wasn't wearing a bra, that her hair was uncombed and her teeth unbrushed. "I must look a sight."

"Would you like a cup of coffee? I think I still have some brewing."

"I'd *love* a cup of coffee."

Jane followed the woman, who was neatly dressed and fully made up, into the burgundy-and-white kitchen. Anne Halloren-Gimblet was tall and slender and maybe a few years older than herself. Her hair was blond and held in place by a black hair band that spelled out the word PARIS in rhinestone letters. She was trying hard not to stare at Jane, but was obviously puzzled by her surprise visit, and possibly even a little frightened. "How do you take it?"

"Black. Lots of caffeine."

Anne Halloren-Gimblet smiled, pouring Jane a large mugful of coffee, and motioned for her to sit down. Jane pulled up a chair by the kitchen table, and gulped her coffee, drinking it down and then asking for more.

"I didn't realize how thirsty I was," she said as the woman patiently refilled her mug.

"Jane . . . you don't mind if I call you Jane, do you?"

"I'd like that . . . Anne," she ventured, and the woman smiled. She doesn't know why I'm here, Jane thought. She doesn't know what to make of me, and she's too polite to ask. She'd like me to state my business, drink my coffee, and leave.

"Jane, are you all right? You didn't look well when I saw you the other day, and—"

"I look worse now, I know."

"It just doesn't look like you. Not that I know you very well," she added.

What do I tell her? Jane wondered, watching the woman's light-green eyes narrow in concentration. Do I risk telling her the truth? That she probably knows me better than I do, that I have no idea who I am, that my husband has been lying to me, feeding me drugs, is about to have me committed. That I escaped by locking my housekeeper in the bathroom, then stealing her car. That I'm here because of a careless remark she made on the steps of a jewelry store on Newbury Street, that I need to know whether my daughter is alive, and that she, who doesn't know me very well, is the only person I can trust to tell me the truth. Is that what I tell her?

"Is there any more coffee?" Jane asked sheepishly, and Anne Halloren-Gimblet emptied the remains of the morning pot into Jane's mug. Jane watched the woman purse, then unpurse, her lips.

"I'm sorry," Anne said finally. "I hope you won't think I'm being rude, but do you mind my asking what you're doing here?"

"I wanted to apologize," Jane said quickly, deciding against revealing the truth, at least for the time being. "For being so rude the other day."

"You weren't rude."

"I was, and I'm sorry. I haven't been feeling too well lately."

"I'm sorry to hear that."

"It's some sort of weird virus. Nothing contagious," Jane rushed to assure her.

"There are a lot of weird things in the air these days," Anne remarked as Jane nodded vigorously. "But you didn't have to make a special trip over here, especially when you're not feeling too well."

"I'm fine now." Jane looked around the spotless

kitchen, trying to look fine, straining to sound casual. "Where's your daughter?"

"Daughters," Anne Halloren-Gimblet corrected, emphasizing the final *s* with a prolonged hiss. "They're at day camp. The bus just picked them up a few minutes before you arrived. Bayview Glen. Do you know it?"

Jane shook her head, recognizing that it felt only loosely attached to her neck, and praying that three mugfuls of coffee would be enough to keep her awake.

"What about Emily?"

Jane felt automatically unhinged at the sound of her daughter's name. "She's at her grandparents' cottage," she stammered, wondering if this was true, and trying not to be overwhelmed by the fact that they were referring to her daughter in the present tense.

"We had a cottage when I was a little girl. I loved it. I used to collect tadpoles and garter snakes."

"Snakes?"

"I was a real little tomboy, though you'd never know it to look at me now." Anne laughed, and Jane recognized that it was more a nervous laugh than one of mirth. I'm making her nervous, Jane thought. "Yes sir," Anne continued, "I was out in the muck every day with the guys. My mother couldn't get me into a frilly dress to save her life. She despaired I'd ever turn out right. Can you imagine, especially looking at it from today's perspective, having a mother who *didn't* want her child to go to university, whose highest ambition for her daughter was that she be a stenographer? Do they even have stenographers anymore?" Anne Halloren-Gimblet shook her head, then carried on, uncomfortable with silence. "When I got married, my mother almost had a fit when I told her I was going to keep my maiden name. She insisted it was as good as living in sin. So, I compromised, went for the hyphen. I was the first woman on my block to hyphenate my last name. Unfortunately, I married a Gimblet."

Jane laughed, but the sound only seemed to make the woman more fidgety. Anne Halloren-Gimblet rose to her feet. "I'm afraid I'm going to have to cut this visit short.

I have an appointment in half an hour," she stated.

An obvious *confabulation*, Jane thought. "I realize I should have called first," she said promptly, "but I found myself in the neighborhood, and thought I'd take a chance you were still home."

"You were out early." Anne Halloren-Gimblet checked her watch.

Jane glanced at the clock on the wall oven. It was barely eight-thirty in the morning. No wonder the woman is nervous, she thought. "I needed some fresh air," Jane told her, standing up, gravitating toward a large piece of Bristol board on the wall opposite the refrigerator. It was covered with snapshots of two very blond little girls, each possessed of the same face though one was taller than the other. "They could be twins," she remarked.

"Everyone says that, much to Melanie's dismay. She points out that she's three years older than Shannon, and at least three inches taller."

Jane quickly deduced that it would have been the younger of the children who was in Emily's class. "So, how did Shannon enjoy school this year?"

"Oh, she can take it or leave it. Actually, I think that if I gave her the choice, she'd never go anywhere. She's a real homebody. How about Emily?"

"She likes school," Jane said, her heart pounding. Was it possible that Anne Halloren-Gimblet simply hadn't heard about her daughter's death? "Have you been on any more field trips lately?"

"I went with them on the tour of the fire department, but everybody was disgustingly well behaved, so it was no fun. I missed you." Her posture became immediately self-conscious, her shoulders folding in on themselves, the fingers of one hand playing with the fingers of the other. "I really have to start getting ready. . . ."

Jane followed Anne into the front hall, knowing she had yet to discover anything conclusive, wondering what she should say or do next. She had to know for sure that their daughters had been classmates *this* year, not last, that as recently as six months ago, she had accompanied their class on a field trip to Boston, that her daughter hadn't been killed in any car accident over a year ago, that Emily was still very much alive.

"Do you think the girls will be in the same class again next year?" she ventured, staring into the living room.

"Well, they've been in the same class since kindergarten," Anne answered, opening the front door. "I'm sure they'll keep them together."

Jane ignored the open front door and proceeded into the living room, passing over the family photographs on the mantel to concentrate on the series of familiar classroom pictures that rested on the closed top of the baby grand piano.

"It's hard to believe how fast they grow, isn't it?" Anne remarked, coming up behind her and looking over Jane's shoulder.

Jane's eyes scanned the classroom photographs, easily singling out her daughter as she moved from junior to senior kindergarten to grade one. And then another picture, one with which she wasn't familiar, one she hadn't seen before.

"I think this one's my favorite," Anne said, lifting the grade two photograph from the top of the piano. "All those great big smiles and no front teeth."

Jane grabbed the picture from the woman's hands, hearing a cry of surprise escape her lips.

"What are you doing?" Anne gasped, fear in her voice.

Jane ignored her, her eyes racing across the children's faces for her seven-year-old daughter, finding her in the back row, her shoulders now slightly stooped like her father's, her smile shy and closed-lipped. "Oh, God, oh, God," Jane cried. "She's alive. She's alive!"

"Mrs. Whittaker," Anne began, instinctively reverting to formalities, "would you like me to call your husband for you?"

"My husband?" Jane's eyes shot to hers. "No! Whatever you do, please don't call my husband."

Anne's arms reached out to reassure her. "Okay, okay, I won't call him. It's just that I'm concerned. I'm not sure I understand what you're doing here, and something's obviously very wrong. Can you tell me what it is?''

Jane could barely get the words out, she was crying so hard. ''Everything okay now. My baby's alive. Emily's alive!''

''Of course she's alive.''

''She's alive. I didn't kill her!''

''Kill her? Mrs. Whittaker, I really think I should call your husband. . . .''

''He told me she'd been killed in a car accident, that I was the one driving, that she died in my arms. . . .''

''What? When? Good God, when did this happen?''

''But she isn't dead. She's alive. She's right here.'' Jane's finger poked at the photograph. ''She was in Shannon's class.''

''Yes, she's alive,'' Anne Halloren-Gimblet told her, and Jane noticed a strange softening of the woman's voice, as if she had decided there was no sense to be made from any of this and therefore no sense in trying. ''She's alive and she's beautiful. So tall. I couldn't believe how tall she'd grown just in the last couple of months. She'll soon be as tall as Miss Rutherford.''

There was a second of absolute silence.

''What did you say?'' Jane asked.

Anne Halloren-Gimblet's voice was so low that it was barely audible. ''I said she'll soon be as tall as the teacher.''

''Their teacher's name is Miss Rutherford?''

A note of fear returned to Anne's voice. ''Didn't you know that?''

''Pat Rutherford?''

''I think so, yes.''

''I had an appointment with Emily's teacher!'' Jane whispered, her amazement audible.

''Yes, well, we all had our private interviews at the end of the school year.''

''I didn't have an affair with Pat Rutherford.''

''I beg your pardon?''

''It was Emily's teacher.''

"Mrs. Whittaker, I'm out of my depth here. I think you need some help."

"I need to use your phone." Jane pushed past the woman and ran into the kitchen, grabbing the white phone off the wall. Anne was right beside her, although she maintained a safe distance between them. Jane could read the fear in her eyes and wished she could say something to reassure her, but she knew that whatever she said would only make it worse. "I need to get in touch with Pat Rutherford. Do you have her home number?"

Anne shook her head. "And the school will be closed for summer vacation," she offered, as if anticipating Jane's next question.

Jane held the phone firmly against her chest. *Pat Rutherford, R. 31, 12:30*, she saw scribbled before her. Pat Rutherford, she repeated silently. Emily's teacher. Not some man with whom she'd been having a sordid little affair.

Had she had any affairs at all?

She quickly punched out 411, answering "Boston" before the obligatory question could be asked. "I need the number of Daniel Bishop. Thank you."

She jotted down Daniel's home number and his work number on a piece of pink note paper, the bottom of which was covered with drawings of sand castles and star fish, the top of which proclaimed LIFE IS A BEACH. Rechecking the clock on the wall oven, Jane decided to try Daniel at home first. "You don't mind, do you?" she tossed over her shoulder at Anne, who hovered in the doorway, poised for flight. If Anne offered any objections, Jane didn't hear them.

Daniel answered the phone on the fourth ring, just as Jane was about to hang up. "Yes?" No *hello*. Just, *yes*? As if he had been expecting her, as if they were already halfway into their conversation.

"Daniel?"

"Yes?" A note of impatience, as if she had interrupted him at something important.

"It's Jane Whittaker."

"Jane. Jesus, I'm sorry. I didn't recognize your voice.

I was just on my way out the door. What's up? Is anything the matter? I tried calling a few times but your housekeeper—"

"Daniel," she began, then stopped. What the hell, she decided, there was simply no easy way to say it. "Daniel, did we ever have an affair?"

Jane heard a slight gasp from the doorway, and imagined that the look on Anne's face mirrored the one on Daniel's.

"What?" Daniel's voice was a laugh.

"I'm serious, Daniel. Did we ever have an affair?"

There was a second's pause. "What's going on here, Jane? Is Carole on the extension?"

"It's just me, Daniel, and I have to know."

"I don't get it. What are you talking about?"

"It's too long a story to go into now. Trust me, Daniel. I'll tell you everything another time. Right now, I need a simple yes or no. Did we have an affair?"

"No, of course we didn't."

Jane closed her eyes, cradling the phone against her ear as if it were an infant.

"God knows I was game," Daniel continued softly. "I think you knew that, but it was never an issue. Jane," he said, as if he suddenly realized he shouldn't have to be explaining any of this, "this conversation doesn't make any sense. Are you in some kind of trouble?"

"Danny," Jane began, "do you know where Emily is?"

"Emily? No. Why?"

"Michael has been hiding Emily from me."

"What?"

"Please don't say anything. Nothing will make any sense to you, and I don't have time to explain right now. I have to find Emily."

"But, Jane—"

"But if something goes wrong, if they find me before I find Emily, and they succeed in putting me away somewhere, please know that I'm not crazy, Daniel. Please try to help me. I'm not crazy. You know that."

"Jane—"

Jane hung up the phone, turning her attention to her reluctant hostess.

"Look," Anne preempted before Jane could say anything, "I don't know what's going on here. And truth to tell, I don't want to know. Either you're crazy or you're in the kind of trouble I don't need, so I'm asking you nicely to please leave. Now."

Jane smiled her understanding and her gratitude, reaching over to pat the woman's arm, but Anne recoiled, and Jane withdrew the gesture, quickly exiting through the still-open front door. Immediately, she heard it close behind her, felt Anne's eyes on her back as she ran toward Paula's car and climbed inside.

She had to find Emily. Michael had her stashed away somewhere. Where? At camp? At his parents' cottage? With friends? Where? And why? Why, for God's sake?

Who could she go to? Who could she ask?

There were her friends: the Tanenbaums, Diane Brewster, Lorraine Appleby, Eve and Ross McDermott, the others whose names she knew but not their phone numbers or their addresses. It would take too long to try to track them down. She didn't have that kind of time. Paula would force her way out of the bathroom sooner or later. She'd find some way to notify Michael. He'd get to Emily, make sure she couldn't be found.

There was only one person who might be able to tell her where Emily was, she realized, fighting with the car's engine, trying to get it to turn over. And that person hated her guts. Hated her because she was convinced Jane had slept with her husband. Because that was what Michael had told her, what he wanted her to believe.

She had to see Carole.

"I'll find you, Emily," Jane muttered, twisting the key in the ignition again and sighing with relief as the engine sprung to life. "I'll find you."

26

PAULA'S CAR STALLED ONCE AT A STOP SIGN AND ONCE at a red light before coming to a complete standstill in the middle of Glenmore Terrace, a few blocks from her home. "No, not now. Don't die on me now. I need you. I need you to help me find my baby."

But the car, like an unresponsive lover, was indifferent to her pleas. She twisted the key in the ignition until she smelled gas and knew she had flooded the engine, that there was no way that the car would restart. "Goddamn you!" She pounded her fist against the steering wheel, then abandoned the car where it stood.

A car behind her honked in protest, but Jane didn't look back, continuing on foot in the direction of her home. It was probably just as well that she didn't approach her house in Paula's car. She would be less easy to spot on foot. Assuming anyone was looking for her. Had Paula managed to break free? Had she managed to call Michael and get him out of surgery? Were they waiting, in ambush, for her now?

Jane crossed the street in a diagonal, feeling the sun hot against her head, then rounded the corner onto Forest Street, still several blocks away from her house. She could sneak between the houses, she thought, trying to force her disparate thoughts into a coherent plan, possibly steal into Carole's backyard without being seen. Was it possible? she wondered, feeling suddenly sick to her stomach and supporting herself against the trunk of a huge weeping willow tree as she threw up almost three mugfuls of coffee.

Her knees turned to strings of spaghetti, and she fell into a crumpled heap on the grass beside the tree. Oh, no, she pleaded at the cloudless sky. Not now. I can't fall apart now. I'm too close. Too close to finding my child. Too close to discovering the truth. Don't let me collapse now.

She imagined Michael and Paula running toward her down the street. Poor thing, she heard Michael whisper to a group of concerned onlookers. She's crazy, you know. Mad as a hatter, she heard Paula confirm. She felt their hands on her arms, wrapping her into a waiting straitjacket, leading her into a nameless van headed nowhere. She saw her little girl disappear forever.

With fresh resolve, Jane forced herself to her feet, ignoring the cramping in her stomach, the pinpricks in her arms and legs, the growing numbness creeping up her neck. If anyone is looking out their windows, she thought, they probably think I'm drunk. Poor Dr. Whittaker, she could hear them cluck. Such a cross he has to bear.

Was anyone watching her? She strained to see a curious face peering through parted curtains, to catch a pair of eyes making a hasty retreat from behind a bay window. She saw no one, felt no one's gaze upon her. I am invisible, she determined, applying a child's logic to calm her nerves—if I can't see them, they can't see me, she repeated as she neared Carole's house. She ducked behind a black car parked on the street just in case her determination failed to convince others.

Her own house looked quiet. The front door was closed. There was no telltale stirring at any of the windows. There were no cars parked in the driveway. Everything looked peaceful, even serene.

Two houses away from Carole's home, Jane picked up speed. Reaching the garage, she lowered her head and ran toward Carole's backyard, her heart racing faster than her feet, her stomach somersaulting ahead of her, her head hanging on for dear life. She attached herself to the side of the house like a clinging vine, pressing her back against the wooden slats, finally collapsing beside a trellis covered with peach-colored roses.

And what would she say to Carole? That Michael had lied to her, lied to both of them. That she and Daniel had never had an affair. That she needed to know what had happened just before she disappeared. That she needed to know where Michael was hiding Emily.

"Who are you and what are you doing in my backyard?"

The voice was harsh, intrusive. Jane looked up to see Carole's father bearing down on her, his ghostly white legs sticking out from beneath a pair of pink Bermuda shorts that had probably once belonged to Carole. The shorts hung on the old man's frail form as lifelessly as clothes on a hanger. His skin was the color of skim milk.

"It's me, Jane Whittaker," she whispered, realizing that she didn't know his name. "Your neighbor?"

"What are you doing in my rosebushes?"

Jane slid up the side of the trellis until she was almost standing. She felt something grab hold of her and twisted her head around, expecting to see Paula or Michael, discovering instead that a thorn from one of the roses had attached itself to Michael's shirt. She gently extricated herself from the thorn, pricking her finger nonetheless, and watched with fascination as a small drop of blood formed a neat raised circle at her fingertip.

"You hurt yourself?"

"I'm okay."

"I'm Fred Cobb," he told her, as if they had been exchanging introductions. They shook hands, the old man carefully avoiding the blood on her finger, even as it made a trail toward her palm. "You here to sell me something?"

Jane looked warily around to ascertain whether they were being watched. "No, Mr. Cobb," she said, wondering if Carole was at home. "I'm not selling anything. I'm here to talk to Carole."

"What about?"

"About my daughter. Emily?"

"Don't know anybody by that name."

"She's seven years old. Very pretty. Long brown hair. You've probably seen her playing in the front yard. Your grandchildren used to baby-sit for her."

"What'd you say her name was?"

"Emily."

"Don't know anybody by that name," he repeated, and Jane wondered why she was wasting her valuable time.

"So, you wouldn't happen to know where she is right now," Jane stated. A long shot.

"Oh, I know where she is."

"You do?"

"She's inside the house."

"The house? Emily?"

"Emily? I don't know any Emily. This is Carole's house."

Jane released a deep breath of air. "Carole's inside the house?"

"Where else would she be? What are you doing here? Are you selling something?"

"Mr. Cobb," Jane began, moving closer to him, watching him take several steps back, "can you tell me whether anyone else is in the house? Does Carole have any visitors?"

"Carole doesn't have a lot of visitors since Daniel left. She was never very good at making new friends."

Jane nodded understanding, both at what he was saying and at her predicament. Clearly she would get no help from Fred Cobb.

"I'm hungry," the old man stated abruptly. "I think I'll tell Carole to make me some lunch." He immediately shook his head, as if he had thought better of it. "No, she'll tell me I just had breakfast."

"I'd be happy to ask her for you, Mr. Cobb," Jane

told him, watching a smile extend the wrinkles at his mouth.

"Would you do that? You're very sweet. Carole hates for me to pester her. She gets very angry. Sometimes she threatens to have me put away."

"I'm sure she doesn't mean it, Mr. Cobb."

"I'm sure she does. But I don't care. Let her put me away, if that's what she wants. It's all the same to me." He made a dismissive gesture with his hands. "Aw, what would you young people know about being put away? You're all convinced you're going to live forever. And stay young doing it." He laughed. "I wish I could be here fifty years from now, see how all you folks make out. That'd be good for a chuckle or two. Anyway, I'm hungry."

"I'll ask Carole about getting you something to eat."

"Why don't you let him ask me himself?" Carole's voice cut through the warm air like a knife slicing through a layer of meringue. J. R. began barking beside her. "Quiet, J. R."

"Damn dog. You gonna put him away too?" Fred Cobb teased.

"There's a leftover cheese sandwich in the fridge, if you want it, Dad."

"What kind of cheese?"

"The kind you like."

"Don't mind if I do," he said with exaggerated politeness, and excused himself to go back into the house as Carole turned her attention to Jane.

Jane's back pressed against the trellis, the rose thorns pricking her flesh through Michael's shirt. She imagined her back stained with little freckles of blood, saw the tiny red spots grow and merge until they formed a large red ball that seeped through the front of her shirt, leaving it covered with blood. "I need to know," she told Carole calmly, "exactly what happened the day I disappeared."

"Why don't you come inside?" Carole offered. "We can talk there."

* * *

"How are you feeling?" Carole asked, once inside her living room.

"I'm not sure," Jane answered honestly, carefully perusing the room, which was painted white and carpeted blue. No one was hiding behind the mismatched furniture. Only dustballs were visible beneath an old wing chair. A large crystal vase filled with mostly dead irises sat neglected in the middle of a dirt-streaked glass coffee table.

"My cleaning lady quit," Carole said, following Jane's eyes. "I can't seem to be bothered finding a replacement. Any suggestions?"

Jane thought of Paula locked in her bathroom, wondered if Carole had somehow found out. She shook her head. "There's so much I have to say to you, I'm not sure where to begin."

"I'm not sure we have *anything* to say to each other."

"I know you think that Daniel and I had an affair. . . ."

"And you're going to tell me you didn't. Spare me. Daniel's already called."

"Daniel called? When?"

"Just a little while ago. He said he had a very strange phone call from you, that you asked him whether the two of you had had an affair. Not knowing about your extremely delicate condition," she continued sarcastically, "he was having great difficulty understanding the nature of your question. I told him that while it must certainly be a blow to his ego to realize just how forgettable his lovemaking really was, it would probably be better for all concerned if we could all put that sordid little detail out of our minds, the way you've managed to do so successfully."

"But Daniel and I didn't have an affair."

"So he told me."

"But you don't believe him?"

"Why would I believe anything he tells me at this point?"

"Why would you believe Michael?" Jane asked in reply.

"What?"

"It was Michael who told you that Daniel and I had an affair, wasn't it?"

"What does it matter?"

"It matters because it's Michael who's been lying."

"Why would Michael lie to me?"

"He's been lying to all of us."

"I repeat, why?"

Jane shook her head, feeling dizzy and lowering herself into the faded cream-colored wing chair. "To drive a wedge between us. To keep you away from me. To keep me from finding out the truth."

Carole made a half turn, as if she was about to leave the room, then sat down instead on the sofa opposite Jane. "The truth about what?"

"I don't know."

"Naturally."

"Something happened just before I disappeared. Something so awful that the only way I could deal with it was by forgetting it. By forgetting everything." She looked to the ceiling. "Carole, how did my mother die?"

"What? Hold on here, Jane. These transitions are too fast for me. I'm having a hard time keeping up."

"How did my mother die?"

Carole took a deep breath and lifted her hands into the air, as if she had decided to give in and go along with whatever Jane wanted. "She was killed in a car accident last year."

"Don't lie to me," Jane admonished, watching the look of shock that crossed Carole's face.

"I'm not the one who tells lies around here, Jane. For Christ's sake, why would I lie about something like that?"

"My mother was killed in a car accident?"

"I thought Michael told you all this."

"He did."

"But you didn't believe him?"

"You didn't believe Daniel," Jane reminded her.

"The circumstances are a little different."

"Where did the accident take place?"

"Not far from here. You mother was on her way into

Boston. Some man went through a stop sign, plowed right into her. You were devastated. You'd been very close."

"Who else was in the car?"

"What do you mean, who else?"

"Who was driving my car?"

"Your mother was driving. You were originally supposed to go with her, from what I understand, but you got called to some meeting at Emily's school, so you had to cancel out. Something like that, I think."

"I wasn't driving?"

"I just told you, you had a meeting."

"Michael told me that I was driving."

"What? Don't be absurd, Jane. Why would Michael tell you something like that?"

"He told me that I was driving, and that Emily was also in the car."

"Emily?"

"He told me that she was dead, that she died in my arms."

"Jane, this is crazy talk."

"But my daughter isn't dead, is she, Carole?"

"Of course not. Of course she isn't dead."

"Where is she, Carole?"

Carole rose to her feet. Jane noticed a new expression creep into her eyes, one she hadn't seen before, and realized it was the same look that had transformed Anne Halloren-Gimblet's otherwise soft features. It was fear, Jane understood, forcing herself to her feet, blocking Carole's exit from the room.

"Where is she, Carole?" she asked again.

"I don't know."

"I don't believe you."

"I don't know where she is."

"Where is Michael hiding Emily?"

"Jane, listen to yourself. Listen to what you're saying. Does it make any sense? Daniel told me you said something about Michael hiding Emily. But why would Michael have to hide Emily anywhere? Listening to you now, looking at you, I'd have to say that if he is hiding her, it's to protect her. It's for her own good."

"No. It's for Michael's own good!"

"Jane . . ."

"He told me she was dead, Carole. He told me that I killed her, that she died in my arms. How do you explain that? Is he trying to protect *me* too?"

"He *is* trying to protect you, Jane. That's all he's ever tried to do."

"By lying to me? By telling me my daughter is dead? That I'm the one responsible? For God's sake, Carole, listen to me. Do you think I'm making this up?"

"I think you're delusional. . . ."

"Delusional?"

"I think you really believe the things you're saying. . . ."

"Delusional? That's one of Michael's words, isn't it? *Delusional.*" She spat out the word as if she had just bitten into something unpleasant. "Michael told you I was delusional, didn't he?"

"Jane. . . ."

"Didn't he?" The look on Carole's face was all the confirmation she needed. Jane shook her head in wonder. "He's really covered all the bases, hasn't he? He's got everyone convinced that I'm crazy, that I suffered some kind of breakdown after my mother's death, and even though I seemed all right to my friends, at home it was a different story altogether. I was always flying off the handle; I threw things; I was violent!" Jane began twisting in small circles, trying to put everything she had learned in order. "And it all makes sense because everybody knows what a terrible temper I have. Everyone has a Jane-and-her-famous-temper story to tell. And how can I fight against him when I'm up to my glassy eyeballs in drugs, so that I can barely get out of bed or speak for all the drool that dribbles down my chin, when I'm so depressed that my happiest thoughts are of suicide?

"Don't you see? He lied to me; he lied to everyone. He told you I slept with your husband; he told me it was just one of many sordid affairs. He made it so that even when I did start putting things together, even when I started twigging to his lies, he could just tell everyone that I was delusional! He didn't tell me my daughter was dead—I imagined it! I'm even crazier than he thought!

"Oh, it's perfect. It's so perfect. Who's going to argue with him when he says I have to be put away? And once I'm institutionalized, and this is the real beauty of his plan, once I'm safely locked away in some snake pit with a fancy name, even if I do eventually get my memory back, even if I do remember the truth, they'll just take that as further proof of my insanity. More delusions they can jot down in their overstuffed reports."

Carole's eyes filled with tears. "But why, Jane? Why would Michael want to do any of those things?"

"Because I know something. Because something happened that I either saw or heard or found out about, something that Michael didn't want me to know about, that he doesn't want me to remember."

"What?"

"You tell me."

Carole's eyes closed in defeat. "I don't know anything, Jane."

"Tell me what happened the afternoon I disappeared. Tell me what happened that day."

Carole paused a minute before speaking. "Michael said you were very upset. . . ."

"Don't tell me what Michael said," Jane interrupted angrily. "Tell me only what you saw."

"I saw you pull into your driveway," Carole began reluctantly. "It was early in the afternoon. My father was having a nap. It was cold that day and I'd been puttering around in the flowers trying to keep myself busy, so when I saw you come home, I thought I'd go over and see if you felt like making me a cup of tea or something, just an excuse to visit. But as soon as you got out of the car, it was obvious that something was very wrong. You were hysterical. That's the only word I can think of. You were muttering, yelling at yourself. I couldn't make anything out. I wasn't even sure you saw me, although you looked right at me. I asked you what was wrong, but you just pushed past me into the house and slammed the door.

"I'd never seen you like that before—oh, I'd seen you angry, I'd seen you lose your temper—but this was different. You weren't even coherent. You weren't yourself. I didn't know what to do. I just stood there for a few minutes, and then I decided to call Michael. I told him what had happened, and he said he'd come home right away. I went back to my house.

"About fifteen, twenty minutes later, I saw Michael's car pull up and Michael rush inside. Well, by this time, I was curious as hell, wondering what was going on. So I kept watch at the window. And a little while later, your front door flew open and out you ran. You didn't close the door and you didn't go to your car. You just ran off down the street.

"I waited a few seconds and then I went over to your house. The door was open but I knocked anyway. When nobody answered, I got a little concerned. I called out Michael's name a few times, and then I heard this moaning, so I went into the sunroom. Michael was on the floor, just starting to get up. His head was bleeding. The floor was spotted with blood.

"I grabbed him, got him into the bathroom, tried to clean him up a little bit, finally drove him to Newton-Wellesley Hospital, where they stitched him up. On the way, he made me promise to tell the doctors he'd fallen and hit his head. He said that you were suffering from some sort of breakdown, that it had been building for some time, that he'd explain everything to me later."

"And then?"

"That's it. You know the rest. You didn't come home. He decided you were probably ashamed and embarrassed, that he'd give you a few days to calm down. He was sure you'd be home once you had a chance to cool off. He called me after he heard from the police, told me what had happened, that you'd lost your memory, that he was going to bring you home."

"When did he tell you about Daniel?"

"Later. And he made me promise not to confront you

until after you were better. We all know how that turned out.''

Jane took a deep breath, then released it, hoping to expel the dizziness she felt creeping over her. ''Carole, please, you have to tell me where Michael is keeping Emily.''

''I don't know,'' Carole told her, and Jane understood she was telling the truth. ''I assumed she was with Michael's parents.''

''So they really do have a cottage?''

''Yes. In Woods Hole.''

Jane knew that Woods Hole was a small strip of land at the tip of Cape Cod, but she had no recollection of ever having been there. It was a drive of several hours and Jane decided that if she had to, she would drive there blind, worry about locating the Whittaker cottage once she got there. ''I need to borrow your car,'' she said, balancing herself on the side of the chair, wondering if she was in any condition for such a prolonged trip.

''What?''

''Let me have the keys to your car.''

''Jane, don't be silly. I can't let you have my car.''

Jane watched Carole's eyes travel to a spot just past her head. She saw Carole's shoulders stiffen and her mouth form a silent gasp, at the same moment she felt someone moving behind her.

''Who is this woman?'' Carole's father asked from the doorway.

Jane thought at first that he was referring to her, then realized, as strong hands gripped the sides of her arms, that the woman to whom Fred Cobb was referring was Paula, that she had somehow escaped her small prison and made her way over. Or more likely, she had been here all along.

''After Daniel called this morning, I went over to your house,'' Carole explained as Paula locked Jane's arms to her sides, ''because I thought something might be wrong. I found Paula in the bathroom.''

''What's going on here?'' Carole's father demanded.

"Carole, who are these people? Are they here to sell us something?"

"No, Dad. Why don't you go upstairs and take a nap?"

"I don't want to take a nap. I just got up."

Jane let her body go limp. "That's a good girl," Paula told her, not relaxing her grip. "There's really no point in struggling."

"Have you called Michael?" Jane asked.

"He's in surgery. I left a message."

So, there's still time, Jane thought, bending at the knees as if their weight was no longer strong enough to support her. Paula's arms sagged to hang on, and in that split second, Jane threw her shoulders back, knocking Paula off balance, giving her just enough time to break out of her forced embrace. "No!" she screamed, hearing Carole's father cry out in alarm as her hand grabbed for the large crystal vase on the coffee table and swung it over her head. Flowers flew into the air, then scattered; dirty water dribbled onto her shoulder and the carpet below; Paula recoiled; Carole shook her head, her father whimpering, hiding his eyes.

And in that second, Jane remembered exactly who she was and what she had tried so hard to forget.

27

JANE WITNESSED HER MEMORY UNFOLD AS IF SHE WERE watching a movie from front row center, the only person at a private screening. She saw the curtains part and the screen fill up with Technicolor images almost too bright for her eyes to stand. Her voice assumed the role of narrator, allowing Carole and Paula to share her lonely vision.

It was morning. Michael and Emily sat at the kitchen table, Michael reading the newspaper and sipping the last of his coffee, Emily dawdling over her cereal, letting her spoon drip milk across the tabletop. Michael peered over his paper to gently scold her. Jane saw herself wipe away the milk and cart the breakfast dishes to the dishwasher, filing each dish in its proper slot.

"So, what have you got planned for today?" Michael asked, as Jane became one with the image before her.

"I have an appointment with Emily's teacher at twelve-thirty," she reminded him.

"Problems?"

"I don't think so. Just parent-teacher interviews they always do at the end of the year. I guess they'll tell me how well she did and what class she'll be in next year, that kind of thing." She patted the top of Emily's head.

Emily acknowledged her touch with a shy smile. "What room are you in again, honey?"

"Room thirty-one." Emily's voice was quiet. Jane noticed that it seemed to get quieter every time she spoke.

"I don't know why I have such a hard time remembering that. I better write it down." She pulled a small piece of note paper from the pad by the telephone and jotted down *Pat Rutherford, R31, 12:30*. "What do you say I make one of my special chocolate cakes when I get back?" she asked, hoping to get a wide smile from her daughter and feeling foolishly proud when she succeeded.

"Can I help?" the child asked.

"Sure can." Jane opened the refrigerator, looked inside. "I better get some milk and some eggs while I'm out." She jotted down *milk, eggs*. "You all ready for school?"

"I can drive her today," Michael volunteered.

"Great."

"Better wear a jacket," Michael called as Emily ran into the front hall. "They're calling for very cool temperatures. That goes for Mommy as well," he said, kissing Jane on the nose.

"Yes, Daddy. Thank you, Daddy."

"You're welcome, smart ass."

"I love you."

"I love you, too. Call me after the interview with Emily's teacher."

"Okay."

Jane followed Michael into the front hall, helping her daughter into her pink-and-yellow-flowered windbreaker. "Have a good day, sweetie-pie." She knelt down, immediately feeling her daughter's arms swoop around her neck, and was loath to break out of the embrace. "I'll see you at school in a few hours." Jane stood up, finding herself in Michael's arms.

"That looked too good to pass up."

She kissed him. "Have a good day."

"Call me."

She stood by the door watching as Michael's car disappeared around the corner, feeling incredibly blessed, thinking that the only thing missing from their lives was the presence of another child. She almost laughed at the irony. Two years on the pill after Emily's birth to make sure that there would be a three-year separation between children, only to have absolutely nothing happen when she stopped. Tests had revealed Michael's sperm count was very low, that Emily had been even more of a miracle than they had originally perceived. It was doubtful such a miracle could occur a second time. So, one child it would be. Thank God, Jane thought, as she thought often, that she had been able to present Michael with such a perfect, beautiful, bright little girl.

Her teacher had sounded worried. Well, maybe not worried exactly, Jane told herself as she headed upstairs to change her clothes. "I'm sure it's nothing to be concerned about," Pat Rutherford had told her, causing her instant concern. Jane had said nothing to Michael. Why should two people worry about something that was nothing to be concerned about?

Jane fished through her closet for something suitable to wear, choosing a simple Anne Klein dress over several festooned with bows and ribbons, dresses that Michael had selected when they went shopping together. He might be a brilliant surgeon, she thought, stepping into the blue Anne Klein, but he had rotten taste in women's fashions. Even his taste in negligees left a great deal to be desired, she thought, pushing the white cotton nightgown he had bought her last Mother's Day to the rear of the closet, never having had the heart to tell him she didn't like it.

She ran a brush through her hair, pulling it behind her and securing it with a jeweled clasp, pleased with her image in the mirror, her well-heeled-matron look, Michael would tease her, preferring her hair loose. She snapped on the simple gold watch Michael had given her for their tenth anniversary, gave her plain gold wedding band an absent twirl, then debated whether to tidy the place up a bit before she left the house. No, she'd let Paula do that tomorrow, she decided, frowning at the thought of the woman Michael had hired to clean the house. Paula had little sense of humor and no time at all for Jane. Jane knew Paula perceived her as a useless dilettante, a spoiled, pampered woman whose life was filled with everything hers lacked. And Paula was crazy about Michael. Even Jane's limited exposure to the overly earnest young woman had convinced her of that, although Michael, bless him, seemed totally oblivious to whatever Paula might be feeling for him.

How would she feel to discover that the two of them had been carrying on an affair? she wondered, then laughed the thought away. It was too absurd to even think about. Besides, Michael would never cheat on her, she was convinced of that. There was no point bothering herself over such unpleasant thoughts. They did both Michael and herself an injustice.

Jane went downstairs, grabbed her purse from the hall closet, and was about to leave when she remembered Michael's admonishment to take her coat. "Who needs a coat?" she asked out loud, opening the front door. "It's June, for God's sake." A cold gust of wind slapped her testily across the face. "It's freezing, for God's sake," she sputtered, returning to the hall closet and slipping her trench coat over her shoulders. "I guess Father Knows Best after all."

Jane spent the morning looking through stores in Newton Center. She thought about calling Diane for lunch, but didn't know how long her meeting with Pat Rutherford might take, so she decided to grab a quick sandwich alone before heading over to Arlington Private School. Why had Pat Rutherford scheduled a meeting at lunch hour? And why today? Hadn't the school calendar listed Friday, June 22 as parent interview day?

She probably can't get them all done in one day, Jane decided, pulling into the school parking lot and getting out of her car, checking the note in her pocket for the correct room. "Room thirty-one. Why can't I remember that? Oh, hell, and I forgot to get milk and eggs. What's the matter with me today?'' She realized she was nervous. ''What have I got to be nervous about?'' she asked herself impatiently, returning the note to her pocket. ''And why am I talking to myself? Somebody's liable to see me and think I'm crazy.''

She entered the school by the side door and quickly proceeded up three flights of stairs, locating room 31 at the far end of the photograph-lined hall. The door was open, and she poked her head inside. The room was decorated with children's drawings and large colorful cutouts of the alphabet. Brightly patterned paper mobiles hung at suitable intervals from the ceiling, and a hamster ran endless silent circles on the pinwheel in its cage by the window. All in all, it was a warm, friendly room that no doubt reflected the personality of its teacher. It was also empty. Jane checked her watch: 12:25.

She was always early. From the time she was very little, her mother had drilled into her the importance of being on time. To be late was to show disrespect for those waiting, her mother had said, though the woman was often late herself.

Jane located one of Emily's paintings on the busy wall—a field of flowers being watched over by a happy sun. If her mother had only learned to take her own advice. Then maybe she wouldn't have had to rush to go shopping before her return to Hartford. Maybe if she hadn't left it till the last minute, if she'd been driving just a bit slower, if she hadn't been running so far behind schedule. . . .

''Hello, Mrs. Whittaker.'' Pat Rutherford's voice was delicate, thin, like the woman herself. ''Have you been waiting long?'' She sounded nervous.

''Just got here.''

''Good.'' Pat Rutherford smoothed her long blond hair behind one ear with her fingers. A large silver loop earring popped into view. ''Thank you for agreeing to see me today. I hope it wasn't too much of an inconvenience.''

"No, not at all. Is everything okay with Emily's schoolwork?"

Jane was expecting a few quick words of reassurance, and was startled when the young woman hesitated.

"Is something wrong?"

"No," Pat Rutherford said unconvincingly, then, "Well, I'm not sure. It's what I wanted to talk to you about, why I asked you to come in today and not with the other parents on Friday."

"What is it?"

"Please sit down."

Jane tried to position herself comfortably in one of the small desk sets in front of Pat Rutherford's desk. Pat Rutherford did not sit down. She paced, occasionally leaning against her desk, her dark eyes unsure where to settle. "You're making me a little nervous," Jane confessed, wondering what the woman could possibly have to tell her.

"I'm sorry. I don't mean to be so tenative. It's just that I'm not sure how to say this."

"The direct approach is usually the best."

"I hope you're right." She paused. "Actually, I'm not even sure I should be talking to you at all."

"I don't understand."

"This is my first year teaching," Pat Rutherford explained. "I've never had to handle anything like this before, and I'm not exactly sure on the correct procedure."

"The correct procedure for what?"

"Normally, I think I'm supposed to report my suspicions to the authorities. . . ."

"The authorities? My God, what do you suspect?"

"But a friend of mine had an unpleasant experience when she did that—two police officers showed up, scared the kid half to death, the whole school was buzzing, the parents were incensed, and my friend almost lost her job. Plus, nothing changed."

"What are you talking about?" Jane sat poised at the end of the small seat.

"I love teaching. I don't want to lose my job. So after

thinking about it for a while, I decided that rather than go directly to the authorities, I'd speak to the school principal first."

"Mr. Secord?"

"Yes."

"What did you speak to him about?"

"I think Emily is being sexually abused."

The words, when they finally emerged, had the force of a dagger to Jane's stomach. She reeled forward, almost tumbling off the small seat. The edge of the desk stopped her, poking into her rib cage. Something was obviously wrong with her hearing, she thought, struggling to regain her composure. She couldn't possibly have heard what she thought she did. "What did you say?"

Pat Rutherford sank into the chair behind her desk. "I think Emily is being sexually abused," she repeated, the words no less deadly for having been repeated.

A gasp of air flew from Jane's lips. She felt her insides being expelled with each breath. It can't be, she thought, then again, no, it can't be. "What makes you think so?" she asked when she was able to find her voice.

"Well, I don't have any concrete evidence, and that's one of the reasons that Mr. Secord was adamant that I not call the authorities. As he pointed out on several occasions, I'm very new at this. There could be any number of reasons for Emily's recent behavior. Just that something tells me that this is it. Everything I've read. . . ."

"Has Emily told you she's been—" The words stuck in Jane's throat. "Sexually abused," she whispered, denying the words even as she spoke them.

"No," Pat Rutherford told her, and Jane sighed with relief. The woman was clearly mistaken, jumping to ill-considered conclusions because of something she had read. "But her behavior recently is consistent with a child who has been abused in this way."

"How so? What kind of behavior?"

Again, Pat Rutherford hesitated. "Well, she's become very quiet of late. She was always a very gregarious little girl, full of enthusiasm, always a smile on her face, and lately she's gotten very quiet. More than quiet, really. Almost sad. Have you noticed that at home?''

Jane had to admit that she had. ''Still,'' she protested, ''that hardly means Emily is being abused sexually.''

''If it were just that, I wouldn't think twice,'' Pat Rutherford concurred. ''There's more.''

Jane said nothing, giving Emily's teacher permission to continue with a nod of her head.

''At recess one day, I saw her in the kindergarten class playing with some of the dolls. That in itself isn't unusual. A lot of the kids like to go there to play with the toys. As long as they return everything to its proper place, there's no problem. But there was something about the way Emily was playing with two of the dolls that made me stop and watch. She didn't see me. She was totally caught up in what she was doing.''

''Which was?''

''She was touching them about the chest and between their legs, rubbing the dolls against one another.''

''Couldn't that be just normal childhood curiosity?'' Jane interrupted, feeling her anger rise. Surely this woman, this inexperienced first-year teacher, had not concocted this preposterous story based simply on childhood experimentation.

''Yes, it could. I thought of that. Obviously, I didn't jump to the immediate conclusion that she was being molested. I thought it was just as likely that she was mimicking behavior she had seen on television or in the movies.''

Jane shook her head. She had always closely monitored what Emily saw on television and accompanied her to the family-rated movies she thought appropriate for a child Emily's age. There had been no such sexual displays. Still, Emily had eyes. She was undoubtedly curious about her own body. And other children talked. ''She probably heard something from one of the other kids,'' Jane offered weakly, fighting to keep control when all she wanted to do was lunge across the desk and strangle Pat Rutherford for her unfounded accusations.

"Mrs. Whittaker, please understand that I'm not saying these things lightly," Emily's teacher said, as if reading Jane's thoughts. "I've been thinking about the best way to approach this for months. Mr. Secord reminded me many times that your husband is an important man in the community, that he's a major contributor to the school's fund-raising efforts. And I know how active you are in school affairs, what concerned parents you both are. That's why I didn't want to put you through any more than I had to. There may be a very logical explanation for everything."

"Everything? So far, I haven't heard much of anything. At least nothing that would make me jump to the conclusion that my daughter is being molested."

"There's more."

Jane held her breath.

"I might have let the whole matter drop except for what happened last week."

"What happened last week?" Jane's voice was a monotone.

"I walked into the class and there was Emily at the back of the room with another little girl. She had one hand on her shoulder, and the other on the little girl's breasts. . . ."

"This is silly. Two little girls touching—"

"It wasn't what Emily was doing so much as what she was saying."

"Saying?"

"She was whispering, 'You're so beautiful. You make me want to touch you because you're so soft and pretty.'"

"What?"

"I know those were her exact words because I wrote them down. I mean, it's not the kind of thing you hear children say to one another. Is it? It sounds like she's parroting an adult, something she's either overheard, or something someone actually said to her. I don't know. I *do* know this is a terrible shock for you, Mrs. Whittaker, and that you're probably very angry with me. I know I don't have any proof at all. But I've racked my brain trying to think what else would turn a normally outgoing child into an introvert, what would make a seven-year-old child so sexually aware. I just can't think of any other alternatives, unless—''

''Unless what?''

''Unless maybe she witnessed her baby-sitter with one of her boyfriends. Is that possible? Maybe she came downstairs when she was supposed to be sleeping, and found your baby-sitter on the couch with her boyfriend. Maybe she overheard what they were saying.''

Jane wondered if this could be possible. Both Carole's children baby-sat for her on a fairly regular basis. Was it possible that Celine had invited a boy over one night when they were out?

''Are there any teenage boys in your neighborhood?'' Pat Rutherford was asking. ''Maybe one of them approached Emily, tried to coax her into something. . . .''

Andrew Bishop's tall, gangly frame shoved itself front and center in her mind. Could it be that Carole's teenage son had tried to molest her little girl?

Jane jumped from her seat with such determination that she almost knocked it over. ''I have to talk to Emily.''

''I was hoping you'd say that.'' Pat Rutherford took a deep breath. ''Emily's having her lunch. I can go down to the lunchroom and bring her up, if you'd like.''

''Please.''

Pat Rutherford exited the room without another word. As soon as she was gone, Jane brought her fist down hard on the teacher's desk, causing a few papers to fly to the floor. ''Goddamnit, it can't be true,'' she repeated. ''It can't be. It just can't be.''

She began pacing back and forth in front of the desk in much the same way Pat Rutherford had paced only moments ago. How could this be? she asked herself. How could it be? There was only one answer—it couldn't. Pat Rutherford had reacted in an extreme manner to an undoubtedly innocent situation that would be cleared up in a few minutes.

A few minutes, she thought, thinking how a whole life could change in just a few short minutes. Here she was, a happy woman with a wonderful husband and a beautiful child, thinking she had the world by the tail, *having* the world by the tail, and in the next minute . . . in the next minute, her world was in ruins. All because of one simple sentence: I think Emily is being sexually abused.

No. It couldn't be.

Was it possible? Was it possible that Carole's children had somehow, possibly inadvertently, been responsible for Emily's strange behavior of late? Could Celine have brought a boyfriend over one night when she was babysitting? Possible, Jane supposed, but unlikely. According to Carole, Celine didn't date much, let alone have a boyfriend, and was constantly fretting that she never would. And what about Andrew? Could he really have been foisting himself on her child? The boy always looked as if girls were the last thing on his mind. He was much more interested in his basketball or his baseball. He never stood still long enough to pay much attention to Emily. Still, he was the logical suspect. Dear God, Jane wailed inwardly, fighting to keep the scream inside her. I'll kill him. I'll kill that damn kid!

"Mommy? Hi, Mommy." Emily ran forward. Jane fell to her knees and scooped her little girl into her arms. "Ow!" Emily protested, and Jane realized how hard she had been squeezing, instantly loosening her grip.

"How are you, dollface?"

"I'm fine. I gave Jodi my apple. Is that all right?"

"Sure, it's all right." Jane pushed a few hairs away from Emily's sweet face, then led her to a nearby desk. "Why don't we talk for a few minutes?"

From the doorway, Pat Rutherford indicated that she would be waiting down the hall. "That's not my desk, Mommy," Emily told Jane, leading her to the second row and proudly showing off her own desk and small attached chair.

Jane twisted her rear end into the small seat. "I need to ask you a few questions," she began, trying to steady her voice. "And I need for you to tell me the truth. Do you understand?"

Emily nodded.

"I won't get mad at you no matter what you tell me. Okay? I don't want you to be afraid to tell me anything. It's very important that you tell me exactly what happened."

"I will, Mommy."

"Honey, when Celine baby-sits, does she ever invite anybody else over?"

Emily shook her head, the hairs Jane had brushed away falling back over her forehead.

"She's never had a boyfriend over when Mommy and Daddy are away?"

"No. She always plays with me."

"What about Andrew?"

"He never baby-sits me."

"He did a few times last year."

"Oh, yes. I remember."

"But he never had anybody else come over," Jane stated.

"No. I don't think so."

"Has . . . has Andrew ever said anything to you that made you . . . uncomfortable?"

"I don't understand."

"Has he ever suggested . . . doing anything . . . that you didn't want to do?"

"I still don't understand."

"Has he ever touched you in a way that made you feel uneasy?"

Emily said nothing.

"Emily? Has Andrew ever touched you in a way that you didn't like?"

Emily's eyes shifted to the floor. Jane fought to stay in control. Inside, her thoughts were raging: I'll kill that bastard. I'll kill that bastard!

"Remember, honey, I need for you to tell me the truth. It's very important. I know that whatever happened isn't your fault. And I promise I won't be mad at you. I know that you're a sweet, beautiful thing and that you wouldn't do anything wrong, so I know that whatever happened isn't your fault, but this is very important, sweetie. I have to know. Did Andrew touch you in a way that made you feel uncomfortable? Did he touch you where it's private?" Jane shuddered. She couldn't believe she was actually speaking these words. Maybe she wasn't, she thought, clinging to the sudden, unrealistic hope that this whole unpleasant episode was nothing but a bad dream.

Jane heard the clock on the wall loudly ticking off the minutes. It seemed like an eternity before Emily spoke. "Not Andrew," she said.

"What?"

"Not Andrew," Emily repeated, refusing to look at her mother.

"Not Andrew? Who, then?" Jane ran through all the various alternatives in her mind. If not Andrew, then one of Andrew's friends perhaps. Or maybe one of the older boys here at school. Perhaps even a teacher. Maybe the dentist she had taken Emily to see several months earlier. Maybe even a stranger. Dear God, who?

"Who was it, Emily? Please tell Mommy. Who touched you, honey? Who made you feel uncomfortable? Please, sweetheart, you can tell Mommy."

Emily slowly lifted her gaze from the floor to look directly into her mother's eyes. "Daddy," she said.

Everything stopped: her heartbeat; the ticking of the clock; her breathing. All sound ceased, replaced by a loud buzzing in her ears. Surely she had only imagined what she knew she had heard. Surely her daughter was lying, supplying any name because her mother had forced her into this untenable position. She was making things up, trying to appease her mother, having been coached by her teacher. Surely, none of this was actually happening.

It was impossible. To think that the man to whom she

had been married for eleven years, this loving husband and respected pediatric surgeon, this goddamn pillar of the community, active in a myriad of charities, loved by virtually all who knew him, that this man could have been sexually abusing his own daughter—no, it just wasn't possible. Furthermore, it was ridiculous. This was the man in whom she had placed her total trust for almost a dozen years, a man who had stood by her through the worst of times as well as the best, who was always there to soothe her when she lost control, flew off the handle, let her emotions run away with her. That he could possibly molest their daughter was a betrayal of such magnitude, that her mind couldn't begin to take it all in. It was impossible. It couldn't have happened. It *hadn't* happened.

If it were true, she realized, watching as tears left a delicate trail across her daughter's cheeks, then where had she been hiding all these years? Who was she that she could have been so fooled? What did it say about her that her husband was not at all the man she'd thought he was? Who was Jane Whittaker if the man she had known all these years as her husband was not the man she'd thought he was at all? What kind of mother did it make her when she hadn't even suspected such abuse? That she'd had to be told by the child's teacher? What kind of person was she? Who was she that she could protect the environment but not her own child? Who was she?

She didn't know. She didn't know anything anymore.

"Are you mad at me, Mommy?"

Jane could hardly find her voice. "No, of course not. Of course I'm not angry at you, darling."

"Daddy made me promise not to tell you," the child continued without prompting. Jane wanted to place her hands over her ears and scream Enough! but it was too late now. She would hear the rest of what Emily had to say whether she wanted to or not. "He said it had to be our secret."

"I know, baby," Jane moaned. "I know." What did she know? she asked herself angrily. What did she know about anything? She swallowed the bile that was filling her mouth, then forced the next question out between quivering lips. "Where did Daddy touch you, sweetheart?"

Please don't tell me, she begged silently. Don't tell me. I don't want to know. I can't deal with it. I can't deal with any of it.

"Here," Emily said shyly, indicating the area of her unformed breasts. "And here." Self-consciously she lowered her hand between her legs. "Sometimes on my bum," she concluded as Jane shuddered.

"When did he touch you?" Jane heard her voice as if it belonged to someone else. She couldn't be saying these things, after all. None of this could be happening.

"Sometimes when I was taking a bath. Daddy would come in and dry me off."

"When you were taking a bath?" Jane heard the relief in her voice. Of course! The whole thing was a misunderstanding. Michael had merely been drying Emily after her bath, the way any parent would do. Everything had been blown out of proportion by an overly zealous teacher and a mother too willing to jump to conclusions. Perfectly innocent acts had been made to look sinister, even obscene.

"Sometimes when you had to go to a meeting, Daddy would crawl into bed with me," Emily continued, and Jane felt the bubble of her rationalizations burst. "He said he was happy he'd made such a perfect little girl." Emily suddenly burst into loud, anguished sobs. "He said it was all right. He said all daddies loved their little girls that way."

Jane took her daughter in her arms, the next question lodging behind her tongue, refusing to come out until Jane almost choked on it. "Did Daddy . . . did Daddy ever ask you to touch him?"

"Sometimes. But I didn't like to."

"Where . . . where did he ask you to touch him?"

Emily pulled out of Jane's embrace, her head dropping, her finger pointing to her groin.

"His penis?" Jane whispered.

Emily nodded. "I didn't want to. I didn't like when it got all wet and sticky in my hands."

Jane swayed, afraid she might faint. "Did he . . ." She stopped. Could she really be considering asking the next question? What further obscenities did she have to hear? "Did Daddy ever do anything else to you?"

Emily shook her head.

"Did he ever hurt you?"

"No."

Jane closed her eyes. Thank God.

"He made me promise not to tell you, and now he'll be mad at me because I broke my promise."

"Don't you worry. I'll take care of Daddy," Jane heard herself say, wondering exactly what she meant. "Listen, sweetheart, I'm going to go home now and pack a few things, and then I'll come back after school and pick you up, and we'll go away for a little holiday, just the two of us. Would you like that?"

"Not Daddy?"

"Not this time, no." Was she really saying these things? "This time it'll just be you and me. A girls' holiday. Okay?"

Emily nodded her head, wiping her tears away with the back of her hand. "Don't forget my blanket."

"How could I forget your blanket? Don't worry, darling, I'll take care of everything." Jane paused, not sure she could move without collapsing. "In the meantime, you play and have a good time, and know that I love you. I love you very much."

"I love you too, Mommy."

Jane showered her daughter's cheeks with kisses. "And Daddy will never touch you like that again. Okay? I promise, sweetheart."

Emily said nothing. Jane understood that the child loved her father, felt *she* was the one who had betrayed *him*.

"You did the right thing, honey. You did the right thing by telling me. Now, you go on back downstairs and finish your lunch, and I'll be here when school gets out this afternoon."

She watched Emily race down the hall and disappear down the flight of steps.

"Did she tell you anything?" Pat Rutherford asked, coming up behind Jane.

Jane started walking down the hall. "I'll take care of it," she said, not bothering to look back, her pace breaking into a run.

28

"GODDAMNIT, YOU SON OF A BITCH! I'LL KILL YOU! I'll kill you, damnit!" Jane brought her fists down sharply on the steering wheel, her screams ricocheting off the closed windows of her car. "How could you do it, you miserable bastard? How could you do that to your daughter? How could you do it?"

Jane sat in the school parking lot, wondering what to do next. She had barely made it to her car before the screams she had been suppressing burst forth, her body no longer able to contain her outrage. It had been essential to get away from Emily. She couldn't allow the child to see the extent of her fury. She needed time to cool off, a few hours to get a grip on her emotions, put a lid on her anger, formulate a plan, decide what she had to do.

Should she confront him? Should she simply storm into Michael's office and make public Emily's accusations, rip the face off his respectable career, his spotless reputation, announce that this protector of little children was really a child molester?

Was it possible that he had molested other children as well? Certainly, he had ample opportunities. His business was tending to the sick and vulnerable. Who was more vulnerable than a sick child? And here was the saintly Dr. Michael Whittaker, in a position of absolute power and trust. He was revered, loved, idolized. Could this same man, this warm and gentle lover, be hiding a heart as dark as any nightmare could invent?

And what did that say about her? How could she have lived with such a man for over eleven years and never once suspected? What did it say about her that she had been so deceived? It was one thing to fool one's colleagues, one's friends and associates, one's patients and one's employees, but none of these people lived with the man, none of them spent every night in his bed, sleeping in his arms.

Jane pictured those arms around her now, then imagined them around her seven-year-old daughter. She immediately felt her lunch rise up in protest, and pushed open the car door, throwing up on the black concrete of the school parking lot. "Goddamn you, you miserable son of a bitch!" she shouted, fighting for some control, losing, slamming down on the horn in desperation. "What am I supposed to do now?"

She wiped her mouth with a tissue she found in her coat pocket, then discarded it on the ground. Polluting the environment, she thought with appropriate irony, deciding against confronting Michael directly. She'd let her lawyers do that once she and Emily were safely away. Right now, she had to sublimate her fury long enough to get organized. She had to go home, pack her things, pack Emily's things, not a lot, just enough, and decide where they were going to go. Downtown Boston, she decided. Check into a hotel for a couple of days, maybe the Lennox Hotel. She'd always liked the Lennox. She could get in touch with her friends from there, get them to recommend a good lawyer.

First she'd need some money. She'd have to go to the bank. They had nine, maybe ten thousand dollars in their joint checking account. It required only one signature to make a withdrawal. That's what she'd do, she decided, closing the car door and starting the engine, pulling into the street. She'd withdraw all their money, let Michael find out about it later, as she had learned about his duplicitous acts—later. By that time, she and Emily would be long gone. The only contact she would have to endure with Michael again would be through their respective attorneys. That was undoubtedly the best solution for all concerned, since if she saw him she would probably kill him.

She drove fast, reaching Center Street in less than ten minutes, parking the car under a no-parking sign directly in front of the bank. She almost knocked over an elderly white-haired woman as she raced to get a place in line, hearing the old lady swear under her breath. Jane was only mildly surprised. How could she be surprised by anything anymore?

It was a small bank, one she visited frequently. She knew all the tellers by name, and they probably thought they knew her. Jane laughed out loud, felt all eyes turn toward her, then lowered her head, wiping away an unexpected tear. How long was she going to have to wait? How slow could people move?

"Is something wrong, Mrs. Whittaker?" the teller asked when it was finally her turn.

Jane stared at the young black woman whose name was Samantha. She said nothing, helpless tears falling the length of her cheek.

"Can I get you anything, Mrs. Whittaker?"

"I want to close out this account." Jane reached into her overstuffed purse and pulled out her bank book, pushing it across the counter.

Samantha studied the balance. "Would you like me to transfer it into another of your accounts?"

"No. I want the cash."

"There's almost ten thousand dollars here."

"Yes, I know. I need it." Jane wiped at her nose with the back of her hand. Damn these tears!

"Mrs. Whittaker, I know it's none of my business, but you seem very upset, and—"

For the second time in as many minutes, Jane laughed out loud. Now everyone was looking at her, including Trudy Caplan, the manager of the bank. Jane ignored their worried stares. "I just want my money."

"Mrs. Whittaker," Trudy Caplan said, taking over

from Samantha. "Maybe you'd like to come into my office and have a cup of coffee." Trudy Caplan was tall and top-heavy, her streaked blond hair pulled into an old-fashioned bun.

"I don't need any coffee. I need my money. And I'm in a bit of a hurry, so I'd like it quickly, if you don't mind." Why was she asking if they minded? It was her money!

"If you're not happy about something we've done—" the manager began.

Why did women always assume they were part of the problem? "It's nothing you've done," Jane assured her quickly. "A friend of mine is in trouble, and I told her I'd do whatever I could to help, that's all. Hopefully, I'll be able to put the money back in a day or two."

That seemed to satisfy Trudy Caplan, who returned her to Samantha's care before heading back to her office.

"We just have to fill out a few forms," Samantha told her.

"Why?"

"Whenever you close out an account—"

"I don't have time to fill out forms. How much money do I have to leave in to keep it open?"

"Five dollars."

"Fine. Leave five dollars."

"And you want the rest in cash?"

"Yes."

"Will hundreds be all right?"

"Sure."

Jane watched as Samantha retreated to the vault and returned with the appropriate number of hundred-dollar bills, which she counted out in front of Jane and then clipped securely into neat little packets. "And seventy-four dollars and twenty-three cents." She dropped the loose bills into Jane's hand and shoved the packets of hundred-dollar bills across the counter.

Jane carelessly stuffed the money into the deep pockets of her trench coat, bitterly offering silent thanks to Michael for suggesting she wear it. Her purse was already too crowded. This was much simpler, at least for the time being. When she got home, she'd change purses, select something larger, more appropriate for transporting all this cumbersome cash.

There was a parking ticket on the window of Jane's car. She tore it up and let the pieces fall to the road. More pollution. Another lost cause, she thought, just as she was a lost cause. A failure as a wife, a lover, a woman. Why else would Michael seek the comfort of a child? Was she so inadequate, so deficient in these areas that she had driven him into the arms of their daughter? Dear God, was it somehow her fault?

She drove home, her tears so copious that she could barely see to drive, her chest heaving, her stomach cramping against the weight of her despair. She had failed everyone she had ever loved, she thought, pulling into her driveway and pushing herself out of the car. She had failed to protect her father from the heart attack that killed him when she was barely thirteen; she had failed to protect her mother, who would no doubt be alive today had Jane only forgone her meeting at Emily's school and accompanied her into Boston; she had failed to satisfy her husband, to be the wife he expected and deserved; and she had failed to look out for her only child, the one person she had made it her life's work to protect.

"I'm a total failure," she mumbled, slamming the car door shut, aware of someone at her elbow. "I'm useless. Worse than useless."

"Jane? Jane, what are you muttering about? Are you all right?"

"What?" Jane found herself staring into Carole's concerned face.

"What's the matter? Are you crying?"

"I don't have time for this!" Jane yelled, pushing past Carole and into her house. She couldn't be bothered trying to explain. There weren't enough minutes, enough hours in the day, to convince Carole that Michael had molested Emily. Who would believe it? No, right now she had to pack her things and get out. She would explain everything later.

Jane dropped her purse on the floor in the front hall

and ran up the stairs toward her bedroom, feeling as if she had invaded a stranger's space. Had she really ever lived here? Was it possible she had ever been happy here? Could she really have shared this room, this bed, with a man she had obviously never known?

She caught sight of her reflection in the mirrored wall of closet doors. Her face was swollen and streaked with tears. No wonder everyone looked at her with frightened eyes. She was a scary sight.

Knowing that she couldn't allow Emily to see her this way, Jane headed for the bathroom, where she washed her face free of makeup and tears and pressed a cold washcloth against her eyes to bring down the swelling. Then she returned to the bedroom and pulled open the closet doors. "Is this why you always insisted on buying me these stupid little-girl dresses?" she screamed, pulling them off their hangers and stomping them under her feet. "Is that why you liked me in buttons and bows?"

She quickly retrieved two black suitcases from the closet of the guest bedroom. One suitcase for her, one for Emily. She'd only take a few things, and if she needed more, well, she had almost ten thousand dollars in her pockets. It was best to start fresh. Wipe away the past. Wipe the slate clean.

She packed only what she considered essential, then collapsed on the bed, the bed she had shared with Michael all these years, feeling his presence encircle her in a tight embrace until she could barely breathe. She felt his lips on the side of her neck, his hands at her breasts, his tongue tracing an imaginary line down her belly. His essence was behind her, on top of her, inside her, until every orifice was filled with Michael, his scent, his touch, his being. I've been a part of you for almost a dozen years, his image whispered tantalizingly in her ear. I'm part of you now.

"No!" Jane exclaimed, jumping off the bed and knocking over her suitcase, watching its contents spill out across the mint-green carpet. "I won't let you be part of me! I won't." She quickly got down on her hands and knees and pushed the clothing back inside the valise, zipping the bag up and locking it, dragging it and the other, still empty bag, to Emily's room.

She left the packed valise in the doorway, carting the other to Emily's bed, then started with the dresser drawers, lifting out Emily's underwear and socks, her pajamas and nightgowns, her T-shirts and shorts. Next she headed for the closet, throwing in as many outfits as she could find, selecting the few dresses Michael hadn't purchased, choosing only those things she had bought on her own. She would take nothing that would remind them of Michael, nothing that attested to his ownership of them, that he had ever been a part of their lives.

I've been a part of you for almost a dozen years, she heard him say again. I'm part of you now.

"No!" she shouted, desperate to get out of the house, to rid herself of the lie in which she had been living. She checked her watch, realized half an hour had passed. God, how much time had she wasted in pointless reveries? She had to get moving, get going, get out.

She pulled the suitcase off the bed and ran with it to the doorway, scooping up the other bag, about to leave the room when she remembered Emily's favorite blanket, the one she had slept with since infancy. It was the only thing Emily had asked for. She couldn't leave it behind.

Jane dropped the bags to the floor and ran to the bed, pulling down the bedspread, searching under the covers for the small white wool blanket with the delicate blue flowers and fuzzy fringe that Emily used to tickle her nose. Where had she put it when she made the bed this morning? "I don't have the patience for this," she cried, locating the blanket under the pillow, suddenly aware that someone was watching her.

"Jane, what's going on here?"

At the sound of Michael's voice, Jane froze, too stunned to react. What was he doing home at this hour?

"Jane, what's happening? I got a very peculiar call from the bank, telling me you all but closed out our checking account, and then a few minutes later I got a frantic call from Carole, telling me you're hysterical, that something is obviously wrong but that you won't talk about it. Needless to say, I got right in my car. I probably broke the sound barrier getting here so fast. Jane . . . are you listening to me? Can you hear me?"

Jane spun around, cold fury escaping from her eyes, no more need for tears. "I hear you."

"Jane, are you in some kind of trouble?"

"Trouble?"

"What happened? You slug another guy in the subway?" He almost laughed. "What is it, honey? What kind of mess have you gotten yourself into now?"

"You bastard!" Jane shrieked, lunging at him, her fingers tearing at his hair, straining for his eyes.

Michael grabbed her hands, locking his fingers around her wrists, keeping her at bay. "For God's sake, Jane, what the hell is going on?"

"Goddamn you, you son of a bitch. How could you do it?"

"Do what? Jane, what are you talking about?"

"I went to see Emily's teacher today, Michael. She's been concerned about Emily's recent behavior." Jane stopped struggling, became very still. Michael looked at her expectantly. "She said she thought there was the possibility that Emily might have been sexually abused."

The look of horror that crossed his face seemed genuine. Was it horror for what had been done to Emily or horror at having been discovered? "What?! By whom? Did she have any idea who it might be?"

"Don't play games with me, Michael," Jane said, her voice cold, unmoved. "It's too late. It won't work."

"Dear God, you think that I—"

"It's no use, Michael. I spoke to Emily. She told me."

There was a moment's silence before Michael spoke. "Somebody's obviously been putting words in her mouth."

"Nobody told her anything, you bastard!" Once again Jane renewed her attempted assault. Once again Michael managed to keep her at bay. "You miserable rotten bastard. How could you do it? How could you molest your own child? How could you rob her of her childhood?"

Jane kicked at him with her feet and he pulled back, suddenly dropping her wrists, as if the mere touch of her filled him with disgust. Jane brought her hands to her face, trying to cover up the horror she was seeing. Inside the dark cup of her hands, her wedding band mocked her. She grabbed at it with the fingers of her other hand, pulling it roughly over her knuckle and hurling it across the room. It bounced against the far wall and landed in a corner.

"Christ, Jane, what are you doing?"

"I'm trying *not* to kill you, goddamnit."

"You're crazy, Jane. I love you, but I've been thinking for a long time now that you're losing your mind." Jane stood rooted to the spot, thinking if she moved again, she *would* kill him.

"*I'm* crazy?!"

"Listen to yourself. Listen to what you're saying. Do you really believe I'm capable of molesting my own daughter?"

"I believe Emily."

"She's a child. Children have active imaginations."

"Emily would never say anything like that unless it were true."

"Why? Are you saying that children don't tell lies?"

"Of course not."

"Are you saying that Emily has never lied? Because if you are, I can remind you of a few occasions—"

"I know she can tell lies."

"But you're sure she isn't lying now."

"I'm sure."

"How? How can you be so damn sure?"

How could she? Jane faltered for a moment. Then she saw Emily, the look of anguish that had distorted her sweet features when she whispered her father's name. "Because Emily loves you. Because it tore her heart out to break her promise to you, her promise to keep what you were doing a secret, damn you! Because I *know* when my child is lying to me."

"Just like you know everything else, right? Just like you know you're always right and everyone else is always wrong. Like when you taunt some jerk on the street so that he almost runs you down, when you scream obscenities at some poor sucker who's only doing his job until he almost punches you out, when you slug some old guy in the subway with your purse because he was rude enough to think he might have the right of way.''

''You're twisting everything.''

''Am I? I don't think so. I think you've been getting worse over the years. At first it was cute. We all thought it was cute. Jane and her temper. Something to laugh about at dinner parties. And then suddenly it wasn't so cute anymore. It was worrisome, almost scary. What would Jane do next? Would she live to tell the tale? I tried to talk to you. I tried to warn you. But nobody tells Jane what to do. Jane Whittaker is a law unto herself. Except that nobody knows who Jane Whittaker is anymore. I've been married to the woman for eleven years and even I don't recognize her these days. Who are you, lady?''

''I don't know what you're talking about. This has nothing to do with anything.''

''Doesn't it? Just who do you think is going to believe this ridiculous story you've concocted? You think that I'll be the only one hurt by these crazy accusations? You think I'm going to sit around and let you ruin my career, my reputation?''

''I don't care about your precious reputation. I care about my daughter.''

''Do I have to remind you that she's my daughter too.''

''I'm the one who should be reminding *you*. How dare you!''

''Oh, don't start with that crap again, Jane. If you want to believe an impressionable child who's probably been coached by her neurotic teacher, then there's nothing I can do to stop you. But I warn you, don't try to make these accusations public because I'll bury you. By the time I'm through with you, they'll be waiting at the courtroom steps with straitjackets.''

Jane fought to keep herself under control, understanding the truth of what Michael was saying. If she did make her accusations public, she would be pitting her seven-year-old child against the father she loved, asking people to believe the word of a little girl over that of her renowned and respected father. Who was more likely to be believed?

What chance did she have? What chance did Emily have?

"All right, listen," Jane began, hearing her thoughts only as they emerged as words. "I won't go public with this. I won't go to the police. I won't say a word to anyone. You get to hold on to your career and your precious reputation. And in return—"

"In return?" His voice was sly, self-satisfied.

"In return, you'll move out. Now. Right away."

"And Emily?"

"Emily? Emily stays with me, of course. I get full custody."

"You think I'd give up custody of the only child I'll ever have?"

"I don't think you have much choice."

"Is that so? Well, maybe that's not the way I see it."

"If you fight me for custody in a court of law, I'll charge you with child molestation. You'll lose everything."

"I don't think so. I think the courts understand how vindictive some women can be when it comes to divorce, how they'll use anything they can, invent all sorts of disgusting, outrageous claims. From all I've read, courts don't look very favorably on hysterical women making unfounded accusations of sexual abuse."

"They're not unfounded."

"Says who? Has a doctor examined Emily? Has anyone found any physical evidence of sexual molestation? Do you have anything other than your daughter's imaginings and the concerns of some unmarried, overwrought schoolteacher?" He paused, allowing time for his words to register. "Are you going to subject Emily to repeated doctor's examinations, to the manipulative, never-ending questions of well-meaning social workers, to some undoubtedly nasty cross-examination by an expert defense attorney? For what? So that some judge can find that, on the basis of the evidence, he has no grounds to convict me of anything other than being an overly indulgent husband to a dangerously unbalanced wife? Trust me, Jane, I think I'll have an easier time proving you're unfit than you will proving me a pervert."

"You're despicable."

"No. Just right, and I think you know it." He looked to the ceiling. "I'll tell you what I *will* agree to."

Jane felt her voice break, wondering at what point she had lost control of the conversation. "What will you agree to?"

"A divorce, if that's what you really want, although it's the last thing I want. I love you, Jane. I've always loved you."

"Then why? How could you? . . ."

"How could I what?"

"For God's sake, Michael," Jane wailed. "You ejaculated in her hand. Can you really deny it?"

"To my dying breath." He smiled. "Or yours."

Jane forced her eyes to his. Surely none of this was actually happening. They weren't really having this discussion. "Is that a threat?"

"I don't make threats, Jane. I'm trying to make peace."

"Oh, I see. Something else I've misunderstood."

"Apparently."

"All right, then, so what *exactly* are you saying? So I don't misunderstand."

"I'm saying that I want joint custody of my daughter."

"What? How can you think for a moment that I'd agree to anything like that?"

"Even if the courts awarded you custody, you wouldn't be able to keep me from seeing her. You know that. I have my rights as a father."

"You forfeited any rights you might have."

"I don't think you'll get many people to agree with you. I think even Emily would tell the court she wants to see her daddy."

Jane looked frantically about the room, desperately

searching for answers, for one single shred of evidence she could offer as conclusive proof. There was none. "Would you agree to supervised visits?"

"No chance. That's as good as an admission of guilt. I didn't do anything."

Jane felt a scream of frustration rising in her throat. "I can't believe what's happened to us. You're a stranger to me."

Michael took a step toward her, his arms outstretched. "I love you, Jane."

"No!"

"I love you. Even now, even after all the awful things you've been saying, I still love you. You're so beautiful. I just want to take you in my arms and hold you."

"Is that the sort of line you used on our daughter, Michael? Is it? Is it, you bastard? Is it?" And then she was screaming, sounds without words, and she was running from the room, leaving the suitcases behind, racing down the stairs, Michael right behind her. He ran around in front of her and blocked her way to the front door. Jane spun around without pause, running to the back door, Michael already there, refusing to let her leave. She found herself in the sunroom, this room she had always loved, that Michael had built for her. Her sanctuary. Her prison, she thought now, tempted to hurl herself through one of the large windows.

And then he was moving toward her, and she was backing up, stumbling against the sofa-swing, feeling it break away from her, her hand fumbling into the air for support, smacking against a brass vase they had brought home from the Orient, raising it over her head as she steadied her feet.

"You really are crazy, aren't you?" he laughed. "I just might go for full custody myself."

And then her arm shot forward, propelled by her full fury, and she slammed the vase against the side of Michael's head even as he tried to turn away. A dagger-like protuberance tore into his flesh, threatening to lift off the top of his head.

Jane let go of the vase, watching it fall to the floor,

her eyes widening in growing horror as blood poured from Michael's head. He staggered toward her, his deathly white face a mask of disbelief and pain. "My God, Jane, you've killed me."

He collapsed against her, his head seeking the refuge of her breasts. Jane pulled away, felt Michael's feet sliding out from under him, watched him fall to the floor, saw the front of her dress covered in blood.

"No!" she cried, pulling her trench coat tightly around her, doing up the buttons with trembling hands. "None of this is really happening." She moved to the door. "None of this has happened." She walked out of the room to the front of the house, refusing to look back. "It's a beautiful day. I have to get out. Go for a walk. Get some milk and some eggs because I promised Emily a chocolate cake. Yes, that's a very good idea." She opened the front door and ran out of the house, not bothering to close the door behind her. "Yes, it's a beautiful day," she repeated as she headed down the street toward the nearest MBTA station. It was a beautiful day. It would be a shame to waste it indoors.

29

JANE LOWERED THE GLASS VASE SHE WAS HOLDING, returning it to the coffee table in front of her, as Paula sank to the sofa and Carole stared at her with open disbelief.

"That's quite a story," Carole said after a lengthy pause.

Jane said nothing, overwhelmed for the moment by the person she had once been. It was as if she had believed herself an orphan all her life, only to be suddenly introduced to the parents she never knew she had, and surrounded by a multitude of siblings. Everything she had ever been, every cause she had ever believed in, everybody she had ever loved, were suddenly all present and accounted for inside her head, fighting among themselves for prominence. Her mother was there, even her father. Her brother, Tommy. Gargamella. Their children. Her friends. The histories they shared. The schools she had attended. Her first date with Michael, much as he had described it to her. Their wedding. The years they had spent together. Her pregnancy. Their daughter's birth. Emily's first birthday. Her first day of school. The last, when she told Emily she'd be back to pick her up at the end of the day.

Michael would have picked her up, Jane realized, not

wanting to picture how Emily must have felt when she saw her father, and not her mother, arrive at the end of the school day. Jane forced herself to confront the unpleasant thought. To deny reality was to risk losing it. Surely she had learned that much.

Her head was spinning, whether from the shock of her memory having returned or the drugs still in her system, she couldn't be sure. She gripped the side of the wing chair for support, ignoring Paula, who remained motionless on the sofa, to concentrate on Carole. "I need you to drive me to Woods Hole," she said.

Carole shook her head. "I can't do that."

"You still don't believe me?"

"I don't know *what* to believe."

"Carole, we've been neighbors for a long time, and I thought we'd become pretty good friends."

"I thought so too."

"But you still choose to believe Michael."

"It's just that I find it hard to accept the things you've just told me."

"That he molested his daughter?"

"He's a pediatric surgeon, for God's sake. His life is helping children, not hurting them."

"I know it's difficult to believe. . . ."

"Not difficult. Impossible," Carole stated simply.

"So you'd rather believe that I'm crazy."

"Frankly, yes. It keeps it a much nicer world that way." Carole ran her hand through her uncombed curls. "And face it, Jane. Forgetting who you are is not exactly the act of a rational human being."

Jane smiled, almost laughed. "I guess I can't argue with that. But I know who I am now. I know what happened that day. I know how much Emily needs me. Now, I can remember how to get to the Whittakers' cottage. I'm just not sure I can make it there on my own. I'm begging you to help me."

Again, Carole shook her head. "I can't."

Jane felt a wave of dizziness wash over her, try to knock her down. She fought to keep her balance. "Then let me have your car."

"What did you do with Paula's car?" Carole asked, though Paula herself said nothing, her eyes glued to the floor, as if the force of Jane's story had rendered her immobile.

"It died a few blocks from here. Please, give me your car keys?"

"Why don't you call the police?" Carole asked in response. "If what you say is true, they're the ones you should be asking for help."

"I will go to the police—*after* I find Emily. But if I call them, now, they'll only want to talk to Michael. He's managed to convince *you* that I'm crazy. How much trouble do you think he'll have with the police? At the very least, they'd waste hours questioning me, hours that Michael can use to spirit Emily away where I might never find her. I can't risk that. I have to find my little girl. I have to know she's safe. Please, Carole. Let me have the keys to your car."

"Is this what you're looking for?" the old voice asked from the doorway.

Jane looked to where Carole's father stood at the entrance to the living room, holding Carole's open purse in one hand, the keys to her car in the other.

"My God, Dad, give me those." Carole vaulted toward her father. As her hands reached out for the keys, Fred Cobb looped them high into the air over her head toward Jane's outstretched fingers.

"Monkey in the middle," he cried gleefully. "Monkey in the middle."

Jane pulled the keys out of the air and raced toward the front door as Carole's father kept his frustrated daughter prisoner with his antics. She reached the plum-colored Chrysler, opened it and got inside, twisting the key in the lock and pulling out of the driveway just as Carole reached the front door.

Jane glanced into the rearview mirror as she pulled away, mindful that Carole had already gone back inside the house. She'll call Michael, Jane thought, checking her watch, knowing that he was still in surgery, that he couldn't be disturbed. Would they disturb him for an urgent message? she wondered, stepping on the gas, automatically checking the gas gauge and noting gratefully that the tank was full. Would Carole call the police to report her car stolen? Would the police be waiting to head her off at the nearest intersection?

She almost laughed, then felt herself dangerously close to tears. No, she wouldn't cry. Not now. She'd cried enough. She had more important things to do, she thought, as fatigue wrestled with her eyelids. "Like staying awake," she said out loud. "Goddamnit, I will not fall asleep. Not now."

She switched on the radio. It was tuned to the local country-and-western station. Jane listened for several seconds to a deep-voiced crooner soothingly proclaim that he'd been loved by the best, then pressed the button to change the station. There was such a thing as too soothing. Any more of the man's rich velvet voice and she'd be sound asleep before she hit the highway. What she needed was some hard rock, something to jangle her nerves and keep her on the edge of her seat.

The announcer, a young man who could only be described as "testerical," announced the latest release by the hard rock group, Rush, and Jane breathed a sigh of relief. She'd have a hard time falling asleep with that music blaring. She turned up the volume, taking no chances, slowing down as she moved through Newton Center on her way to Highway 30, not wishing to risk being stopped for speeding.

That would be great, she thought, heading north on Walnut Street. Not only did she not have her driver's license with her, but she was driving a stolen car. That would make for an interesting police report, to say the least. More fodder for Michael, she realized, in a less light vein. More evidence that she was an unfit parent.

She turned east on Highway 30, headed toward Boston. After that it would get a little tricky. She'd have to transfer to Highway 3, eventually get on Highway 28. Michael usually drove whenever they visited his parents' cottage. While she was familiar with the route, she was unfamiliar with the actual driving, and didn't know how long she could keep functioning. Hopefully, instinct and adrenaline would be enough to get her there in one piece.

The drive, once she reached Boston, would take approximately an hour and a half, maybe slightly longer, depending on the traffic. It was only ten o'clock now. She would get there in time for lunch. Would Michael's parents offer her a hot meal? She giggled, then cautioned herself against getting giddy.

What kind of reception *would* she get? What had Michael told them? How much did they know?

Good old Dr. and Mrs. Whittaker, Jane thought, picturing them standing side by side, though not touching, never touching. You saved that for your son, didn't you, Mrs. W.? All those cozy little baths together long past the age where it was still appropriate. Not that she suspected Mrs. Whittaker of molesting her son. No, Jane was confident that her mother-in-law would be properly horrified at the very idea. But however innocent those communal baths may have seemed, however innocent they undoubtedly *were*, Michael's mother had failed to define her boundaries, making it difficult, if not impossible, for her son to understand his.

The senior Dr. Whittaker, a Ph.D. in science, had always been friendly enough on the surface, but essentially he was a cold and distant man who had been a largely absent father, although he was more accessible as far as his only grandchild was concerned. Jane called him Bert, but she'd always had the distinct impression he would have preferred the more formal title of Doctor. As for his wife, Jane thought of her only as Mrs. Whittaker, but the woman, tall, meaty, overbearing, had insisted on Mom. Jane had opted for Doris, and from that time on, the relationship between the two women had been as stiff as Doris's hair, although the woman was never less than polite.

The reception she would get from those two would be decidedly lukewarm. Possibly even hostile.

Jane breathed a sigh of relief once she hit the highway. She had made it this far, surely she would make it the rest of the way. The traffic was good, moving at a steady clip. She determined to go no faster than the designated speed, preferring to arrive a little late than chance not arriving at all. For once in her life, she would have to be patient.

And what of her own parents? she wondered.

She remembered her father as a not very tall, rather round man, with a soft voice that still managed to resonate authority. He was the principal of a high school in Hartford, a dedicated man who joined his teachers on the picket line to show his support when they went on strike against the school board, and refused all his life to buy anything from Germany, against which he had spent almost two years fighting in the Second World War. When he died suddenly of a heart attack at age forty-four, Jane had put her own grief aside to comfort her mother, who tended toward hysteria even in the best of times.

Her mother had a quick wit and a quicker temper. She was flighty and demanding and exasperating, and it wasn't until Jane was safely out of her teen years that she was finally able to accept her mother in spite of her many faults, or maybe because of them. At the time of her death, the two were probably closer than they had ever been. When she died, Jane had cried for both her mother and her father, letting her grief overwhelm her for several days and then quietly pushing it to the back of her mind.

How dared Michael use this tragedy to further his own ends!

Jane allowed her anger to fuel her just enough to stay alert. Had Michael really expected to get away with his plan to discredit her? Had he really expected to convince everyone, herself included, that she was crazy and needed to be put away for her own protection? Or had he been hoping that she would spare him the trouble and simply kill herself? Had he ever really loved her at all?

Strangely enough, she believed he had, that, in fact, he still did. His expressions of love were genuine, she understood, just that his instinct for self-preservation was greater. He couldn't possibly allow her to make her accusations public, just as he couldn't allow her to limit his access to his child, who was, after all, an extension of himself. No boundaries.

He had come very close to succeeding, she realized with a gasp, reading the sign at the side of the highway that indicated Sagamore was sixty-two miles away. After Sagamore, it would be another twenty miles to Falmouth, and then only a few more miles to Woods Hole. She had to concentrate. Concentrate on the road ahead. She couldn't allow her thoughts to distract her.

Still, she wondered, what had gone through Michael's head after she'd taken off? Where had he thought she'd gone? And when she hadn't come back, when she hadn't tried to contact him, when she'd made no moves to find out where Emily might be, what had he thought then? Had he assumed he had frightened her away? That his threats, combined with her attack, an attack that had sliced his head open and required almost forty stitches to close, forty stitches with which to impress the hell out of any judge in a custody dispute, had sent her scrambling? Had he thought, as Carole had suggested, that she would come back after she calmed down? After she had time to think it over and admit the error of her ways?

And what must he have thought when the police called, told him that his wife was sitting on an examining table at the Boston City Hospital and seemed to have no memory? Is that when he had started cooking up his diabolical scheme? Buying time with the lie that she was visiting her brother, formulating his plan, kicking it into action, so easy to fool everyone with his reputation and his bag of doctor's tricks. So easy to substitute one medication for another. Using her mother's death and her own quick temper to his advantage. Letting the pieces fall naturally into place.

How long would it have worked? How long before her brother came to visit, saw what was going on, and rescued her? Jane scoffed. By the time Tommy hit town, she would have been weaving baskets in some private hellhole, too strung out on drugs to even acknowledge his presence. He would have expressed concern, even dismay, but Michael would have soon managed to persuade him, as he would have undoubtedly persuaded all their friends, that it was better for him to go back to his own life, that he would continue to look out for Jane's best interests, that he would keep in touch.

And Emily? What would Michael have told her? That her mother had run off, abandoned them? That it was only the two of them now, that they had to stick together? Would he stress loyalty, the importance of keeping certain things secret? Would he continue to dry her after her baths and comfort her when she missed her mother by crawling into her bed at night to hold her? Would he suggest that she might be more comfortable in his bed? Would he tell her how beautiful she was, that it was her fault for being so beautiful that it made him want to do these things to her? These vile things! Jane thought, realizing when she saw a police car on the side of the road that she had been accelerating, and pumping on the brakes in an effort to slow the car down before she was caught in a radar trap.

She glanced at the police car through her rearview mirror, sighing with satisfaction when she saw he was letting her pass. She'd have to be more careful. She'd have to concentrate on her driving.

Jane looked to the side of the highway, noting that the scenery was changing as she headed down the Cape. Normally, it was a drive she cherished, leaving the city, anticipating the country air. Woods Hole was a tiny village at the tip of Cape Cod, sparsely populated and largely overlooked by tourists and cottage owners for the more fashionable islands of Martha's Vineyard and Nantucket. Most people thought of Woods Hole as the place where you either got on or off the ferry. They paid Woods Hole little attention, which was just fine with the Whittakers, who had never been very comfortable with crowds. In truth, Jane had always loved the small cottage that was secluded behind a gathering of tall trees, not far from the water's edge.

She rubbed her eyes, forcing them wide open, her thoughts returning to Michael's scheme. What if she had regained her memory? What then? She knew the answer to that one only too well. It would be her word against his, and who was going to take very seriously the ravings of a woman who couldn't keep track of her own identity? If her memory hadn't returned until after she was safely locked away, then even had she eventually been released, it would be too late. Too many years would have passed. Too many fresh crimes would have been committed. Emily would be lost to her.

Had Michael molested other children as well? Was it possible that he used his position of power and trust to abuse other children?

Jane recalled the afternoon she had burst into Michael's office, had cooled her heels in the waiting room until Michael was free to see her. She remembered the little girl who sat whimpering on her mother's lap, crying that she wanted to go home. How quick they had been to dismiss her cries. How deaf they had been to her pain.

Had she been as insensitive to her own child?

She had tried to be the perfect mother, just as she had striven all her life to be the perfect little girl, the perfect student, the perfect employee. She had taken an active part in Emily's education, gone so far as to attend classes in effective parenting. But while she might have been an effective parent, Michael was the one who had very early captured Emily's heart. Jane had found herself occasionally jealous of the easy rapport they shared, the natural warmth and ease that Michael brought to fatherhood. She always considered herself a good mother, but Michael was a *natural* father. When had natural become unnatural?

Jane made the transition onto Highway 28 with a minimum of drama. A simple lane change eliciting a few palpitations of the heart and it was done. FALMOUTH, 20 MILES, the sign read, and she clutched the wheel tighter, and picked up her speed just a little. The next half an hour seemed to pass as slowly as the days of "The Young and the Useless." Every second was an hour; every minute was a day. And then suddenly there was the turnoff for Woods Hole, and Jane looked around to find herself in the middle of the country.

She could see the water of Buzzards Bay, wondered whether Emily would be swimming when she arrived. Or would she already be gone? Would Carole have succeeded in contacting Michael? Would he have managed to reach his parents? Had they already taken off for parts unknown? Perhaps she had even passed them on the highway, going in the opposite direction. Perhaps it was already too late.

"Please don't let it be too late," she prayed, turning the car down a small dirt road, the trees surrounding her, allowing her to approach the cottage in relative anonymity. Jane pulled the car into a makeshift driveway of small white stones several cottages away from the unvarnished wooden cottage that was the Whittakers'. She had always thought the Whittaker place the perfect cottage. Not a country home by any stretch of the imagination but a real cottage, small and basic and smelling of the woods. Not too fancy, nothing elaborate. The Whittaker cottage had running water and an indoor toilet, but that was about it in terms of modern amenities. Jane smiled when she thought of all the happy times she had spent here, recalling the photograph of her and Michael cavorting on the beach that Michael had brought with him to the hospital. The smile froze on her lips as she quietly opened the car door and stepped outside.

As soon as her legs touched the ground, her knees gave way, and she collapsed onto the blanket of hard white stones, one hand still clinging to the door handle. She stayed in this position for several seconds, unable to gather enough strength to pull herself up. Just a minute to catch my breath, she told herself, forcing her eyes to stay open, to look around, to assess her situation.

She was alone. No one seemed to be watching. Probably because it was a weekday, not as many cottages were around, although she heard human voices in the distance, the sound of children's laughter. Her child?

The image of Emily splashing about merrily in the water only yards from where she stood propelled Jane to her feet. The country air will hold me up, she determined, letting it fill her lungs, taking a few tentative steps forward.

She kept to the stones, avoiding the grass at the side of the road, on guard against the garter snakes that liked to sleep in the sun. She remembered one afternoon when they had all been here together, three generations of Whittakers, she the only real outsider, and she had forgone a dip in the bay in favor of a lawn chair and a good book. She had been on the verge of nodding off when she saw movement by the side of her chair. Knowing it was a snake without having to look, she had screamed and jumped up, both feet planted not so firmly in the middle of the lawn chair. She expected the snake to simply slither away, more afraid of her than she was of it, at least that's what the Whittakers kept telling her. But the snake, an ordinary black garter snake with a yellow stripe down its thin back, had stopped and lifted itself up to almost its full height, staring right at her, as if mesmerized by the sound of her screaming.

Snakes are deaf, Michael subsequently informed her, after racing from the waterfront to her side to see what all the screaming was about. By that time, the snake had taken off. It must have been a frog, Michael insisted at the dinner table. No, it was a snake, Jane told him. I know a snake when I see one. And Michael's parents had chuckled and exchanged knowing glances. No question about whom they believed.

Jane lowered her head and crept toward the Whittaker cottage. There was no car in the driveway. What did that mean? That they were out? That they'd gone visiting for the day? That their son had already managed to get in touch with them and told them to take Emily and clear out? Please no, anything but that, Jane pleaded, glancing to either side, then running up the several steps to the cottage's front porch.

The cottage was quiet. Standing outside, cautiously approaching the window, Jane heard no sounds emanating from the interior. Holding her breath, she peeked in the window into the still living area.

The room looked as she had always remembered it, its interior walls the same as the exterior, its furniture colonial except for the ultra-modern thirty-inch television set to the right of the central fireplace, the living room opening into the dining and kitchen areas, no doors except to the three small bedrooms and single bathroom at the rear of the cottage. Gentle folk art lined the walls: two peasant women gossiping in the sun, children fighting at their feet; men playing poker on an old barrel top, cigarette smoke wafting from between stained teeth; an old woman in a rocking chair, surrounded by a variety of cats. Everything still, as if patiently waiting for something to happen.

Could they have already left? Was she too late?

Jane peered inside, spying fresh fruit in a wicker basket on the dining room table. That didn't necessarily mean that they were still there, she realized. Surely, if Michael had phoned, they would have just left everything.

She had to get inside; she had to find out for herself.

She tried the door, was unsurprised to find it locked. The Whittakers always locked the door, even when they were only going to the beach. You could never be too careful; you never knew who might be trying to break in, grab that thirty-inch TV.

Jane crept around the side of the cottage to the back where the three bedrooms were huddled together. The windows were open, protected by screens. Jane searched the grass for a thick branch, finally locating one and ramming it against the screen in the master bedroom until she succeeded in pushing it out of its frame. She looked around, praying no one had seen her, then pushed the window up and crawled inside.

She landed on the queensize bed just as she heard the alarm go off. Oh, no, good God, no! she thought, feeling faint, wanting only to sink inside the well-made bed. Then the alarm stopped, only to start again, and she realized it wasn't an alarm at all, but the telephone.

The telephone was ringing.

She made no move to answer it. Was it Michael? Had Carole reached him? Had he returned Paula's earlier message? Was he calling to warn his parents of her impending arrival? Or was it simply a friend calling from the city, someone who felt like visiting for a few days? Or maybe a neighbor, calling to report a suspicious-looking person lurking around. Whoever it was, the party being paged wasn't home. Had they cleared out before her arrival?

Jane jumped across the bed and pulled out the drawers of the small dresser on the opposite wall, silently counting each ring of the telephone. Five rings . . . six . . . seven. The dresser was filled with clothing, as was the closet. Still, the Whittakers might have left everything behind, reasoning they could always come back later.

Jane took several giant steps into the bedroom that Emily usually occupied, finding a number of her clothes hanging neatly in the closet, a few toys lined in orderly fashion across the top of the bureau. Ten rings . . . eleven . . . twelve. Emily's pajamas were under her pillow, and a small stuffed bunny rabbit sat perched on the top.

Jane moved about the cottage. A child's still-damp bathing suit hung over the side of the tub in the bathroom, and the refrigerator, while far from full, hadn't been emptied. It was possible they were still here.

The phone stopped after twenty rings. Someone was obviously very anxious to reach the Whittakers. Jane checked her watch. It was almost noon. Where could they be? She walked into the living area, letting her body collapse into an oversized orange-and-brown-striped wing chair. Despite the heat, the cottage felt cool, soothing. She leaned her head back, feeling the cushion support her tired head and wondering how long she would have to wait.

In the next minute, she was asleep.

30

SHE AWOKE TO THE SOUND OF THE PHONE RINGING.

Jane jumped to her feet, her head spinning, her heart pounding. She checked her watch, noting with alarm that almost twenty minutes had passed since she had unwittingly closed her eyes. How stupid she was! How unbelievably careless. To have come this far only to fall asleep! Had the Whittakers returned from their outing only to find a real-life Goldilocks asleep in their chair? Had they bundled up their grandchild and fled the scene?

The phone continued to ring. Three rings . . . four. Then another sound, the sound of a car door slamming. A woman's voice: "Is that the phone, Bert?"

Jane stared at the phone, debating whether to yank it out of the wall, running into the kitchen instead and flinging open one of the drawers beneath the counter where she remembered Michael's mother kept a large pair of scissors. "Be there," she cried, and they were. Grabbing the scissors and brandishing them before her like a weapon, she returned to the living room and cut the phone wire in the middle of the sixth ring.

"I don't hear anything," a man's voice said from somewhere outside the cottage door.

"Well, you're so slow, they probably hung up. Where are you going, young lady?" the woman admonished.

"You have to give your grandfather a hand with the groceries. Give her that little bag, Bert," Doris Whittaker said clearly, her voice reaching into the dark recesses of the living room, where Jane stood frozen to the spot.

"There you go, Emmy," a man's voice said. "Think you can manage that one?"

"Oh, Grandpa. It's not heavy at all."

Jane clutched tightly to the scissors in her right hand, realizing she had left the kitchen drawer open, but knowing she didn't have enough time to close it, ducking behind the tall wing chair in the far corner of the room as she heard the key turn in the door. The sun streaked across the floor and up the wall behind her head as the door opened. How long before they noticed the phone wires had been cut? How long before they noticed the open kitchen drawer and the missing pair of scissors? How long before she could grab her child and flee?

"Where should I put it, Grandma?"

"Put everything on the kitchen table," Doris Whittaker called as Jane heard Emily skip across the room.

Jane had to bite her tongue to keep from crying out as she caught a fleeting glimpse of the little girl she hadn't seen in almost two months. Emily wore fluorescent-pink shorts and a multicolored T-shirt, her hair brushed back into a high ponytail from which hung a multitude of brightly colored ribbons. Her toes protruded over the ends of last summer's white sandals. My baby, Jane thought, my beautiful little girl. How was she going to rescue her? How was she going to rescue them both?

"For heaven's sake, would you look at the way that silly checkout boy packed this bag," Doris Whittaker was complaining as she made her way through the cottage, her husband following right behind. "He put the fruit at the bottom, so that all the peaches will be crushed. A fine how-do-you-do. Weren't you watching him?"

"That's your job," retorted her husband, lowering his heavy bag to the table with a grunt, and heading for the rear of the cottage. "Somebody left a drawer open," he said in passing, absently pushing it shut as he went by.

"Well, we better get this unpacked and see what the

damage is. We may have to turn around and drive back."

"Can I go swimming now, Grandma?"

"Not yet. Aren't you hungry?"

"Not really."

"Well, I'm starving, so we better eat. How about a baloney sandwich?

"Okay. And an ice cream?"

"Only if you eat all your sandwich."

What should I do? Jane wondered, debating whether she should simply stand up, scissors in hand, and announce her presence, or wait until Emily was alone in the room and then spirit her off. She heard the sounds of unpacking, of cupboards being opened and closed, of groceries being put away. She remembered similar outings when she'd been part of the action, not a silent witness to it. Was there anything more peaceful than a hot summer's day at the cottage, where even the act of putting away groceries was a testament to serenity?

"What happened to the phone?" Emily asked, her little girl's voice breaking the spell, catapulting Jane back into reality.

"Not now, Emily. I want to finish getting these groceries unpacked."

"But look what happened to it." Jane pictured Emily holding up the severed wire.

"What are you talking about?" A pause, followed by footsteps. "My God, what did you do?"

"I didn't do anything," the child protested.

"It looks like it's been cut," Doris Whittaker pronounced, her voice growing wary. Were her eyes even now scanning the room? Where they focused on the tall wing chair in the upper left corner of the room? Could she see Jane hiding behind it? Did she know? "Bert, come in here."

"I'm in the bathroom," came the muffled reply.

"Well, hurry up. There's something funny going on."

Jane heard the toilet flush.

"For God's sake, Doris, can't a man go to the john around here?" Bert Whittaker demanded, the word "john" sounding foreign on his lips. "What's so damn urgent that it can't wait a few minutes?"

"Someone's cut the phone wires."

"I didn't do it," Emily protested.

"That's strange," the senior Dr. Whittaker mused. "Has anything else been touched?"

Jane heard them moving about, heading toward the rear of the cottage, taking Emily with them.

"I don't like the feel of this," Doris Whittaker proclaimed.

"Everything else appears to be in order."

"My God, Bert, look at this! What happened in here?"

Jane understood that she had discovered the broken screen by their bedroom window. She knew that she had little time left.

"It appears that someone broke in," Bert Whittaker exclaimed.

Jane heard the sound of distant drawers being opened and closed.

"But they didn't take anything. The television, the radio—they're still here. Our clothes. Even the money in the piggy bank," Doris Whittaker said, returning to the kitchen and checking on the contents of the large glass jar. "Why would anyone break in just to cut the phone wires?"

"My stuff's still here," Emily called out, running back into the kitchen.

"It's probably some kids playing a prank," Bert Whittaker offered weakly.

"Some prank! This is breaking and entering."

"Doris, calm down, you're scaring the child."

"I'm not scared, Grandpa."

"No? Well, good for you. You're a smart little girl."

"Did you say someone had left a drawer open in here?" Doris Whittaker suddenly demanded of her husband.

"Yes, I did." A short pause. The sound of a drawer opening. "This one."

"My God, my scissors are gone."

"Well, they probably used them to cut the phone wires. We should go to the police."

"Bert—"

"What?"

"What if it isn't a burglar or some kids?"

"What do you mean?"

Another pause. "Emily, why don't you pack a few things into an overnight bag, and we'll go to the Vineyard for a couple of days."

"But Molly said she might come over to play this afternoon."

"You'll play with Molly another day. Please don't argue. Do what I say. That's a girl."

"Really, Doris, don't you think you're overreacting?"

"I don't think we've been visited by any burglar," Doris Whittaker stated, dropping her voice to a whisper. "I think it's Jane."

"Jane?"

"Ssh! Keep your voice down. Do you want Emily to hear you?"

"What makes you think it's . . . her?"

"Think about it for a minute. It's the only logical explanation. Why would someone break into the cottage and not take anything? Why would they cut the phone wires unless they were afraid that someone might reach us, warn us she was coming? Think about it, Bert. It has to be Jane. She came to get Emily."

"If she *was* here, then she found the place empty and left."

"She wouldn't leave," Doris Whittaker pronounced. "If it's her, she's still around here somewhere. We have to get out before she comes back. Emily! Emily!"

"I'm packing, Grandma."

"Forget it. We have to leave right away."

"I need my bunny."

"Not now."

"But I want him."

"We'll buy you another one."

"I don't want another bunny."

Jane recognized the threat of tears in Emily's voice.

Don't cry, baby, she wanted to call out. Don't cry.

"I want Hopalong."

"We'll buy you a dozen bunnies later. Now, get moving."

"This is crazy," Bert Whittaker was saying as they started across the room. "Why don't we just go to the police?"

"First we'll call Michael, find out what's going on. If I'm wrong, there's no harm done."

"I don't want to go to Martha's Vineyard," Emily cried. "I want to go home. I want to see my mommy!"

Jane suddenly pushed herself up to her full height and stepped out from behind the orange-and-brown-striped chair, blocking the path to the door, the scissors hidden behind her back. "I'm right here, angel."

"Mommy!"

Doris Whittaker gasped and her husband looked faint, but Jane barely paid them any heed as Emily wriggled out of her grandmother's grasp to fly into her mother's arms. Jane scooped her daughter up with her left arm and smothered the child's face with kisses.

"Oh, my beautiful baby. My sweet angel. My big, beautiful girl."

Emily wrapped her arms tightly around her mother's neck, squeezing so hard that she almost knocked Jane off balance. "Where *were* you, Mommy? Where were you?"

"I'll explain everything later, sweetie. I promise."

Emily pulled back her head to stare into her mother's eyes. "I love you, Mommy."

"I love you too, baby." Jane's arm could no longer support her daughter's weight, and she was forced to lower the child to the floor.

"Come here, Emily," Doris Whittaker commanded, moving immediately toward the little girl and grabbing for her arm.

"Don't touch her," Jane screamed, her right hand shooting out from behind her back to reveal the knifelike scissors in her clenched fist. "Don't touch her or I'll kill you. I swear it."

"Mommy!"

"You're crazy!" Doris Whittaker shouted. "Look what you're doing to her. You're scaring her half to death!"

"I'm sorry, sweetie. It's the last thing in the world I want to do."

"Put down the scissors, Jane," Bert Whittaker said softly.

"Sorry, Bert. I can't do that."

"Just what is it that you want?"

"I want to take my daughter and get out of here."

"You know that we won't let you leave here," Doris Whittaker stated, her chest puffing with a false bravado her voice betrayed.

"This isn't your fight, Doris," Jane told her evenly. "Don't get involved."

"Emily belongs here with us."

"She belongs with her mother."

"So you can fill her head with lies? So you can make up more disgusting, awful stories about her father? Make her believe your sick fantasies?"

Jane looked toward her daughter, saw that her eyes were filled with confusion and fear. "Emily, please trust me, honey. You know I'd never do anything to hurt you, don't you?"

The child nodded without hesitation.

"Don't listen to her, Emily," Bert Whittaker cautioned. "Your mother's been sick. She's not the way you remember her."

"I'd like you to wait for me in the Chrysler that's parked in the driveway a few cottages down," Jane continued, ignoring Bert's interruption.

"The kind of purply one in the Stuarts' driveway? Grandma wondered whose car that was."

"Yes, that's the one."

"When are you coming?"

"In two minutes."

Emily's eyes traveled warily between her mother and her grandparents. "I'm afraid."

"Don't be afraid, sweetie. I promise I'll only be a few minutes."

Emily hesitated, and Jane understood that she was remembering the last time her mother had promised to join her soon. "Okay," Emily announced finally, running to the door, then coming to an abrupt halt at the sound of her grandmother's voice.

"Your daddy wants you to stay here with us," Doris Whittaker told her forcefully. "You don't want to hurt your daddy's feelings, do you, dear?"

Emily said nothing, silently reaching for the doorknob.

"Aren't you at least going to give your old grandma and grandpa a kiss and a hug good-bye?"

Emily looked toward her mother.

"I don't think that would be a good idea. At least not now," Jane told them, wondering what she would actually do if it came down to a physical altercation.

"Are you going to start filling her head with lies about us too?" Doris demanded, her husband retreating into the silence with which he had always been more comfortable.

"Go on, sweetie," Jane told her daughter. "I'll be right out."

"I'll *throw* you a kiss," Emily compromised, raising her hands to her mouth and making a loud, smacking sound with her lips. Her grandfather automatically raised his hand to catch the airborne kiss. "Bye-bye." Smiling shyly at her mother, pointedly ignoring the raised weapon in her hand, Emily opened the cottage door and ran outside.

Doris Whittaker threw her shoulders back and lifted her chin. "You won't get very far. We'll get to a phone, call the police. Unless you're planning to tie us up before you leave," she added, her voice dripping with sarcasm.

Jane lowered the scissors to her side, though she kept it pointed at her in-laws. "I think I know what Michael has told you," she began, "and I want you to know that . . ."

"We're not interested in your lies," Doris Whittaker shouted, blocking her ears with the palms of her hands.

"How dare you make up such awful stories! How dare you defile our son's good name! Only a crazy person would do such a horrible thing."

"It's your son who's been lying to you."

"I won't listen to such garbage."

"Did you talk to Emily? Did you ask her?"

Doris Whittaker ignored the question, if she heard it at all. "Don't think you're getting away with this. We'll stop you. You're crazy. If there was ever any doubt, this little stunt proves it. My son will keep his reputation *and* his daughter. The next time we see you will be in a court of law."

Jane Whittaker walked to the cottage door and opened it. "I look forward to it," she said.

31

"Do you have any jacks?"

"Any jacks?" Jane looked over the cards in her hand, then back across the kitchen table at Emily. "No. No jacks. Pick a card."

"You're supposed to say 'Go fish.'"

"Sorry. I keep forgetting. Go fish."

A look of dismay settled on Emily's delicate features.

"What's the matter, sweetheart?"

"Are you starting to forget things again?" the child asked.

Jane gasped, immediately lowering her cards to the table and reaching across to take Emily's hands in her own. "Oh, no, sweetie. I'm fine now. I promise."

"For sure?"

"For sure. Absolutely. Cross my heart."

"Sometimes I forget things too," Emily said, as if to reassure both her mother and herself.

"Everybody forgets things from time to time," Sarah Tanenbaum announced, walking into the room, wearing a rose-colored bathrobe, her uncombed hair secured away from her face by two tortoiseshell combs. "But your mom is all better now. You don't have to worry about her. Now, who's ready for breakfast?"

Emily laughed.

"I think you mean lunch," Jane told her friend, in whose kitchen they were sitting.

Sarah groaned. "Why didn't somebody wake me up?"

"We decided you needed your sleep. It's not easy having full-time boarders."

"Are you kidding? I love it." Sarah poured herself a glass of orange juice and drank it down in one smooth gulp. "I'm hoping you never leave."

"There's coffee in the pot, and you're very sweet, both you and Peter. I can't thank you enough."

"We're thrilled to have you. We've never had a little girl stay with us before." Sarah brought her mugful of coffee to the table and sat down, directing her comments at Emily. "My boys are all grown up now. Or at least they think they are."

"We'll be out of your hair before they get home from camp," Jane assured her.

"You'll stay until everything is settled. End of discussion." Sarah took several long sips of her coffee, and fidgeted with one of the combs in her hair. "So, what's on tap for today?"

"Diane's taking Emily to a movie."

"And to McDonald's," Emily added with enthusiasm.

Jane jumped slightly at the mention of the name, recalling her brief incarnation as Cindy McDonald. "Sally Beddoes is coming over in about an hour, and Daniel said he might drop by," she said, trying to steady her nerves, knowing her future depended on how in control she was perceived to be.

Sarah hurriedly downed the last of her coffee. "Then I better get dressed. Can't have a man seeing me in this condition."

"What about Peter?" Emily asked. "He's a man."

"Peter's my husband; he doesn't count. Besides, he's out playing golf. Can you imagine teeing off before eight A.M.?" She shook her head. "Men and their games." She and Jane exchanged rueful glances before Sarah left the room.

Two weeks had passed since Jane had reclaimed both her daughter and her life. Sarah and Peter had graciously invited them to share their home, Michael refusing to leave the house on Forest Street. Jane doubted she could return there, in any event. Too many memories, she thought, and laughed out loud.

"What's funny?" Emily asked.

Jane hesitated, picking her cards off the table. "What's funny is that I *do* have a jack in my hand." She handed the card to her daughter, who seemed oblivious of the fact that Jane had laughed *before* she picked up her cards. Emily immediately pulled three more jacks out of her own hand and arranged the four cards into a neat little pile, next to several such stacks.

Like neat little bundles of hundred-dollar bills, Jane thought, suppressing an involuntary shudder, growing impatient with her habit of relating everything to her recent past. Would a Big Mac be forever synonymous with her ordeal? Would she see stacks of money in the most innocent of children's games? Would she ever be able to look at a picture of model Cindy Crawford again without breaking into a sweat?

"Do you have any sixes?" Emily was asking.

Jane carefully perused the cards in her hand. "Go fish," she pronounced decisively, feeling a renewed sense of well-being.

She had been examined by a host of doctors since her memory returned. They were monitoring her closely while gradually weaning her off the drugs in her system, and she was seeing a therapist twice a week. She was well on her way to a total recovery, they pronounced. Thanks to Sarah's gourmet cooking, she had even managed to put back a few of the pounds she had lost, and her skin was no longer the color of ashes. She had stopped drooling and her coordination was back to normal. Nor did she have to fight to stay awake, although it was true she tired easily and often went to bed at the same time as Emily. And she'd cut her hair into a more sophisticated style that stopped at her chin and was better suited to her face than the longer hair Michael had always preferred.

Her body tensed at the thought of her husband's preferences. How had she failed to notice that he had always liked her best, been his most loving, when she was at her most girlish, her most needy? Those awful adolescent-style clothes he had bought for her, the desire to see her in soft pastels over bright colors and sophisticated blacks, that awful white travesty of a nightgown he had told her was sexier than any of the garter belts and stockings she had purchased on her own.

The doorbell rang.

Emily jumped off her chair. "I'll get it."

"No, I'll get it," Jane insisted, grabbing Emily's arm. "I need to stretch." She pushed herself out of the chair and through the modern glass-and-chrome kitchen toward the front door, feeling her knees shake.

Every time the doorbell chimed, each time the phone rang, she was afraid it might be Michael announcing he was there to reclaim his only child. Although he'd agreed, through his lawyer, to stay away from her and Emily until the district attorney decided on whether or not there was sufficient evidence to lay charges, Jane always felt him lurking along the periphery of her vision. She knew Michael was too diabolical, too angry, to allow her any prolonged peace of mind. If he'd been relatively quiet these past two weeks, it undoubtedly meant that he was plotting something. Unless he was so confident that no charges would be laid and that he would eventually secure custody of his daughter, he felt he could afford the luxury of appearing patient and cooperative.

Jane stared through the peephole of the Tanenbaums' front door at the uniformed courier. She slowly opened the door, studying the young man's careless good looks, knowing she had never seen his face before.

"Package for Jane Whittaker," he said through his nose, thrusting a piece of paper at her to sign. "Print your name next to your signature," he instructed, and Jane did so, loath to take the small package from his hand.

"Thank you," she said, retreating back inside the suede-papered front hall, holding the package in front of her as if she were afraid it might explode.

"Is that Diane?" Sarah called, coming down the steps

and joining Jane in the foyer. She was dressed in beige pants and a white T-shirt, and her freshly combed hair brushed against the side of Jane's cheek as she leaned over her shoulder. "What is it?"

Jane shook her head, and the two women walked into Sarah's white-and-coral living room. "It's not ticking," Jane said, trying to disguise her apprehension with a laugh.

"You think it's from Michael?"

Jane nodded. "Who else?"

"Do you want me to open it?"

Jane hesitated. "No," she said finally. "I'm not going to panic every time I get an unexpected package. I will not give Michael that kind of control over my life ever again."

"Atta girl!" Sarah said as Jane tore open the plainly wrapped parcel.

Inside was more wrapping, this time a silver foil topped with a royal-blue ribbon. A small card peaked out from beneath the blue bow. "Sorry I missed your birthday," the note read, typed and unsigned. Jane's eyebrows raised as if of their own volition, and she quickly dispensed with the silver paper, opening one box only to discover another, smaller box inside.

"Well, it's not a car," Sarah deadpanned as Jane lifted the small jeweler's box out of its larger container.

Jane gently pushed back the top of the small box. "Oh, my God," she said, staring at the beautiful band of heart-shaped diamonds.

"An eternity band," Sarah whispered, and Jane shuddered at the implication.

"What's he trying to pull now?" Jane wondered out loud, recalling the morning that Michael had dragged her into the jewelry store on Newbury Street. A chance meeting with Anne Halloren-Gimblet had proved all the chance she needed. Newbury Street had been her road to salvation.

Was Michael sending her this ring to reassert his dominance over her? To remind her of his power?

"I'm ready to go," Emily called, skipping into the

living room, then looking around in confusion. "Where's Diane?"

"She's not here yet," Sarah said as Jane snapped the ring box closed.

"Then who was at the door?"

"Someone delivered a package to the wrong house," Jane told her, returning the small box to the bigger one and setting them down on a nearby coffee table.

The doorbell rang again.

Nobody moved.

"Isn't anybody going to answer the door?" Emily asked.

Sarah marched to the door and peeked out. "What do you know? Two for the price of one." She pulled open the door to reveal both Diane and Daniel on the other side.

"We pulled up at the same time," Diane announced, coming forward to hug Jane. "You look terrific. I love your hair."

Daniel hung back, almost shyly. "How are you, Jane?" he asked from the doorway.

"I'm good," she told him honestly.

Diane turned her attention to Emily. "You ready for our big date?"

"I've been ready for hours."

"You have?"

"Since breakfast. Mommy and I have been playing cards. Sarah just got up."

"Thanks a lot, kid," Sarah said, laughing. "I forget there's no such thing as secrets when you have a small child."

There was a moment of awkward silence.

"So, give your mother a kiss good-bye and off we go."

Emily reached up to give her mother a big kiss, then was reluctant to let her go. "Will you be all right?" she asked.

"I'll be fine."

"Don't worry, sweetie," Sarah told her. "We'll take good care of your mommy."

"Will you be home when I get back?" Emily asked.

"I'll be right here."

"Promise you won't go out."

"I promise."

"I have a good idea. Why don't you come with us?" Emily suggested, grabbing Jane by the hand and jumping up and down.

Jane's eyes appealed to Diane for help.

"Your mom will come with us next time. I kind of wanted to spend some time alone with you, just the two of us."

"Besides, then I'd be stuck here by myself with Daniel," Sarah said, making a face, and Daniel laughed.

"He can come with us."

Jane lowered herself to her knees. "I don't think so, honey. I'm expecting someone soon who it's very important I talk to. But you go," she continued over the child's protests. "You've been looking forward to this for days, and so has Diane."

"But . . ."

"I'll be fine. I'm not going anywhere. I promise I'll be here when you get back. Now, off you go, or you'll be late."

Emily kissed her mother's cheek, then buried her head against her shoulder for one last hug before releasing Jane from her embrace and taking Diane's hand.

"I'll bring her back safe and sound," Diane assured her friend, leading Emily down the front walk.

"Have a good time," Jane called after them, watching Emily crawl into the front seat of Diane's car and immediately secure her seat belt.

"I'm going to make some more coffee," Sarah said, closing the front door and expelling a deep breath of air.

"Can I do something?" Jane asked.

"You can entertain your guest." In the next instant, Sarah was gone and Jane and Daniel were sitting on opposite ends of the deep coral sofa.

"Is she always so afraid to leave you?" Daniel asked.

"She's like my little shadow, which is understandable after what happened. We sleep in the same room and I have to sit with her every night until she falls asleep. Sometimes I fall asleep before she does." Jane smiled. "Truth be told, I'm not sure if it's her need or mine."

"Does she ask a lot of questions?"

"She did initially. She wanted to know exactly what happened, why I didn't come for her when I said I would, where I'd been, how it was possible to forget who you are, what it was like."

"And what did you tell her?"

"The truth. Or as much of it as I felt she could understand. I'm still not sure *I* understand everything that's happened." She paused. "When you live with a man as long as I lived with Michael, you make certain assumptions. It's a shock to learn that those assumptions have no validity. It destroys your equilibrium, makes you question everything." She looked into Daniel's dark-blue eyes. "Do you know what Michael told Emily?"

Daniel shook his head.

"He said that the things she told me made me so unhappy I got sick and had to go to the hospital. Can you imagine laying that kind of guilt trip on a seven-year-old child?" She scoffed. "I guess it's no worse than anything else he did to her." She brushed aside a wayward tear. "But we'll work through it. We're both seeing therapists, someone Dr. Meloff recommended. She's very good. I think she'll be able to help us." She paused, looking toward the kitchen, knowing that Sarah was taking longer with the coffee than necessary. "How about you? How have you been?"

"Good. Well, no, that's not entirely true," he continued in the same breath. "I've been on a guilt trip of my own, I guess, thinking that I should have kept in touch, that I should have sensed something was very wrong that morning I saw you, that I shouldn't have called Carole that morning after you phoned . . ."

"*Why* should you have known anything was wrong? Are you psychic? How could you possibly have known? And it was the most natural thing in the world to call Carole. . . ."

"I could have blown the whole thing." Daniel jumped

to his feet, walking to the front window and staring out at the street. "It was because of my phone call that Carole found your housekeeper. It was just dumb luck that they weren't able to reach Michael in time to stop you."

"But they didn't. They didn't stop me. They won't stop me now."

Daniel returned to the center of the living room, lowering himself into a white wing chair. "Where do things stand?"

"It's hard to say," Jane admitted. "The D.A.'s office is still investigating. They haven't been able to locate Pat Rutherford. Apparently she's traipsing through Europe, and won't be back for another week. And Mr. Secord, Emily's principal, is firmly in Michael's camp. He and Michael had a long talk when Michael picked Emily up at school that day, nursing his bandaged head." She shrugged. "It won't be easy."

"But you *are* confident? . . ."

"We have someone who might be willing to back up my charges with allegations of her own." Jane checked her watch. "Her name is Sally Beddoes and her daughter is one of Michael's patients. She's coming over in about an hour."

"Coffee's ready," Sarah announced, carrying a large Lucite tray into the room and depositing it on the coffee table, nudging the silver-wrapped boxes out of the way.

"I'll get that," Daniel said, moving the small box to the end table beside him, reading the card. "Somebody's birthday?"

"Michael's idea of humor," Sarah said, showing Daniel the diamond eternity band.

"Some joke." Daniel snapped the ring box shut with the same measure of disdain Jane had showed earlier. "Doesn't the man understand you've filed for divorce?"

"I think it's all part of his strategy," Jane said, putting her thoughts into words. "The loving husband right up to the end."

"But he's still fighting you for custody," Daniel stated more than asked.

"We're meeting with the lawyers on Monday to see

if we can reach some sort of agreement." Jane took a cup of coffee from Sarah's hand.

"I'm surprised you're even willing to meet with him after everything he's done!"

"What has he done?" Jane asked, widening her eyes in mock innocence. "I'm the one who lost her memory and took a trip to ga-ga land. I'm the one who's violent. I not only tried to kill him, I threatened our housekeeper with a knife and his parents with a pair of scissors. Everyone's only too happy to testify on his behalf."

"But the drugs he was giving you . . ."

"I stole them from his bag. He only injected me when I was violent."

"And the doctors—"

"—will testify that I was suffering from hysterical amnesia, which I don't think is going to win me many points with the judge. They weren't there when Michael was giving me the wrong medication. It's his word against mine. As far as they're concerned, he was nothing but the most caring of husbands. And he's one of them, don't forget. They're not going to be too eager to speak ill of so respected a colleague."

"Even Dr. Meloff?" Sarah asked.

"All he knows is that the woman he examined was in the middle of a hysterical fugue. He was white-water rafting when the shit hit the fan."

"You're saying Michael might win?"

"I'm saying he has a good chance if he decides to fight me."

The doorbell rang.

"I'll get it," Jane stated, fighting a feeling of apprehension in the pit of her stomach. Was Diane bringing Emily back already? Had the child been too upset at the thought of leaving her mother for a whole afternoon? Was Diane bringing her back to prove that her mother was exactly where she said she would be?

Or was there another surprise from Michael?

Jane recognized the woman standing outside as Sally Beddoes, the mother of the terrified child she had encountered in Michael's waiting room. She quickly pulled open the door. "Mrs. Beddoes," she said, ushering the woman inside and surreptitiously glancing at her watch. "I'm sorry. I wasn't expecting you for another hour."

The woman glanced nervously toward the street. "I'm early, I know. I can't stay long. My husband is waiting in the car." She motioned toward the black Ford idling at the curbside.

"He doesn't have to wait outside . . ." Jane began.

"He wants to. I told him I'd only be a minute."

"A minute? Mrs. Beddoes, we have a lot to talk about."

"Won't you come inside, Mrs. Beddoes," Sarah urged, coming to Jane's side as the phone started to ring. "I just made a fresh pot of coffee."

"No, really, I can't stay." It was obvious that the woman wasn't going to budge from the front hall.

"I guess I better answer that," Sarah remarked, looking toward Daniel. "Danny, you want to help me answer the phone?"

Daniel immediately jumped from his chair and followed Sarah into the kitchen.

"Mrs. Beddoes, I'm not sure I understand. . . ."

"I think you do."

"Please don't say what I think you're about to."

"I'm sorry, Mrs. Whittaker. I know you were counting on me, and I hate to disappoint you this way. . . ."

"Then don't. Please don't," she added, her voice a whisper.

"My husband and I spent hours arguing about it last night. He's adamant, I'm afraid. He won't let Lisa testify."

"But Dr. Whittaker was molesting her!"

"We have no proof of that."

"Don't you believe what she told you?"

Sally Beddoes stared guiltily at her feet. "*I* believe her. But who else will? Who else will believe a four-year-old child with a known terror of doctors?"

"You're forgetting she won't be alone. My daughter will also be testifying. A judge won't be so quick to dismiss the charges if there are two of us. And the district attorney is going through my husband's files, trying to determine if there were any other children he might have molested.'' Jane could hear the note of desperation creeping into her voice. She knew that so far the district attorney had turned up no one willing to come forward.

''Lisa has been through so much already in her young life,'' Sally Beddoes was saying, fighting back tears. ''She's undergone six major operations since she was two years old. Don't you understand? It would be wrong for us to subject her to more medical examinations, to the questions of district attorneys and the badgering of lawyers. She's had enough trauma for one lifetime. We just can't put her through any more.'' Her eyes sought Jane's. ''Please, try to understand.''

''I do,'' Jane told her honestly. ''I do understand.''

''I'm so sorry.'' Sally Beddoes ran down the front walk to the waiting car.

''Oh, God,'' Jane moaned as the car pulled away, hearing Daniel and Sarah behind her, and collapsing into Daniel's arms. ''Oh, God. Without her, I don't stand a chance.''

''Don't give up now, Jane,'' Sarah urged. ''You have truth on your side.''

''The truth is I'm going to lose my little girl!''

''No, Jane. We won't let that happen.''

''Oh, really? What are you going to say when Michael's lawyer asks you under oath about my marriage? You're going to tell him that you always considered it a marriage made in heaven, that Michael was as loving and considerate as any man could be, that I must have told you a million times over the years how lucky I was, how much I loved him. And what about that night you came to dinner, when I passed out and had to be carried upstairs? How do you think that's going to look to a judge?''

''We'll make him understand,'' Daniel offered, but failed to sound convincing.

''Don't think Michael won't use you too. Don't think he won't use all my friends against me.''

"Carole will testify that Michael lied to her about our supposed affair," Daniel reminded her.

"Was Michael lying or merely repeating the lies I'd told him?" Jane countered. "Trust me, he has all the bases covered."

"There must be something you can do," Sarah muttered.

"There is." Jane headed for the bedrooms at the rear of the large bungalow.

"Where are you going, Jane? What are you going to do?"

"It's time for me to disappear again. Only this time, I'm taking Emily with me."

"Jane, you can't do that," Daniel pleaded, following after her, stopping her before she reached her room. "Michael will find you; he'll track you down and bring you back, and then for sure he'll get custody."

"That's a chance I'll have to take."

"Jane, let's sit down for a few minutes and talk this thing through," Sarah urged.

"You can't spend the rest of your life running away, looking over your shoulder. What kind of life would that be for Emily?" Daniel asked.

"What kind of life would it be if Michael wins custody?"

"But where would you go?" Sarah demanded. "How would you live?"

Jane hung her head, unable to think of a satisfactory reply.

There was a loud knocking from the front hall. "Excuse me, is anybody home?"

"Who the hell is that?" Sarah asked.

Jane was the first into the front hall, drawn, as if magnetized, by the familiar voice. It can't be, she thought. No, it can't be.

Paula Marinelli stood just inside the entranceway, her face as sober as ever. "The door was open . . ." she began.

"What are you doing here?" Jane demanded, wondering how much Paula had overheard.

"Michael told me you were here. I thought wc should talk."

"I have nothing to say to you." Was there no end to this woman's presumption? Were there no lengths to which she wouldn't go for the man she idolized?

"I think you better leave before I call the police," Sarah told her. "You can report back to your boss that Jane is doing just fine."

"I'll do that," Paula said as Jane fought the urge to jump at her throat. "But not until I've said what I came here to say."

"In that case," Jane told her, curious in spite of herself, "I guess we'd better sit down."

32

THE FIRST THING JANE NOTICED WHEN SHE MET WITH Michael in his lawyer's office was how fit and confident he appeared. There were no bags under his eyes to betray a lack of sleep. His hands were steady; his voice was warm.

"Hello, Jane," he said easily.

"Michael," Jane replied, smoothing the folds of her beige Armani pantsuit, and trying not to spit in his face. She shouldn't have come here, she thought, stifling the urge to run from the expensively furnished room. She should have taken Emily and fled, instead of listening to her friends, instead of risking everything. What did she think she was doing? Did she really expect Michael to give up without a fight?

"How have you been?" Michael managed to look and sound concerned about her welfare.

"Much better," she stated between gritted teeth, aware that Michael's attorney, Tom Wadell, was studying her from behind his large marble desk. He's waiting for me to make a mistake, maybe lose my temper, fly off the handle, anything that would give them more ammunition to use against me in court.

"Can my secretary get you a cup of coffee while we're waiting for Ms. Bower to arrive?" the lawyer asked, smoothing his bald head with long, manicured fingers.

"No, thank you."

"Since my wife's attorney has been unfortunately delayed," Michael began, and Jane bit down hard on the side of her tongue to keep from screaming, "perhaps Jane and I could take this opportunity to have a few moments in private."

Jane shook her head in amazement, unable to find her voice. What was Michael trying to do?

"I don't think it's an unreasonable request," Michael added quickly, looking to his lawyer.

"Mrs. Whittaker?" Tom Wadell asked.

"I certainly wouldn't want to appear unreasonable," Jane said, not bothering to disguise her sarcasm.

Tom Wadell rose from his high-backed, burgundy leather chair. "I'll be in the conference room. My secretary is right outside the door . . . in case you need anything."

In case you have to scream for help from this demented woman, Jane understood he meant, watching him shut the door behind him. Automatically she took a step back.

Michael looked hurt, almost offended. "Just what is it you think I'm going to do to you, Jane?"

"What's left?" Jane asked in return.

"I thought we could talk to each other like two adults. . . ."

"Interesting concept for a man who prefers children."

Michael looked to the floor. "You're not making this easy."

"I must have forgotten to take my Haldol this morning."

Michael's eyes slowly lifted to hers, his mouth a frown. "I know what you think I've done, Jane, but—"

"Oh, spare me, will you, Michael? Save your lies for the courtroom. If this is what you wanted to talk about—"

"I want my wife back."

"What?!"

"I love you, Jane. I know you don't believe that. I know you think I'm some kind of monster, but you have to believe that I love you, that all I've ever wanted is everything we once had. I just want this nightmare to be over and for you and Emily to come back home where you belong."

Jane sank into the burgundy leather sofa on the wall across from Tom Wadell's desk, hearing the air whoosh out of the wide seat. Was she losing it again? Could these words really be coming out of Michael's mouth?

Michael reached into his pocket and pulled out the small jeweler's box Jane had returned to him, via the same courier service he had used, the day before. "I bought it for you, Jane. I want you to have it."

Jane felt her fingers curl into tight fists at her sides. Was this his plan? Was he hoping that she'd strike him?

"I miss you, Jane. I miss our life together. I miss our daughter."

"The daughter you told me was dead."

Michael ran a steady hand through his hair. "I know that's what you *think* I told you. . . ."

"I see. So now my hearing is suspect as well."

"Jane, you were completely irrational. Hysterical. How can you be sure of what *anyone* told you?"

Jane closed her eyes, said nothing. *Could* she be sure?

"I love you, Jane," he said, sitting beside her. "I know what you think I've done, to you *and* our daughter, but I also know that with time, and with proper therapy, you'll come to understand that nothing happened the way you think it did, that I never did any of the things you're accusing me of."

"And Emily?" Jane asked. "How long before she understands?"

"Emily is seven years old," Michael explained patiently. "Nothing would make her happier than to see her parents back together." He reached for her hands.

Jane watched his long surgeon's fingers stretch toward her own. Then she lifted her gaze to his face. She traced the wayward lines of his nose, studied his full lips, his fair hair, his pale-green eyes, trying to piece all the parts together into one recognizable whole. But he was more of a stranger to her now than when she'd met him in Dr. Meloff's office two months earlier. "Touch me and I'll kill you," she said evenly.

Michael immediately pulled his hands away and jumped to his feet, clearly shaken. Jane wondered whether it was her words or the calm way she had delivered them that had spooked him. "Are you threatening me, Jane?" he asked, shaking his head in seeming amazement.

In that instant, it occurred to Jane that the office might be bugged. Had she blown everything? Oh, God, where was her lawyer? What was taking the woman so long?

"That's exactly the attitude that got us into this mess," Michael was saying. "There's no room in your life for compromise, for working things out peacefully. Why should you compromise when you're always right? You know everything, don't you, Jane? No sir, nobody can tell Jane Whittaker anything. She knows it all. She has all the answers. She calls the shots. Nothing gets done without her approval. You always have to be in control, don't you, Jane? You have to make all the key decisions: where we go; who we see; what we do; when we make love; *how* we make love. . . ."

Jane fought to piece together the puzzle of his sudden accusations. "Are you trying to say it's *my* fault that you molested our daughter?"

"For God's sake, Jane. I never molested Emily!" He raised his hands to the ceiling, as if appealing to a higher order for help. "She wandered into the bathroom one night when I was taking a leak. You were off at one of your meetings. She was curious, as any child would be. She asked if she could touch me. I didn't see any harm in it. It was all so innocent. I had no idea of the repercussions. . . ."

"So now it's Emily's fault."

"Why are you so consumed with assigning blame?"

"Why don't you go straight to hell?!" Jane snapped, her voice louder than she expected.

There was a knock at the door. "Everything all right in there?" a woman's voice inquired.

Michael walked to the door and opened it, a look of anguish on his face. "I think you can ask Mr. Wadell to come back now," he told the concerned-looking secretary, disappointment clinging to every word. "It doesn't appear that we're going to accomplish anything on our own."

"Nice touch, Michael," Jane said, amazed by how well he had played her.

He looked at her as if he had no idea what she meant, and Jane found herself wondering whether she would stand any chance at all against him in court.

"Look who's here!" Tom Wadell exclaimed, leading Jane's lawyer inside the office and motioning for everyone to sit down in the grouping of chairs across from his desk.

Jane's lawyer was a transplanted Floridian named Renee Bower who had moved to the Boston area after a brief stint in New York. She was an attractive woman whose soft exterior belied the toughness at her core. She gave Jane a brief nod of reassurance as she settled in, clearly not intimidated by the opulence of her surroundings. "Sorry I'm late. It took longer at the D.A.'s office than I expected."

"I think we should get right to business," Michael stated after they were introduced.

"We're open to any reasonable suggestions," Renee Bower told him.

Tom Wadell cleared his throat. "My client has no desire for a protracted and bitter court battle. Also, as a concerned father, he has no desire to see his daughter separated from her mother at this traumatic point in her life. He feels enough damage has been done to the child already, and has no desire to add to her suffering. He is, therefore, willing to allow Mrs. Whittaker custody of Emily."

Jane's eyes shot to Michael's. Could it really be that he was finally listening to his conscience, that he would spare them all the agony of a court hearing?

"And in return?" Renee Bower was asking.

"In return, your client drops all allegations of sexual abuse against Dr. Whittaker."

"My client gets sole custody?"

"Dr. Whittaker gets generous access."

"What does that mean, *generous access*?" Jane interrupted, leaning forward, her earlier elation starting to dissipate.

"My client would see his daughter on alternate weekends and every Wednesday night. Also one month each summer and one week at Christmas and Easter. Other holidays to be divided equally between both parents."

"Never," Jane said angrily. "I will never give you unsupervised access to Emily."

"You really expect me to agree to see my daughter for only a few hours a week in the company of some social worker who'll be watching my every move?" Michael asked.

"That's the least of what I expect."

"I see. And you're willing to gamble? Because if you don't accept my offer, Jane, and I think your lawyer will tell you it's a damn good offer, then I'll fight you for everything. By the time I'm through with you, you'll be lucky if you ever see our daughter again." He paused, letting the full weight of his words sink in.

Jane looked toward Renee Bower, but the woman was staring directly at Michael.

"You really think you can make your obscene charges stick?" Michael continued, standing up and circling the room. "That the D.A., given the evidence of your hysterical amnesia, will take your word over mine? That any charges will be laid? That I won't be completely exonerated? And after that, when we face off in a custody dispute, you think that any judge is going to take the word of a woman who, in addition to forgetting who she is, has a history of violence that includes whacking her husband over the head and beating up on total strangers? Does that sound logical to you?" He paused, though, clearly, he wasn't finished. "And what about Emily?"

"Emily?"

"Yes, Emily. Don't you understand the harm you'd be doing by forcing her to testify against her own father in court?"

Jane shot to her feet, her chair teetering on its back legs, as her lawyer sought unsuccessfully to steady it. "How much harm *I'm* doing?"

"If you don't care about me, Jane, if it doesn't matter to you what these outrageous accusations will do to *my* life, then at least can't you think about our little girl?"

"You bastard!"

"Jane," her lawyer cautioned.

"How dare you," Jane hissed, slamming her fist on the cold marble desk top, watching Tom Wadell pull back in alarm. "How dare you try to twist this around."

"Banging on the desk, Jane. That's a good start. What's next on the agenda?"

"Jane," Renee Bower warned, "don't lose it."

"Maybe we should reschedule this meeting, give you some time to consider our proposal," Tom Wadell offered, rising to his feet.

"Just give me a moment to get this straight," Jane asked. "I want to make sure that I understand everything." She began pacing, Michael quickly resuming his seat to get out of her way. "You avoid the publicity and fallout of an unpleasant trial; you get to keep your position at the hospital and your dazzling reputation; in return, I get sole custody of Emily. I get to look after her on a daily basis; you get to molest her on Wednesday nights and every other weekend. . . ."

"Jane, for God's sake." Michael brushed his hair away from his forehead.

". . . Not to mention a week at Christmas and Easter and a whole month in the summer."

"I don't see that this is getting us anywhere." Tom Wadell began gathering his papers together.

"You really expect me to go along with this?" Jane stopped directly in front of her husband. Was she planning to strike him? God knew nothing would give her greater satisfaction.

Michael inched his chin slowly toward her, daring her, taunting her. "I foolishly thought a compromise might be in all our best interests."

Jane fought to keep her hands at her sides, to keep her fingers from scratching at her husband's eyes. And suddenly she saw Emily reflected in those eyes, and she understood that her best hope for winning, her best revenge, lay in remaining calm. How strange, she thought, that in this instance, hope and revenge should amount to the same thing.

"Oh, it's in *your* best interests, all right. And maybe even in mine," she said, returning to her seat. "But not in Emily's." She looked to her lawyer, who reached over and covered Jane's hand with her own. "Besides, it's way too late for compromises now."

Michael laughed bitterly. "And what does that mean?"

Jane let her lawyer speak for her. "I've just come from the D.A.'s office," Renee Bower stated. "He's prepared to bring criminal charges against you."

Michael's glance shot to his attorney.

"The D.A. knows those charges will never stick," Tom Wadell said with confidence. "I can't imagine he'd actually go to trial on the word of an impressionable child and her, pardon the expression, seriously unbalanced mother." He smiled at Jane as if he had just paid her a great compliment.

"It's not just our word anymore," Renee Bower told him. Jane watched the smile freeze on his face.

"What does that mean?" Michael demanded.

"If you'll excuse me a minute," Renee Bower offered, "I think I can clear this up." She rose from her seat and exited the office.

"What the hell is this about, Jane?" Michael demanded.

"Relax," his lawyer advised. "Ms. Bower is famous for her theatrics."

In less than a minute Renee Bower returned, Paula Marinelli at her side.

"Paula?! Thank God!" Michael exclaimed. "We've

been trying to get in touch with you all week.'' He jumped up and grabbed her hand, leading her toward his lawyer's desk. ''Tom, this is Paula Marinelli, my housekeeper, the one who helped me look after Jane. She knows better than anyone the shape Jane was in.''

''You might be interested in hearing what Ms. Marinelli has to say,'' Renee Bower suggested, signaling for Paula to proceed.

''How could you do it, Dr. Whittaker?'' Paula asked quietly, her voice a monotone. ''I trusted you. No, I thought you walked on water. How could you betray me the way you did? How could you hurt my little girl?''

Michael's face went from white to ashen. ''Hurt her?! My God, I saved her life!''

''Yes, you did,'' Paula acknowledged, ''and for that I'll always be grateful.''

''Suppose you tell us what you told the D.A.,'' Tom Wadell said, his eyes reflecting his grasp of the situation.

''When my daughter, Christine, first started having nightmares,'' Paula began, looking directly at Michael's attorney, ''I thought it was just something children go through. I didn't pay them much attention, not even after my mother told me she thought there was something more to it. When Christine told me that she didn't want to go for her checkup because the doctor *touched me funny*, I didn't think anything of it. When she persisted, I told her that Dr. Whittaker only touched her where he had to make her well. I refused to listen to what she was really saying. Once, I even spanked her for making up such terrible stories.''

''Tom, this is ridiculous,'' Michael interrupted. ''Do I have to listen to this crap?''

''I think it might be a good idea for you to sit down,'' his lawyer advised.

Michael sank into his chair as if he were an inflatable doll with a hole in its side. Jane could almost hear him losing air.

''When I heard Jane's story,'' Paula continued,

"when I heard what Dr. Whittaker had done to his own little girl, I realized that everything Christine had told me was true. I was so shaken, I couldn't move. I felt as if someone had reached in and cut out my heart." Paula shook her head in disbelief. "I believed this man over my own child. I ignored her cries for help because I trusted him. I've always done everything he asked me to do without question. I kept his wife drugged and cut off from her family and friends. I gave her pills and injections, sometimes round the clock, if that's what he told me to do. I watched her suffer and I did nothing about it because I believed him when he said it was for her own good. Now I know he's a liar. I know that he molested his daughter and he molested my little girl, and I'm ready to testify to that under oath. I look forward to testifying to it. *That's* what I told the district attorney."

There were several seconds of absolute silence during which no one seemed to breathe.

Renee Bower was the first to speak. "I think we've given these gentlemen a lot to digest." She got to her feet. "Why don't we give them some time to think things over." She looked directly at Michael's attorney. "You'll call me?"

Tom Wadell nodded silently.

Michael buried his head in his hands as Renee Bower led Jane and Paula from the room. Nobody said a word until they were out on the street.

"How can I ever thank you?" Jane asked, turning to Paula.

"Are you kidding? I'm the one who owes you."

Jane reached out and hugged the other woman to her chest. "Take care of your little girl."

"You too," Paula whispered before hurrying off down the street.

Jane watched her until she turned a corner and was out of sight. "What now?" she asked Renee Bower.

"Well, the criminal charges are out of our hands."

"And Emily?"

"I don't think we'll have any more problems there."

Renee looked at her watch. ''It's a little early for lunch, but I'm kind of hungry. How about you?''

Jane felt a smile fill her face. ''When in doubt, eat,'' she said, throwing her head back and laughing out loud. ''Let's go. I'm starved.''